THE MORNING STAR SHINES BRIGHTEST

MARIE DORON: A DAUGHTER OF THE COUNTRY

R.R. HILL

Black Rose Writing | Texas

The author grants the final approval for this literary material.

First printing

This is a work of fiction. Names, characters, businesses, places, events, and incidents are either the products of the author's imagination or used in a fictitious manner. Any resemblance to actual persons, living or dead, or actual events is purely coincidental.

ISBN: 978-1-68513-738-0
LIBRARY OF CONGRESS CONTROL NUMBER: 2025948412
PUBLISHED BY BLACK ROSE WRITING
www.blackrosewriting.com

Printed in the United States of America
Suggested Retail Price (SRP) $19.95

The Morning Star Shines Brightest is printed in Garamond Premier Pro

*As a planet-friendly publisher, Black Rose Writing does its best to eliminate unnecessary waste to reduce paper usage and energy costs, while never compromising the reading experience. As a result, the final word count vs. page count may not meet common expectations.

Dedicated to the bravest woman I ever met and my number one fan.
Thanks, Mom!

To my children and grandchildren who, without which,
there would have been no reason to strive!

THE
MORNING STAR
SHINES BRIGHTEST

CHAPTER ONE

Oregon Country – Shoshone Lands
January 1814

Marie Dorion stood over the steaming cook pot. Despite a light snowfall, she felt warmed by the pot and the fire crackling below it. The smell of gravy, wild onion, and elk meat wafted to her nose. She breathed deeply while stirring the pot, then spooned some of the liquid for a small taste. *Needs salt.* A few snowflakes floated down around her. As she worked on the pot, she kept an ear perked for sounds of her children's laughter and glee, which told her they were playing nearby. *It's when I can't hear them that I need to worry.* She turned toward the joyous sounds, and finding the children snowball fighting, she smiled. All their lives in the snowy wilderness, and they could still find joy in the bitter cold playground of the Oregon Country wilderness.

She turned her gaze from her boys to the edge of the tree-lined meadow, looking for the return of her husband Pierre and the men who were out trapping with him. They'd been away for two days, and she expected them any time. She also kept a watchful eye towards the woods for any incoming threat. A day earlier, a Nez Perce warrior had come into camp. His words were ominous. The Shoshone were talking war against the white invaders. They were in Shoshone country and the Shoshone and her people, the

Ioways, were not friends. A century before, the Ioway had clashed with the Shoshone over contested hunting grounds on the Great Plains.

The first booming report of gunfire rang out. Her head swung in the direction of the sound. *Sounds of gunfire traveled for miles. Maybe they've shot some meat. One more squirrel and I...* She looked down into the boiling pot.

Then another BOOM! Then another.

Maybe a herd of elk.

More gunshots sounded. The hair on the back of Marie's neck stood up.

That's not right.

She dropped her cooking spoon and broke into a run toward the boys. She slid on the snowy surface and dropped to her knees before them. Their faces showed surprise at her sudden appearance. "Boys!" She grabbed their arms to get their attention. "Jean." The little boy's eyes drifted. She shook him, her voice raised. "JEAN! PAUL. LOOK AT ME! LISTEN!" She took a breath to steady herself. "We're going to the woods." Her voice quivered. "We're going to the woods." She rose and, tightening her grip on each boy's arm, she took off in the opposite direction of the gunfire.

"Mama," little Paul whined. Mama, stop." He stumbled as she pulled him across the uneven, snow-clad surface. Every time he started to fall, his mother pulled him upright. The four-year-old's little legs churned as fast as they could.

BOOM, BOOM came from behind them. Her head jerked a glance over her shoulder. No one was following.

Reaching the woods, Marie moved between the trees until she finally found what she was looking for. Underneath the root ball of a mammoth fir tree was an opening to what she surmised was a coyote den. "Get in." She pointed at the opening. The boys hesitated. "GET IN!" She pushed them forward. The boys stumbled down the cratered depression left by the roots when they were pulled from the ground. Once both boys were in the den, she covered the opening with branches strewn around the forest floor. Down on her knees, looking between the branches, she said, "Wait here. Don't make any sounds. I'll be back soon." She began to get up.

"Where are you going," asked her seven-year-old son.

"Jean Baptiste." She hesitated for a bit, cutting off a rebuke. Taking a deep breath, her countenance calmed, she began again, "I'm going to find Papa. Those gunshots," she said while pointing, indicating where the shots had come from. "They've got some food down, and I need to go help." She got up, hoping they'd accept her lie without question. Walked a few steps. Checked to make sure the boys were not visible. Seeing Jean's face peering out between branches she raised her hands, palms pointed toward the boy, "Stay." Then she put a finger to her lips. "Shhhhhhh." Turning away she broke into a trot, careful not to slip on the snowy ground. She stopped at their tent in the meadow. Hanging from the center pole was a pistol, a leather pouch of mini-balls, and a powder horn. She stuffed the mini-balls and powder into a satchel and swung its strap over her head, positioning it on her left shoulder, then grabbed the rifle, which was leaning against the pole and ducked through the flap of the tent. The fire sizzled as the pot boiled over.

Marie melted into the forest, moving through the stand of pines, the branches had blocked last night's snowfall, leaving only a pine needle carpet to walk on. She floated over the landscape like a ghost, carefully eyeing the ground to make sure not to snap a branch with a careless step. She had not gone far when she saw the hulking, staggering figure. He was leading a horse. She raised her rifle aiming toward the man. The light was dusky, but she recognized the shape of Giles Le Clerc. Lowering her rifle, she ran to him. "Giles! Where is Pierre!?"

Le Clerc leaned against a tree. "Shoshone. Back that way." He pointed to his left.

She saw his hand holding his stomach and his blood-stained shirt. "Oh my God, you're hurt! Put your arm over my shoulders." Grabbing the hand draped over her shoulders and wrapping an arm around his waist, she let out a small grunt as she lowered Le Clerc to the ground into a sitting position. Then kneeling in front of him, she lifted his shirt. Seeing a gash oozing more blood than she could remember ever seeing flowing from a person still alive, she let out a gasp.

Le Clerc spoke in hushed tones just above a whisper. "I'm hurt bad. Done in. Get to Reed. You know the way?" His head hung down.

With a hand, she lifted his chin until his eyes met hers. She saw fear, confusion. Caused, she assumed, by his terrible wound. *He sees what's coming. I need to distract him from his bleeding and the pain.* She wondered what he had been through. *It must have been terrible.* Then, smoothing his hair, she said in a lowered voice, "We'll all go back to John Reed's post together." She noticed he appeared to be caving in, probably from the massive blood loss. "Here, lay down." Using all her strength, she helped Le Clerc lay down.

"Leave me. They're everywhere."

"What about Pierre?" she asked again. She looked at the wooded surroundings, expecting Pierre and his trapping partner Jacob Reznor to come walking up at any moment. *Maybe they were pursuing the attackers.*

"Do me a favor."

Marie nodded. "Of course."

"Tell my wife how I died."

"You're not going to die. I won't let that happen." Marie rose and began gathering moss from the trunks of nearby trees. She used the moss to pack the gash in Le Clerc's abdomen, hoping to staunch the bleeding long enough to get him back to camp.

Le Clerc spoke, his voice just above a whisper, "They're dead."

"Who's dead?"

"Your husband is dead. Reznor too." Le Clerc swallowed. "I saw them die. Clubbed down and scalped. Shoshone."

Her chest tightened, breaths came in gulps. Her eyes watered, but she stifled the desire to sob. *Not now. Later.* She sniffled and rubbed at her nose with her sleeve. Marie pushed these thoughts from her mind and continued packing the wound, trying to save Le Clerc. Mostly the moss was stemming the flow of blood. There was little left to do but wait and hope he would regain his strength enough to walk. "Where does your wife live?"

"Red River colony. We've got a small farm." He coughed. Blood bubbled around his lips. His breath was ragged, and he wheezed when he exhaled.

"Do you have children?" Marie realized she didn't know much about the man lying in front of her. He had closed his eyes, and she leaned in close to his face. He was still breathing. She patted his face lightly to wake him up.

"Do you have children?" There was no response. Marie grabbed his hand. "Giles! Giles!" There was no response. She checked for breathing again. There was nothing. He had slipped into death.

Marie got to her feet. Looking down at the man, "Adieu," Marie whispered. *Go to God.* Then looking through the pine boughs above to the sky, she said the Prayer of Commendation. She crossed herself and walked toward where she had left the boys, rifle slung over her shoulder.

She hadn't gone far when she heard the sound of voices, men's voices. Their words were unintelligible. They were likely Shoshone. She'd heard the language before, talking with Sacajawea in St. Louis. Marie had mostly communicated with her in French but occasionally the Shoshone woman had used her native tongue when she didn't have the words in French or English. The men were coming from the direction of her camp. She felt her chest tighten, her heartbeat pounding. If they'd found it, they could be looking for her and the boys. Kneeling, she raised her rifle to firing position. Her hands were sweating as she gripped the cold steel barrel of the rifle and fingered the trigger. She could hear Pierre's words to her when he taught her to shoot, "Aim for the heart. Squeeze the trigger, don't pull it." She was aware of her breathing and slowed it with a deep breath. *Aim for the chest. Don't look in the eyes. The eyes are life. The chest is a target.*

A figure stepped into a small gap in the trees. Marie put the bead at the end of the barrel onto the chest of the figure and squeezed the trigger. The rifle butt bucked hard on her shoulder, and a cloud of smoke belched from the barrel. Marie, stood, moved to her right and clear of the smoke. She could see a figure crouching over a crumpled body on the ground. She began to reload when the crouching man saw her. He rose to his feet and broke into a run toward her, spear raised, his war cry filled the air.

No time.

Marie dropped the rifle then grabbed the pistol from her belt. Turning her body to present a slender profile, she raised the pistol to eye-level. The gap between them was narrowing, enough that she could see his craggy features formed into a snarl on his face. The man raised the spear and planted his feet to make the throw. Marie aimed the pistol and fired.

CHAPTER TWO
RENDEZVOUS

Three Months Prior
October 1813 at Fort George
Mouth of the Columbia River

Marie Dorion sat on the dock. Wind, coming off the fast-flowing river, swirled over and around her. Blowing from the east, the wind kept the usual fall storms from sweeping in from the ocean. The prior weeks had seen gloriously bright, sun-filled days with the bluest of blue skies, unusual for this country so late in the fall. Her long tresses whipped behind her like dark silken ribbons rising and falling with the gusting wind. Despite the sun, the lateness of the day brought a coolness that raised goosebumps on her flesh, and she rubbed her arms. Her gaze drifted toward the river the natives called *Wimahl*, The Big River, and her fellow fur traders called the Columbia. The surface churned and roiled, topped by white caps. Evergreens, sweeping uphill from the river, swayed on the distant bank and blanketed the faraway ridges and mountains. Burnt-orange alder leaves among the firs and pines spoke to the uniqueness of the biome of this territory.

She pushed herself up to stand, arms folded over her chest, and thought, *God! Splendid!* She felt warmth spreading over her and a smile creasing her face. Having lived in the harsh conditions of the Canadian Shield, at times, and at other times on Canada's vast plains, she could not have dreamed such a place existed. Here was a land of unbounded forests, towering mountains, and, of course, *Wimahl* and its expansive network of tributaries, which was the defining characteristic of this country, the giver of life-sustaining water.

The sound of geese squawking made her look to the sky. She hated geese. They were foul animals. She couldn't understand why, but the Englishmen here loved a goose in the pot; for her, chicken was much preferred as its smaller size made it easier to handle than a goose. Crack the neck. Pull the head off. Let it bleed out, and the job was practically done. The goose, on the other hand, had a thick neck that needed an axe. And then came the tedious work of plucking the down and pin feathers. *A mess.* A goose was hours of work for her, but so was feeding 130 men. To accomplish this feat meant the post's cookhouse was almost continuously in operation. One meal ended and the preparation for the next began almost immediately.

Marie drew in a deep breath, scanned the lush surroundings, and thought about the places where she had grown up, which could not have been more different. From an early age, her environs had been anything but lush. She thought how her father would've loved this place. In her mind's eye, she saw his bearded face and straggly reddish-brown hair. Her father, Jean Paul, a French-Canadian, was a Nor'wester, the nickname given to the men of the North West Company of Montreal, the preeminent fur trade company operating in Canada at the time. She felt an ache in her heart as she remembered her father. His death, which had come suddenly, had been a shock to her. He was so strong but had gotten caught in a blizzard and was missing for days. The word she got was that they had found his frozen body inside an ice cave he had built to get out of the weather. Jean and Paul were named after him and she wished he had been around to see them grow. Not her first boy though. He had been named for Pierre. He'd only lived a few weeks.

She looked at the sky. *Lord hold him in your arms until I can get there. Amen.*

A gust of wind pushed her a bit, bringing her back to more immediate concerns. She looked at the paper in her hand and read the last words scrawled on it. Her face wrinkled.

"My love. Meet me at the spot tonight. I need to see you. Please come."

She crumpled the note in her hand. *He's not listening, Why would he?* John had been an important part of her life for almost three years—since St Louis. His big grin and Scottish brogue had comforted her through all the hardships of walking across half of the continent. "Aye, lass," or, "Aye, sweet Mare...." His gentle manner and authentic kindness had drawn her to him and raised more than a few eyebrows, including her husband's. Cutting John suddenly out of her life seemed cruel, yet she knew it was necessary. She buried her face in her hands, her head gently rocking back and forth.

There is just no way that this works.

After a time, she looked up to the sky.

How did it come to this?

She knew the answer.

Because I was weak and I encouraged this. I needed this.

She felt a familiar jag in her chest, guilt over her feelings for John, a Scottish gentleman of the Nor'westers.

She wondered if it was possible to love two men. Is the heart so fickle that both men couldn't enter? She felt a smile as she thought about what the Father would say. But she also knew Moses had two wives.

Why can't I love two men? Solomon had 700 wives or something like that. When did he sleep? A chuckle slipped out.

Do I even love Pierre?

She knew she was tied to Pierre by marital obligation, by giving birth to their children and yes, by her Catholic beliefs and the teachings from the various priests and nuns she'd met in the Canadian wilds.

But she also had other influences in her life—strong beliefs that governed her decisions. She felt that her mother's people, the Ioways, would allow her to end the marriage by simply walking away from it.

A salmon breached the surface, splashing as it went back underwater. Searching the river, she let her eyes drift over the white caps and across the river to the distant bank covered in fir trees, the mountains to the east, and the fireball sinking in the west. Smiling broadly, she drank it all in. Sunrise to sunset, day after day, had been this way for millennia. Before humans were here.

The water and the wind worked in concert to carve a path across the earth, making contours for the water to follow, exactly what the river needed to fulfill its unrelenting goal – to disappear into the ocean then be reborn in the snow and rains that swept inland from that same ocean. It was the cycle of life – *Wakan Tanka*, the Great Mystery. Hyacinth danced in the air and tickled her nose. A smile made a brief appearance across her face. She breathed in deeply: the air, the river, the forest. It smelled of wetness. Of algae. Of fish. *It is a good smell,* she thought; *it is life.*

Marie uncrumpled the note in her hand and reread it. He'd put it where only she would find it – the kitchen pantry wedged between a couple sacks of flour. He knew she would be there baking before the expedition set out. She held the note to her lips, kissed it, and threw it into the river. She watched it float away toward the Pacific.

Her gaze shifted to the fire-red sky; the sun was sinking slowly into the ocean. Her hair flowed in streaks of black across her brown cheeks as she looked over her shoulder — she could see the forest surrounding the fort on three sides. Trees of mammoth size, twenty-five feet or more in circumference at the base, had been felled to clear the site for the fort. The stumps had to be blasted with gunpowder or burned out by fire.

Yet the forest lurked, towering, shadowing, its recesses dark and foreboding. It was where the wild things lived. Howling beasts roamed within. In the dark of night, deer and elk trembled in the underbrush. The natives had learned to utilize it for shelter, food, and even medicine. But the forest, while giving, was also unforgiving, and going into it held no guarantee of safe return. The trees in this area were so tall, their limbs so dense that beams of sunlight struggled to light the forest floor. Forests, she knew, had a hundred different ways to kill.

The sun-emblazoned fur-trade post stood in contrast to the dark woods. It represented order, juxtaposed against the chaos of the wilderness. She thought of the Garden of Eden, how men for millenia had sought to conquer the wild by civilizing it. *Was this good or had humans destroyed the grand design of the Creator?* Astor's fort had been a first step in civilizing the wilds of the Oregon country. They reaped its bounty of pelts then shipped them to distant ports in China and Europe to make fashionable hats and other garments. But then war between Britain and America broke out, and she heard the scuttlebutt in the dining hall that the British Canadian North West Company used this uncertainty and the threat of British naval power to negotiate a buyout of Astor's enterprise for pennies on the dollar. With the acquisition, Astor's fort became Fort George, named for the reigning British monarch. She recalled the fort's change of hands. The denizens of the fort, those remaining to work for the new owners, and some of the nearby natives, such as Chief Concomly, huddled in the freezing wind and rain in the courtyard to watch the ceremony at which the Stars and Stripes came down and the Union Jack was hoisted up the fort's flagpole.

Now, Marie heard the sounds of a fiddle floating over Fort George's ramparts. Men in the courtyard belted out a favorite song. Amongst the frivolity, a solitary sentry manned the catwalk, his gaze always outward toward the edges of the forest where danger might emerge. The gate's two halves, crafted from the massive fir trees cleared away to make room for the fort, stood open. Just before dark, they would be closed.

She glanced at the five canoes loaded with bales wrapped in tanned-hides, tied up at the left side of the dock. They built each canoe on an oaken frame with cedar planks riveted and glued with a pine-pitch resin, making the canoe water-tight. Cedar and pine wafted in the air. The canoes rode the tide, rising and falling with the river's waves. She noticed the white-corded lanyards twisting about in the wind. She sighed. The thought of leaving the relative safety and comfort of the fort for a sojourn into uncharted and potentially hostile territory was unnerving, especially with two small children in tow. But she was resigned to the fact that they'd leave in the morning. Pierre would be the interpreter for any natives they encountered and guide for the party once they left the river and moved toward the place where they would establish the new post. She'd go, and the boys would go because, well, they always went.

She looked down at the water, feeling her body slump. Her insistence on keeping the family together had brought her and the boys across the continent from St. Louis to Astoria. She thought the journey would end his drinking. She'd been six months along when they left. Out in the vastness of the Oregon country's high desert, the labor pains started, low in her back.

She had kept walking for a time, even rode some. Eventually, it was time. Time to build a shelter in which to have her baby. Pierre and the boys remained with her while the rest of the party moved on. They had to move. Keep to a timetable. The family could catch up once the child came.

Laying on the earth inside the hastily constructed shelter, Marie pushed and pushed, sweat poured, her stomach muscles, hell, every muscle in her body screamed to give out. If she quit, she'd lay on the dirt floor of that shelter, made of buffalo hide and branches, and bleed to death. So, she pushed and strained, every muscle in her core stretched to breaking. She scratched and clawed, grabbing fistfuls of dirt. She fought to bring this life into the world. This person she loved without knowing, without touching or feeling, but that had been an integral part of her for the last nine months.

The baby lived only a short time. The vision of that tiny mound of earth, her daughter's earthen grave, on that flat, open prairie was always with her. Seemingly the only bump in the land for miles and miles. She'd prayed the Rosary over their daughter in her grave and then turned and walked away. She hadn't looked back. A tear streamed down her cheek. She swiped at it with the back of her hand.

Standing now, she repeated a ritual she performed often. She loosened some strands, and her buckskin dress dropped to her feet. On her chest, a silver cross dangled from a simple leather thong tied behind her neck. This she never took off, ever! She stepped out of the garment and dove into the choppy water. Her muscles tightened at the shock of the instant cold. Her skin tingled. Reflexively, she kicked off the sandy river bottom, gliding to the surface, breaking through. Her breath came in shallow gulps. Her chest was tight. Stroking her arms, she made her way through the chop of the whitecaps. She felt like she was flying over the water, fast as a flat rock skipping. Eventually, she tired. Treading water, she looked around to get her bearings. In the distance, she saw a Chinookan canoe with two paddlers heading toward the north shore. They didn't notice her.

She swam toward the dock. Reaching it, she put two palms on the deck and lifted herself out of the water. The wind blew over her, raising goosebumps. Water dripped from her. Still, she sat on the edge of the dock, curled so she could wrap her arms around her knees with her legs bent. After a time, she rose, turned to the sunset, and prayed naked, with arms outstretched and eyes closed. The wind caressed her. Her nose filled with the scent of the world – the river, the forest.

Wakan Tanka, I come to you cleansed of the day's sweat and toil. Washed away are the earth's soil and dust. Let me walk in beauty. Let me remember to thank the sun, the bringer of light, the giver of warmth. May my eyes always appreciate the orange and purple of the sunset. Wakan Tanka, may the sun come again.

Dropping to her knees, she held the silver cross and said the *Pater Noster* in Latin. Finishing the prayer, she crossed herself and began to dress. Her worldview developed under the scrutiny of two parents with opposing cosmologies. Her mother took her to visit her relatives, where she and her sisters learned The Way of The People. There, she learned Ioway customs, rituals, and religion. Her father sent her and her sisters to the Catholic school, when one was present, and took her to church. She remembered walking down the muddy streets of the little villages of the Canadian Shield and the Great Plains, hand in hand, towards the ringing bell in the steeple. Her mother did not go. Marie remembered her saying, "For me the Great Mystery does not live in a house to visit on Sundays. The Great Mystery is in everything, every blade of grass, every tree, it's song is in the sound of the trickling water of the river." When they were in remote areas without a church her father sat with his daughters, in front of a fire and read passages from the Bible. The girls also took turns reading aloud.

Now, walking the wheel-rutted road toward Fort George, looking up at its ramparts, the Union Jack fluttering on the flag staff, her childhood days seemed like a hundred years ago. The sentry walked the wall. She stopped at the dirt pathway that ran parallel to the shore, weaving among the trees. Looking at the pathway, which disappeared into the woods, she knew John would be there, waiting for her. That way consisted of hard-packed dirt that never really dried because of the denseness of the trees and brush. It also led to perdition. However, the fort on the road ahead of her offered refuge. The blessings of divinity. She listened when the Father said, "Heaven on earth is found in the embrace of a faithful husband with his dutiful wife." But also Pierre was there, probably angry and sullen with a jug in his hands.

Marie decided and once the sentry turned his back, she took a sharp right and followed the trail deep into the woods. In the dappled lighting of the setting sun mingling with tree branches, she saw the Oregon grape's bright yellow blooms lining the pathway. Marie bent down and pulled some. Breaking off the roots from the rest of the plant, she stuck them in a pocket of her dress. These would be ground into a powder, which, when applied to cuts and other wounds, would ward off infection. Further down the trail were white-flowered trillium, which, once ground into a paste, was handy for controlling bleeding. Good things to have where they were going.

She came to a downed tree across the path. The trunk smelled wet, and a moldy scent reached her. She stretched her hands up and vaulted to the top of it. Pieces of the log crumbled away as she landed. She squatted on all fours like a cougar, ready to pounce. Once she got over and onto the ground, she found a conk or large white fungus growing out of the deteriorating log. She broke this off. These were valuable for transporting fire. She would dig a hole in the conk, insert an ember, and the ember would smolder all day until they stopped to camp for the night; at which point, she would use it to start a fire for the evening meal.

As she got deeper into the wood, the sound of the river dissipated slightly, and she noticed a curious reddish glow coming from within the heavily treed shoreline. Her heart quickened along with her breathing. The nearer she came to the end of the trail, the soft red glow turned to a flame-driven yellow. Then she heard crackling sounds. A pop of an ember bursting. Fire!

The man knelt over the fire, adding sticks, and the flame grew taller.

He looked up from his work. Seeing her, he smiled. "Hello. Something comforting about a fire, eh Mare!" Rising, he walked to her, and she continued toward him. They came together. He was barrel-chested, some might say stocky, but she thought of him as solid. Gently brushing her hair away from her face, "Aye, sweet Mare. You're a beauty, lass," came the familiar Scottish voice. The way he trilled her name, Maaaiirrre, made her shiver.

"Yes John. A good fire wards off the chill!"

"Are ye cold lass? I have a blanket."

"No. I'm fine."

"Ye sure. Your hair's wet and you smell a bit like algae." His eyes twinkled and he smiled at his clever wit.

"Sweet talker." Came Marie's sardonic reply.

They moved and sat on a four-point blanket of the finest Scottish wool, which laid on the ground a few feet from the flames. The rough material scratched her skin in places, but she glowed with warmth all over. She looked at the bearded face beside her, the gentle, blue eyes she loved to gaze into.

"I was surprised to find a note from you. I told you last time that we need to stop this." She paused and waited for his reaction.

"Aye, I know what was said." He let his head hang down toward the ground. "But I can't let ye go! I don't want tooo."

Worry caused deep lines to crease his forehead. Marie took his face in her hands. "There's no future in this for either of us. I'm a married woman in the eyes of the universal Catholic Church." She looked into his eyes. "It's not what I want either, but...," her voice trailed to nothing. "I've gone over this in my head thousands of times. It always ends the same. I stay with Pierre and you move through life alone." She paused, her eyes scanning his cragged, lined face. "It's not fair to you."

He nodded. She could see the pain her words caused, and he looked beaten, defeated, sick. "I see," he said, getting to his feet and pacing around the campfire. "There's a whole vast world out there. We've barely scratched the surface of this place. After this job, I'll go back to Scotland. It's the only way I'll...." He choked off the rest, clearly not trusting his voice.

"My lone wolf!" She smiled. "*Sunkmanitu tanka*! Always running wild, eh?"

"Big wolf, huh?" He smiled.

"You understand Lakota pretty well."

"Run around this country long enough, it rubs off." His smile faded. "I've been frostbitten, starved, stabbed and clawed by bears but nothing I have gone through has cut me as hard as the words you just spoke to me. They cut my heart. A place no one or no creature can reach." He looked at the ground for a bit.

Seeming eons passed in silence.

John fidgeted with a stick he'd picked up from the ground, "We'll be leavin' in the morn'." He blushed at the obviousness of this statement. He returned to the blanket and, sitting next to her, looked into her eyes. A strand of her hair escaped from the rest, hiding her face. He reached out and moved it off to the side. It was still wet from her swim. Taking some long strands, he slowly let them pass through his fingers. He looked into her eyes, and her heart beat faster.

"Always taking care of me."

"Since I first met you. Watched the way you hiked across the continent, chased two little ones over those thousands of miles, packed the company's gear, skinned elk and deer, cooked, bandaged wounds, all of it, I knew you didn't need to be taken care of." He paused to let his words sink in, then added, "Just loved."

She touched his arm, "I've not felt love until I met you John."

He nodded. "I do. Always will."

Her hands rested on his arm. She didn't know what to say, so she said nothing.

Finally, he broke the silence, "Mare, ye know I picked him so I would be near ye, and that's all."

Her face flushed. "Careful, sir! My husband will be about!" She grinned. "Talk like that might give rise to his temper."

"Aye, if he wasn't passed out cold in the dining hall, he would probably give me a good thrashin' if he seen me here with ye. Heard my lovely whisperings." He took her hand and kissed it. "You're a beauty, my love!"

I love you too. She couldn't say the words out loud. He'd never said the word out loud before. Love. She looked at his face that was now relaxed, his eyes glinting. He lowered her hand but kept ahold of it. They gazed at one another for what seemed an hour, but was in reality several seconds, lost in each other.

Marie finally broke the trance, "Oh my God! The boys!" She started to get to her feet.

"Don't worry, Mare. They're with Cadotte. He was teaching them to whittle when I left."

She felt relief sweep over her. It was replaced by a feeling of pity for Pierre, but she also knew she was helpless to fix him. She wondered why she could not have met John first. Her head rested on her forearms, which rested on her knees.

"Raise your head, love. This is not your fault." A vein popped up in his forehead, "Man in a bottle like he doo. Can't trust 'im. Not even to look after his kids." He looked away, up at the fir trees towering over them.

"Well, I'm here with you. Not exactly..."

He looked her directly in the eyes, "You can put all of this on you if you want. I can't stop you. But remember, he's the drunk. He's the man who beats you."

"Yes, he does all that." She paused, "But maybe I'm the cause of his drinking. And you know I have a smart mouth I can't seem to keep in check." She forced a smile.

"Being a drunk is weakness, manifest. Being a woman beater is...inexcusable." He took her hand in his. She straightened up to look at him. "I'll be the one thrashin' 'im if he goes for ye agin. Who'd miss the lout if...?" He didn't finish.

Her forehead creased slightly. She studied his face. "My sons would miss him." Her voice had an edge.

His face reddened. His gaze dropped to the ground, "Shite!" He paused. "Ye know I ain't that sort anyway."

"I know." His beard perfectly framed his ruddy complexion and sparkling blue eyes. "You're a good man, John. I know you'd protect me if it came to it." She saw the shame in his eyes fade, and his face relaxed.

He looked into her brown eyes. "How'd a man like him end up with a woman like you?"

"Pierre was not...," she searched for the words, "...like he is now. I was...." She looked away from him, out at the river. Suddenly, she grabbed her chest and feigned a swoon. "Ah," she mimicked an anguished sound, "Amor shot his arrow into my heart!" She fell backward, lying flat on the ground. John rolled onto his side near her. "Before he drank, he was quite...something. A proud Lakota warrior!" She paused, rolling on her side to face John. "But that was long ago."

"Aye, loove at first sight it t'was then?" A pang of jealousy touched his chest.

"Yes. The first time I saw Pierre, he was sitting on a big chestnut stallion. What a sight for a young girl!" She let out a breath. "His long black hair flowing behind him as he rode by."

"Now he's got that top-knot doo-dad goin'! Quite the look! Where'd he get that ring that holds it all together? New York?"

She lifted her head. "Don't you start!" She smiled at John, pointed a finger, and added, "Anyway, back then, he was a bit more...I dunno, something. When he rode by that day, he looked at me, and our eyes met for just a few seconds. Next thing I know, he was asking my father if he could court me."

"That's a strong move. I kinda admire that." He paused then added, "Never thought I'd say that one!"

"I think it was more about having been out in the wilderness for a few months!" She smiled; let out a chuckle.

John moved, pressing against her. They gazed at each other. No words passed. He had a question but was afraid of the answer. He thought it was strange that he had fought Indians and grizzly bears, wandered lost in blizzards, and been so hungry that he had eaten beaver pelt because there was nothing else to eat, but he was afraid of words, the words she might say to him. But he needed to know. Finally, he broke the silence, "Soo ye goin' ta stay with him?"

She pulled away from him to sit. Taking a slow breath, in and then out, she thought of the best way to tell him what had been in her heart. "I took an oath before the Lord."

"That's not wha' I asked ye, lass." John moved to sit so he could stare into her eyes.

"Yes, John, for the boys. And..." she looked at her hands folded in her lap. "I couldn't stand the guilt if something happened to him because I left." She hesitated unsure if she should share more. *He deserves to know.*

She looked down at her folded hands. "We lost a child, a son. Measles." She looked to see his face.

"I'm so sorry." He reached to embrace her.

"Pierre was crushed. So was I. He went into the bottle and never came out. I left God but I came back." She paused considering her next words. "I thought the expedition out here would help him. Ya, know the wilderness is Pierre's home. When Mr. Hunt hired him to guide the company I thought that might be the spark. It wasn't." She looked at John, "Did you know that Pierre was facing jail time in St Louis?"

"No. What did he do?"

"Ran up a bar bill he couldn't pay. Hunt took care of that. I was so thankful."

"I didn't know any of this."

"I know you didn't. How could you?" She swallowed before continuing. "I eventually found God again. I promised that I would never leave him. Never stray if he would just take my boy in to his loving embrace until I could get there." She hesitated, "So I am bound by the Lord to keep His commandments and His pronouncements about a woman's duty to her husband."

John averted his gaze. He couldn't look at her. His chest tightened, jolted by a jagged pain. With a quaking voice he said, "Does the Lord require ye to be beat regular? I can't believe..." He heard the volume of his voice rise as the anger welled inside him. He breathed deeply to get some control.

"John. You don't know the anguish this decision has caused me. I've been over it and over it, and it always comes back to the boys and something one of my favorite priests told me a long time ago." She paused. "Father Chardin told me no one knows the mind of God." She paused as she surveyed his eyes, dark and loving. "There's a plan. I believe that, and we all play our part."

"Thas one hellauva plan your god has you involved in. In my country, we used to be locked into religious zealotry. Then a young boy came along, a certain Thomas Aikenhead born of a wealthy family, maybe twenty or so, a university boy in Edinburgh. He taught us all a lesson; he did."

"What did he do?"

"He died. Swinging at the end of a rope on the road from Edinburgh to Leith."

She let out a gasp. "Why?"

"God."

"What'd you mean? God?"

"He was a university boy. Filled with ideas about things. There is no God, he said to the wrong people. They tried him and took him out the next mornin', and, surrounded by clergymen, they stretched his neck, hung him from a tree, they did." He hesitated. Looked up at the stars. "He was killed for his ideas, thoughts." John heaved a sigh. "But out of this tragedy came men like Frances Hutchison and David Hume. They showed us that we have control of our own destiny if we will just take it." His outstretched hand closed as if grasping the air. John cleared his throat.

They avoided each other's gaze for a time. In the dark, the light of the fire was all they had to ward off the cold and darkness. Marie shivered.

John grabbed a blanket that had fallen off to the side and put it around her.

"Better?"

She nodded. Despite herself, she longed for his touch; she pushed the blanket off, revealing her upper body.

He gently traced along her shoulders and neckline, along her collarbone. They shared a deep yet tender kiss.

Pulling slightly back John said, "We better get back afore you're missed."

She sighed deeply. "No one's looking for me," she said lying down. She opened her blanket, inviting him in.

"But you said..."

A smile spread across her face. She put a finger to her lips. "Ssshhhh."

CHAPTER THREE
LATE FOR DINNER

Marie waited just inside the tree line for the sentry striding on the catwalk to make the turn and begin the slow walk on the south wall. Glancing skyward, she saw the full moon shining; it lit up the land almost like day. She studied the multiple undulations of the ground between the woods and the Fort. There were rows of peas running up the poles of tripod structures. Corn stalks glistened in the moonlight. Pathways cut through the rows of crops. She decided she could walk through the rows of corn as they were tall enough to conceal her movements, plus the aisleways were cloaked in dark shadows. She would harvest some of these vegetables for the stew that would feed the Company on their first day out on the river. Seeing the sentry's back, she walked into the clearing and was instantly bathed in moonlight. She grabbed a woven basket, then tore ears of corn from their stalks, adding peas, carrots, and potatoes to her basket as she moved toward the Fort from moonlight and then to shadows whenever the sentry appeared on the catwalk.

As she gathered food, she thought of her time tonight with John. Despite the cold, clear night, she felt a warmth surge over her. She stopped and gazed upward, searching for the Bear within the stars. When she spotted it, she traced the outline with her forefinger. "Thank you for John. Thank you for his love. I love him too," she whispered at the sky. She decided then to tell him how she felt. *But is it right when it can never be anything?* She thought of him out there in the cold. He was spending the night at their rendezvous spot so as not to garner the sentry's attention. Seeing two people outside the wall that evening would raise suspicions.

Marie made her way through the garden, which spread over two acres of the forest clearing. Sections were neatly organized, with narrow paths between each to provide easy access for gardeners and their equipment. Vegetables that complemented each other were in the same rectangular sections: tomatoes with basil and onions. Marigolds were interspersed amongst these vegetables to ward off beetles and aphids. She came to the section that she most needed. It contained carrots, rosemary, and sage, as well as cabbage. Grabbing another small, woven basket, she loaded what she needed for the morning's meal.

Being out this evening had put her behind.

What was I thinking?

There's so much to do.

She forced these thoughts from her mind and came back to thoughts of John, the main character in her passion play. A smile creased her face.

She would enlist Jack and Tom, two Owyhee servants from the Sandwich Islands assigned to maintain the post's vegetable garden. They also ran the dairy and worked in the kitchen and dining hall. She glanced at the barn where the two men lived, along with the cows, chickens, and pigs.

While they worked, Jack would tell her tales of the Islands. Tom chattered away in his native language, and Jack would translate for her. They had filled her head with visions of paradise: lush vegetation, sandy beaches, and warm, gentle breezes that caressed everything it touched. She supposed that growing up in a land such as the Islands had made these men disposed to gardening.

She recalled her time with Jack and Tom, not their real names, but appellations assigned because their names were too difficult for British, Americans, and Frenchmen to pronounce. She smiled as she strolled through the garden, her thoughts shifting from John to these two Owyhees. She marveled at her luck in having three men in her life who moved through the world, displaying a sense of humor and cheerfulness that took the edge off this hard, wilderness existence.

She had learned that Jack and Tom had been sold to Astor's Fur Company by the Hawaiian King Kamehameha and had arrived with Astor's seaborne expedition onboard the Tonquin to what would become Fort Astoria. In a sense, these Owyhees were enslaved but no more than any of the men who trapped and traded under contract to the Company. Everyone who found their way to Astoria had to do the time promised. These indentured ones had total freedom of movement. If they ran away, which some did, they soon found they were hundreds of miles from the nearest settlement with nowhere to resupply. They usually came back in a few days, a look of hunger and privation marking their countenances.

As she strolled, carrying her baskets, she was thankful for these two men from Owyhee who had made a lush garden of cool-weather crops such as peas, cabbage, beets, carrots, and much more. She had lived at many remote settlements and could not recall ever having such a variety of critical foods to supplement the meat—and fish-based cuisine. She knew they were one missed supply ship from being in real trouble and that this garden, for all its simplicity, was a potential lifesaver for the people of this wilderness station.

"HALT!"

Marie stopped instantly. She stood still, looking up at the sentry on the catwalk at the front gate. He leveled his musket at her.

"Who are you?"

"Marie, Mr. Smith. Let me in, please."

"You oughtn't be outside the walls this time of night. Coulda shot you for an Injun."

"Wouldn't have been far off, would ya?" She laughed nervously, knowing she looked more like one of the Clatsops that lived nearby than one of the white men inside the walls. "I know. I needed to get some vegetables. You're right."

Smith motioned and barked at someone, and, in a few moments, Marie heard the gate creak open. She slipped through the small gap.

"Take a man with you next time," Smith growled at her.

The gate closed behind her. "I will, sir. And thank you." She called over her shoulder.

Take a man with me! Ha, she thought as hooting, hollering, and fiddle music was coming from the dining hall. *Like any of them would be in shape to escort me.* She glared at the structure and then went around to the back of the building. Following the path next to the hand-hewn planks that formed the outer wall structure, it led her to the stairs that went to the kitchen, located in the basement.

Entering the kitchen, she noticed an overwhelming heat from the fireplace. A metal shield attached to the stone-lined back of the firebox reflected heat into the room. A brick oven was located to the left of the firebox. She smelled biscuits baking. She saw blackened tools, hooks, ladles, and a coal rake. Jack and Tom were bustling around; dishes clattered, crystal glasses clanked. Steam rose from a kettle of water simmering on the stove.

Marie, with Jack and Tom, spent their days in some aspect of food preparation. They were called upon to produce meals for as many as a hundred men of the fort. Breakfast was ready at daybreak. When the sun was overhead, the bell rang to announce that it was time for dinner. Whereas the first two meals of the day were informal, supper was meticulously set before the officers and gentlemen in the Great Hall at dusk. Linen tablecloths woven in English mills, fine China, crystal, and silverware graced the tables. Italian wine and Jamaican rum slaked the men's thirst. The common workers ate in the outer courtyard. A tarp was strung overhead in rainy weather.

The system of feeding the people of the fort was complex. Hunters were out constantly, ranging through the forests. Bringing in meat was their sole reason for being there. The garden was a five-acre plot in which every inch was utilized to produce various cold-weather vegetables. A grand Hereford bull had been shipped in from England and had mingled with the cows that were brought in from Spanish California. A calf or two was born every spring. This small herd produced milk, cheese, and butter for the Fort.

Occasionally, these cattle supplied meat. This was rare as the husbandman, a Scot named Finan McDonald, was careful to keep plenty of meat on the hoof in reserve, only acquiescing to a slaughter when the herds population became overwhelming for the available land. The surrounding woods provided mushrooms and wild asparagus or maybe rhubarb or berries for pies. They bartered for fish with the natives. The Pacific Ocean nearby provided shellfish such as clams and crabs. Oysters came from bays that formed in river bends and coves.

Jack turned, "Hello, Miss." He bowed towards her slightly. She bowed in return.

"Hello."

"The water is almost ready," he nodded at a Dutch oven hanging over the flames. "You're late."

"Yes, sorry. I got delayed."

"That's what late means. Yes?" He smiled.

Her look went straight to the gap in his front teeth. "Yes. Dumb thing to say." Her face reddened.

His rounded face seemed to hold a perpetual smile.

What's going on behind his brown eyes?

Several candles lit the room from candle holders attached to the wooden beams that supported the floor above and, by extension, the building itself. The candle holders had tin-backs that reflected light and kept the beams from catching fire. She walked to a table. Setting her basket down on the varnished tabletop, she got to work with a knife. Jack and Tom chattered. Before long, the kitchen smelled of elk meat and vegetables slowly simmering.

Jack walked to the pot and took a spoonful of broth. "Needs salt and rosemary."

He smiled.

He disappeared into a storeroom where they kept the spices in earthen jars. He soon returned, and using a pot handle hanging from the mantle, lifted the lid of the Dutch oven and dropped in the ingredients. He stirred the pot for a bit, and then, scooping a ladle of liquid, he tasted it.

"Ah, perfect!" He smiled at Marie.

"They done eating up there?" Marie looked up at the ceiling to indicate the dining hall above.

"Yes. Your husband very, very drunk. He asleep." Jack averted his gaze.

"I heard." Marie continued, "Are you hungry? I'll make you something." She heard Tom tittering in the background, followed by something spoken that was unintelligible.

"Tom say we eat enough to be very fat." Jack chuckled.

"Ah, but I bet you didn't have this." Marie walked to a tall, wooden larder on the opposite wall. Opening the doors, she retrieved a deep white dish. She turned towards the two Owyhees. "Apple pie." She smiled at the men and motioned for them to sit at the small table. Slicing two pieces, she put each on a plate and set them before the men. She then retrieved two cups of coffee from the pot simmering on the stove.

Tom always has coffee on the stove.

Marie smiled as the two men wolfed down their pie and slurped their coffee. "I made it for a friend, but he won't mind if you boys have some too."

Jack looked up. "Miss Marie, you leave in the morning?"

She nodded yes.

"Tom and I knew the three that went last year." Jack looked at her. Tom lowered his head to his food. "One was Tom's cousin. They don't come back."

Marie looked at the floor as a mouse scurried. She watched it disappear into a crack in the wooden floor. Then she looked back at Jack. Her hands moved to rest on the back of her waist.

"Be careful."

Marie grinned as she removed her apron. "Goodnight, boys. I'll see you in the morning." She turned back a bit when she reached the top of the stairs. "Throw a couple of sticks in the firebox before you go to bed. I want that stew to simmer most of the night."

Emerging into the courtyard, she glanced up at the night sky. She couldn't locate the Bear but prayed to the night, anyway. She thought about the lost Owyhees. The scuttlebutt at the Fort assumed they had become lost in the wilderness and starved to death or had run into hostile indians out there. "Watch over my boys. Keep us safe. I thank you," she murmured. She continued looking at the star-filled sky for a while longer. Crossing herself, she walked across the yard to their quarters. She shivered against the cold air.

Her thoughts came back to John. *I hope he's warm.*

CHAPTER FOUR
THE ADVENTURE BEGINS

Marie sat in bed in the small box of a room she shared with Pierre and their two boys at Fort George. The dying embers in the fireplace dimly lit her surroundings. Eyes wide open. Her body tense. She'd heard something--she wasn't sure what--but something had raised the hairs on her neck. A life spent in the wilds of North America kept her on a razor edge. Her mind always drifted between sleep and wakefulness, staying cognizant of her surroundings. There was a small table with a stub of a yellowish candle in a tin candleholder with a broad base and two loops for easy carrying. Their whole existence was guaranteed by fire. Fire for warmth. Fire for cooking. Fire for light.

Log walls with mud and straw plugged gaps needed re-packing from time to time to keep the coastal winds and rain out, as well as invasive rats and field mice who seemed to like the straw. The furnishings were spartan; besides the small table was a mattress on the packed-dirt floor, which functioned as a bed for the boys. A wooden chest held their worldly possessions, primarily clothes but heirlooms like her father's hunting knife and a small axe. She was saving those for the boys. There was also a quilt her mother had sewn, a gift every married couple should have; she had told Marie as she handed it to her the morning of the wedding.

When she returned from the river last night, she found the boys sleeping in her bed. She and Pierre had a bed made from hewn logs, fir cross-slats, and a linen mattress cover stuffed with elk hides. She listened for the sound that had awakened her but only heard the light, rhythmic breathing of the boys. No sunlight shone through the small window. Any sound that awoke her was potential trouble, and ignoring sounds could lead to disaster. She glanced at the empty mattress on the floor to see if Pierre had made it home.

Why do I bother?

Finally, hearing nothing out of the ordinary, she slipped into her clothes, which included a pair of linen breeches, a white, long-sleeved cotton shirt, and a blue sash tied around her middle. When she went out into the wilderness, she dressed like the men dressed and noticed a few glares from some in the company. Ignoring them, she opted for comfort for the long canoe rides and freedom of movement. You never knew when linen breeches might be necessary for a quick escape. A long dress was too restrictive. Besides, no one said anything negative about seeing a woman in men's breeches, at least not directly to her. They didn't dare. She was the source of their food. Marie pulled on leather boots that reached her mid-calves. She tossed some sticks on the embers, making the fire crackle. Jean Baptiste sat up in bed. "Mama?"

She looked at the boy. "Go back to sleep, my love."

"Where are you going?"

"I need to start the fires in the cookhouse. There will be food soon. Lay down and stay with your brother. I'll be back." She grabbed her red woolen coat, then turned and slipped out the door that opened to a central courtyard inside the fort's walls. The moon illuminated her pathway to the kitchen. Its reflection made the moonlight brighter as it bounced off the frozen white grass. She strode toward the dining hall across the way, crunching with every step, enjoying being the first one up and moving around. She liked the solitude as she worked. In an hour or so, she knew the air—which was sweet and cold in her lungs—would fill with wood smoke and the acrid stench of coal burning in the blacksmith's stove. Men would be bustling about as the sentries raised the flag. Finally, the bell would ring, calling all hands to breakfast.

The bright moon had rendered the candle's light impotent. She blew it out. Crickets chirped. An owl screeched from a tall tree somewhere close by. The river ran. But she heard nothing out of the ordinary.

About midway to the dining hall, something caught her attention. Out of the corner of her eye, she saw something move within the deepest shadows of the courtyard -- where the northern wall of the stockade and the fur warehouse met. Her head snapped around to the area of the motion, studying it for a few seconds. She glanced up at the catwalk. No one was there. She assumed the sentry was sleeping it off in one of the bastions. A clanging sound like a pot dropping on the floor and something rustling brought her attention back to the shadows. She peered into the dark, struggling to see what was hiding inside. Her first thought was that natives had slipped over the wall to steal whatever they could find. She knew the people here were fishermen, not hunters, so they had little to trade with. Unlike the natives in the east, these river Indians would not go out and hunt beaver for the furs. This was a constant source of frustration to the North West Company fur men, who were counting on the natives to bring in pelts. The Tonquin that had carried half of the founders of Astoria had been bulging with trade goods, axes, blankets, and glass beads to encourage the natives to hunt. After years of interacting with white traders and developing a taste for the white man's goods, these river Indians remained fully satisfied with their fish and root agronomy.

She slipped the knife out of the sheath tucked in her sash and crouched low, creeping toward the shadow-filled corner; her body was tensed in readiness. He emerged from the shadows, a hulking figure. Marie gasped, and reflexively, she gripped the knife handle tightly in her sweaty palm, ready to take an upward thrust. Her father had taught her to master the upward thrust, teaching her to strike in a way that is harder to see coming as it is further from the eyes of the attacker.

"Dammit, Archie," Marie blustered out. "I could have killed you!"

"Pie," Archie said matter-of-factly. "Pie." He held out the empty pot for her inspection.

Marie looked over at the man with a cherubic face. He lowered his gaze, as usual. A heavy wool blanket enveloped him. "What are you doing out here? It's freezing cold!"

Archie's face scrunched into slight wrinkles, and his head tilted slightly. "Pie."

"C'mon." Marie re-sheathed the knife and took Archie by the hand.

She pushed on the heavy wooden door to the dining hall, and as they entered, she first noticed the smells of last night's revelry: tobacco smoke, rum, elk fat, and the acrid smell of vomit mingled with urine. Having skinned buffalo, beaver, and almost every other kind of animal, she had smelled worse things in her life. The hall comprised one large room with a small kitchen annex. A rectangular table with benches on all sides filled the center, leaving a bit of space to pass between the table and the walls. At either end of the table were oversized oaken chairs with curved wooden arms and cushioned backs covered in red velveteen material bordered by ornate carvings at the top. They reserved these chairs for the wintering partner and his right-hand man. The benches were for the clerks, traders, who tended to be British, primarily Scots, and the interpreter, Pierre. Not seeing any passed-out bodies in the chairs or under the table, she kept an eye out for puddles of vomit or other bodily fluids.

"Sit." She pointed at a bench and, hearing nothing, turned back to find that Archie had not followed her. Retracing her steps to the door, she opened it to find him standing in the cold, wrapped in his blanket, holding out his eating pot.

"Pie," he said.

"Archie, get in here," she commanded.

He just stood there. He was not allowed in the Great Hall unless invited to be made fun of or to fetch food for the table.

"C'mon," she pointed toward the interior.

Archie shook his head.

"ARCHIE," she barked in a louder, whispering tone. "NOW!"

Sensing her anger, he walked inside. His shoulders slumped; his head hung as he shuffled in. "SIT," she said firmly, pointing at a bench.

They had found Archie, his last name was Devlin, wandering in the wilderness. A letter in his coat pocket was the only testament to his full name. Further, they learned from the letter that he had come west from St Louis with a group of American fur hunters under Manuel Lisa. The letter addressed to Miss Ida Freeholder of Spartanburg, Connecticut, suggested that she and Mister Devlin were betrothed. After that, Archie's biography became filled with barracks rumors and innuendo.

Marie had caught snippets of conversation amongst the men who said Archie's sleep time mumblings suggested he had gotten separated from the main party somewhere in Blackfoot country and had spent a few years living among them. Because Blackfeet's treatment of trespassers was harsh, he had to have avoided their wrath in some way, as he lived with them. However, he may have aimlessly wandered until he lucked upon a Nez Perce village. It was further surmised that the Nez Perce, who were notably more friendly towards whites—having learned of the trade in the whites' goods like steel-bladed knives, axes, pots, and pans, and of their god—fed him and fattened him up and then pointed Archie towards white civilization.

Marie looked at Archie in the dim light of the Great Hall. She thought it odd that his vocabulary in his sleep was vast. Yet when awake, pie was the only word he uttered and only when he was hungry. As she watched him, she wondered what he had endured that was so terrible as to cause him to withdraw into himself so thoroughly. "Wait here," she commanded.

She lit the wall lamps and then went into the kitchen. She got a fire roaring in the fireplaces firebox. The wood crackled with a bursting fire. Breakfast would be simple, and the party would eat several miles upriver a stew of elk meat, potatoes, and peas that Marie had made the previous evening. She quickly got the kettle and the stew ready to travel.

She heard "Pie" continuing to be demanded from the dining hall.

She walked back into the dining hall from the kitchen. "Archie, be patient." Cowed, Archie looked down at the table.

Marie's eyes snapped toward a gurgling sound from the other side of the room. Walking toward the sound, she saw him lying on a bench. Just underneath him was a puddle of his vomit. He sprawled with his arms and legs flung out to either side. Her stomach knotted.

She gasped at his name. "PIERRE!"

Nothing stirred; no response came. She stomped down the interior staircase to the kitchen, grabbed a pitcher of water from a countertop, and returned.

"PIERRE! GET UP DAMN YOU!" Her flood of cold water struck his face and chest. She stood over him, her free hand on her hip. "Your topknot came out!"

"GAWWDAMMIT!" He sat up, spitting. He looked up at her, "WHAT?!" He shook his head, wiped his face with his hands, and then flung his hair back over his shoulders. He looked at the ground. Then, seeing what he wanted, he retrieved his blue-beaded hair band from his vomit.

Resting on an elbow he said, "Oh good morning my dear," Pierre smiled and fluttered the fingers of his right hand at her.

"Don't good morning me!" Came out in a harsh, whispering voice. She breathed deeply, wanting to control her emotions, then said calmly, "Clean up your vomit and your clothes. Go down by the river to do it. I don't want the boys to see you like this."

Pierre looked up at her. Blinking. He used his fingers to clear his eyes of sleep.

Marie clapped her hands twice to get his attention. "Be quick about it. There's a pot on the stove. Take it with you. Put it by the canoes."

Pierre stumbled to his feet, brushed dried vomit off his clothes, and went out the door, giving it a good slam as he left.

Marie fought back tears. She retreated to the kitchen, put a hunk of elk in a cast iron pan, and added some gravy. It cooked over the fire for several minutes. Finally, she set a plate of hot food in front of Archie. He looked up at her and said, "Pie."

She looked into his eyes, took off his hat, and ran her fingers over his matted hair. "Yes, Archie, pie!" Looking at him, "You men are such simple creatures. A full belly and a woman in your bed and you're happy as school boys in a play yard. Isn't that right, Archie?"

He smiled at her and dug in, ravenously using his hands to stuff meat laden with gravy into his mouth.

As she watched him eat, she wondered again what had happened to him. What had he seen? What had been visited on him? What had he suffered at the hands of men or nature? The wilderness was unforgiving. She would never know and prayed that no one she knew would ever meet such a fate again. She also prayed for Archie to come back, for his mind to heal. To go home to Miss Ida Freeholder of Spartanburg, Connecticut, and to raise a family and enjoy their lives together. That is what she prayed for that morning alone with Archie in the dining hall of Fort George in the Oregon country. That and other things that she held secreted in her heart, things that were just between her, the Lord, and her Bear guardian.

• • • • •

Across the compound, in a room almost directly opposite the dining hall, a candle burned in its holder sitting atop a simple wood table, rough-hewn wood crafted from downed timber, refuse from the remnants of the trees that had once abounded in the area that now constituted the grounds of Fort George. John, fumbled with some papers in his hands—a letter to his brother in Scotland.

He read the letter for a fourth time.

My Dearest Jamie,

I hope this letter finds you well and healthy and a lass or two at your side to ward off the cold, Highland nights! May that health and well-being of your house extend to my son. Please hold him close and let him know his Da thinks of him often and loves him much. I know it has been some time since my last post and you have my deepest regrets. Give Mother my love, and as for Father, well, my feelings on that matter hardly need to be recounted here! In your last letter you had stated your hope that my feelings toward him might have softened with time. Let me assure you they have not and never will. Regardless, I think of the rest of you often and look forward to the day we might at last raise a toast to a free Scotland, may she win her freedom from tyranny.

I write to you now to declare to you my love of a beautiful woman. She is of this land. Black hair and eyes the color of coal. Her brown face is framed by a sleek jawline and high cheek bones, a perfect nose runs to full lips. Her skin is soft and warm. She carries with her the smell of hyacinth as if she bathes in it. She laughs easily but alternately is given over to her passions. When provoked she is a tigress, but this is rare. Deep inside is the heart of a blessed saint. Caring. Loving. Lastly, I must confess before you and God himself, she is married, and Lord help me I love her so.

I won't justify my actions to you. Just know that I would lay down my life to save hers and that of her two small boys. Sometimes, alone in my bed, I chuckle at what the fathers of the seminary would think. Do you recall I was their star pupil for a time? When I thought I would give my life in service to God? They would certainly look upon me with scorn. Although Father Mensies I think would be different. He was always the reasonable sort. Sought to understand, not condemn. I liked him. I can hear him now, "Tell me what you be feelin' son? The Lord will listen if you ask him for guidance." He asked me that question once and I told him I was there because I was not the eldest, I would not inherit our father's lands. That path was for you, Jamie, my brother, my twin. And I felt that I would make a poor servant of the Lord.

I went on to tell him that I didn't know what the Lord's up to but I believe he might not care all that much about us and it's kind of silly that we think he does. Really, do we matter so much that the Creator of the Universe has nothing better to do than watch over our every move? I saw plenty in Edinburgh – the starving people walking the streets, begging for table scraps. A disgrace! I've seen plenty since to indicate to me a lack of attention on His part.

On the other hand, I am in a place that certainly God himself created. It is lush and green with giant trees that stretch to the sky. Pines, the trunks of which are as big around as a crofters small house! I cannot even describe these to you, but they would certainly set your mouth agape Just let me say that when we were clearing land for the fort, we'd have two men with axes and wedges, they'd stand on planks jammed into the trees themselves, six feet off the ground. They'd be whacking away, sometimes for days, before the behemoths would fall. Then we had to blow the stumps, massive things, with gunpowder or burn them with fires that smoldered for a week! The mountains here are tall like the Alps in France. Not far from here a mountain called St Helens belches smoke and fire from time to time. There's a river, a mile wide, which with its tributaries feeds the land. If there ever was an Eden certainly, this is it.

Even after the years spent bracing against the bitter sting of blizzards sweeping across the Canadian Shield, feeling the ache of starvation when the supplies at a distant outpost ran out, a regular occurrence, fighting off wolves, bears or the natives, I still thank the Good Lord every day that I came out of our dear mother a couple of minutes after you. Otherwise I'd be the eldest and would be the Laird! Sitting in my library dreaming dreams of adventure instead of living the adventure!

Brother, please send word of yourself as well as of our mother. It has been so long; I wonder if she is still alive? It's been, eleven years ago when we last looked in each other's eyes and gave a last embrace. Do you remember, at Stornoway, the night before the ship sailed? We drank to everything but the ghost of William Wallace, although I was so drunk, we may very well have, and I just don't recall it!

My hair has some gray mixed in with the reddish-brown. My beard is sprinkled with it too. Some wrinkles around the eyes. I have done well in this fur business. I go now to do one last task and in two years' time will come back to my beloved homeland and gather my son. We will start our life and I will show him how life works in the Highlands of our beloved land. I fear the woman I mentioned, my love, will remain with her husband and so while I will come home wealthy in earthly measures, I will be poor as a street sweeper in l'affairs d'amor!

I will close now. We leave soon for the interior of this land. The dalles du mort, rapids of death, await, as do the natives, who are mostly friendly but, from time to time, can stir up trouble. Mostly this is for show. A chief trying to gain standing with his people by getting more trade goods. It's almost laughable as most of the time they are bought off with a plug of tobacco and a few colored-glass beads.

Ah I have been remiss in not mentioning that you may continue to draw from my account at the Nor'Wester headquarters in Montreal for the boy's needs.

Respectfully and Affectionately Yours,
John

He blew on the paper to dry the ink, then after a moment or two, rolled the parchment and, using the candle, sealed it with wax, making an imprint with his signet ring. He inserted the papers into a metal tube and then sealed it with a cap. This dispatch would go with the other documents and reports for the company headquarters in Montreal. From there, it would be put on a ship for Scotland and into his brother's hands in six months or so.

He felt a twinge of guilt that he had not thought of the boy's mother in some time. John was the boy's name, his son's name. He would be eleven now. Thirteen by the time he returned to collect him. His mother had passed from a fever, the white man's pox. He remembered her brown skin, soft to the touch and sweet-smelling.

He had loved her.

But not in the same way that he felt for Marie. That thought made him feel sad, guilty, and conflicted. He felt he owed his wife's memory better than he had given. He sat staring at the burning candle.

He remembered the night she died. She was burning with fever, and he sat up with her, putting cold, water-logged rags on her forehead. She moaned and flipped around to get comfortable. No comfort was to be found. Not in the cold rags, not in his soft voice speaking words of encouragement; nothing worked. Finally, he had drifted off to sleep, sitting in a chair beside her. He woke to her screams. Jolted awake, he saw her running out the door. She ran to the ice-cold lake a few yards from their cabin and flung herself head-first into the water. "The shock killed her," he thought.

John shook away these thoughts. He picked up a second document, read the heading, "Final Instructions for the dispensation of my estate." He repeated the process he had done with the letter to Jamie just a moment ago. He picked up the candle, dripped some wax on to seal the document to prying eyes. *You never know,* flashed through his mind. *Dangerous country.*

A thought of Marie pushed these thoughts away. A smile started.

CHAPTER FIVE
UPRIVER

When Marie got down to the dock, she found Pierre sitting on a bale of goods wrapped in a tanned-hide. His head hung, forearms rested on his knees. His head bobbed as if he were sobbing. Marie hung back not wanting to have him know that he had been crying. She saw him wipe at his face, then she approached. "See you got yourself cleaned up."

"Yep. I dunno why I can't..." Pierre's voice trailed off.

"I miss him too," she said. "People will be about soon. Best go get your gear."

He rose and walked toward the fort's front gate. She watched until he was out of sight.

Marie stood on the dock. Soon all would be hustle and bustle but for now she enjoyed the quiet of the pre-dawn world. The full moon bathed the scene in light. Before long men straggled down from the fort, carrying their personal gear in bags, some slung these over their shoulders.

Before long there was a throng of men, all busily getting the canoes ready to go. She took a quick mental accounting of the men going out that day—the *voyageurs or coureur de bois*, of course; these French Canadians were the crucial personnel. If you weren't working an oar or guiding a canoe, you were cargo. The bowman or *avant* held a pole, which he used to push away from rocks and divert floating logs from the craft. He called out directions to the steersman that moved the craft away from threats such as currents leading to whirlpools and fluxes that smashed against rocky shores. There were four rowers, two on either side of the canoe and, in the aft, the steersman who operated the rudder.

Marie's attention was suddenly diverted, "Mama, Mama!" She spun towards the voice of her son, Jean Baptiste. The little boy ran into her waiting arms. He looked up at his mother. Marie stroked the boy's long, black hair.

"Bonjour, mon amour! Où est ton papa et ton frère?"

Her oldest son turned from his mother's embrace and pointed toward the fort. Marie's gaze followed, and she saw Pierre and Paul coming down the cart road, holding hands. She heard little Paulie's voice, "Papa. *Je suis fatigue!*" At that, Pierre picked the little boy up and snuggled him in his arms. Paulie laid his head on his father's shoulder and closed his eyes.

"Guess he's not an early bird!" Pierre smiled at Marie.

"You'd know that if you were ever up early!"

"Let's not start again, all right!?" Pierre's smile disappeared.

Marie took Paulie, who had fallen asleep, just as Cadotte walked up.

"Bonjour, Madam," Cadotte bowed slightly to Marie. "And what do we have here?" He patted Paul's back lightly.

"He's a bit tuckered out."

"Tuckered out! We've not even begun!" Cadotte said with a jolly laugh.

"Someone may have kept him up late whittling last night." Marie's eyes twinkled at the giant voyageur. He started to offer an excuse, but Marie stopped him with a pat on his forearm. "Thank you for doing that. They love spending time with you."

Cadotte's beard covered most of his face, but she saw his upper cheeks redden. "Ah, and I love them as well! They are good boys." Cadotte turned his look toward Jean Baptiste. The little boy was looking up at him. "Are you ready to try again?"

Jean Baptiste nodded, *"Oui, Gran Pere."*

Marie smiled, loving that the boys thought of Cadotte as their grandfather. She stifled a laugh as she remembered that Paul only called him *"pere,"* to which Cadotte laughed his big laugh and said to him, "I am fat like a pear, no!" Then he wobbled around, holding his hands out wide and pretending that he would topple over at any second.

Cadotte retrieved a small coin from his pocket. He held it up between his thumb and forefinger. "Ready?"

"*Oui.*"

Cadotte's two big hands swirled around quickly, and he opened his hands to reveal that the coin had vanished. "Where is it?"

Jean Baptiste's eyes grew wide in amazement. "I don't know."

Cadotte reached into the pocket of Jean Baptiste's jacket and came out with the coin between two fingers. "How did this get in there?" Cadotte feigned mock surprise. He held up a small wooden figurine of a horse. "Hmm." Cadotte laughed at the little boy's dumbstruck expression.

"The coin?" Jean Baptiste inquired.

"You will figure it out one day." He tousled the boy's hair.

The steersman for her canoe was Francois Cadotte. Marie was relieved by this. She was comfortable with Cadotte and his ever-present smell of tobacco smoke, she rarely saw him without a smoking pipe in his mouth. His teeth were tobacco-stained and this showed when he smiled, and he had a big, unabashed smile. She found him kind and gentle; he had the soul of a poet with a sweet baritone singing voice. He carved wooden whistles, taught the boys to play them, and quoted the love poems of the Roman Catullus. They were swarthy odes of lust and passion that, fortunately, he cleaned up for his young audience.

One night, not so long ago, she had found Cadotte at a fire by the river. He turned at the sound of her approach.

"Do you mind if I sit with you for a bit?" she had asked, recalling the river lapping on the sandy shore, a starry sky above.

"Please." His hand gestured for her to sit on a nearby log.

"It's a good fire," Marie offered.

"Yes, it keeps the chill off."

"I heard you reading to the boys today, and I wanted to thank you."

He chuckled, "Yes, Catullus. They're very smart. Jean Baptiste has a lot of questions."

She smiled. "They are full of energy and curious minds and mouths that only stop when they are asleep." For a moment, they were quiet. The sound of the river was omnipresent, like a low roar that was always there and only noticed when it disappeared. "Where did you learn to read?"

"In my village, there was a priest," he told her. "He insisted that the boys and girls of the village know how to read. He had no books except the Bible, so he borrowed from his wealthy parishioners. I was taught to read by God, Herodotus, Cicero, Catullus, and others."

"Catullus certainly loved Lesbia," Marie said.

"You know Catullus?" He asked, looking surprised.

"I've read some. I had a priest too." She chuckled.

"I see." He puffed on his pipe. "Catullus was a lost soul." Cadotte looked into the fire. "Young men can be such silly things. I know. I was one!" He jabbed a thumb at his chest and laughed a big laugh.

She looked at the large, bearded man. He was barrel-chested with a round belly, and when he laughed, it came from somewhere deep within him. Smoke curled around his head.

"We don't know whether it's love or lust sometimes." He stopped for a moment. An ember burst, sending flaming sparks upward. "He turns on her, you know?"

Marie offered a blank look.

"Lesbia. When she spurns him."

"I must have missed that part in the story." Marie smiled.

He looked at her. "Ah, yes Madame Dorion. It is true. He becomes something ugly. Such is the power of love."

"How does a man know when it is love, Francois, or any of us?"

"You must know, Madame, your husband, he makes your heart sing, no?"

Marie considered this idea. How should she respond. Her gaze shifted from Cadotte to the fire, and she wanted to say to Cadotte, to confide in him, that no, her husband did not make her heart sing. Instead, she thought of John. "Yes," she smiled, "he makes my heart sing." And then, "How about you? Does your heart sing for someone, Francois?"

He took a deep drag on his pipe, savored the flavor, and then slowly released the smoke from his mouth. His body heaved and a sense of ease spread over him as he gazed toward the horizon. At the river. The mountains.

"There was a girl once. Ah, she was a beauty! She had beautiful, long brown hair that glistened in the sun. It was the color of cinnamon. Her laugh was like a bird singing. Her blue eyes sparkled with joy." Then Cadotte went quiet and stared into the fire.

Marie fell silent, allowing Cadotte some space to think. He seemed about to say something important. The sound of the river, the crackling of the fire, and the chirp of crickets were all there was.

He breathed a sigh. "She was a whore. I loved her very much." Marie saw his eyes watering. "I got into the trade to buy her freedom." He hesitated. "I was a foolish boy who did not understand things." He did not look at her. Instead, he pounded his pipe on a rock to clear the bowl. Taking a pinch of tobacco from a packet he'd taken from his pocket, he repacked the bowl. He grabbed a twig from the ground and lit it in the fire, quickly transferring the flame to his pipe.

"Did she spurn you?"

Cadotte did not answer, puffing on his pipe. Smoke billowed around him as his gaze met hers, "You know, Lesbia and Catullus were doomed from the start. Their love was illicit. A married woman carrying on so..." He didn't finish. He shifted his gaze away from her to the fire.

Marie wondered if he knew. She blushed. They'd been careful. Or at least she thought they had.

John Reed's booming voice brought her back to the present. "Let's get 'em loaded, gents!"

She shook off the memory as she handed little Paul to Cadotte and watched them walk to their canoe. They were easy to follow because the smoky cloud surrounding them was like a rain cloud. She continued scanning the men.

John had selected a group of Iroquois from eastern Canada to work the oars, and once at the site for the new post, they would also hunt beavers with the French-Canadian trappers. Tom and Jack came down to the dock to see them off. She recalled Jack's warning from the previous night about how three Owyhees had not returned from an expedition that had traveled to the area they were headed to on this trip. John had told her the men of the company considered their disappearance an insult. And that kind of aggression toward the company—inflicted a year earlier—could not be forgotten or left alone.

"No one kills a Nor'Wester and gets away with it. Owyhee or no."

They had to return and lay claim to the area as North West Company hunting grounds. "That's why we're a goin'! That and the Americans have been sniffing around a bit too close for my liking!"

"Basically, we're going to wave the Union Jack. Is that it?"

"Something akin to that, aye." John looked away.

Marie spotted the five gentlemen or officers of the company going. They huddled together, talking, until they received the order to mount up. One was Dugald MacTavish, who would accompany them in setting up their post. He would do the clerking, accounting for goods distributed to the natives and furs brought in, counting the ninety-pound bundles of fur for shipment back to Fort George. MacTavish, a tall, lanky lad with bright red hair, had deep connections in the company.

To Marie, MacTavish seemed young in terms of his level of responsibility. She had asked John about this, and he explained the young man's pedigree. "His great-uncle Simon MacTavish, a Scot from the Highlands, was a chief founder of the company, and by God, the kid would pull his weight. Learn the business from the bottom up. He's due to inherit, you know?"

"Really?"

"Aye. Old Man MacTavish doesn't have an heir. Ain't even married. That young man has the blood of Simon Fraser and Alexander Mackenzie runnin' through his veins, and the old man is determined to make sure that he carries on the family's Scottish heritage with dignity."

"That's a lot of pressure on one so young," Marie had observed.

Marie almost jumped out of her skin as the command to "LOAD UP" was shouted.

One of the fort's cannons was touched off. KABOOM. The signal that the expedition was to commence.

Upon its departure from Fort George, John Reed's party numbered fifty-one souls, the minimum number needed to face the Indian threat on the lower part of the river. Thirty of the party with three canoes would follow the river, where it turned north and continued to Canada. From there the party would take trails and the canoe routes of the Red River watershed and the Great Lakes until they arrived at Montreal, led by the four officers whose contracts were expiring. They would have several voyageurs, including Cadotte, and some clerks who were also leaving the Nor'West Company service. They would hole up at Fort Colville until spring, launching their canoes when the rivers were gorged with snow runoff, and then continue to Montreal.

With six trappers, along with Dugald, Pierre, Marie, the boys, and Archie, John Reed would continue on horseback to establish the trading post. This is where Pierre would earn his keep. His command of French would facilitate horse trading with the Nez Perce.

Just before the canoes launched that morning, John Reed said, "Me and my twelve followers. Kinda makes me like Jesus, don't it?"

Marie rolled her eyes and said, "Yes, you remind me of my Lord and Savior every day!"

The sound of Archie approaching shook her out of her thoughts. "Pie!" He held up a pan containing the remnants of the pie she had baked and served to Jack and Tom the night before. She saw his huge smile and crumbs around his mouth.

"I see you got your pie!" She laughed heartily. Her head tilted backward. She grabbed Archie by the shoulders and pulled him in for a hug. "I love you, my boy," she whispered in his ear. Standing back but still holding his shoulders, she said, "You are an angel. Are you sent to me from Heaven, Archie?" She looked into his eyes.

"Pie."

Pierre overheard their conversation. "Jesus, would somebody get him some fucking, PIE?"

"Don't be an ass, Pierre! He's had an injury."

"He looks fine to me!"

"It's the kind of hurt you can't see!" Marie's eyes flared at her husband.

When the first oar dipped into the water, it was still dark. Despite some wispy cirrus clouds, the nearly full, gibbous moon glistening off the water managed to light the way enough. Marie saw a pattern in the clouds, to her they looked like a spider web crossing the sky. Each canoe had a lantern lighted and hanging from its mast for extra lighting. No sails today as the wind of the previous day was gone. The river was like glass.

The two boys, arranged on either side, laid their heads on Marie's lap. The gentle rocking of the canoe soon put them to sleep. Packed around them were the supply packs filled with what they would need to survive for the next six months, plus glass beads, blankets, traps, axes, and knives for trading with the natives.

Pierre, cleaned up but still groggy, sat in front of her, facing backward in the canoe. His elbows and his forearms rested on his upper legs. As an interpreter and guide, he wasn't required to row.

Looking down at the two boys, Marie stroked their hair gently, humming a song.

"What's that song?" Pierre demanded, looking at her sideways, a hangdog expression on his face.

"I don't know the name," Marie replied. "My father's men sang it as they rowed."

"Stop it!" He glanced sideways at Cadotte, sitting in the steersman position.

"Monsieur, the boys sleep. You shouldn't yell," Cadotte offered calmly.

Pierre shot a look at Cadotte. Sizing the man up, he went on, a bit calmer, sunk his head in his hands, "A man can't think."

Marie stopped humming.

Then, it was silent, except for water sluicing around the oars.

Cadotte broke the near silence, saying in his native French. "It is *En roulant ma boule*, Madame Dorion."

Marie looked at the hulking steersman. He wore a black wool cap, his pipe stuffed into his coat's breast pocket. "What?" Marie was confused.

"You know, the song you were humming...*Derriere chez nous y-a-t'un etang. En roulant ma boule.*" He sang quietly, his deep bass floating over the air. "I do not want to wake the little ones."

With a quick nod, "*Merci.* It will be a long trip for them."

"Gives me time to teach them before...." Cadotte's voice faded to nothing.

Marie nodded at him, her lips tightening. She looked away at the river and brushed a strand of hair from her face with her right hand.

The little fleet of canoes rowed on. The *voyageurs* sang to the rhythm of oars striking the water. Marie couldn't make out all the words to their songs, but she heard enough to know they were about lost love, drinking bouts, and fighting- all the things these men knew well. As they rowed steadily, driving their fleet eastward, Pierre let out a snore.

The horizon was brightening. Marie could see the mountains in the distance—jagged purple shapes against the yellow glow of the sun behind them. On the shore, she saw occasional fires near the wooden huts of native villages. These huts were of the same design, rounded, dome-shaped structures, a frame covered in the bark of Yew trees native to the region, designed to ward off the torrential rains that would soon come. Children would run to the edge of the water and wave at them. Marie waved back.

At full daylight, the sun beaming off the water and blue sky overhead, Cadotte, crewing the lead canoe, made a slow arcing turn toward shore— the string of canoes behind them followed suit. The jolt of the canoe hitting the sandbar woke the boys. Five-year-old Jean Baptiste rubbed his eyes. He glanced around, taking his bearings. While Marie struggled to lift the pack with the food, Jean Baptiste had clambered over the side. Standing up to his knees in the water, he lifted his three-year-old brother Paul over and onto the shore. Holding hands, the two boys walked up the sandy beach. Marie rose a bit, "Jean, you and your brother stay close!"

"*Oui, Mama!*"

She smiled at the way Jean Baptiste looked after his little brother.

They turned and ran down the strip of sandy beach bordered by tall fir trees and brush. Their giggling filled the air like birds singing in the morning. Happy to be free of the canoe's confines.

She returned to struggling with the pack and shot a disgusted look at Pierre, still sleeping.

"Madame, please allow me," Cadotte spoke softly. He grabbed the ninety-pound pack with one arm, hefting it like a pillow.

From down the riverbank came the booming voice of John Reed, "Arseholes and elbows, laddies! Ain't got all day!" Everywhere, men were scrambling to beach their canoes and light their pipes for a good morning smoke in front of a roaring fire. Each man was issued a draught of rum. The rum helped with the aches that came from hours bent over an oar in a cramped canoe.

Marie wrestled a cast-iron pot near the base of the fire so she could start preparing a meal for the weary travelers. Wood smoke blew in her face, causing her eyes to tear up. She closed her eyes against the stinging as she moved away from the fire. Soon, she could hear the bubbling sound of a gruel made with elk marrow, gravy, and peas, which would be spooned over bread.

Archie arrived and said, "Pie."

"It does smell like pie, doesn't it?"

She whistled, and the men stopped their conversations, banged out the smoking refuse from their pipes, and lined up to spoon some of the gruel into cups or whatever they had at hand to hold the runny mixture. That chore done, Marie scanned the beach for a sign of Jean Baptiste and Paul.

"Where are those boys?" Standing with hands on her hips, Marie asked loudly, but to no one in particular. She raised a finger and thumb to her lips and whistled. The loud, shrill sound resonated through the air. She waited expectantly, but nothing happened. Her chest tightened, and her stomach twisted and churned. She felt herself walking down the beach in the direction the boys had gone. *It has only been a little bit.*

Before she realized it, she was running, scanning the forest for a sign of them. She perked her ears at the slightest sound. Nothing. She looked back at the way she had come. She could see the men sitting and eating on the beach.

Realizing she was almost panicking, she took a deep breath and slowly let it out. Her muscles relaxed as she searched for the boys using tracking skills she had honed over the years.

Just need to be logical.

She walked back—now paying attention to the sand—and eventually found small footprints heading into the woods. She followed them to the edge and found a trail. No rain this late in the fall had made everything dusty, but she saw the faint outlines of the boys' footprints heading deeper into the woods. Following the trail, she occasionally checked the sand for the boys' footprints. Before long, she noticed something else on the path. She bent down on her knee to look. Cougar track! She could tell it was fresh as it lay in the groove the boys had just made. They were being stalked!

She jumped to a sprint, simultaneously withdrawing the knife from her belt. The steel of the blade sang as it came out of its sheath. Every sinew in her body was strained as she flew through the woods. "JEAN," She yelled over and over.

Then came the reply, "MAMMA, MAMMA!"

She rounded the turn on the trail, stopping suddenly, assessing the situation. The cougar, she guessed, had to be about seven feet long and over a hundred pounds. Not huge, but it was still powerful enough to take down two small boys. She could see the animal's muscles rippling under its smooth coat. A bit of drool leaked from its mouth—it was hungry. Marie judged it was about ten feet away and slinking toward the two boys. "Jean!" She said firmly yet as calmly as possible. "Throw your rock at it, raise your arms, and yell as loud as you can. You too, Paulie." Marie crossed herself.

The two boys looked at their mother as she spoke. Jean Baptiste raised the rock to throw it.

"Aim for its nose. Hit it in the face."

Jean Baptiste threw the stone and hit the animal on the bridge of its nose. The rock glanced off, flew over the animal's forehead, and dropped with a thud. The big cat screamed and drew back three quick steps, its feet kicking up the dust from the forest floor. Marie used this opening to jump to a spot closer to the boys where she could intercept the cat if it made a move, but she wasn't sure if she would be quick enough to block his lunge.

Jean Baptiste yelled, "Yay!" Jumping up and down at his accurate throw, he raised his arms and loudly shouted.

The cougar let out a screeching yell at its prey and backed up slightly. Its head tilted to one side as the commotion in front caused it to evaluate the situation.

Paul was behind Jean Baptiste, and he started jumping and waving his arms as well. Marie crept in an arc around the cat, hoping to move between it and the boys while trying not to appear threatening and cause the cat to spring at them. As she moved, she gripped her knife tighter; the steel blade glinted in the dappled light of the forest. She had to act. Crouched low, her leg muscles rigid, she prepared to spring.

CHAPTER SIX
ENCOUNTERS

Marie's head turned toward the sound of snapping twigs coming from the darkened forest. She sensed movement in the recesses and dim spaces between the trees. Whatever was creeping forward, Marie had to expand her attention to include her boys, the cougar, and the approaching new threat.

The cougar's long, sleek body was in hunter mode, with its muscles rippling beneath its coat of glistening fur. It disregarded the new threat and, regaining its composure, moved slowly forward—undeterred by the waving of arms and the shouting. It was now mere feet from the boys but newly agitated as it turned toward new sounds coming from its right, sensing imminent danger. Focusing his attention on the movement, it let out a low snarl, bearing its white fangs. Its mouth was foaming in anticipation of a meal and its incredible luck at having so many choices for supper.

A woman dressed in elk-skin leggings and a tunic belted around her middle stepped out from the shadows. She was tall and slender. Long black hair flowed around her face and over her shoulders. She had the mark of Chinookan royalty – a flattened forehead. Shadows obscured her face, but Marie registered a nose ring and copper square-shaped earrings, which confirmed her royalty. Her left arm was bent in front of her and parallel to the ground. Her right hand, which held a spear, was cocked back so that her right hand was even with her right ear. With her legs bent, she stepped cautiously forward. Her eyes shifted from Marie to her target.

The cat became overwhelmed with the sensory input. There were multiple threats, and it was surrounded. Operating on instinct, it chose the most negligible threat and, with fierce eyes, focused on the small prey before it. In an instant, its body tensed. Marie saw the cat's haunch tighten, readying to spring and began yelling and waving her arms. She ran and threw her body in the path of the lunging cat. Jean Baptiste's scream pierced the air as he raised the stick, readied to strike. The cat soared toward him in mid-air as the woman from the woods ran forward two steps and let her spear fly, catching the cat in its midsection. The spearhead drove deep, shattering ribs, tearing open flesh, and lodged in the animal's beating heart. Its scream howled loud and shrill as it thudded to the ground and skidded to a stop near Jean Baptiste. As it exhausted its last breath into the dust, inches from Jean Baptiste, the boy felt the warm breath on his toes.

The boys were still like statues. Jean Baptiste clutched the stick, which shook. Paul peered out from behind his brother; tears ran down his cheeks. Both were looking at the dead animal in front of them. Marie ran to them and, kneeling, wrapped them up in her arms. She looked up at the woman, who moved quickly toward the downed animal. The woman placed a foot on the animal and yanked on the spear. It came free after a couple of tugs, and she set the butt of the spear on the ground. She leaned the spear so that the spearhead came to her eye level and began wiping the spearhead clean with her free hand. She wiped the blood on her buckskin dress. The spear's shaft was five feet long and carved from the limb of a spruce tree. The spearhead was chiseled obsidian, a black glossy rock formed by volcanic eruptions many millennia ago. It was inserted into a notch at the top of the shaft and then secured with a leather strap coiled around it.

"That's some spear," Marie said. "What is that spearhead made from? I've not seen rock like that around here."

The woman held the spear before her and looked up at the spearhead. "It's from the People upriver. To them, it is a gift from Loowit."

Marie's face turned as her eyelids narrowed and her forehead wrinkled.

"The smoking mountain!"

"St. Helens," Marie said.

"She belches fire. These rocks form from what comes out of her. We trade salmon or some of our baskets for it." Then, turning her gaze to Marie, "I am Ilchee. Daughter of Concomly. Wife of Kiesno." The woman's chin jutted up while she spoke.

In better lighting, her face is visible, and Marie said, "I've seen you at the fort." Marie stood up. "I am Marie."

"I know who you are, Madame Dorion. You and I have met before. My father and I did much business with the whites at the fort. Do you recall?"

"Yes. I remember, but I didn't think you would remember me."

"How could I forget you? It was raining, and I was wet from the trip across the river. You offered me some dry clothing and tea." Ilchee paused. "You were very kind."

Marie blushed. "Well, thank God you came along now. I don't know what.... We were in trouble. I couldn't get between them." Marie's eyes watered. She tried not to think about what might have been.

"I'd been tracking that cat for several miles. It has been stealing pups from our village." Ilchee swung her gaze at the boys. "You should stay close to your mother! This time it was a cat. Could've been the Boq! They are everywhere!" Her arms spread wide.

"The Boq?" Marie asked.

"They are big and hairy! Ugly beasts. Their bodies are like men, but their heads are like wild animals, and they roam these forests looking for little boys to eat for dinner!" She saw the boys' eyes open wide. Ilchee laughed. And then, jumping and raising her hands in a claw-like fashion, she yelled, "Boo!"

The boys grabbed Marie's legs tighter. Marie laughed, too, and tousled the boys' hair. "Oh, my brave boys!"

"Mama, I was brave," said Jean Baptiste.

Marie knelt at eye level with the small boy. "Yes, my son. You were very brave and protected your brother." She moved her hand to his face, stroking it lightly.

Ilchee stood silently, giving Marie time to comfort the boys. After a minute or two, she spoke. "You're going upriver?" She shifted her weight from one foot to the other; her right hand held her spear, the tip pointing straight up and the shaft resting on the ground.

"We're putting a new post in. Past where the river turns north," Marie confirmed.

"That's Snake country." Ilchee's forehead wrinkled in confusion. Her smile faded. "The Snake people are fierce warriors. You call them Shoshones or Shoshone."

"I've been in their villages on the way out from St Louis. We traded for pack horses and dogs to eat. Seemed friendly."

"That was then. This is now, and much has happened between the whites and the People of this river and beyond!"

Marie's face tightened; fear gripped her stomach, twisting it into knots. Her head tilted sideways. Her eyes never broke contact. "What's happened?"

"The troubles last summer?" Ilchee asked. "You must have heard."

"Yes, the two that were hanged," Marie confirmed. "He was a young officer named McGill, out with a fur brigade for the first time. He was a hothead, and he ordered the hanging of two Shoshone tribesmen for stealing some of the company's property, mostly colored glass beads. Baubles used to trade for beaver pelts and other furs. They also absconded with a pack horse."

"I've heard whisperings." Ilchee had finished cleaning her spear, and she held it next to her like a Medieval sentry guarding the entry to a castle.

"Whisperings?" Marie asked.

"Yes. We trade. We gather. We talk. You come here seeking the pelts to become rich! But you know so little."

"Believe me, I'm not getting rich here!" Marie re-thought her approach. "What should I know?

"That we are all connected here on the river and beyond."

"Don't speak in riddles. Please. What am I taking my sons into?" Marie pleaded through the worry that etched itself on her face, the furrow between her brows carving out a new wrinkle.

Ilchee could sense Marie's desperation. "The Shoshones are proud people. It was an insult, and they will want blood." Ilchee spoke matter-of-factly.

"We have fifty men. Well-armed and used to dangers." Marie lied, knowing that most of their party would split off for Montreal, where the Columbia turned north. She felt terrible lying to this woman, their savior, but she balanced that by knowing it might be a valuable rumor to spread upriver.

"You have fifty men against the Shoshone nation?" She made a sound, "Phumpf. Your white arrogance is...." Then, "The Shoshone can gather a few hundred of their warriors. Others will come too! Blackfeet. Bannock."

Marie brushed off the reference to whiteness. The last thing she felt was a part of the whites. "What do you suggest? We turn back? Hide in our fort, behind our walls?"

"I think you should never have come in the first place."

"That may be so," Marie offered.

"Once you get above the Cascades, my father can no longer protect you," Ilchee said.

Marie recalled the talk among the gentlemen, the officers at the fort, regarding Chief Concomly's arrangement for his daughter to marry an upriver rival. They had said this marriage to Kiesno, chief of the Multnomah tribe, had been a masterstroke of political maneuvering, one that gave Concomly influence amongst the people of the lower river, from its mouth up to the series of rapids known to the whites as the Cascades. It was said that his influence made Concomly important to the white traders, first the Americans and then the British. They all looked to Concomly to facilitate the trade. To calm the natives so that the fur traders could safely walk the land, Concomly was rewarded handsomely, mainly with the finest manufactured products England could produce. Nothing was held back.

During a council at the fort, where she, Jack, and Tom worked as waitstaff, she witnessed Concomly's newfound power. The chief had noticed a gentleman of the fort named Gabriel Franchere writing and took a fancy to his pen set, a blue glass-blown stylus with a steel tip, and his leather-bound notebook. It had been a gift from his sweetheart upon his departure from Montreal several years before. Reluctantly, they forced him to turn over his pen and paper despite Franchere's heated protests. "He can't even write!" He also talked about losing his drawings and notes taken over several years in the territory. Marie remembered the beaming Concomly, showing his new gifts to the members of his entourage.

Ilchee added, "Look out for yourself and your own. Keep the boys close and have a rifle close to hand."

Lines creased Marie's forehead. Her face was stern, and she clenched her jaw muscles. She reached out a hand. Ilchee took it and held it for a moment.

"Travel well!"

"Boyos, come now. We've got to get back. They will be wondering about us." Feeling like she needed to say "thank you" again, only a squeak and then a nod with a tight-lipped expression emerged. Ilchee nodded.

They walked up the path leading to the river's sandy shore. Marie looked back to see that Ilchee had kneeled by the cat, a gleaming knife in her hand.

Nothing is wasted.

Once back to the sandy strip by the river, Marie looked ahead and saw the men re-loading the canoes. "Boys, on your knees." The two boys kneeled, as did Marie. With folded hands and bowed heads, Marie gave thanks, ending with "Amen." The two boys rose. Marie cleared her throat and gave them a stern look. "One more to the Bear who watches over us, too." The boys kneeled, and Marie, with her head raised to the sky, her arms spread wide, began chanting the Bear song. "With you, I walk in a strong way. With you, my power comes. Keep me strong to defeat those who come against me."

When thanks had been given, she rose to her feet. Her hands brushed the sand off her pants.

"Why do we pray to the Lord and to the Bear, mama?" Jean Baptiste inquired.

She looked at his wrinkled-up face, staring through his long dark hair. "We're hedging our bets."

She saw that confused him. "It's hard to know which has the stronger medicine out here. Understand?"

Jean Baptiste nodded that he did.

"Okay, let's go now."

Looking down the beach, she saw Pierre walking toward them. When he got within a few feet, he asked, "Where have you been!?"

"You're awake." She brushed past him.

He grabbed her arm, spinning her around. "I asked where you've been!" His voice shook. She saw a vein pop in his forehead. She'd seen that before and knew a storm was brewing inside him.

"LET GO OF ME!" She pulled away from him and continued walking.

He ran after her, moving in front of her. He grabbed her again, this time by both arms. "I AM TALKING TO YOU!" Paul began crying.

She wrestled free of his grip and picked Paul up. "You're scaring him. Why don't you quiet down?"

"Don't tell me to quiet down! A man can inquire about his family, can't he?" Pierre's face was twisted; his eyes enlarged. He leaned in toward Marie.

"I thought you were more interested in what flows from the bottle than your family."

She looked at Pierre, but her mind was on more urgent matters.

I've got to tell John about Ilchee's warning. Dammit, Pierre, if it weren't for your drinking...

But then, she would never have met John.

That thought made her sad.

Pierre probably would have died drinking or been thrown in jail because of his debts from drinking.

Pierre said nothing. He turned and looked out at the river.

Marie could no longer muster anything like sympathy; seeking to cut the conversation short, she blurted out, "Honestly, Pierre, we were picking berries."

He turned back toward Marie and the boys. "Well?"

"Well, what?" Marie shot back.

"Where are the berries?" He held out his hands for some.

"Couldn't find any. Guess the bears got them all." She brushed past him, holding Jean Baptiste by the hand. She wheeled around, "Don't ever touch me again, or I swear, Pierre..."

Just then, Cadotte appeared. "Is there a problem, Madame Dorion?" He glared at Pierre.

"No, Francois. There's nothing here."

John yelled from down the beach, "Let's load up! Time's a-wastin'!"

* * * * *

Several minutes later, Cadotte pushed their canoe away from shore. It glided smoothly, dipping slightly in the back when the giant Frenchman jumped aboard. An east wind buffeted them, raising a chop in the river. Whitecaps were visible everywhere now and slowed their progress mightily. The big Frenchman sang *En roulant ma boule*; his baritone voice floated on the breezy air. His oarsmen kept time, their strokes matching the beat of the music. The men in the other canoes joined in.

Sitting with the boys beside her, Marie scanned the far riverbank, looking for what she knew not. *Trouble could be lurking.* The breeze was warm on her face. Across the river, she saw a stand of oaks, their leaves blazing orange against a background of green firs and pines. Sun glistened off of the water. She wondered if she should tell John about her conversation with Ilchee. There hadn't been the time before they relaunched.

He would know. Certainly, he wouldn't bring her if it weren't safe.

She decided to talk to him after they made camp for the night.

Her thoughts came back to the boys. She held them close to her. Paul laid his head on her lap and slept. She looked again out over the landscape. "This must be what Eden was like," she mused. Eden with several hundred Indian warriors waiting for their chance to kill you!

CHAPTER SEVEN
THE TRANSITION

Marie found the combination of the *voyageurs'* singing, the warm sun, and the rocking movement of the canoe irresistible. She had drifted into a state somewhere between dozing off and full-on sleep. The west wind, kissing her cheeks and blowing through her hair, brought her out of her semi-conscious state. She spun her head to look behind them. A west wind could mean weather was coming off the ocean, but the horizon was clear.

Before long, Cadotte called out the command to unfurl the sail. He was hoping to rest his men by taking advantage of wind power. One of the middlemen, LeClerc, turned to unstrap the sail from the mast. The wind caught the canvas sheet, which fluttered and then popped to full deployment. This new propulsion source sent the canoe gliding over the white-capped chop, making the ride bumpy. The paddlers, resting their oars across their laps, awaited Cadotte's commands to guide the canoe as needed. The voyageurs had been in constant motion. Singing and rowing to the rhythm. Never missing a beat. Marie noticed that the other canoes had also deployed their sails and felt thankful for the men to rest. With her boys onboard, she wanted these men to be at their best.

The wind pushed them onward, and they made good time, even going against the river's current so that by mid-afternoon, the first canoe touched the sandy bank of a place known by the fur trappers and traders that plied these waters as Jolie Prairie. They'd made ninety miles that day.

Marie stretched, letting the warm sun wash over her. Hours in the cramped space of the canoe with two boys crowding her had left her body stiff and aching. Her feet sank into the soft sand as she trudged up the steep, sandy bank, making every step a struggle. The boys, full of energy, ran ahead. Marie was joyful that her boys' energy, bottled up by several hours in a canoe, was now given vent.

Marie trotted a bit to keep them in sight. "Stay close," she yelled after them. Within seconds, they had disappeared over the top of the embankment. She was on edge both by their close call and by the words of warning Ilchee had spoken. She needed to find time to talk to John about what she had learned.

Now, topping the embankment, she saw the boys rolling down a grassy hillside; their giggling sounds filled the air. Marie saw a sun-splashed plain covered in long, green grass, with sprinkles of blue flowering plants scattered around. Oaks and white-barked birches sparsely populated the hillside and in the distance she saw a lake with oak trees scattered about. Beyond the lake, an undulating plain rose toward foothills covered by fir and pine trees.

While Marie wandered around, taking in the new surroundings, a camp of pitched, white canvas tents sprung up, arranged in a square with a fire pit in the middle. The fur trade was about rank and separation by social class, so the officers and men like Pierre, who brought a wife and children with them, rated a tent. Voyageurs slept by the river under their tipped-over canoes that formed a roof against rain and wind, but that was about all. The unlucky men would spend the night walking the perimeter, watching for any encroachments of natives or wild animals.

Marie heard the crackle of the fire and saw a spark fly as a knot burst into flames. She looked around her at the meadow where they would camp. It smelled of oak trees, fall wildflowers known as camas, and grass. A sweet smell of grass intermingled with the onion-like odor of the camas plant. Their offensive smell was balanced by its beautiful blue flower. The whiff of onion reminded her it was time to put dinner together.

She sent a *voyageur*, a man named Smith, to the river for water. Smith was one of a few Americans in their group. She didn't know him well, as he was quiet and kept to himself, but she had made up a story about him but didn't know why. It was probably because of his mysterious ways or the scar that etched his forehead from what could have been, perhaps, a glancing tomahawk blow. He looked like a rough character, like a rogue bandit from a Walter Scott novel she had once read. While thinking of Smith, she cut up hunks of salted elk meat, then retrieved a bag of dried radishes and peas from one of the supply bundles. She had carefully labeled the bundle in big black lettering in English and French and had directed its placement in the canoe so that she would have ready access to her cooking gear upon settling in for the night. As she worked, Smith came back to her mind. She imagined he was a man on the run from his past. The fur trade was an excellent place to hide; many men made up names for themselves. And Smith? "Really? That was the best he could do?"

She nearly jumped when Smith came up behind her and said, "Here ya go, Madame Dorion." He had surprised her at his quick return. She muttered a quick "Thank you," avoiding eye contact as she was afraid he might somehow know what she was thinking. The hair on the back of her neck stood up a little.

Watching him walk away, she thought, "Something is going on with that man."

She dumped the water into the pot, which sat on rocks beside the fire. Flames licked at the black outer shell. Then came the cut-up meat. She dumped the dried vegetables in and left the pot to simmer. She had learned food preservation techniques from her experiences with her mother's family, the Ioways, and while working alongside her mother and sisters out in the wilds of Canada. Mostly, they had preserved fish and meat. Roots were their vegetables. Eventually, she had learned the valuable art of making pemmican, the meat and berry concoction that, when dried, formed a high-protein meal for *voyageurs* on the move.

Marie's latest home at Fort George presented different environmental issues that hindered and helped food production. It's somewhat mild yet cold and damp climate, with rains and wind slashing off the ocean, made the growing season short, maybe about ninety to one hundred and twenty days during the middle of summer into September. However, the loamy, mossy soil made a fertile planting bed, so once the sun warmed the soil properly, the seeds in the ground virtually exploded. Despite this unpleasant climate, the fort's garden produced peas in abundance and other cold-weather crops such as cabbage, radishes, and carrots. Combined with meat, these formed the bulk of the dietary intake for the fort's population. Of course, there was salmon, always!

Jack and Tom brought in the bounty in the fall, and Marie used the fresh produce as much as possible. Potatoes, carrots, and other roots were stored in barrels in the fort's cooler below the kitchen. Whatever couldn't be consumed quickly was dried for later use. Peas, pumpkin slices, cut-up squash, and beans were hung on strings from the kitchen ceiling until thoroughly dried.

Marie's thoughts came back to dinner. She moved the kettle closer to the rocks next to the fire. Satisfied that dinner was well in hand, Marie went to the river to find Archie.

"Archie," she called out to him. He looked up from his work of unloading a canoe. "Come here," she yelled and waved her hand as a signal to come to her.

Archie approached her on the run and breathlessly uttered, "Pie?"

"Not yet. I'll show you."

Marie and Archie walked to the pot. "Look," Marie said to him, pointing into the pot.

Archie stepped hesitantly toward the pot and peered over its lip. Then he looked back at Marie, his face scrunched in puzzlement.

"When it boils...."

He looked confused.

Marie rolled her arms, spinning around each other. "When it boils." Marie nodded at him to gauge his understanding. She used one hand like a spoon, raising it to her mouth. "Bluh, bluh, bluh." She made the sound of boiling gravy.

Archie smiled broadly. "Pie!"

"Yes, when it boils…," she pointed into the pot. "Bluh, bluh, bluh. Pie. Okay? Here." She handed him a stir stick, a long-handled stick with the shape of a small paddle at the opposite end. "You stir." Okay?

"Okay," he nodded.

"You watch and stir," she said, backing away and pointing at the pot. "No sneaking!" She wagged a finger at him as she spoke. She smiled at him.

Archie nodded again.

"Good boy!" She thought it was a weird choice of words. Archie was a full-grown man. Somehow, she didn't think of him that way but couldn't understand her feelings about him. "Maybe it's because he's broken that I treat him like a child," she mused.

Marie glanced at the grassy hillock where the boys were rolling downhill in a somersault fashion. Pierre was with them.

Marie strolled through camp, looking around.

John was working at writing on the top of a turned-over shipping crate in his tent. She felt herself turn towards him and then turn away. "Now's not the time."

Ilchee's words weighed heavily. "Maybe after supper." She turned away and found a dirt track close to their camp. At her first step on the trail, she felt a weight leave her, an unburdening. She discovered the path ran east toward the distant mountains. Primarily for her, it just led away.

Pierre loves the boys. He's a good father when not drunk. She glanced up at the blue sky and let out a sigh. Her shoulders sagged a bit in resignation. *But he is often drunk.*

As she strolled, she used this alone time to consider what had occurred. This time to escape without physical or mental demands was a gift she granted herself whenever possible. But only when she felt she wouldn't be missed because, in her mind, she was always in service. The children constantly needed something. Paul still needed his diaper changed, but those incidents were getting less and less. Jean Baptiste had shown him how to pee on trees, so now little Paul ran around with no pants, peeing on things that caught his attention. Marie chuckled at the memory of the grimace on Pierre's face when Paul had peed on his favorite saddle. She had worried how he would react since he could explode with rage at the slightest provocation. She'd incurred his wrath, taken his beatings. But he never hit the boys, ever.

"Good for the leather," was all he said as he walked away.

Her service to Pierre was on an entirely different level. He was barely less work than the two boys. His neediness, both emotional and physical, always needed to be satiated. She took care of his traps, clothing, knife, powder, and ball kit for his rifle. If she missed a step, a trap spring unoiled, his knife dull, anything amiss, there was hell to be paid. Worse than the beatings were the way he berated her for some triviality. "YOU don't take care; WE don't eat or worse!" He would yell, pointing at a rusty spot on a trap or an infinitesimal piece of dirt on his clothing. He had the power to shame her, and she hated that about herself.

While he entrusted her with the care of his field kit, one item was off-limits: Pierre cared for his rifle. He oiled and cleaned the weapon daily. He would tell the boys, who sat at his feet and watched him work, "The rifle is the only thing standing between you and the wilderness. The wilderness wants to kill you. The rifle protects you. Take care of it, and it will take care of you."

As for lovemaking, she was done.

But then again, as much as she loathed the idea of Pierre's touch, she wanted to give herself to John freely and with enthusiasm. He was gentle yet solid. Strong. Marie found herself longing for him at various times of the day. She watched him and how he commanded his men—in control. Yet he allowed them to make decisions and act as they saw fit. She'd been around the fur trade long enough to know that the Company frowned on independent action. That's how Indians got hanged for stealing baubles.

Then there was her responsibility to the expedition, the men; they required food and looked to her to prepare it.

Out in the field with the fur brigade, things changed somewhat. Breakfast was a quick affair, food on the run. Her first task would be to get a fire going and put out ready-made biscuits already dried like hardtack. She fried up bacon and served it mostly cooked, laying it on the biscuits. Grumbling men would file by and grab the food. They didn't sit. They ate on the move. Mornings were about getting loaded and shoving off in the canoes while the stars shone brightly overhead.

Dinner would come a few hours upstream. Tomorrow, after a few hours on the water the canoes would pull in at a spot known as *The`* Prairie. The meal consisted of tea, some pemmican, and pipe smoke to fuel their incredible feats of endurance.

There was more time for supper, and this meal, while served on trenchers of hard, stale bread or wooden platters instead of fine China, was usually hot and provided the majority of the calories for the day. The men would be sitting around, "smoking and joking," as John would say—resting weary bodies, sitting on the ground using packs as a backrest.

The air would be cooling, the daylight dimming, the forest night noises gathering, crickets chirping, and owls hissing as Marie worked over the fire-heated pot. At her signal, usually a whistle, the men filed by, holding out a wooden cup or bowl or platter, whatever they had, and she would put meat, gravy, sotted bread, and vegetables onto or into their container. She served them with a smile and a kind word for each man. Despite the daunting, physically demanding work they performed every day, their grit impressed her. For the officers and gentlemen, she would carry the pot to their dining tent and serve the food on fine China while the clinking of crystal wine glasses filled the air. After serving them, she saw to the boys, and lastly, once she had finished cleaning and packing away all the cooking equipment, it was her turn to eat.

As Marie moved down the path, she felt a chill in the shady spots as the late afternoon sun faded. Huge oaks with fire orange leaves, which rustled in the faint breeze, dotted the mostly grassy plain. The trail skirted the edge of the lake and continued to the east, parallel with the river now a quarter of a mile away, by her estimate. As Marie passed by the lake, she saw a green-headed mallard swimming. A drake with five little ducklings trailing behind her followed the mallard. The sight of the struggling ducklings brought a smile to Marie's face. "Awkward things," she thought. "So fuzzy and cute." She watched for a bit but then moved on to find their nest, which she located after a few minutes.

The serenity of her bucolic surroundings was soon interrupted by the booming report of a rifle off in the distance. *Hunters.* One of the first tasks taken care of upon setting up camp for the evening was to deploy the hunters to scare up some food from the local environs.

Marie noticed a patch of plants with blue flowers, which she immediately recognized as the camas plant. Knowing the culinary value of this plant, she strode off the trail and began pulling these by the root. The edible bulb would be ground into mush and fried with some elk or deer fat to make fry bread that the men loved. It filled them more than any hunk of meat could. If she could find enough berries or a bee's nest, she would mash the berries and drizzle the juice or honey over the fry bread.

"These will dry for a few days, and then they'll be ready," she decided.

She gathered several of these plants, so much so that she had to take off her outer elk-hide shawl to bundle up her bounty. Leaving the bundle behind, she moved further on the trail, deciding to pick it up on her way back rather than lug it with her on her walk. As she walked, she breathed deeply and noticed a hint of hyacinth. The sweet fragrance dancing on the breeze reminded her of growing up around the Great Lakes. Fall was her favorite time there. After the heat of summer had dissipated and before the frigid north winds began to howl.

The sounds of leaves rustling brought her back to her present. She loved the fall here, too. The sun shone brightly during the months just before the rains came off the Pacific. An almost constant wind freshened the air during the day and the cold frosts of night. And everywhere, like home, there was water: lakes, the big river, and the ocean.

Trees flourished.

The hills and mountains were carpeted with firs and pines. Under that canopy, an entire ecosystem of ferns, moss, and creatures like frogs and skeeter-bugs played in the wetness of the land. Birds sang sweetly, their trilling sound bouncing off the walls of trees. Ivy slowly scaled inch by inch up the mighty firs, year after year. Rabbits bounced along. Deer and elk grazed in the occasional open meadow or nibbled on the leaves of smaller deciduous trees. Wolves howled at the moon, and of course, cats—cougars slinked through the forests, taking whatever moved.

She looked skyward. It had turned from blue to a deeper hue, something like purple, and the evening star appeared in the eastern sky.

Marie dropped to her knees and looked at the ground.

She said her daily Our Father, and then, spreading her arms and looking to the sky, she conversed with *Wakan Tanka,* the Great Mystery of her people. She thanked the Mystery for the water, the air, and the food that the Earth Mother provided and that the Mystery made possible. She asked that the Bear continue to watch over her and her children, keeping them strong regardless of what lay ahead. They must be brave. Was Ilchee right about the upriver tribes, she wondered?

Rising to her knees, she turned back for the camp. The light was dusky now, and the shapes of things in the distance faded to indistinguishable shapes. As the stars came out in abundance, she came to where the wilderness ended, and the camp began. She stopped. She wanted to turn back, to escape the pressures and her mundane existence. The boys were in her mind as she took that first step. As she entered the tent ring of their camp, the world descended onto her shoulders. Looking towards the gathering of men, she saw the fire blazing brightly. The men had eaten, and someone had brought out a harmonica. The *voyageurs* sang their bawdy love songs loudly. Jean Baptiste and Paul danced and swayed to the music. The bottle had started to make the rounds. "Oh Lord," she thought, and then she saw Pierre lying on his side, watching the boys dance and laughing at the words to the song. She glanced at John's tent and saw him still working away at writing. "That must be some report." She decided to fix him a plate and take it to him.

Pierre saw her, and they had a moment of eye contact. They both smiled and then Marie turned away.

· · · · ·

A woman's voice came, saying, "You seem a world away."

John Reed looked in the direction of the voice. "Aye, Mare." He rose and walked toward her, stopping short, realizing eyes were everywhere. Yet he yearned to tear through the inches of air between them and wrap his big arms around her. Propriety, however, ruled his behavior. It was not his reputation he worried about, but hers. "What have ya there?" He nodded at the plate in her hands.

"I brought you some food."

"Very kind of ya, lass." He took the plate--covered with cloth--from her hands and set it on the table behind him. "Enjoy your walk?"

She thought she had secretly stolen out of camp. "How'd you know?"

"I pay attention. Might need to rescue you again." A smile spread across his face.

"Huh. Well, I think it's time for me to rescue myself." She recognized that the statement might be misconstrued. She changed the subject. "What were you thinking about?" She paused a bit and pointed at his tent flap, "When I walked in."

"Ah, my brother in Scotland."

"You've never mentioned him."

"He's my older brother. He's the laird of the manor." He collected his thoughts for a moment. "He's very protective, worries about me. When we were young he'd keep me from getting thrashed by the rougher kids that were about."

"I see. My Jean does the same for little Paulie."

He nodded at her. "Yeah, like that. He still does. My brother. He's the oldest, so he's to inherit." He looked at the ground and grunted. "May have already. It's been a long time since I've had word from home. My father saw to it that I got sent off to university to follow a path chosen by him. My brother always looked in to make sure I had everything I needed."

"Quite a family. And your parents?"

"Far as I know, they're still alive." He hesitated. "I've others ya know. Got three younger brothers and a sister."

"Well, when you go back, they'll be so proud of what you've done here. You won't be showing up with your hat in your hand. You've done well." She wore a smile and brushed her hair back, exposing her neckline to him.

"Aye, lass, but right now, all I'm thinkin' is takin' you to my bed." A smile broke out. His eyes sparkled as he moved a step or two closer to her.

He could feel heat from her body radiating toward him. "What were we talking about?" He laughed at his own joke.

"I was saying that your family will be proud of you."

"Sure, if gold in the bank is a measure of a man's worth." John uncovered the plate in front of him. "Eggs? Where'd you get these?"

"I found them in a duck's nest by the lake. Eat!" She was quiet while he took the first bite. Then she searched her mind for something to talk about that would move the topic from their liaisons to another subject. "What did you do at university?"

"I was in the seminary. God, these are delicious." He pointed his fork at his plate.

A smile came to her. She put a hand to her mouth before a laugh could escape.

"Pretty funny, eh?"

"I'm sure you would have been a wonderful comfort to old maids and widows, Father John. Comforting them in that way you do." She wore a broad grin.

His face turned flush. He looked down at his feet. "I save my charms only for damsels in distress." He looked up, beaming a huge grin. "Didn't ya know?"

"Think you're funny, do you?"

He shrugged and looked at his feet, one of which was being used to trace patterns on the dirt floor.

John grabbed the fork on his plate and sat on the stump he used as a chair. He began to wolf his food down. She'd made some fry bread at the fort before they left and had saved one for him before the men had taken them all. It had a smear of huckleberries on top.

Watching him eat, she smiled while enjoying the pleasure of his truly satiated hunger. She longed to walk toward him, and as she moved, her body tingled, imagining running her hands over his broad shoulders, kissing his neck. The tightness of his body would relinquish control as her hands moved over him. She envisioned him reaching back to willingly guide her from behind him and then slowly lay her on his table as he devoured her with his lips, tongue, and mouth as voraciously as he was going after the food on his plate.

When he looked up from his plate, he saw her smiling and looking at him. "What? Haven't ya seen a starvin' man eat before?" He snorted a half laugh. A piece of food flew from his mouth, and he continued eating, hoping she hadn't seen or wouldn't say if she did.

"I've no napkin," he said with a smile.

Marie glanced around to see who might be nearby. Seeing no one, she moved to his side and, taking his left hand, she put each finger in her mouth, one by one. She held his hand for a moment. Smiling at him, "Better?"

"Oh, yes, lassie. Vastly better." He started to rise to his feet.

With a hand, she gently pushed down on his shoulder as if to say, "Sit." Her smile faded. "I need to talk to you."

He noticed the change in her appearance. Her face was now wrinkled with concern, and her eyes had lost their playful sparkle.

She went back to the other side of his table. "John, the boys and I met a woman in the woods earlier."

"Where? Who?" He stopped eating and looked at her.

"When we stopped for dinner, the boys wandered off, and I went looking. She saved us from a cougar that had the boys up against a tree."

"Who was she?"

"Ilchee. Concomly's daughter. You've seen her at the fort."

"Aye. For sure. She's a tall one. Sturdy." His eyes sparkled.

She must have seen the glint in his eye. "Easy, boy. I know you like 'em tall!"

"Don't forget sturdy," he added.

They both laughed at that.

"You're the devil himself! What did they do with you at seminary?"

"I got expelled for getting caught in a broom closet with one of the cleaning gals. She was a fine one. Big lungs!"

"Don't be a pig!"

He chuckled. "Forgive me. I forget myself."

"You're a wonderful man. I don't take offense." She paused for a minute. "She told me there's trouble upriver."

"What?" John stood up. Threw his fork down. It clattered on his ceramic plate. "Damn that Concomly! Fuckin' Indians. Can't trust...." He broke off his statement.

Her arms flew wide as she spoke with her hands, "Whoa, John! You forget yourself!"

"I didn't mean...."

"Me? You meant all the other Indians but me?"

"I'm an idiot. Forgive me."

"Just remember, I've got Ioway blood running through me, so watch yourself." She could see his head hanging. "Now, think for a minute, would you? His daughter warned me. Why would she do that if her father was up to no good? Why would Concomly risk his position of privilege with the whites? Huh?"

"Okay. I'm listening." John looked her in the eyes.

"Ilchee said the Shoshone, or as you would call them, the Snakes, are mad about the incident last year." She saw the confused look on his face. "William McGill? The hanging`?"

"Oh God, that bloody fool!" John's face had turned red, and a vein popped on his forehead. "Damn it!" He took a deep breath. His face slowly regained its natural coloring. "We sent`m back to Montreal on a ship, remember?"

"Maybe you should've shipped him to the Indians instead."

"I'da been all for that, but not McKenzie." He cleared his throat. "Concomly came to the fort. Demanded McKenzie hand him over so he could be taken to the Snakes to satisfy the relatives of the dead man."

"Seems like a just solution."

"Yeah, except the boy had powerful friends. His uncle is Alexander McKenzie. Fuckin` fur trade royalty."

"And another white man gets away with murder, literally." Her arms folded across her chest.

"Aye." John nodded. He stared down at the ground for a few seconds. Then, looking at her, "It was arranged for him to be smuggled out on that British Navy ship that was here last fall."

She shook her head. "Damn!" She looked at the tent's ceiling, exhaled, then brought her gaze to him. "John, I just need to know we are not taking my boys into danger."

John Reed folded his napkin and placed it on his plate. Then he rose and moved around the table, taking her in his arms. "Sweet Mare. We've been in danger since we left St. Louis three years ago."

"I know, John. There're no guarantees out here. But as a mother, I have to know we will not all be slaughtered in some revenge killing!"

"Mare, I'll not let anything happen to ya and your boys while I am drawin` a breath."

She rested her head on his chest. His strong arms were wrapped around her, holding her close. She breathed him in. The smell of the river and the woods covered him. It was familiar. She breathed deeply, letting out a slow exhale. Her eyes were closed. She whispered, "Thank you."

He stroked her soft, shiny hair. The warmth of her body radiated into him. He let out a sigh. "Oh Mare, if only...." He quit speaking, his eyes darting to the tent door.

Then, the tent canvas rustled. A figure stood in the opening with the flap pushed aside. He swayed on his feet. "Well, this is a fine thing, isn't it?" He tossed a near-empty bottle to the ground, where it clattered on rocks.

Marie broke away from John, spinning toward the voice. "You're drunk! Where are the boys?" she demanded.

"Looking for their whore of a mother, I'm sure!" Pierre, with that snarling look he gets before he strikes, pulled his knife from his belt and, crouching with arms held out at his sides, moved toward John and Marie.

CHAPTER EIGHT
AFTERMATH

It was the birds that woke Marie. Their light tweeting singsong skipped through the air of that fuzzy-gray dawn, like a rock skimming over the surface of a glassy pond. Enough light filtered into the tent so she could make out the shapes of the two boys lying beside her under the buffalo robe. Their outlines rose and fell with the rhythm of their sleep breathing. Rolling slightly back, she instinctively reached out to Pierre, but her hand swiped at the air.

Her head snapped toward where Pierre would have been. It was then the events of the previous evening flooded her mind with images. Her stomach cramped a bit. "Damn fool!" She let out a heavy sigh. She replayed it in her mind's eye, saw herself spinning away from John's embrace and taking Pierre to task. She'd pointed her finger at Pierre's chest, "Don't be an idiot!" The gleaming steel blade of Pierre's knife reflected the candlelight in John's tent.

She remembered John's words. "Aye, lad, there's no call for all this!" John stood with one hand behind his back. She soon discovered this hand gripped his pistol handle, which he had thrust into his waistband.

Marie replayed the words that John had said. These words spun around in her head.

"I love her! And I'll not let ya harm her. Ever!"

She'd not considered his words of love at the time, but as she lay in the tent beside her two sons, she was thunderstruck by his repeated profession of love for her.

"She's a possession to ya. Nothin' more," John had continued.

"SHE'S MY WIFE!" Pierre yelled and moved toward John, knocking her sideways to the ground.

The officers and *voyageurs* had been having a good time, singing loudly to a violin's undulating strains, oblivious to the events inside John's tent. She recalled there had been sounds of a fiddle, harmonica, and general revelry filling the air. This added to the confusion Marie had felt at the time. So much joy outside and so much anger within the tent.

John had pulled the pistol from behind him. Pierre had stopped abruptly once it came out.

"Easy, laddie," he hissed. "No one would fault me for shootin' ya where ya stand." She heard John's words in her mind and saw his finger on the trigger. His hand had been steady. "And to tell ya true, nothin' would give me more pleasure."

Pierre had gathered himself. Stood tall and said, "Then she'd be all yours, wouldn't she?" Pointing his knife at Marie, who sat on the ground, he added, "And my sons. YOU'D TAKE THEM TOO?!"

He had waited for an answer. An answer that never came.

"I'll die first!" She had been surprised by Pierre's voice. It had shaken a bit as he spoke.

"Take one more step with that knife, and you'll get your wish. I assure ya!" John had said coolly.

Marie did not remember getting to her feet. But she did remember the look on John's face as he held his pistol on Pierre. He was calm as a pool of water. A slight grin had creased his bearded face. His steady hand extended the pistol level at Pierre's chest. She remembered thinking, he's made up his mind to shoot him dead.

The two men stared at each other for what seemed an interminable time. She had just been ready to get between them when Pierre feigned a lunge. Then came the distinctive sound of a pistol's hammer striking the tinder box. No familiar ignition of gunpowder, just a click. Pierre smiled, recognizing his good fortune, "Gotta keep your powder dry, John," he said. Then he had crouched low and went in for the kill.

A child's breathing brought her back to the present, taking her focus away from those frightful images. She raised her head a bit and looked out of the parted flap of the tent. She could see one star in the early morning sky.

"God, why do I feel like the glue holding everything together?" She wanted to run away and be free. The thought of escape made her feel light, but within seconds, she felt shame and guilt. She reached out to Paul, caressed his silken hair, and slid her hand down to his back.

"Momma will never leave you," she whispered to the two boys. One of them made a chortling, throat-clearing sound. A snorting snore followed, and Marie giggled.

As she lay warm under the buffalo robe, she realized two things. First, the men were up and breaking camp; she heard movement and clattering of tin and metal in the tent circle. Second, she had to pee. She braced and crawled out from under the warmth of the robe. Cold air sent a shiver throughout her body. Scrambling to her feet, she made her way to a bush.

When she emerged, she saw the men walking toward the river, white bundles on their backs. The bundles typically weighed 90 lbs. This standardized weight helped evenly distribute the loads in the canoes, facilitating the watercraft's mobility as they shot the rapids churning through the *dalles du mort* basalt rock formations. She knew she was putting her life and her children's lives into the hands of these *voyageurs*. She trusted their skill as excellent oarsmen. They had seen the worst of what North American waterways had to offer. Many water features had the names of the *voyageurs* who had died trying to run them. A properly loaded canoe was an essential yet critical element in successfully navigating the treacherous waterway known as the Rapids of Death. Marie knew they were less than a half-day away from the Dalles.

She scanned the grassy meadow where they had camped. There was nothing but a smoldering heap of ashes where there had been a square surrounded by tents. Elk bones and an empty rum bottle laid in a heap. The tent she had shared with the boys was the last one standing. Quickly, she turned away from what had been and moved to the tent to rouse the boys.

Within minutes, Marie had a white canvas bundle on her back, and a tump strap encircled her head at about the hairline. This device moved the weight of the load to the carrier's spine, taking the strain off the shoulders and lower back.

The two boys groggily trod alongside her. They came downhill onto the sandy riverbank. The river smelled cold and fishy. Cadotte approached her. "Let me lift your burden, madame." He walked to the canoe and dropped her pack into it.

Marie scanned the beach looking for Pierre. There was no sign of him. "Boys, go get in the canoe."

She watched the boys run toward Cadotte, kicking up sand as they went. The big Frenchman yelled out, "Come here, my boys! Uncle Cadotte will load ya!" He didn't push the *gran pere* title on the boys. She smiled as the boys squealed with laughter upon being picked up and placed gently in the canoe. Cadotte threw a blanket over them.

"Do the magic trick," yelled Jean Baptiste. Soon, Paul joined the rhythmic chant, "Magic trick. Magic trick."

"Okay, my boys. Ready?"

The two boys nodded.

Cadotte retrieved a small, carved figure of a dog from the pocket of his woolen jacket. He held it up between his forefinger and his thumb. "See?'

The boys, wide-eyed, nodded in the affirmative.

Cadotte enveloped the figurine in his hands. He moved them rapidly, in a circular motion. Then he opened his hands to show that it had disappeared.

Paul called out, "Where'd it go, *gran pere*? Where did it go?" Jean Baptiste waited quietly.

"Well, my dear Paulie, it's right here." He reached over to the young boy's left ear as he spoke. "Here it is!"

Paul squealed in delight at the sight of the little dog. "Can I have it!? Can I have it!?"

"Here you go, my boy!"

Cadotte noticed Jean Baptiste, watching him. "Do you wonder where your figure is?"

Jean Baptiste shook his head, "No, *gran pere*. I know you have something for me as well."

Cadotte laughed a big, throw-the-head-back laugh. "You know your *gran pere* so well." He reached over and took off the boy's cotton toque; it was red, and the upper half flopped down towards his left ear. "You see?" Cadotte held up a small wooden carving of a duck. "Quack, quack," he said, handing it to the boy. Cadotte tossed his knit cap back as well.

Marie checked on the boys.

"Look, Mama, I got a dog from *gran pere*," Paul said, beaming and showing her his prize. Jean Baptiste held up his little dog carving.

"You boys stay here. I'll be back." She walked toward John's canoe. What she saw made her stop still in her tracks. Pierre was shackled to the mast of the canoe. She turned her gaze from Pierre to John, who barked orders to his *voyageurs*. John saw her, and a smile broke across his bearded face. He strode over to her.

"What's going on?" Marie fired out at him, pointing in Pierre's direction.

John turned to look where she pointed, "Him? Your husband assaulted an officer of the company. There's consequences."

"John!" She stopped talking. Her eyes closed, and she took a breath. "You know where we are going."

"Aye, I do."

"*The Dalles.* We get into trouble; he'll go under, tied to this thing," she pointed at the mast.

John glanced at Pierre and then back to Marie. "Good riddance to bad rubbish, I say." He saw the look of disapproval on her face. "He pulled a knife on me, Mare! For the second time, I might add!" A vein popped in his forehead, his face reddened, and his arms swept around as he spoke.

Marie folded her arms and gave him a sideways look. "Do me two favors."

With hands on his hips, John brought his gaze up to hers and huffed an outward breath of resignation, "Aye."

She retrieved a bundle of papers from the bag at her side. She handed the tied bundle to John and said, "Put this in the mail sack for Montreal."

John took it and examined the address. Then he read it aloud, "Miss Ida Freeholder of Spartanburg, Connecticut?" He looked at her, "What the hell is this lass?"

"Just put it in the mailbag for Montreal. And untie Pierre before we get to the rapids. He can't swim. Give him a fighting chance." She spun and walked to her canoe. Cadotte extended a hand, which she took as she stepped into the canoe, then nestled in with the boys.

John had watched her all the way. Shaking his head, he muttered, "I'll be damned." He stepped into the canoe and approached Pierre whose eyes grew wide as he saw John coming with his knife drawn, Pierre's own knife.

"Ya gonna kill me with my own knife?" Pierre's body stiffened.

"Relax, asshole." John bent down and cut the leather thongs that kept Pierre connected to the mast. John turned to take his spot in the middle of the canoe.

"Why'd you do that?" Pierre rubbed his right wrist.

John looked over his shoulder. "Your guardian angel came to me in my sleep." He smiled and winked.

Pierre, who had spent the night tied to an oak tree, turned red with rage. "GODDAMN YOU!"

John's smile faded. He tossed the knife in its sheath to Pierre. 'You've come at me twice with a knife and lived to tell about it. You do it again; I'll shoot you dead." John turned away. Yelling to his bowman, "Let's go, Robespierre!"

"Yeah, if your powder's dry," Pierre called after him.

The comment rankled John. Hair stood on his neck. He knew how to keep fresh powder in his weapons. "Damn," he thought. "Would've solved a lot of problems." But then he wondered if Marie would've rejected him for killing Pierre, even in self-defense.

There was a large man at the bow of the canoe. He pushed the canoe into the river. As the canoe glided away from shore, the voyageur, who went by the nickname of R.P., jumped onto the canoe's bow, and assumed his position. Soon, he was at work with an oar guiding the bow into the main channel. Once the canoe was pointed appropriately, the men behind him began to row in unison.

John took the letter out of his coat pocket. He reached for a metal box and lifted its lid. Its hinges creaked. He tossed the bundled letter into the box among a couple hundred other pieces of paper. These were correspondence concerning the operations at Fort George and personal letters home from the homesick men who would remain in the Oregon country.

The oars cut the calm river surface in perfect unison, keeping rhythm with the *voyageurs'* song. John's French was functional at best, but he got the gist. He'd heard this one occasionally throughout his travels in North America. It was about a buxom barmaid in Montreal who had broken many a man's heart. Many had come up with offers of marriage. Wealthy men were turned away. *Voyageurs* too. She finally accepted the proposal of the local Anglican clergyman. A gangly, bespectacled man with a bad case of acne! Oh, *Mon Dieu*, as the song goes, who would marry such a beast! And now, when the *voyageurs* return to town, they spend their time at church instead of the bar. He chuckled to think of *voyageurs* attending a protestant church, as these Frenchmen were almost exclusively Catholic.

"I guess love is blind," John thought. He turned around slightly and looked at Pierre over his shoulder. "Yeah, it is," he thought as he turned back to the bow.

• • • • •

Marie and the boys rode midway in their canoe. The vessel glided over the river's surface, rising and falling over the white-capped waves. The sun struggled to break through a layer of fog that shrouded the river. Right behind her, Archie worked at whittling something resembling a fife or flute, and Cadotte's baritone voice sang out from the stern. Cadotte's eyes scanned the surface for logs and other debris. Anything smashing into a canoe would be disastrous.

They were off the shore at *Thé* Prairie a couple of hours later. The lead canoe turned toward the popular stopover. It was here that fur brigades stopped for breakfast on the outbound journeys, where inbound brigades, who'd been months in the wilderness, stopped for the night to celebrate with whatever alcohol remained, bathe in the river, and, in the morning, put on their best clothes, before starting on the final leg of their journey.

Recognizing they were abreast of *Thé* Prairie, Cadotte yelled the command, and his oarsmen steered their craft for shore. This would be a quick stop for pipe smoke, tea, and maybe some pemmican.

Marie let the boys run over to some huckleberries, telling them to pick as many as possible. "If you do well, I will make you a pie," she promised. She spotted Pierre off sulking by himself, chewing a piece of pemmican and sipping what she supposed was tea. With everyone in their places, she sat down in the lush grass of the prairie. She looked upriver. The fog was lifting, and she could just see the first basalt cliffs of the Gorge. Here, the river narrowed a bit, and a little further on, say fifty miles or so, there were a series of rapids where the river crashed over and around more basalt formations – the Dalles. On the way out from St. Louis they had run these same rapids. But this time, going upriver, they would be forced to get out of their boats more often. That would make them vulnerable to attack.

While she thought of what was coming, her natural motherly intuition kept alert for her sons. As long as she could hear the boys chattering, they were good. It was when it got quiet that she worried. She could hear them arguing about their seats when they returned to the canoe. They both liked to be as close to Cadotte as possible, to listen to him sing, bark out commands to his rowers, and maybe tell them a story about his life in the wilderness, his life as a *coureur de bois*. She'd had to chastise Cadotte when his tales became too vivid for her liking. "Remember, they are just small boys." The big man hung his head at her critique.

She listened to the boys argue and thought to mediate but decided against interjecting into their squabble. Instead, she lay in the grass and stared at the sky. Her thoughts went back to things she'd heard while traveling from St Louis about how this country and the lands beyond had been formed in such an unusual way.

Two scientists had been sent from the east with the overland expedition. They were both from England and sponsored by the Royal Horticultural Society. One of these men, Thomas Nuttall, would recap his day's observations around the fire almost every night. Mostly, his talks were about plants or animals of the area, but when they got to the river gorges of the west, the topic changed almost exclusively to geological observations. Marie could not recall the exact terms he had used, but he had talked extensively about seeing layers in the rock formations. He suggested that these were from different volcanic eruptions over millions of years. "There were, of course, the massive eruptions caused by shifts of tectonic plates deep within the earth that, combined, formed the volcanoes of Mt Hood and Mt St Helens, but hundreds of smaller volcanoes all contributed ash and lava. We're traveling in an area of the world that millions of years ago was on fire!"

Nuttall's hair was a wild red mass that had been dried and frayed after months of traveling overland. Marie recalled that he looked like a wild man in the firelight. His movements, which seemed agitated and twitchy anyway, were accentuated by the dancing fire.

"Sounds like Dante's Inferno," John had said.

"Dante never imagined a hell like this, Mr. Reed. I assure you," Nuttall said.

One night, Nuttall's last at Fort Astor, the men were gathered around the table in the Great Hall for the evening meal. The room hummed with the sounds of men murmuring through mouths full of food and drink. Nuttall was to get on a ship the next morning, which that night lay at anchor in the bay west of the fort. It was headed for Shanghai to drop off furs, and then, loaded with spices, silks, and other goods, would arrive in London six months hence.

At one point, Nuttall rose from his seat and repeatedly clinked on his glass with a spoon. The murmurs finally subsided when he spoke, "Quiet, please. Quiet." After a pause, he continued, "Thank you. To my hosts, Mister Hunt, Donald Mackenzie, and the officers and men of Fort George, I want to say thank you again for your hospitality and for putting up with me on this grand adventure across the continent of America." He raised his glass. "A toast then to all of you. To Marie for a wonderful meal tonight and the many she prepared on our journey." He looked at Marie, who let a small smile crease her face. Nuttall raised his glass to his lips and sipped his wine. Turning to the ship's captain, who occupied the seat of honor at the head of the table next to Hunt and Mackenzie, "Captain Talbert, thank you for the ride home!"

The captain nodded, and after all had sipped their drinks, he said, "Modesty prevents me from taking all the credit. The Royal Horticultural Society is paying me handsomely, I might add, for bringing you and your samples back home!" The captain's face broke into a wide grin. Polite laughter was heard amongst the clinking of glass.

Nuttall said, "Thank you just the same.' He sat back in his seat to raucous cheering and clapping.

Donald Mackenzie rose and spoke next. "Dr. Nuttall, it was our pleasure to have you accompany us. Please do tell the captain here about your theories on the formation of the land in this part of the continent." Mackenzie turned to Captain Talbert and said, "This is really quite fascinating."

Nuttall's face lit up. He always enjoyed the opportunity to speak about his findings. Sitting at the table, he spoke at length about the scablands they had come through after their descent through the Rockies. Marie explicitly recalled his discussion of floodwaters ripping across the lands, carrying debris for hundreds of miles. His descriptions were biblical in scale, and Marie wondered if something similar could have happened in the lands of the Old Testament.

Nuttall continued, "Great ice dams formed and broke over a few thousand years, let's say. Water rushed forth over the lands, carrying with it all that stood in its path; rock, soil, and everything was wiped away. Like it had never been. The land became a clean slate. Over time, these floods made the great channel that we call the Gorge."

Someone spoke out in an alcohol-induced slur, "That gorge from volcanoes and a flood?"

"Not a flood. A whole series of floods over thousands of years. It's truly the hand of God at work!" Nuttall's eyes were wide, and his face blushed with a fervor approaching fanaticism.

The screech of an eagle soaring over the river snapped Marie back to the present. She looked to the sky, from where the eagle's call came. Sitting up, she watched it dive down low toward the water. It skimmed the surface with its talons. Suddenly, the great bird slowed to an almost stop. It dipped into the water for what seemed to Marie to be the span of a heartbeat. She watched the bird slowly pick up speed again, and as it rose, she could see a thrashing salmon locked tightly in the eagle's grip. She watched the bird rise until it was out of sight.

"C'mon, lads, let's get back to it!" John called for the breakfast to end and the journey upriver to resume.

Marie yelled for the boys to come. They ran up to her, their mouths and cheeks streaked with the purple stain of huckleberries. Marie put her hands on her hips, "Show me your hands." She almost burst out laughing at the sight of purpled, stained fingers. "Well, I guess you ate more than you picked, right?"

The two boys nodded.

"Off ya get then." She feigned a bit of anger, but mostly, she was disappointed because she'd been hoping to get a nice pie together somewhere along the way. As Marie watched them go, John approached her.

"Here you go, lass." He handed her his pistol, a bag with lead balls, and another with powder.

"What this?"

"You know where we're goin'," John said matter-of-factly. "We're always surrounded; at the fort, out here." He moved his right hand in a sweep of the forest. "The trees have eyes. Right now, we're being watched. Messengers are running upriver to report our coming." He looked her in the eyes. "If arrows start flyin', shoot at anything that moves."

Marie took the pistol and the two bags and put them in her satchel. "Did you load this one?"

"Huh?'

"The one you held on Pierre last night. Wasn't loaded."

"Powder was damp. He's lucky by a damn sight!"

"Or you're lucky I stopped him from using that knife on you after the misfire."

"That was a nice takedown, fo' sure. Remind me not to make ya mad!" John's face broke into a smile, and just as quickly, the smile faded. "Look, if I can't be there for ya, that'll mean I'm..." He pointed at the pistol as his words trailed away.

"What happened to 'It's gonna be fine?'" She smiled slyly and gave him a wink.

"'Ya know how it goes out here. Probably nothin' to worry about, but just in case."

"You just be careful, you hear?" Marie turned and walked away. Within a few minutes, she and the boys, along with Archie, Cadotte, and the oarsman, were aboard the canoe pointed upriver. Due east. The *voyageurs* sang. Marie cuddled the boys to her. Archie continued to whittle.

"*Gran pere*," Paulie cried out. "Sing us a song!"

Cadotte hesitated to respond, lost in thought. Then his face lit up, and his deep baritone voice could be heard, "Frere Jacques, Frere Jacque..."

"Again, again, *gran pere*!"

Cadotte repeated the song from his childhood a few times until he noticed young Paul was asleep, his head resting on his mother's lap.

Marie scanned the vast river in front of them. The towering walls of the Gorge were now plainly in view. On the near shore, maples, oaks, and birch trees were lit up in bursts of orange that mixed and mingled with the evergreens. The sound of the white canvas sails unfurling brought Marie's attention back to the river. The sails, once deployed, snapped tight against the onrushing west wind, pushing their craft fast over the chop of the river towards the east.

They passed sand islands with flowing green grass. Small birch trees dotted the islands' landscape. Come May, Marie knew this island and the many others in the river would be submerged under several feet of water. The spring thaw brought the outflow from snow melting in the nearby Cascade Range. Marie was happy to see the *voyageurs* getting a respite from their labors. They would need their strength for what lay ahead.

As they went further upstream, the river changed from a wide expanse to a narrow channel. To her it was like the walls of the gorge closing in. Basalt cliffs rose high above the river until the only view of the sky was directly overhead. Beacon Rock came into view. It was a monolithic, volcanic plug named by Captain Clark just a few years ago. She watched seagulls swarming around the Rock, gliding on thermals created by the wind sweeping over the river and battering into the Rock, forming an upward gush of air. Her ears heard the unmistakable sound of millions of gallons of water rushing through a rock-filled space a few hundred feet wide. The resulting roar was echoing off the walls of the Gorge. It was a low roar that Marie recognized at once. Her body stiffened a bit, and she pulled the boys close. She had heard the sound many times before. It was the siren song of the rapids, the *dalles*, the basalt tubes, and whirlpools where death lurked at every twist and turn. The rush of water over and around rocks sent a cacophony upward; the airwaves were alive with the roar.

Then she thought of Ilchee's warnings and knew soon they would be battling more than the river. *How many would die this time,* she wondered.

CHAPTER NINE
THE DALLES

The boys slept; their heads lay on her lap. She stroked their hair, soothing them into deeper sleep, while her eyes focused on the nearby riverbank to her right. The pistol lay on a leather-wrapped bale of cargo in front of her. It was loaded. One of the boys murmured. She looked down and whispered, "Sleep, my baby. Mama's here." Then, she lifted her eyes to the riverbank and saw a flitting image in the brush about halfway up the bank. Was it an animal, maybe a deer? Then she saw it again. A brown splotch moved gracefully, barely making a sound.

A deer would be crashing through the brush, she thought. *And would run away from humans.* This, whatever it was, moved parallel to the river.

"Cadotte?"

"I seen 'em, Miss. Just keep your eyes straight ahead. Probably a scout. Nothing more."

Cadotte started up with a rowing song. The other men joined in, rowing to the rhythm. Oars in perfect synchronization. Their craft was gliding through the water now. An eyewitness would barely guess their canoe carried close to a ton of cargo, all neatly packed in 90-pound bundles, not to mention the weight of the nine human beings riding inside.

They rounded a bend in the river, and Marie saw the wind spray from falling river water over the rocky channel ahead. Then came the arcing movement as the canoes headed for the bank and the first portage of the trip. This one would be short—maybe half a mile. Several men with rifles would guard the trail through the lava rock as the remainder carried the packs and canoes along that protected trail.

After disembarking, she and the boys stood on the rocky riverbank, the roar of the water drowning out all sounds. The boys were quiet, watching the beehive of men and packs moving towards the east to the other side of the rapid below.

Marie looked down the bank and saw John in an animated conversation with Pierre. John's arms were waving and pointing at the packs. Pierre stood with arms crossed. Then she saw her husband lean in. The roaring water prevented any words from reaching her. Soon, she saw John toss his hand in the air and walk toward her.

John raised his voice to be heard over the river, "Mare, that husband of yours, he's quite a wee frilly, ain't he?"

She looked at John's face; it was flush. His voice had a hard edge.

She leaned in.

He leaned toward her with his right ear.

Yelling, she asked, "Did he just inform you that he's an interpreter and guide and doesn't haul packs?"

He stood straight and yelled, "Yeah, although not as politely as you just said it! Something about those packs and my arse was the general gist of the conversation. Anyway...." John tossed a hand in a swirling arc, then, pointing at her, said, "You and the boys are waiting here. Johnson and McCrory are waiting here also."

Marie glanced at the two men and noted that each was armed with a rifle and had a hunting knife hanging from their belts. McCrory tipped his hat to her. Johnson managed to smile.

"They're two of my best with a rifle, and they've seen some scrapes against the Blackfeet and still got their hair."

Johnson lifted his hat, rubbed the sweat off his balding scalp, and set his hat back down.

Marie looked at John and burst out in laughter.

"Well, they ain' been scalped anyway!" His eyes were smiling at her. They sparkled because of her. "Keep your pistol in hand and the boys close," he yelled. "I'll be back for you soon."

She watched him walk away until he disappeared around a rock wall. Then she looked around at the few scattered packs and the canoes, which weighed several hundred pounds by themselves. These would require a man on each end and two on each side. She decided that when the first canoe was moving up the trail, she and the boys would be right behind it.

Marie and the boys sat on the hard, rocky surface and played a sign-language game she used to teach them how to communicate with the natives they might encounter. They were the children of parents who were the children of Lakota and Ioway mothers. They needed to know where they came from and who they were. She made the sign, pointing her index finger at the boys and then at herself. She saw their eyes intently watching her. "We," she said, "will." Then, her right hand moved like a blade cutting the air in an up-and-down motion. "Wait," she finished. "Understand?"

The boys' heads nodded to indicate understanding. She turned to look at Johnson and McCrory. McCrory cradled his rifle, looking toward the brush and timber above them on the bank. "If trouble was coming, it would come from there," Marie reasoned. Johnson was out of her sight but soon came stumbling out of the brush.

"You were gone long enough," McCrory said matter-of-factly.

"Call of nature, my friend," the American replied. He looked at Marie, his face blushed a bit. "Sorry, ma'am."

Marie was looking up at the blue sky. She saw a red-tailed hawk floating above. How easily it moved through the air, floating on invisible currents.

Her eyes returned to earth with the first whooping sound erupting from the timberline. It was muted by the cascading water and announced the presence of three rushing warriors. A spear came whooshing through the air, striking Johnson in the throat. His rifle dropped to the ground as his hands reached for the spear. Blood flew through the air. Marie would always remember the look of surprise in the dying man's eyes as he fell backward with a heavy thud. McCrory swung his musket toward the oncoming warriors. His weapon belched smoke and fire as it erupted, sending a metal ball crashing into the skull of the lead warrior. Bone, blood, and flesh exploded from his forehead. The warrior landed on his back. Dead.

The other two hesitated, looking at their companion. McCrory began the reload process. Ball and wadding loaded in the barrel. Ramrod pushing them down. Stopper in the powder horn pulled. Powder added to the pan of the flintlock. Before he could finish, the two warriors were on him. McCrory wrestled one to the ground with his musket clattering on the rock. He pulled his knife, and his hand plunged toward the warrior underneath him. The third warrior spun toward Marie and the boys, looking at them menacingly. Marie was aware of Paul's crying. Jean Baptiste was silent. A menacing spear balanced in the warrior's right hand as he moved toward them, crouched low.

Marie grabbed the boys and physically lifted them into the canoe. She yelled to Jean, "You and your brother stay in the canoe. I'll come get you!" Then she pushed the canoe out into the river. Turning back to shore, she brought her pistol up to eye level. She held her free hand up, palm toward him, "Stop!" The warrior, who had moved within mere feet of her, stopped dead in his tracks upon seeing the pistol leveled at him. He stood up tall and still.

Marie took out her knife and sliced open a bale near her. "I hope there's something in here. Please, God!" She reached her hand in the bale; it had strings of beads. She raised them, "See." Then she tossed them to the warrior, who caught and examined the beads. "Take," she pointed at the bale. The warrior moved closer to get a look. Marie backed away, never taking her eyes off of him or lowering her pistol. "Take," she said again. "Then go!"

He called his partner to halt and motioned for him to come over.

"Let him up," she yelled to McCrory, who had pinned his foe to the ground.

"But they killed Johnson! That can't stand," McCrory pleaded.

"We've killed plenty of theirs. We'll let them go, and they can take this bale of beads and buttons with them."

McCrory looked down at the Indian on the ground. Straddled over the top of him, McCrory moved his knife quickly, slicing off a piece of the left ear lobe of the man under him. The man winced and shot a hand to his wound. Blood gushed out of the cracks between his fingers. "Something to remember me by." McCrory spat the words out, and then, getting to his feet, he grabbed the Indian by his leather shirt and pulled him to his feet. The man stumbled toward his fellow warrior. McCrory picked up his musket and leveled it at the two Indians.

"I say we got 'em where we want 'em."

"Yeah, except if you miss or I miss, I got two kids in a canoe with no mother. Besides, use your head for something else than a hat rack. We kill these two; there's-what do you figure-a hundred more where they came from? A thousand?"

McCrory scratched his capot for a minute on that one. "They're fuckin' fish-eaters. Not afraid of 'em!"

"Tell your friend Johnson that! Look, who knows how many are now running this way. The gunfire would bring warriors, and we: you and I," Marie waved her pistol towards McCrory and then back at herself, "are going to hold them off? God knows how many? That math doesn't work out in our favor. This way, we got one dead Indian and one dead white man, and they got a bag of goodies. I think that makes things square in their eyes." She let that information settle for a bit. "Now keep a watch out. I need to go get my boys." She looked at the two Indians, who seemed puzzled at what to do next. "Shoo, shooo. Go, go!" She wagged her pistol at them, signaling what she wanted.

The warriors turned abruptly and walked away, dragging the dead warrior and leaving with just a few strings of brightly colored beads.

"Guess they figured you were going to shoot 'em, so they high tailed it!"

"Nothing like an angry woman with a gun to get men moving in the right direction." Marie scoffed.

When she dragged the canoe with the two boys ashore, John rounded from the rocky labyrinth. He looked at a dripping-wet Marie, then McCrory and the contorted body of Johnson lying on the ground. He strode over to the prostrated fur man. Felt for a pulse but retracted at the cold feel of the dead man's skin. "FUCK!" He went to McCrory, taking powerful strides, "What in the fuck happened here?" He pointed at Johnson.

"They jumped us. Johnson caught the first spear. I shot one, had one of 'em down, and was ready to do him in when she stopped me!" McCrory pointed to Marie.

"Mare?"

She answered, "Yes, John. They killed one of ours, and we killed one of theirs, and I figured that was a draw they could live with. I had two kids in a canoe in the middle of the river to think about. Plus...."

He cut her off, "You're a mother. I'd expect that's how you'd think."

"Don't say mother at me like it's a dirty word!"

"Mare, ya know that's not...."

"Just say thank you for saving us. That'll do." Her face was darkened; a vein popped in her neck. She turned and led the boys from the boat to the river trail and across the portage to the new embarkation site. Along the way, she, holding Paul's hand, who in turn had the hand of Jean Baptiste, pushed past *voyageurs* returning for their second load.

When Cadotte and MacTavish came along, Cadotte saw her temper flaring in her eyes; her face, usually soft-featured, was rock hard. Such was the force with which she walked that he stepped off the narrow, sandy track that had been worn through hundreds of years of use.

"Madame Dorion, what is the matter?"

She stopped, glaring up at the big man, "The matter? Never mind." She looked him up and down, "You won't get it either."

Cadotte watched her go, leading little Paul by the hand and Jean Baptiste trailing. He heard the little one calling, "Mama *j'ai faim! J'ai faim!*" They rounded a corner and were gone.

"C'mon Mr. MacTavish there's more bales to get."

"I work in the counting house. I'm not a toter of bales!"

"Mon dieu." Cadotte shook his head.

· · · · ·

Marie and the boys reached the point of embarkation. Leather-wrapped packs were stacked on the beach. Canoes would come next. She knew she had an hour or so before they'd be ready to sail again, so she quickly got a fire going using dry grass and twigs for tinder. Using her fire striker, a flint with a steel shank, she sent a shower towards the pile, which started smoking. She waved back and forth to encourage the small flame in the dried grass, which quickly spread to the twigs. She began putting fry bread together and simultaneously cared for and built the fire into a crackling, popping heap. Before long, she had the bread baking in a blackened cast-iron pot, which she nestled in the glowing coals at the side of the fire. She heaped embers from the fire on top of the pot to speed up the baking process. Next to the bread pot, she had started a pot with elk flank braising.

The boys sat on the sandy beach, watching her work. "Just a while longer," she said, looking at the two boys. In a few more minutes, Marie removed the embers from the lid, lifted it, and loaded two cups of fry bread with a layer of gravy and meat.

Paul, using his hands, devoured gravy-soaked bread. The gravy was smudged around his mouth. Jean Baptiste quickly finished the bread in his bowl and began gnawing on a hunk of elk flank.

He must be going through a growth spurt. He eats as much as a man!

As word of the skirmish spread up the line, one of the officers in the party, a Scot named Mr. Alexander Thompson, ordered sentries posted. Five men were arranged in a picket line between the tree line and the packs. Two or three were taking the time to have a smoke. Marie was surprised by their casual attitude. Cradling their rifles in their arms. Smoking. *They should have their rifles ready,* she thought. She scanned the tree line above them. Nothing. The packs were arranged in stacks according to which canoe they would be loaded into. On one end, Marie had rigged a prop stick weighted by rocks to hold a fire-blackened pot inches over the flames. The smell of smoke mingled with the scent of elk meat stew.

"Mama, *je n'ai plus...*" Jean Baptiste started.

"*En anglais s'il vous plait.*" Marie arched an eyebrow as she spoke.

"*Oui,* mama!" Jean laughed at his impetuousness.

Marie laughed as well. "Seriously, Jean?" She said in a mock, stern voice. Moving a hand from her work to her hip and pursing her lips.

The little boy laughed all the harder. "May I have some more meat, please?"

His sweet laughter filled her heart with lightness and joy. "Perfect!" Marie moved to the pot and stabbed a hunk of meat. Walking to Jean Baptiste, she pointed it toward him, hot fat dripping onto the ground. He grabbed the hot hunk of meat from the knife point and hungrily began gnawing on it. Juice ran down his chin, and the boy swiped at it with his shirt sleeve. Marie cleaned the knife blade and re-sheathed it so that it hung at her hip.

Marie glanced at little Paul. She looked at the fry bread crumbs and gravy smeared all over the child's face. She burst into laughter and knelt to wipe the child's face with river water she had collected in a pail. Paul squealed at the coldness of the water and fought to get away from his mother's swiping hand.

"There," she said, admiring her work. "All clean." She smiled at Paul and tousled his hair.

The crack and boom of a flintlock rifle, the Baker Infantry rifle was predominant in the group, startled her. Marie's head snapped toward the sound as her hand pulled the pistol out of her belt. She glanced up at the tree line to see a naked white man running toward them.

John's voice rang out, "Don't shoot, ya damn fools!" John strode toward Miles Stuart, the sentry, who was holding the smoking rifle. John grabbed the gun out of the other man's grasp. "Can't ya see he's one of ours!?"

The confused Stuart stammered, "He don't look white to me."

"Ah shite, ya idiot." John looked at him like he couldn't fathom such stupidity. "Go get 'im a blanket, damn ya!"

Miles Stuart turned on his heels and scrambled precariously over the basalt surface to the packs. He returned to John with a blanket and held it out to him.

"Not me, ya dolt!"

Stuart blinked.

John pointed with Stuart's rifle, "Him! Wrap him up and then bring him to me."

Marie turned to look at the grimy, naked man coming down the hill. He was waving his arms over his head, speaking in gibberish, and drooling like a mad dog. Still, she thought, *he looks familiar*.

Marie watched as the man, now wrapped in a wool blanket, was led to her cooking fire. He was emaciated. She quickly ladled some elk and fry bread into a metal drinking cup. He sat in the sand, and when she handed him the cup, he hungrily went after the bread, then dug with his fingers in the cup, retrieving hunks of meat, which disappeared into the man's mouth. He made grunting sounds while he ate.

"More." He held out the cup to Marie. His hand shook, and Marie had to hold on to the cup to get more food into it.

She watched the man attack the second cupful with renewed vigor. His hair was long and stringy, and he had a heavy, graying beard. He looked over the cup at her with gray-blue eyes. His free hand shoveled food into his mouth.

Marie arose and walked to John. "He's been through something awful."

"Aye. Poor devil." John paused for a moment. "You recognize him?"

"There's something about him, but no," she said. "Should I?"

"That's John Day. Been missing since we split up in Hells Canyon over two year ago."

"Holy Jesus!" Marie crossed herself, "How did he survive?"

"Look at 'im. Did he survive?" John looked at the frail, emaciated John Day; then his gaze landed on Marie again. "I gotta get these men movin'. We're sittin' ducks here. We'll be camping on that sandy island out there tonight," John said, pointing to the island in the middle of the river. "Gives us cover in case our friends come back for a fight."

"You expecting more trouble?"

John had shifted his eyes from Marie to the tree line above. "Always am."

He paused and looked her in the eyes. "Can you stay with Mr. Day? Talk to him? See what you can find out," he said. He had a worried look. "Lass, we got a canoe with damage. Some of the boys will stay and fix it. You'll be good here till I come back. Okay?"

"Sure. Just don't forget us over here." She smiled thinly and winked.

"Not to worry, my dear. Fat chance I'll be forgettin' 'bout you. I'll be leavin' your husband and two men to guard you as well!" He winked back at her. "Speak a' the devil!"

Marie followed his gaze to see Pierre rounding the bend with a tump strap on his forehead and a pack on his back. Right behind Pierre were Dugald MacTavish and five men carrying the first canoe. The overturned canoe rested on the shoulders of the men: two in front, two mid-canoe, and two on the stern.

"Make a lark of it, did ya!? Have a nice sightseein' jaunt?" John, with a wry smile, called at Pierre.

"Go fuck yourself, Reed!" He slung his pack to the ground. "I ain't your damn pack animal."

John gestured with a hand towards the boys, who were busily eating their food, "You should be watchin' your language in front of your boys. Settin' a good example and all. Least today, they get to see you upright."

Pierre glared. His face grew flush, and a vein popped in his forehead.

John scoffed, then turning to the men milling about, said, "Let's go, boys. Load the canoes as they come in. We're beddin' down on that island o'er there." He flung a hand toward the river. He turned back and pointed at Pierre. "You stay here with Mare and your boys. Pick two good men with rifles to stay with you. We'll be back shortly." He turned to go.

"John!" Marie called out. He turned to look and saw her pointing toward the tree line.

"Holy Mother of God!"

Slowly emerging from the tree line came Indians. Led by an elder, the warriors followed. They moved down the hill. All were painted for war.

CHAPTER TEN
THE WASCO

John assessed the situation. He quickly calculated the number of men who stood as their enemy. It was sizable. He turned to Cadotte. "Bring your boatmates...and your rifles," John paused, then added, "Bring the pouch too!"

Cadotte's right brow arched, and the big man replied, "*Oui, Monsieur* Reed." Then barked commands in French. The middlemen and the *Avant* came quickly, with rifles in hand. They walked past Marie and the boys.

Marie looked at the faces of these men as they passed. They were leathered. They wore beards. Eyes squinting, they showed no fear. There was not a hint of doubt that they could meet any challenge. Each wore a long knife on their side. She was sure they would not hesitate in hand-to-hand combat if it got down to it.

John watched Cadotte get his men ready, then after a moment, his look turned toward Pierre and said, "Need you too!" as he waved him over. John hated to admit it, but Pierre's translation skills would be critical. He recalled how Pierre had saved the party back on the trip out from St Louis when they had run into a sizable Lakota hunting party that was none too pleased with the white men transiting their hunting grounds, let alone scaring the game away with their presence and noisy fire sticks.

As Pierre walked over, Alexander Thompson also approached John. Thompson was an officer who had come out with the original overland party. John was sorry to see him returning to the east, but his contract with the company was up, and he had a wife and children to return to.

"Be careful," Thompson said. "I'll get the men busy setting the bales up as a perimeter in case the talking doesn't go well."

"Aye, sir. We're aiming to avoid the shooting, so...."

"You beat it back if it starts going wrong. Can't lose ya."

"Aye," John hesitated. Looking beyond Thompson, he saw Marie feeding the men and the boys chasing after one another in a game of tag. His gaze returned to the man before him, adding, "Sir, please keep the woman and the boys within your sight."

Thompson turned to look at Marie. She was busily dishing food out to the men who'd spent the last hour lugging baggage and canoes overland. Turning back to John, he said, "She'll be safe." He touched John's shoulder, looked him in the eye, and added, "You have my word."

John nodded at him, then turned, walked to his men, and, brushing past, led them to the oncoming mob of warriors.

Marie's stomach tightened as she saw the three men with whom she depended most leading the way. They were walking toward a mob of God only knew how many warriors – she figured around a hundred. Most of them were armed with bows and arrows. Some had spears, and she saw rifles sprinkled around the group.

Her attention went to a man walking out in front, the leader, she supposed. He wore a hat made of woven reeds with three eagle feathers sticking up in the back of the hat. His buckskin shirt was covered in bright beadwork, and he wore a chest plate of elk bone with blue and red beads interspersed. A little behind and to the side of the headman stood a short, slender woman. She was adorned with oyster shell earrings and a necklace of long tube-shaped dentalium shells. The necklace was off-white and had multiple strands hanging around her neck. She wore a headband of small round shells and sinew, bright brass ringlets hung by strings on her forehead. Marie could tell from her adornments that she was somebody important. The warriors stood a few feet behind the headman.

She went back to join her boys. Mr. Thompson was organizing the construction of a perimeter. Marie crossed herself and said a quick Hail Mary. Peering over the bales, she watched the action. Pierre's arms were moving as he spoke, but she could only catch a word here and there. She saw him make the sign for peace, his right hand moving slowly parallel to the ground. Then she heard him say, "Peace."

The headman's arms moved wildly. He kept pointing at the woman, and Marie picked up words as he spoke. She heard the Chinook Jargon word for dead – *memaloost*. He yelled it! The men behind him were stirring.

She saw John motion one of the men over and say something, and then the man ran back to the newly constructed perimeter.

"What's going on up there?" she asked LeClerc as they all stood, looking on.

"Ah Madam, it is big trouble."

"What, LeClerc?"

"The dead Indian? That woman was his bride. The old man is not happy that her future husband is now a corpse."

LeClerc grabbed a bale from the perimeter wall and set off. He turned back to Marie, "Stay down. Hide the boys!" And then he was gone, carrying the bale up to where John, Pierre, Cadotte and the rest stood.

John gave LeClerc a sideways glance as the trapper set the bale down. Then, looking at Pierre, he said, "Tell him we are sorry for his misfortune and that of his daughter. And that we have gifts here for him." While Pierre translated, John pulled his knife and cut the bale open. He reached into the bale and brought out an axe for the chief. John moved forward and presented it to him with a flourish, bowing slightly as if he were presenting the fine saber of a defeated emperor to the King of England.

"For you," John said. He turned slightly to Pierre. "Tell him it is for him."

"A gift," he said in Chinook Jargon to the old chief.

The chief reached out and took the wooden handle of the axe in his hands. He turned the smooth, varnished handle over and over, considered it, and then said in halting English, "It good gift." A big smile spread over his face.

John smiled at him and then reached into the bale again. This time, he retrieved a wooden box and slid the lid open to reveal blue, red, and green glass beads. "Here," John held the box out to the young woman. "For you."

The woman looked at the chieftain, who had nodded at her. She stepped forward and took the box. Seeing the beads, her face broke into a smile.

"*Merci.*"

She lifted the box toward the white men and then returned to her place. John noticed the men in the background were milling around. There was some grumbling.

"LeClerc, take a man or two and bring up two more bales," he demanded.

"*Oui, monsieur.*"

"Pierre, tell him that we are friends of Concomly. And that Concomly would be very disappointed if we could not go on our mission."

Looking at the chief, Pierre delivered the message in Chinook jargon. "Concomly, *tillikums.*" He added in English, speaking slowly with careful annunciation of his words. "Concomly is a friend of the whites, English and French. We go upriver. To build a fort. Trade with the Snakes and the Walla Walla and the Yakama!" Pierre made the sign of the river, his hands moving like a wave through the air, followed by using his two hands to make a paddling motion and then pointing upriver. "Canoes. *Cooley chuck,*" which meant river. Then Pierre started the paddling motion again.

Suddenly, a furor arose in the back. Then shouts came from the rear of the gathered warriors. John noticed a tall native man making his way through the crowd. He shoved one warrior out of his way and then another. As he burst out of the throng of warriors, his flintlock came up to level and was pointed directly at John. The man, his sneering face painted black for war, shouted some words to the chief while glaring at John. The old man yelled some words back and barked again. The younger man shifted his feet and gripped his rifle tighter in his sweaty hands. John saw his finger on the trigger.

"What the fuck is this all about," John whispered to Pierre.

"The dead Indian. I heard the Chinook word for brother."

"Oh, for fuck sake. What's he want?"

"If I had to guess, probably not glass beads!"

John and Pierre watched the two Indians squabble back and forth. They both shouted alternately. The chief's hands and arms waved around as he yelled. The warrior's gaze never left John.

"What are they saying?" John asked Pierre.

"I don't speak their language." Pierre's face twisted. He was straining to hear the words floating back and forth. "I dunno. I heard Concomly's name. That's about all I can tell you. But in all native cultures, hell in all cultures, there's an unwritten code about vengeance, an eye for an eye."

"Shite!" John considered the situation. His hand came up to his chin. He scanned the mass of natives in front of him. After a few moments, John muttered, "Fuck it!" He handed his pistol to Cadotte. "If anything starts up, you make sure that the chief and the warrior are the first dead bodies to hit the ground. You understand?" Cadotte nodded. "Give me the pouch." Then John looked at Pierre. "Come with me and leave your weapon," John said.

He began walking toward the chief.

Pierre followed.

"My heart is filled with sorrow today," John said with a strong, unwavering tone. His hands came to his chest. "Two of our brothers are dead."

John looked at Pierre, who jumped in with a string of Chinook jargon, using this trade language to convey emotional concepts as best as possible.

"Your brother," John looked at the tall warrior, "died with a strong heart, a heart filled with honor. He walked the strong path of a defender of his people." John thumped a fist to his chest twice. He heard Pierre's voice echoing beside him. "My brother has fallen, too. He had a wife and children at home. I will need to tell of his sad fate. It is a terrible thing for us all."

John hesitated as Pierre's words fell on the mob of warriors. "The coyote, the trickster, wants to cause trouble among us." John used the coyote, a familiar symbol of treachery in these people's mythology. He scanned the crowd. "We can speak with our firesticks, but it would make the gods happy if we spoke with our words as friends." John's arms spread wide toward the sky, and his gaze drifted upward. His glance came back to earth and swept over the crowd. He saw people wavering. The crowd was shuffling, milling, shifting their weight from foot to foot, and looking at the ground. There was general murmuring. Some lowered weapons.

John walked to the woman and got on one knee. He took her hand and spoke, "All I can offer you is these trinkets. I know it doesn't make up for..." his voice trailed off. Pierre translated instinctively. John handed the pouch to the woman. She loosened the strings that held the bag closed. She removed a necklace of pearls. Her face broke out with a smile, showing a full, white-toothed grin. She held the necklace up for the elder to examine. "*Merci!*"

John turned toward Pierre, "She speaks Frenc, maybe? Ask her what her name is?" Pierre rattled off the words: "*Quel est ton nom?*"

"*Je m'appelle* Kimana," the woman said in French. "I am of the Shoshone people, promised in marriage to the son of Pawashtimane." She nodded toward the chief, who was examining the necklace closely. "But he is gone now." Her face gave away no hint of emotion; she stared at John.

John spoke over his shoulder, "What'd she say?"

"Her name is Kimana. The chief's name is Pawashtimane, and I think she said the dead man is Pawashtimane's son. She speaks too fast. Couldn't get it."

Cadotte spoke up. "She said she was given to marry Pawashtimane's son."

John rose to his feet; he walked back to Pierre. "Shite, the dead man is the headman's son. That tall warrior with the rifle pointing at us...? The chief's son, too?"

Pierre said, "Makes this whole thing complicated."

John looked at Pierre. "Talk through the woman. French is better than jargon for sorting out this mess."

"Be better to have my wife talk to her," Pierre offered. "A woman speaking with another is liable to get you better information."

John cringed at the word "wife" coming out of Pierre's mouth when speaking of Marie. Like she was his property. Even more than that, he hated to admit that Pierre's logic of having a woman engage with Kimana was probably correct. John nodded and looked at Cadotte. "Aye, bring her up."

• • • • •

"They want me to do what?" Marie asked Cadotte. She wore a look of incredulity, mouth agape, her eyebrows knitted.

"They need you to speak with the Indian woman," Cadotte pointed at the mass of humanity before them.

"What about Pierre. Or Franchere? He's French for god's sake!"

"Franchere's not in the company. He stayed behind." Cadotte paused and then added, "It was last minute."

"LeClerc?"

"I don't know, Madam Dorion. I am given an order to bring you. I think they want a woman to talk to her."

Marie weighed out the situation for a full minute and said, "Okay. I'll go, but you, Francois, must remain here with the boys." She pointed a finger at him.

The big *voyageur* went over to the two boys, and in one bending movement, he swooped them off the ground, each boy riding up in his two massive arms. "I shall guard them with my life, Madam!"

"See that you do," Marie said matter-of-factly. Then, turning, she walked up to where John and Pierre stood.

John turned toward her and watched the last few feet of her approach. He smiled and said, "We're in a real mess here. What Pierre has pieced together is that the dead man is the son of the chief, and the woman is the daughter of a Shoshone head man who has betrothed her to the dead man to strengthen ties and all that kind of political horse dung."

"Who's that tall one over there?" Marie nodded at the large warrior, restrained by several members of the chief's inner circle. She noted he had long silver spangles dangling in his hair, which hung to his shoulders, and he wore a simple, narrow leather band that encircled his head. Around his neck, he wore a necklace of long white, tubular shells that held a round medallion made of tiny beads intricately embedded. These white beads formed an exterior border with a red circle surrounding the image of a black-bodied stick-figure thunderbird with yellow wings and bulging blue eyes. The thunderbird was in a field of white. The warrior wore a wide, dark-brown leather band around his left bicep. He was dressed in buckskin leggings and no shirt. A medallion dangled around his neck and hung down almost to the top of his stomach.

"Trying to talk in jargon is hit or miss, but I think he's the dead man's brother," Pierre offered.

"I see," Marie nodded as she spoke.

"Like Pierre says, the jargon isn't getting us where we want to go. I'm hoping you can speak with the girl; she speaks French, and maybe we can find out what is going on," John instructed. "Her name is Kimana."

Marie nodded and then turned and approached the young Indian woman. Standing in front of her, she leaned in and whispered, "*Viens avec moi*," while holding out her hand. Kimana reached out and clasped Marie's hand, and the two began to walk away.

First, there was murmuring, then a clamor arose within the ranks of the gathered tribesmen, and the chief yelled out, "*KO PET!!! KO PET!!!*" He raised his arms as if seeking attention from all those present.

Aware of the tumult behind her, Marie turned back to John and Pierre. "Tell him we are going over to those trees to talk privately," Marie called, pointing at a small copse of white-barked, quaking aspen trees whose leaves were turning from green to orange. I want her to speak to me without fear." She and Kimana kept walking.

They came upon a log of a fir tree, and both sat, turned in at an angle to each other.

At a distance, John and Pierre watched. "What do you think they're discussing?" John asked, covering his mouth with the fingers of his right hand. His left arm folded across his chest, and his fingers rested on his bicep.

"Fry bread recipes, probably." Pierre scoffed, "How the hell should I know?"

John cast a glance at him but ignored the remark. He and Pierre continued to suffer in an awkward silence for what seemed an eternity. John watched Kimana speak and gestured back, pointing at the crowd of warriors. Marie's voice could be heard, but the words were unintelligible. She gestured with her hands as if she were using the sign language of the trade to convey points or seek clarification. At last, John felt a significant release of tension from his shoulders as he saw Marie and Kimana get up and walk back to their respective sides.

Marie walked up. She saw John's chest heave, followed by an exasperated exhalation. Pierre looked at her while stroking the beard of his chin. His head was tilted to one side, and his other arm was crossed in front of him. *Pompous ass,* she thought.

"Well, we've got a huge problem," Marie started.

"Go on." John's face grew grave. His forehead was wrinkled, and an eyebrow was arched.

"Kimana is the eldest daughter of the Shoshone shaman Washakie. She was promised to chief Pawashtimane's son," she nodded towards the elder standing before the mob of warriors. She noted that Kimana had returned to Pawashtimane's side and that the two were conferring. Marie continued, "Or more specifically, to Pawashtimane's dead son."

"What about that very large Indian over there? The angry one?" John couldn't resist a slight smile.

Pierre spoke up. "That's the dead Indian's brother. I already told you that, John!"

Marie heard that edge in his voice; Pierre didn't like having his work questioned. "Actually, that's not what was meant when you heard the word for brother being floated around."

"No? So, who is he, Marie?" Pierre's voice took on a demanding tone. His face was flush, his mouth twisted into a crooked smile and his voice shook as he tried to contain his mounting rage.

"His name is Cameahwait. He is a popular warrior with his people—the Shoshone, he's not Wasco. Kimana said he was sent as her chaperone and protector until the wedding ceremony. It was also clear by the way she averted her gaze whenever she talked about him that she has some kind of tie to him."

"What do you mean, tie?" John asked.

"I am not sure what's between them, but something. Can't put my finger on it."

She saw a look of confusion creep over John's face. "Maybe she's concerned about disappointing Cameahwait. I'm guessing here. Could be that since this marriage has turned into a fiasco, his honor will be questioned by his people. They may think he has bad luck, and his word will no longer carry weight by the council fires. This is a big thing for a warrior." Marie hesitated for a moment to let that sink in. "But that's not his biggest issue."

"No? What is it then?" John asked.

"The Indians that McGill strung up last year?" Marie looked John in the eyes. At first, they showed nothing but continued confusion over the entirety of the situation she had described. "Do you recall?"

"Aye, I do."

She pressed on, saying, "One of the men that McGill ordered hung was Cameahwait's brother." With these words, she saw John's eyes light up. It was a moment of clarity for him, and she saw that he understood the situation.

CHAPTER ELEVEN
COOLER HEADS

Chief Pawashtimane and Kimana were conversing. Kimana pointed toward John, Pierre and Marie, speaking in an animated fashion, she used lots of hand gestures. Finally, the chief spoke in a loud voice to the assembled throng. His words were echoed by Kimana, who translated Pawashtimane's words into French. Marie translated for John and Pierre. Pawashtimane was calling for a time of grieving and a time for the angry voices to calm. Further, there would be a council tomorrow to which the white men would be guests. As Marie softly spoke within earshot of the men, they heard Cameahwait yelling something at Pawashtimane in the background, thrashing against the four warriors restraining him and dragging him back toward the tree line behind them.

John and Pierre stared in awe as the Indians retreated. "What's happening there," John asked nobody in particular.

Pierre said, "He's not happy. He just called Pawashtimane a coward and an old woman. Pawashtimane's inner circle is showing him out." He paused. "My Shoshone is better than my Chinook Jargon." He shrugged. "We should keep an eye on him."

"That's the smartest thing you've said all day," John retorted and then, with a huff, added, "I don't mean Cameahwait. I mean, Pawashtimane ordered a break in hostilities quickly. It was almost like he was afraid or something."

"Afraid? Of what? He's got a hundred or more men to our ten or so. Doesn't make sense," Pierre shot back.

"Maybe Concomly's wrath?"

Marie saw the two standing nearly toe-to-toe, glaring at each other. She stepped between them, "Holy Jesus, do you both have to have the last word?" She paused. "They will send a messenger in the morning with word of when the council is gathering. If you two can calm down, I will tell you exactly what Pawashtimane is afraid of." She looked at one and then the other. They were expecting an answer. "I'll tell you after camp is set up and we have all eaten." She pushed ahead between them, gently nudging each with a shoulder as she passed. "Grow up!"

"Lovely," John added with a touch of sarcasm. Then, "Let's get the men moving." He clapped his hands, rubbing them together. Then he looked at Pierre and said, "Maybe I need a new interpreter?" John walked away and could sense the heat of anger coming from behind him. He let out a small chuckle.

Within an hour's time, they had moved the men, the canoes, and all the baggage to a sandy island located above the rapids in the middle of the river. Marie lit a cooking fire and got busy preparing the evening meal. She sensed the men were somber. They were quiet. No bellicose banter or even good-natured joking. No violin playing. Only John Day's incoherent ramblings could be heard against the sounds of the river. She looked at him. He was strolling back and forth, moving away from the perimeter. Talking but to no one in particular. *Poor man.*

She was determined that this meal should be something sumptuous to replenish the bodies of the men who had struggled so mightily against the flow of the giant river and toted the heavy bales of supplies and the canoes over the portage. This meal should restore their bodies as well as their souls. They had suffered the loss of one of their own and now had to deal with the emotions of loss, and on top of that, there was the dread of being surrounded in enemy territory with their future anything but certain. She was sure no one would sleep that night.

One of the hunters, a tall Iroquois named Miles, had managed to rig a makeshift fish trap using rocks, sticks lying about, and driftwood. He brought in three good-sized salmon and a small sturgeon using this trap, shaped in the form of a V—broad at the end that pointed upriver and narrow at the other end. He deposited them near Marie's feet. "Here you go, miss. A little somethin' for dinner," he said with a wink.

"Thanks. And you gutted them, too. Appreciate that."

"Happy to help, ma'am." The hunter turned and walked away.

Marie cut the heads off the fish and set them aside to dry. Once they had dried out properly, she would keep them in a bag in her kitchen kit for a fish stew later. She worked now with a knife, fashioning sticks into spits on which she would have the salmon roasting over a fire. She had decided to hold the sturgeon back for another day. She would cut it into strips and set them out for drying along with the fish heads. She had a pot near the base of the fire that cooked up a sweet bread pudding. Another pot simmered with elk meat, sweet potatoes, and gravy.

She was intent on her work and didn't hear the footfalls of the approaching man coming up behind her.

"Nice work out there today."

Her head snapped around. Her glare turned to a smile. "Oh, shit, John, you startled me!

"Sorry Lass. Just wanted to say thanks." He knelt. Their eyes met. "That's not entirely true. I mean, I wanted to see you. Make sure you're good."

"I'm good, John. Thank you for checking."

"I can't get over it."

"What's that? Your immense ego? My extraordinary beauty?" She laughed.

John's face broke into a smile. He looked at her. *She always knows how to make me laugh.* "Well, yes, both of those things, but I was more thinking about why Pawashtimane just broke ranks and went away so quickly. Seemed odd."

"Well, let's just say I planted a bug in his ear!" She gave a quick, exaggerated smile and added, "Now go away before people start talking."

He looked at her. "Just tell 'em I put in my order for dinner." He chuckled and, turning on his heels, walked away.

Marie had lain the boys down in a hastily thrown-together tent.

"Mama, tell us a story about the Bear god," Jean Pierre pleaded.

"Please, Mama," Paul echoed the request.

Marie wanted to tell the boys it was time for bed and that she was needed elsewhere. "Well, I will tell you how the Bear started the world."

The two boys screamed out, "YAY, YAY," in unison.

"Okay, okay. You need to lay quietly and listen." Settling in, they used the buffalo robe for a mattress and covered it with their coats. Marie lay next to them. "The Bear awoke one day. Winter was over, and he came out of his cave. He discovered that while he had slept, the world had changed. Instead of green, leafy trees and soft, lush grass, everything had dried out. The trees were dying everywhere he looked, and the rivers where he got his fish for his meal were running, but only the barest trickle of water was evident."

"Mama, what happened?"

"Hush, my love, and listen." Marie waited to make sure the boys were quiet. "He walked through the land and found a desert everywhere. Finally, he came to a Ioway village. The People were despairing because they, too, could not find anything to eat. So, he asked the chief of the People, 'Why is everything so dry?' And he learned from the chief that the snows had not come, the Spring rains had not come, and the land had shriveled up."

Marie heard the sounds of heavy breathing, sleepy breathing. She knew they would be out any minute. She softened her tone; her voice became deeper and took on a velvety quality. "The bear left the village and came to a tall mountain. Now, he knew this was a sacred place because it was said that *Wakan Tanka* dwelt at the top of this mountain. Looking up at the mountain, the bear saw flashes of lightning and rumbles of thunder and assumed that this was the home of the Great Presence. He knew the People believed this Presence to be the Ruler of all that could be seen, even the stars in the Heavens." Marie listened for a moment and heard the breathing of sleeping boys. She kissed each boy on the forehead and then got quietly to her knees and slid through the crack in the tent that served as a door.

Cadotte was seated outside the tent on a log washed up on the island. She shot him a quick glance, and he nodded. With Cadotte standing watch, she went looking for Archie. She thought it strange that he hadn't approached her for "pie." She looked among the men eating. All were within the perimeter, yet each man was watching for approaching natives between gulps of food. She noticed the sun was going down, its blazing orange reflecting off the river. She shivered a bit against the cold air caressing her skin. *Where is that boy?* She walked to the north side of the perimeter and spotted him sitting on a small sand hill with tufts of long grass. To her surprise, he was sitting with John Day. "Well, there you two are!"

Archie looked up at her. His eyes watered slightly, and his look portrayed an emotionally awash man. They cried out for soothing words. Marie knelt by the two men, handing Archie the plate of food she had brought and was about to stand to get a plate for Mr. Day when she saw Archie offer his plate to the older man. Day had a confused look on his face. Archie made the motion of eating by repeatedly raising a hand from the plate to his mouth.

"That's very kind of you, Archie. I want you both to eat. Food soothes the soul when it is in anguish. But before you eat, let's say thanks." She began, "Our Father Who art in Heaven..." To her surprise, John Day began echoing the words. She looked up briefly but continued. "...but deliver us from evil...For thine is the kingdom and the power...Amen." She heard John Day say Amen as well.

She looked at both men. Day took the plate back, ate a few bites, and then handed it back to Archie, who took it without hesitation and began to eat voraciously. Marie spoke softly. "You two share a common experience, an experience that no one in this company understands, as well as the two of you. You should help each other. Lead each other back."

John Day opened the shirt that had recently been given to him. He turned to Archie and pointed at deep scars on his chest. Marie guessed that they were the result of torture. Burns that were inflicted with hot metal, like knife blades. Archie looked at the marks, and his eyes grew wide as he stared at the wounds. He then opened his shirt, revealing similar scarring. Marie felt a few tears run down her cheek. She had never thought to ask Archie if he'd been hurt; she just assumed it was so, and now, there was the evidence. Even now, she wondered if she had asked him if he would have shared. John Day reached over to the young man and clapped his big left hand onto Archie's shoulder. They looked into each other's eyes. Marie was shocked to see Archie shake his head and clasp the older man's shoulder in return. The sun was almost down, and the world was cloaked in a heavy dusk. She bowed her head, folded her hands, and said a prayer of thanks for this miracle she had just witnessed. "Your hand, Father, is in all good works such as this. Watch over these two men. Help them heal. Please help them to regain what has been lost. Amen." She crossed herself.

She left the two men and walked back to the main perimeter. Marie was adrift in the wonder of God—the wonder of the world.

"WHO GOES THERE!?"

Marie was stunned back into reality. She crouched low and held her hands up, "It's me! Marie Dorion," she said. "Don't shoot!"

A man's voice replied, "Walk in slowly until I can see your face."

Marie took a tentative step forward, half expecting to be shot. Eventually, the man with the rifle stood from behind the perimeter, which was constructed with leather bales and driftwood. "C'mon in," he said as he lowered his rifle. "Almost shot ya," he said matter-of-factly.

"Almost got killed," Marie responded. "Thanks for not shooting me."

"Next time, let someone know you're going out. Hear?"

"Yes. It was dumb. Won't happen again. By the way, John Day and Archie are out there. Pass the word. Don't want either of them shot."

"Yes, ma'am."

Just then, John's voice rang out in the darkness. "Mare? Need you over here."

Her gaze moved to the voice. No campfires were lit, which gave the company a feeling of being hidden from attack. Marie saw three figures in the dark. She could only make out rough shapes but assumed two of the blobs were John and Pierre. She approached the men, who were obviously involved in a serious conversation. "Look, we've got to turn back. There's one dead; these Indians are not friendly, and who knows about the tribes upriver."

She recognized the voice. It was Alexander Thompson. Earlier that day, in front of the Indian mob and then again on the sandy island that evening, he'd gotten the men to build the perimeter and then positioned them for the defense—military training.

"Nay, we aren't goin' back because of a few angry natives. You know Montreal's been belly-achin' over our poor harvests."

"Yes. However, keeping your scalp has its own rewards, right?" Thompson asked.

"They say the beaver run so thick in the rivers over there a man can use 'em as steppingstones. Don't even get his boots wet! And by God, we're goin'." John hesitated a bit and then said to Thompson, "Sides, you need to be gettin' back to that pretty wife and those kiddos."

"Yeah, and I want to get back in one piece. I'll take the next ship around the Horn."

John chuckled, "You'd spend the sail bent over the rail heaving your dinner. You ever sail around the Horn?" He didn't wait for an answer. "Rough is what I've heard. So rough the men lay in their bunks for days cause the pitch and roll make it so a man can't walk. They piss and shit themselves too. Is that how you wanna go home?"

"You're starting to make a trip through hostile Indian country sound good!"

"That's the spirit!" John clapped Thompson on the shoulder. "When you're back home in front of the fire, you can tell the kids stories of fighting Indians in the Oregon country. You'll be a hero!"

"I'm already a hero. This limp? An American Mini ball at Ticonderoga."

Marie entered the conversation, "As the mother of two little boys, I'm with Thompson here."

"Who asked you!?" Pierre's tone had a bitter edge.

John felt himself tighten, his fists clenched into balls, as he said, "Hey, watch yourself. If it wasn't for Marie, we would have no idea what's going on here."

Marie suppressed a smile.

"We're not turning around. Too much at stake to quit now." John paused.

"The moon will be up in an hour or so. We could slip away. We'd be miles upriver before they knew we were gone," Pierre offered.

"I can't have a hostile Indian tribe in our rear. No, I've got to meet him tomorrow and make things calm. Then we can leave." John paused. "Mare, what's the bug you planted with Pawashtimane?"

A smile spread across her face. "I told Kimana that you carried death in a bottle."

John's face scrunched into a look of wonder. "What?"

"You remember when the men on the *Tonquin* were killed by the tribes up north?"

"Sure."

"We were all worried about the local Indians around the fort. Remember?"

"Yes." John's eyes grew wide. A smile broke out on his face. "Son of a bitch!" Then he remembered himself. "Sorry, Mare."

"What is she talking about?" Pierre asked.

"McDougal," Thompson said.

"Exactly." Then John added, "That's quick thinking, Mare. Quick thinking indeed."

"I'm not following," Pierre stated.

"Are ya daft man? Think back. Remember McDougal calling Concomly and his leading people to the fort for a talk?"

"Yes. So?" Pierre retorted.

"He told Concomly that he had the fever in a bottle. That he could release it if they didn't behave. He had a bottle with some white powder in it; I think it was talc, or baking soda, or some such. He waved it around, making sure they all saw it." John hesitated to let that sink in. "Mare just threatened 'em with unleashing a pox upon them! Fucking brilliant!"

· · · · ·

Marie lay down with Jean and Paulie that night; lying on her back, she listened to the gentle breathing of her sleeping boys. Looking at the starry sky, she prayed to the Lord and offered thanks to the Bear in the sky. A breeze blew across her, which caused her to shudder, and instinctively, she pulled the buffalo robe higher on her body. She kept thinking about Kimana's curiosity about John, which seemed unusual. She had told Marie that she felt he was a good man and would make a good husband. Marie wondered if it was obvious to all that she and John were...something. She thought about that for a minute, too. *What were we? What are we doing?* Marie had tried to steer the topic back to Kimana and the predicament she found herself in. But Kimana always swung the conversation back to John and what a good husband he would make.

It was then that Marie became firm in her decision. *Oh my God!* After two years of conflicting emotions about John, she finally knew what she wanted, and it was John—not Pierre, John. The clarity made her body race with excitement. *AT LAST!!!* She knew.

And Kimana knew it, too. Did Cadotte? Had she been a fool to think that no one knew what was happening between her and John? This whole time, everyone knew!

She wanted to go to him now. Nestle in his arms and tell him everything, how she felt, and how she wanted to be with him in Oregon, Montreal, or Scotland. The where didn't matter, just that they would be together. But she would wait. She couldn't leave the boys, and what if someone saw her entering his tent? What if Pierre saw? *Probably drunk anyway.*

As her eyes fell softly closed that night, her last thought was, *I will tell him tomorrow.*

CHAPTER TWELVE
POTLATCH

The river's glassy surface was shrouded in a wispy mist that clung close to the surface. Marie could smell the morning humidity as she threw the buffalo robe off, leaving the boys covered. Peeking out of the tent, she glanced at the stars. The moon was still up, and Venus was in the eastern sky. She breathed deeply; the moist air smelled sweet like hyacinth. Looking toward the southern riverbank, she could make out the figures of John, Pierre, and Thompson standing near the bale perimeter. They were huddled together, conversing.

As she walked up, the men turned to her. John smiled, "Mornin' Lass!" John thought about the familiarity of how he addressed her. *What will Pierre think.* He blushed. Sleep well?"

"Not really. The ground was hard, and the boys were rolling around." She looked at Pierre. His face wore a scowl. She started to say something to him, to acknowledge him, but instead, her smile faded, and she looked at Thompson saying, "Good Morning."

"Good morning, Madame Dorion." He gave her a small bow.

She nodded at Thompson and smiled. *He definitely has that ramrod-straight bearing of a British officer.* "What's the plan today?" she asked no one in particular.

"We're waiting for our friends across the way," John said, nodding toward shore.

Marie pointed toward a misty patch on the river. "I don't think you're gonna wait long!"

The three men looked where she was pointing. Out of the mist came a canoe with two warriors rowing slowly and methodically their way.

"The chief's men," Pierre said.

"How do you know?" Thompson asked.

"The bow and stern of the canoe swoops upward, and the blue and black image of the raven, its eyes, see forward and behind."

"Is that significant?" Thompson asked.

"The chief is expected to protect the people. The raven on bow and stern represents his all-seeing wisdom." Pierre's tone was even, but his face twisted into a scowl.

The two oarsmen pulled their oars out of the water, letting the canoe glide closer to shore.

"Keep your rifles ready, boys. No firing unless I say!" John never took his eyes off the Indians in the canoe.

The men near him heard the command and spread the word up and down their line.

John intently watched the Indians in the canoe, hoping for a clue or sign of their intentions. The man in the aft of the canoe raised his hand, a gesture of peace. Then the man yelled out, "*Potlatch. Potlatch.* You come." He motioned with a hand.

John waved at the man, then turned to Marie, Pierre, and Thompson. "Looks like we're going to a party!"

$$\cdot \ \cdot \ \cdot \ \cdot \ \cdot$$

The sun was high in the sky, and there was a gentle west wind blowing, which despite itself was still capable of driving the canoe, carrying John, Pierre, Thompson, and Marie to the *potlatch*, off its course, so much so that Cadotte was constantly ordering corrections to account for it. "Paddle harder, damn you," he would bark at the *milieu* on the port side. "Keep this damn thing moving in a straight line!"

Marie looked at the *milieu* or middleman struggle to paddle hard enough. She thought he was too scrawny for the job and doubted if he weighed as much as her. He was shorter. Miller was his name. She thought he came from Germany. Every time Cadotte barked, Miller turned to scowl, his face twisted in rage, his sweat-soaked hair hanging over his eyes. The wind kicked up waves on the river; this caused the bow to rise and fall and the entire canoe to pitch from side to side.

Over the din of the river and the wind, Cadotte cursed at his men, especially Miller, to work harder. "C'mon, lads, put your back into it."

Marie imagined that if Cadotte were in ancient times, he could have been a centurion on a Roman galley using his whip on the rowers to get them to work! She thought he would make a fine Roman centurion. She smiled. Now, he used his tongue instead of a whip. *Seems more humane.*

Marie considered the *potlatch* they were going to and had to work to suppress a giggle. She hadn't quite told John everything that Kimana had said to her yesterday and had tried to get him alone for a private word, but Pierre made sure that they were never alone. Finally, she'd given up trying to tell him of her revelation and told him to clean up his beard and brush his clothes.

Marie's gaze turned to John, sitting mid-canoe. *Cleans up well.* Her smile faded. She had been fond of John for many years and knew he was in love with her. All she had to do was look into his eyes. The way he looked at her and the way he touched her spoke volumes. Maybe she should have ended their affair long ago, but she hadn't been strong enough to do it, and now she knew why. Last night's epiphany may not have been heaven-sent, but it struck her like one of God's lightning bolts, making her realize that she could never end things with John - be the good and dutiful wife to Pierre —because she loved John. It was that simple. And even though her years of being educated in the Church and learning that what she was feeling was wrong, she wondered, *How could a loving God punish someone for loving someone?*

The canoe's rocking movement snapped Marie back to the present. They were near the shore, and she saw the two heralds of the chief standing on the riverside to guide them to the village. As the canoe glided unassisted, Miller laid aside his oar and sprang over the gunwale into knee-high water. The bowman jumped out, and the two pulled the canoe's bow until it grounded on the sandy beach. He then ran to Thompson and carried him to land, keeping the gentleman's shoes and clothes dry.

They followed the two natives into a wood and along a beaten path. Marie picked up a hint of wood smoke and knew they were not far from the village. In a few moments, they emerged from the wood into an open clearing in which sat a longhouse, a large, narrow, long wooden structure where the natives had community gatherings, feasts, and other celebrations. Smoke was pulled through a hole in the roof's peak about midway between the entrance and the very back of the building. Smaller huts were arranged on either side of the longhouse. Marie's attention turned to sounds, barking dogs and squeals of children playing, that floated through the air.

Chief Pawashtimane, Kimana, and a horde of natives were gathered near the entrance to the longhouse. Off to the side was Cameahwait. He stood with arms folded across his chest. In his arms was cradled a long rifle. He sneered.

Chief Pawashtimane started the conversation. Kimana translated, "Chief Pawashtimane welcomes his guests, the children of the mighty Father in England, King George III." Marie, standing beside John, quickly translated Kimana's words.

"Tell them we are happy and delighted that the children of this vast Garden of Eden and the children of the King are friends and are walking the path of peace!" Marie and Kimana worked on translating. Marie recognized the term "Garden of Eden," would need to be explained. She waited explained this to Kimana, "Do your people know the word paradise?"

"I can explain what is meant," Kimana replied.

Walking up to some children standing in front of the assembled villagers, John stepped forward and began to talk to them softly. Marie watched him moving from child to child, passing out peppermint candy sticks; he patted heads and smiled. He noticed that none of the children was eating the candy. The children looked at the candies confusedly.

"Ah, me laddies and lasses, it goes like this." John demonstrated by putting a candy stick in his mouth and sucking on it. Some of the children followed his lead and tried the candy. Smiles broke across their faces. Others looked hesitantly back at their mothers. Receiving nods of approval, they began eating the candies. Smiles abounded. John came to one little girl at the end of the line of children. She was crying, and he knelt at her eye level and said, "For you, my crying angel, I have a special treat."

The little girl sniffed, and wonder overcame her desire to cry. John took a packet of waxed paper out of his bag and unfolded it to reveal a small square of dark chocolate. "Here, " he raised the paper toward the girl. "For you."

The little girl took the square of chocolate and bit into it, as it melted in her mouth her eyes lit up and she let out a giggle of joy.

"Good, eh?" John asked. The little girl nodded; chocolate smudged around her mouth. John tussled her long, dark hair. "That's a girl!"

John strode back to Marie and the rest of the group.

"Nice," Marie whispered.

Chief Pawashtimane said a few words, then turned and entered the longhouse. Kimana followed, but the remaining tribesmen waited for the whites to enter before they entered.

John said to no one in particular, "I guess it's dinner time?"

"Brilliant," came Pierre's sarcastic remark somewhere behind the group.

"Well, I thought I'd get a jump on the translation. Might take you a bit to get it straight!" came John's rejoinder.

"Boys quit arguing!" Marie smiled. *They're worse than Jean Pierre and Paulie.*

"WOMAN, no one asked you!"

Marie wheeled around, and, grabbing Pierre's coat lapels, she said in a quiet, forceful voice, "Don't ever call me 'woman' again. I have a name!"

She saw disbelief; his eyes widened, bulging a bit.

"Especially don't call me your woman!"

Her eyes met his. Her face betrayed a rage that she had tamped down for years. It all came bursting to the surface as she pushed off, releasing her grip. Pierre stumbled a step or two backward. She turned and walked with John and Thompson into the longhouse, walking beside the men, not behind them.

Pierre regained his balance and followed behind the group.

She felt John staring at her; pointing a finger at him, she said, "Don't say a word."

"Who me?" John replied, his face registering mock surprise. "What would I say that you didn't, Marie?"

The oar-men had been told to stay with Cadotte, rifles loaded and ready for a hasty retreat if needed.

Upon entering, Marie saw a raised stage-like area at the far end of the building, and Pawashtimane and Kimana sat alone. John, Marie, Thompson, and Pierre were directed to benches on the left side of the dais. A large fire burned in the middle, a man dressed in only buckskin pants, his hair cropped short, occasionally threw large chunks of wood on to keep the flames roaring. His short haircut showed that he was a slave. Hair represented virility and manhood. Cutting the hair sent a message that he was something less. Judging from his tall, lean body, she guessed, based on his lean, tall build that he was Shoshone or Bannock—definitely a Plains Indian, not a river dweller. Marie's attention went to another man who came to the fire-tender and barked commands. Her gaze left the fire pit as she watched the trail of smoke rise, in curlicue fashion, from the fire to a hole in the ceiling twenty feet overhead. Around the room, torches were attached to tall poles which supported the beams that held the roof.

A commotion coming from the entrance drew Marie's attention. Twenty or so men and women entered. They were dressed in ceremonial robes of a woven material that she guessed was like cotton; that was how it appeared to her from a distance. The robes were of vibrant reds, blues, and yellows. The men wore wooden masks decorated similarly; the most prominent features were a wolf-like creature's bulging eyes and teeth. Most of the carved surfaces had blue and white covering. They paraded in and took a position at the front right, near the dais. Marie guessed they were holy men or part of the tribal council.

Other groups began filing in and taking seats on woven mats on the floor. They sat in arcing semi-circular patterns on either side of the hearth and its bursting flames. Marie listened to the low murmur of voices as all became seated. Before long, Pawashtimane stood, and Kimana joined him. Pawashtimane gave a welcome, turning first to the men and women at his right, then to the assemblage, and as he spoke - his words floating over the air and echoing off the longhouse walls and ceiling - Kimana translated the chief's words into French and Marie translated those words into English.

"He is welcoming the gathering of his people. He welcomes the Wolf Society members and calls them his wise counselors. Those would be the group in the robes to his right. He welcomes the white children of the great King in England."

John, Thompson, and Pierre sat quietly listening to Marie, their eyes on the chief.

The chief and Kimana continued, and Marie translated, "He has come to realize the great power of the whites. He has heard from their friends up and down the great river of the power of the whites. Their sticks of lightning, their forts, their great numbers. It is with this knowledge that he welcomes us today, and he calls for gifts to be given to all to mark this great day of peace between his people and the children of the King."

Marie located Cameahwait in the back toward the entrance. He was without his rifle, and the only thing he wore along with his buckskin was his perpetual scowl. His arms were folded across his chest. However, she considered it a good sign that he was not vocalizing his displeasure. *This may work out yet.*

John leaned in toward her and whispered, "This is going well. I'm crossing my fingers that it stays this way. Big ugly back there is behaving too," he nodded at Cameahwait.

Marie smiled. She looked at Cameahwait and noted the paint on his face. A four-inch band of black ran from his right temple to his left, enveloping his eyes, burning hatred amongst this field of black. The black was bordered with red running along the top of the black band, and the bottom was bordered with white. His forehead was white, and streaks of red ran in individual streams down his right cheek. Around his neck was a dandelion shell choker. His ebony locks flowed to his shoulders; he cradled his rifle like a mother cradled a baby. "I'm not sure he's in a peaceful, loving mood," she whispered to John.

"Why do you think that?"

"Look at the war paint."

John scanned Cameahwait's face. The warrior sneered at John. "Aye. He does seem a little crotchety for sure." John chuckled, then said, "Me and that one is going to tangle one day."

Marie glanced at John, then her eyes moved to continue watching Cameahwait. She noticed a glint of metal on his chest. She'd seen that medallion on Cameahwait yesterday and before that she had seen Concomly wearing one during a dinner in his honor at Fort George. Concomly was proud of the medal that he had received from Captain Clark, a few years before Marie and the overland party had reached Astoria. *How had Cameahwait gotten a Peace medal?*

She watched as native women moved through the crowd, handing out gifts in woven baskets to the less fortunate of the tribe. She couldn't tell, but she guessed the baskets probably included grains, roots, dried salmon, and maybe elk jerky. These would help get the people through the approaching winter. Small trays of dentalium shells and ornate leather pouches went to the robe-wearers, and they each revealed the contents of their bag, showing a hand-carved pipe and a pouch of tobacco. There was a general buzzing of human chatter in the room. Pawashtimane rose from his seat on the dais. He called out for quiet while motioning with his two hands for all to quiet down. Then he began to speak.

Kimana's voice called out the chief's words. "The great Chief Pawashtimane has one more gift to give. He is greatly pleased to have the children of the Great King here with us today. Despite the tragedy of yesterday. The deaths of two men. One being his son, which causes him great grief. But he recognizes his son was a young man and young men are given over to their passions. He should not have attacked the King's children and so he wishes for peace, and to give a gift that will bind the two peoples together in peace until the time when the lights in the sky go dark. The Great River runs dry. The salmon comes no more, and the birds no longer fly."

John leaned into Marie, "This oughta be good."

Kimana called to John, motioning with a hand she bade him to come to the chief's side.

John looked at Kimana and, pointing at his chest, mouthed, "Me?"

Marie nudged him with an elbow. "They want you up there."

Pawashtimane said something curtly, and Kimana started walking toward John. She reached out, inviting him to take her hand and come with her. As Marie watched the two walk to the dais, she felt uneasy. Her chest tightened, and her pulse quickened. She moved to the edge of the log bench she was sitting on.

Then, with John and Kimana standing before him, Pawashtimane handed John a leather bag, like the ones he had passed out to the Wolf Society robe-wearers a few minutes before. John took the bag and opened it. He removed the pipe and admired its carvings of birds, elk, and salmon on the long stem. The bowl was carved to represent the mountain god Loowit, which was appropriate as Loowit occasionally belched smoke and threw out ash. John turned to the crowd to show the beautiful pipe.

When he turned back to Pawashtimane, he said, "I have nothing to offer you in return except my friendship and the promise that I will always strive for peace between our people."

The chief and Kimana looked at him blankly. While John had been speaking, he didn't notice that Marie had come up to a point a few feet behind him. She quickly translated the words into French, and Kimana relayed the information to Pawashtimane.

Marie watched for a reaction. The chief's eyes brightened, and he smiled and raised his hands to the air. In his language, he said, "Oh Sahale...giver of the light, the salmon and caretaker of the people, anoint this marriage with your blessing." He then moved to John, took Kimana's hand, and placed it in John's hand. "Let there be peace!"

Marie's heart felt crushed as she realized the chief's meaning. She did not need a translator to know Pawashtimane had just betrothed Kimana to

John. From the back of the great longhouse, she heard the screams, yells, and threats of Cameahwait in perfect French, "I CURSE YOU OLD MAN. YOU ARE A DOG! A WOMAN!" Cameahwait started for the chief, but the chief's men tackled him and then dragged him out the door.

She watched as the chief's bodyguards flung aside the hides covering the doorway to the longhouse. Cameahwait's yelling was heard well after he had disappeared from the building. Then she turned to John; their eyes met. Her mouth was agape, and her mind spun as she tried to understand what had just happened. The thunderous pounding of feet and hands in approval and the loud trilling of the women overwhelmed her senses.

She wanted to scream.

She looked back at Pierre, who wore a twisted grin and a smirk that said, "You're mine!"

She wanted to vomit.

She looked again at John, whose expression was one of a man caught in a nightmare he couldn't get out of.

He was trapped.

And they both knew it.

John's face was twisted and flush as his emotions swung between anger and desperation. Looking at Kimana, "This is a mistake." He saw her face looking inquisitively at him. "Christ we don't even speak the same language!" He knew he had to tread carefully. Upsetting the chief could bring a hundred arrows hurtling at the small knot which formed his delegation. *Marie. I have to protect her. Maybe if I can give the chief another alternative.*

John started to say something to the chief, to refuse this offer of marriage, but Marie cut him off. She spoke directly to Kimana. "John, uh, Mister Reed wholeheartedly accepts Chief Pawashtimane's generous offer of a bride. He has been alone too long. He needs a partner and is excited to be your husband."

Kimana's face lit up, and her face broke into a smile. She spoke excitedly to Pawashtimane.

Marie started again, saying, "It will be nice to have another woman on our journey. To share in our work."

The chief called for food to be served, music to be played, and dancing to begin.

John approached Marie and said, "What the hell are you doing?"

Marie looked John in the eyes. She took both of his hands in hers. "I'm saving our lives, John. Saving all of our lives."

He saw a tear running down her cheek. "This changes nothing! I love you and will to the day I die." John walked around in a circle. Not knowing what to do but needing to move to relieve the anxiety that was wracking his body. His hands we on his hips. "This is not going to happen! Do you hear me!?" He almost doubled over at the pain shooting through his gut. *Can't show weakness. That's trouble.* His face was twisted angrily. Marie was talking to him but it was as if he was underwater and her words were a gurgling, watery mess of sounds that were unintelligible. Finally, he cleared his head and heard her speaking to him.

"John! John!," she shook him, grabbed his hands. Then got him to look into her eyes. "IF you love me and you love my boys you have to do this or we're dead. All of us." She let go of his hands. "Do you understand?"

"But I don't....," John's words trailed off as he understood what he needed to do. Then he looked at Marie, "Mare," he pleaded.

Thompson interjected, "Reed, she's right! I've fought in every kind of war you can think of. My professional opinion of this situation is we don't have enough firepower to survive an attack here. Hell, there's not enough firepower if every man at Fort George were here." Thompson let those words sink in. Then looking John intently in the eyes he added, "You've the chance to save many lives if you do what you know deep inside you need to do. Or we can fight our way out of here and fight all the way up the river and many of us, if not all of us will die, and so will many of the natives."

John stood engaged in a stare with Thompson. He then turned to Marie, arms held out with palms up, his face wrinkled in anguish and said, "Mare?"

"Take care of your wife." She turned and walked out of the longhouse. Once outside, she wiped a tear from her cheek and took a few minutes to gather herself, clear her head. She looked up at the sky. "Lord," she said out loud. "If you'll pardon me saying so, dear Lord, you've got an interesting sense of humor." She chuckled irrationally through her tears, realizing that there was nothing she could do. The decision was made. And because of that, John had to begin a life without her. She wiped at another tear and then walked to the canoe.

Emerging from the trees, Cadotte was the first person she saw.

"Ah, Madame Dorion! How are things going up there?" He nodded toward the trees.

"Fine, Francois. Just fine." She looked back at the trees, then back at him. "Make room for one more in the canoe."

CHAPTER THIRTEEN
REALITY SETS IN

The following day, Marie awoke to the sound of gear being bundled and men grumbling over the early start. She felt a stabbing jolt in her upper torso. *John had a wife.* She stared at the stars over her. *How? I hesitated. That's how.* She considered yesterday's events and wondered why she hadn't made a more concerted effort to speak with John before they left for the *potlatch*. *Wouldn't have mattered. He couldn't have refused.* She threw off the buffalo robe and thought about getting Kimana to help with the morning meal but decided to let the newlyweds be for a bit. It would be a small, cold breakfast anyway, and she felt she could handle it. Retrieving the tea kettle, she went to the river and dipped water with it. Before long, she added tea to the boiling water. The men filtered by, and she splashed tea in their cups and handed each a biscuit with a piece of pemmican.

Cadotte stepped up. "Good morning, Madam Dorion!" She didn't respond as she offered him some pemmican and held the ladle filled with tea. Cadotte stared at her.

"Your cup." Her tone was curt. It had an edge.

"Mada…"

"Your cup," her voice was low, but it came out in an even sterner tone. Cadotte looked at her while holding out his cup.

"*Merci beaucoup.*" He turned and walked away.

When John stepped up, he didn't look at her. Just held out his cup. Marie said, "Good Morning!" She used the happiest tone she was able to muster. He glanced at her and moved on.

The sun was beginning to creep over the distant peaks to the east when the first canoe pushed off with John and Kimana sitting side by side. Marie and the boys rode with Cadotte, who sang a French rowing song. Marie had heard it before but didn't know the name. It was a song about lost love. *Ironic.*

Looking at the horizon, Marie recalled from her childhood readings how the Greeks described the sunrise as the rosy fingers of dawn. Her favorite was the *Iliad.* Paris's heart loved so intensely that he risked everything. She found that amount of commitment to love admirable, even if he was stealing away with a married woman. Helen had been unhappy and mistreated. *Just like me.* Helen was royalty, yet just a step above being a slave. *Just like me.* A smile came to her lips as she unwound the parallels in their lives.

The river was choppy. In the dim sunlight, Marie saw whitecaps. The good news was that the wind was coming from the west, and the sails were deployed. She could hear the occasional snapping of the canvas. *They would make good time.* Her thoughts drifted to John and Kimana. Marie wondered if she should tell John how she felt and that she loved him. After running through the possible outcomes, she decided that John knowing of her love would not do anyone any good. Not her. Not John. And definitely not Kimana.

She glanced over to the banks on the south side of the river and followed the landscape up to the top of the bluffs. The summer had been dry, and the rains had not yet come. The land was parched, and the grass was yellowed and sunburnt. The only greens were the reeds right next to and in the river and the sage that dotted the land.

Suddenly, a glint caught her eye. Sunshine reflecting off metal came from the top of the bluff. Not taking her eyes from the spot, she said, "Cadotte?"

"*Oui, Madam?*"

"I saw something up on that bluff-top over there." Her finger pointed at the spot.

Cadotte turned his gaze in that direction. "I don't see anything, Madam."

Marie continued looking. After a time, not seeing anything unusual, she offered, "I'm probably imagining things."

Cadotte looked at Marie. Their eyes met, "*Oui, mon cher*. This is possible when we have upsets."

They held their gaze, and then Marie looked away. "I'm going to rest."

"*Oui, Madam*." Cadotte looked back to the bluff. A shadow of something was there, and then it wasn't. "Whoever it is, he is not good at stealth." Cadotte looked at Marie, who had lain down between the boys. "You may not have such a good imagination. But it is probably only a Wasco scout keeping tabs on us until we leave their lands."

• • • • •

They camped on a sand island in the middle of the river that night. They had made good time; John had said to her in the food line, with the help of a *ventis secundis,* a following wind. These were his first words to her all day. *He liked to show off his Latin when he was in a good mood.*

"Tomorrow, with a good wind, we will reach the turn north in the river," he told her.

Marie knew he was preparing her. Cadotte and the others would turn north, while John would lead the rest of the group into a veritable wilderness where few whites had gone before.

"You should get your goodbyes said tonight. The boys, too." John nodded at her and then walked away carrying two plates.

"John," she called after him.

He turned, and their eyes met. In the firelight, he could see a tear on her cheek. The creases in his face lessened a bit.

"I..." Marie couldn't trust her voice. She brushed at tears on her cheek.

"I know," he said. Then he turned and walked into the darkness.

• • • • •

She found Cadotte later that evening. He was sitting on a drift log in front of a fire. Smoke trailed from his pipe bowl.

"I like the river at night. I will miss it very much," he said without turning to look at her.

"How did you know it was me? Coulda' been an Indian."

"It is an Indian. That is how I knew it was you. The rest walk around, clomp, clomp with their heavy feet. You walk like a ballerina. Like a queen!"

"A Ioway princess, you mean? " she laughed and then sat on the log next to Cadotte.

"Yes, Madam, a Ioway princess." He smiled and puffed on his pipe.

"Tomorrow…"

"Let us not talk of unpleasant things, Madam."

"Alright. What will you do in Montreal? You don't seem like a city boy to me."

"I am going to the Red River colony. Have you heard of it?"

"No."

"Well, Madam, they say it is a place with such rich soil that even an old steersman like me can reap a bountiful crop. Can you imagine? Even a poor, old paddler like me can grow enough food to keep a family and then some. The company is giving me a hundred acres. A Hundred Acres! I will be like a king!"

"Sounds nice, Francois."

"I'll find a nice Ojibwe bride, and we will make many babies. And I will grow old and fat watching my children play, and I will remember you and your boys always! Then, when my children are grown, I will die in a warm bed, not out here on river rapids or some frozen lake or with an arrow in my chest." Cadotte let out a chuckle and puffed again on his pipe.

Marie stood. She started to leave but then placed a hand on his shoulder. "I will miss you. The boys will miss you."

Cadotte put his hand on Marie's. "Disappointments come to us all. But the pain that you are feeling now will pass with time. You'll be stronger for it." Marie patted his shoulder.

"You're a good man, Francois." She turned and walked back to her tent.

She gazed up at the stars and found the Bear. "Keep us safe."

CHAPTER FOURTEEN
THE SHOSHONE

Cameahwait's horse splashed across the small creek that ran from north to south near his father's village. When he was within a few hundred feet of the outer ring of teepees, dogs began barking. People who had been bustling and going about their day noticed the solitary rider. Spotting a familiar figure, the people came out to greet him. Women trilled. Children ran about laughing and playing. Cameahwait felt an almost instant irritation at all the fuss. He had to suppress his desire to call them all fools and send them scattering away. He swung down from his tired mount. They had covered many miles to get back to his father's village. He handed the reins to a small boy and commanded him to turn the horse out with the herd.

"My son!" Came his father's voice from the murmurs of the gathering crowd. The man, called Komkomis by his people, made his way to the front. He grasped Cameahwait's arms and said, "You have been gone many days. Come and take some food at your mother's kettle, and we will talk."

"Father," Cameahwait began, "the whites, they..."

The old man's face wrinkled; a vein appeared on his forehead. "We will speak of this privately."

Cameahwait, carrying his rifle, his shoulders slumping, followed the older man to his teepee. As they approached, Cameahwait saw his mother at the fire. She tended to a steaming pot hanging from a pine limb tripod and tied at their junction with a strap of buffalo sinew.

Upon seeing her son, she smiled and said, "Welcome, my son. There is meat in the pot." Her wooden spoon held a chunk of elk meat. Looking at her son, then her husband, her smile faded, and worry creased her forehead. Cameahwait took the meat and bit into it ravenously. Game had been scarce. He'd managed to get a rabbit two days ago.

"Come," his father said as he nodded toward the opening in the teepee. "Now, son, finish your meat and then tell me your story. There had been no runner from Pawashtimane. I was concerned when you were so late, and no word came of the marriage. I thought maybe..."

Cameahwait quickly swallowed the last of the food, "The whites, Father, they attacked the village."

"The whites attacked Pawashtimane's village?

"Yes."

"Why?"

"Why do these people do anything?" Cameahwait's voice became louder as he spoke.

"You did not fight?" The older man's tone was curt, almost harsh.

"Father, Pawashtimane refused to fight. He lay down like a dog in the dirt. Licking their boots. I was the only one who stood against them, but they had many men and rifles."

"I see."

"The whites tried to take me too, but I was too fast, too elusive." Cameahwait continued, "These people killed your son, my brother! WHY?"

Komkomis looked into the flames of the small fire in the center ring. "Yes, they killed my son. However, remember they brought your sister back, too."

"And now SHE's dead." Cameahwait's arm came out as he pointed a finger at his father's chest. "The white man only brings death, Father!"

"Sacagawea was taken by the Lakota, not whites."

"Those pigs sold her to the whites."

"ENOUGH!" Komkomis took a moment and breathed deeply. "She's dead." The old man looked into his son's eyes. "Your brother's dead." He hesitated before going on. "These things are of the Great Mystery. The Great Mystery gives. The Great Mystery takes. It has always been." Komkomis hesitated, waiting for his words to sink in. "And what is your answer? More death?"

"The whites have divided. Some go to build a fort on our land. On Shoshone land! I trailed the whites as they went upriver. Their group has split. Some following the river as it runs toward the land where winter lives." Cameahwait referred to the land that the whites called Canada.

The old man said nothing. He stared into his son's eyes. Cameahwait, his stomach clenching, felt the need to break the silence. "I want to take twenty warriors and go find those that aim to put up a fort and hunt in our country. We need to protect what is ours," Cameahwait pleaded.

"Get some rest. Clean up. Tonight, you will speak at the council."

His father rose and left the teepee. Cameahwait watched him go.

CHAPTER FIFTEEN
NEZ PERCE

Three Months Later

Lying next to the slumbering boys, Marie watched sunlight creep over the distant peaks, and the rosy-fingered dawn soon splashed across the snow-laden valley floor. The far-off peaks looked like a jagged, granite wall—*monuments to the gods*. Marie slipped out of the covers. Instantly, she felt the chill in the air and shivered. This morning, she would begin to work on the camas root she had gathered on their way back to the post. She ground the camas into flour using a flat stone as her base and another smaller stone as a pestle. She mixed in some elk fat and water from melted snow and soon had a pan of fry bread cooking over fire-blackened rocks.

As she worked, her mind drifted back in time and relived the last few days. She thought about how much her life had changed from now to a week ago, when Pierre, Marie, and the boys had left the trading post along with Jacob Reznor, a wiry American who had stayed on after the British takeover, and another trapper named Giles Le Clerc, one of the French Canadians who had come when the North West Company bought out Astor's men.

God, if only we'd gone a different way to another spot or even delayed our departure by a few days.

But Pierre had said, "Now is the time! The beaver will be many, like nothing we've seen before!" His eyes had shimmered with excitement. It was winter, and the beaver fur would be thick, which drove Pierre to leave when they did. Thick beaver fur meant a thick purse. There was lots of money to be made.

They had set out with two pack horses with a month's provisions to look for beaver. As they'd left, she remembered turning to look back. Smoke floated out of the chimney. John and Kimana were standing by the front door of what served as the Indian trade store of their newly constructed trading post. John gave her a wave. She returned it with a half-smile.

Pierre had led them up a small river that generally headed north-east.

Breaking from her thoughts of a week ago, she checked the bread in the pan. Using a finger, she tamped lightly down on the middle of the bread.

Needs a bit more.

For some reason, on the trip out, she had paid attention to their direction of travel but didn't really know why. At night, she would check the position of Ursa Major—*thank God I did.* By day, she noted the position of the sun.

The hunting party had found an area of small streams that fed into a larger river. She remembered Pierre saying, "This place will have plenty of beaver." His eyes were bright and smiling, something she did not see often except when liquor or money was involved in the proposition. The three men had set out the following morning.

Thinking back now, in her mind's eye, she could see the men riding away. She remembered that day had been cold, as were the two days that followed. The children had spent much of these days playing in the snowy meadow and running in the woods. She wasn't concerned as long as she could hear their laughter and playful cries of joy. When these sounds disappeared, she would yell, "Not too far!" With this caution, the children would return to the fire, warm themselves, and run back off to play.

She remembered the men had been gone for two days when a Nez Perce warrior appeared. Marie saw him riding his Appaloosa slowly along the river, moving toward her. She kept her eyes on the warrior and a hand on the pistol in her belt. "Boys, go to the hiding spot," she yelled out. She had found a downed fir tree with a dugout spot under its root ball. She remembered telling them, "This is where you go when I say to hide. Okay?" She had looked Jean Baptiste in the eyes. He would take his little brother to the hiding spot.

The Nez Perce stopped a few feet in front of her. Sitting atop his horse, he made the sign of peace, a hand parallel to the ground, moving from left to right. "I am here in peace. You need not fear me," he said in flawless French.

Marie's hand stayed on her pistol. She nodded. She noticed a silver cross hanging on a chain that encircled the warrior's neck. She felt her body relax slightly. "You speak French well."

The warrior replied, *"Oui, madame,"* while he swung down from his mount. "I am Nez Perce. My people have traded with French trappers for many years."

Marie followed his movements. He walked to the river and, bending down, scooped up a handful of water. Raising his hand to his mouth, he drank. With his thirst slaked, he stood. "Food?" he asked in French.

"Yes. I have some elk in that pot by the fire. Help yourself." She nodded her head toward a blackened cast iron pot. The warrior squatted and sliced off a hunk of meat using his knife. He ate hungrily.

He wiped at his mouth with his sleeve. Though gnawing his food, he spat out, "Où sont les hommes?"

"The men are out hunting. I expect them back directly," she lied.

"Many Paiute and Shoshone war parties around. Talk of white men coming. Make war talk at the council fires."

Marie tried to mask her fear. *He just said they'd traded with the French for years. Why is war coming now?* "Why now? We've been among your people for a long time."

"You've become dangerous. Hanging boys. Now word comes that you've killed many downriver, the people of Pawashtimane!"

"That's a lie! We left them the way we found them. Alive!"

He let out a small grunt. Stared into space as if considering, evaluating this new information. "You should leave this place," he said.

"Why are you warning me?"

"I'm Nez Perce. Shoshone enemy." The warrior chewed a hunk of elk. "We are friends of the whites. They gave us the book. Saved many Nez Perce with your medicines." The Indian stood. Marie studied him from head to toe. He wore buckskin leggings with a heavy deer hide coat dotted with beadwork of blue, white, red, and leather boots that reached halfway up his calf.

"What book?"

"Long ago, the French came. One was a priest. He read from the book. He healed people—Whiteman's fever. Then, the Frenchmen left. Around the council fire, we talked about the book. We talked about the power of the white man's god."

"Ah, the Bible!" Marie let a chuckle slip out.

"Yes. Bible."

"What was decided at the council about the book?"

"Four of our wisest men went to seek readers of the book. They walked many miles until they met an old friend, Captain Clark. You know Captain Clark?"

"I've met him. In St Louis."

"He sent a holy man to continue teaching us from the book." The Indian held up his cross. "He gave me this." The Indian strode to his horse and, with a leap, was astride his mount. He turned his horse to go the way he had come. "You should leave," he called over his shoulder.

Marie watched the Nez Perce ride away. She recalled being stuck, not knowing what to do. She remembered squatting by the fire, staring into the flames. Another day came. There was no sign of Pierre, Le Clerc, or Reznor.

"Mama," said Jean from beneath the buffalo robe. Marie was roused back to the present, the aroma of the fry bread wafting in the air.

"Yes, darling boy?"

"Is Papa here yet?"

"No. He's not come yet." She checked the bread. Satisfied it was done, she broke some off and handed it to Jean. "Eat."

Marie's mind drifted away again to the recent past. It hardly seemed real to her. She and the boys had waited at the camping spot by the river. She had scanned the bank of the river almost constantly; her anxiety about what the Nez Perce had told her was weighing heavily on her mind.

Then she had heard the gunfire, which broke her out of her malaise. Gunfire had been her call to action that day. She had hid the boys in the hiding spot, grabbed her rifle, and took off to find Pierre, Reznor, and Le Clerc. She hadn't gone far when she spotted Le Clerc.

Marie saw him clearly in her mind's eye now. Bloody and dazed, he had asked her to tell his wife that he loved her. She had watched him die. Before he died, he told her Pierre and Reznor were dead. After he passed, she wrapped his body in a blanket and covered him with rocks from the river. She crossed herself, said a quick prayer for Le Clerc, and poured a dram of whiskey on his grave.

She recalled the fight with the Shoshone warriors. Her body slumped inward as she thought, *I had never killed before. But my boys.* She pushed the images of the dead warriors away.

Instead her thoughts turned to escaping, how she had quickly broken down their camp that day and loaded the necessities she would need for the trip back to Reed's trading post. She packed light to quicken their pace and travel quietly. No pots or traps or anything metal that would clank and give away their location. She had the boys on a horse and walked ahead of them, leading the pack horse. She recalled that she had said the Prayer of Reparation over and over as she walked and prayed also for the souls of the warriors she had killed. She tried to comfort herself. *It was them or us!*

She and the boys had spent some time looking for Pierre, weaving their way along the winding river's bank. The bank was a mix of snow, sand, and round smooth rocks of various shapes and sizes, making walking difficult. Birch, with its characteristic white bark, sparsely populated the area. Marie occasionally checked the river for signs of traps but found nothing. They came across an old fire pit about five miles from their original campsite.

She had tied the pack horse to a small birch tree and walked to the pit. She felt the coals and charred wood pieces.

Cold. We need to leave before we're discovered.

"Mama, I'm hungry," Jean said.

"Me too, me too," Paul joined in.

"Where's Papa?"

Marie looked to the river and then at the two boys sitting on their horse. In the rush, they hadn't eaten. A canvas bag she hung from the side of a larger pack contained fry bread and elk meat. Marie opened the tie strings and got some of each for the boys. Walking to them, she handed the food out.

"Wait here. Eat. I'm going upriver to find...." She hesitated. "I'm going to get your papa." She turned to go, stopped, and said to the boys, "Whatever you do, don't yell for me. I'll be back soon." She would make better time without the horse plodding behind her.

Jean shook his head. "But what if you don't come back?"

Marie looked him intently in the eyes. "I'm coming back." Not wanting to continue the discussion, she turned and briskly walked to the river. Her rifle slung over her right shoulder, she followed it for a half mile. She continually searched the water for stakes that held beaver traps; she checked for the scent of castoreum, the liquid bait that attracted beaver to the trap. Nothing. She searched the bank for anything that showed Pierre had been there, footprints or horse prints in the sand. Finally, she stopped. *Nothing.* She had breathed deeply. "Pierre, where are you?" She had asked the air. If he was truly dead, she owed him a proper burial.

When she returned to the boys, they still sat on their horse.

"Mama!" they yelled almost in unison. She'd untied the pack horse, and they turned back toward the post. They had stuck to the trees, avoiding the open areas and trails. She'd had to stop and tell the boys to be quiet more than once.

Eventually, she tried to make it a game.

"It's like hide and seek."

"Why?" Paul had asked.

"Because, dummy," came a rebuke from Jean Baptiste.

"Hey, hey. No dummies here. We're trying to hide from Papa. See if he can find us."

"Why?" Paul wondered again.

"It's a game. Remember when you played with Papa at the fort?" She looked at Paul. "Hide and seek. Remember?"

Paul giggled lightly. "Hide and seek," he squealed.

They hadn't encountered any warriors and had gotten back to the post in a couple of days.

A popping ember brought her back from her daydreams. *Some dream.* She squatted over the fry bread. Took a bite of it. The warm, soft bread felt good in her mouth. It was then she remembered she hadn't eaten yesterday. She glanced over at the buffalo robe. Looking now at two sets of eyes peering at her, she handed each boy a hunk of bread. Her glare said: "Eat!"

"Stay here." Standing over them she gestured with a downward push with both hands. Stay down.

Marie moved off again toward the smoldering ruins of John Reed's outpost. The air was heavy with the smell of smoke. There hadn't been time for a palisade, just a couple of quickly tossed-together cabins built before the winter weather arrived. Blood trails littered the snow. From this, she surmised that whoever was here—John, Kimana, Archie, MacTavish, the clerk and maybe one or two others—had put up a fierce fight. The rest of the men would have been out hunting beaver. Probably dead, too. Tracked down and finished off, one by one.

Marie moved charred timbers that had tumbled from the walls to the ground, off to the side. When she saw the toe of a boot sticking out from the rubble, she began frantically tossing debris aside, and then, seeing him, she let out a small gasp; involuntarily, her hand went to her mouth. He was under the fallen roof of the outpost, his rifle next to him. She gently brushed aside debris from his face and upper body. There was a gash on his cheek just above his beard line. She touched him—her John Reed—and pulled back from the icy feel of his skin. Then, she stroked his hair gently. He still had his scalp. It looked like he was sleeping and would awaken at any moment,

Like after the night they'd spent on the prairie, "Eh, and a good mornin' to you, lassie!"

Mon amour.

Oh, John. I'm so sorry. She caressed his hair. For how long, she didn't know.

· · · · ·

The ground was covered with snow and frozen hard. Like it was with Le Clerc, whom she had buried a couple of days ago, there would be no burial in the traditional sense. Instead, she placed timbers and rocks over John's body. It was not a proper tomb, but the best that could be done. She brushed sweat from her brow.

Hope it keeps the wolves away.

She placed the last rock on the mound and marked it with a simple cross. Then she gathered the boys and said, "Take off your hats."

The trio stood silently for a time. Marie bowed her head. Her words came amid sobs as she said, "Yea, though I walk through the valley of the shadow of death, I shall fear no evil...."

She made the sign of the cross and said, "*In nomine Patris et Filii et Spiritus Sancti, Amen.*"

Looking toward the sun-filled sky, she said, "He was a good and loving man. Father, please take him to your arms. Forgive him for his sins. Let him dwell in your Kingdom forever and ever. Amen."

Her cheeks reddened when she realized she had recited a Latin prayer over a Scottish Presbyterian.

Forgive me, John.

Marie got the boys back to their camp. She got them busy helping prepare for their trip.

"Start picking stuff up and putting it in that canvas bag over there," she told them as she pointed toward the bag. "I'll be back."

Marie strode over to the cabin where she had found John. Stepping onto the wooden porch, a flash caught her eye as she went through the doorway. She stopped and whirled toward it. Hanging on the entryway from a nail was a Lewis and Clark peace medal. She took it down, gave it a quick look over, and then stuffed the medal in her pocket. Moving quickly through the cabin, she set aside burned timbers and scavenged for food and equipment.

She prayed she wouldn't find anyone but searched the rooms for Kimana and anyone else who may have been with John. She came across Dugald MacTavish. He had been beaten beyond recognition but his red hair was present on the side of his head where he hadn't been scalped. Standing over his body Marie whispered, "So young." She hastily piled the timbers, that had once formed the counting house's walls, and rocks from the now crumbling fireplace, over his body. She gave the sign of the cross and said a prayer for his resurrection.

She continued searching the area for others but no one else was present. *If she survived, Kimana would probably be a captive. She's young. Can work. Bear children.*

In sifting through the remains of the post, she found a bag of flour, some pemmican, some wool trading blankets that had burn marks but could still be used, a steel trap, and a cooking pan. She hefted the pan. It was cast iron, heavy, and felt good in her hands. Finally, she stood and scanned the ruins, then gazed at the sky. The sun was fully up, and she wanted to get underway before the Shoshone came back.

One thing she knew for sure. No one from Fort George would be coming to look for them any time soon. Maybe a search party might be sent when they didn't show up in the spring with their winter harvest of beaver pelts. She wasn't interested in waiting around to find out. The Shoshone were probably looking for them. They had to move north, but there was no established route. This was unexplored territory. No other fur brigades had been in this area before, at least not since the Owyhee had been killed there a year ago. And no one returned from that expedition with a map or even knowledge of any landmarks, rivers, or mountain passes.

Thinking of the dead, Owyhee trappers took her back to Fort George for a moment. She wondered how Tom and Jack were. She hadn't thought about them for a long time but realized she missed their smiles, their happy chittering in the fort's kitchen. Recalling that Tom's cousin was one of the three Owyhee that were killed, she wished she would have asked more questions about that missing expedition. Maybe the natives knew something. Maybe Kimana did. Even Ilchee may have heard. There was a trade network throughout the region and information traveled along with woven baskets, dentalia shells, and dried salmon.

No need to dwell on things that she could've done.

She and the boys were on their own. Scanning the distant mountains with both boys on one horse, she checked the packs to confirm they were securely tied to the pack horse. As she worked, she took stock of the supplies they had. She figured they had about a one-week supply of food in the packs. She pushed the pistol further down into her belt. She wore a leather pouch, its strap draped over her opposite shoulder, containing medicines, roots, and powder in a small compartment. She had separate bags for the pistol ammunition, .45 caliber balls, and John's rifle, which shot a hefty .64 caliber ball. She kept the pistol and rifle loaded at all times. The pistol would be her first line of defense, and since it was adequate for only close-in targets, it was kept in her belt all the time. The rifle, on the other hand, which was secured in a leather scabbard on the pack horse, would be used for longer-range threats or hunting.

"Jean, you keep control of that horse." She looked at him in the eyes.

"Yes, mama," came the child's reply.

"Hold on tight to your brother, too."

"Yes, Ma'am."

She took the pack horse's reins and made clicking sounds at the horse, "C'mon boy." She tugged lightly on the reins. The horse plodded forward. As she walked, her mind wandered back to their supply of food. She would dig out camas root to supplement their stock, but they would have to scavenge, trap, and fish. She used the weapons at her disposal for food but saved her limited powder for defense. If they got lucky, they might get a deer or two or find wolf or bear kill, sort of like wild animal leftovers, after the predators had finished their meal. After that, they would eat horse meat as a last resort.

Why was John's rifle not taken? Those things are like gold to the Indians.

She spent some time thinking about the trade post and how she found it. Had John been killed under the weight of the roof falling?

Maybe that is why they didn't take the rifle. They didn't see it. They didn't see John either. That's why he wasn't scalped.

As she walked, she tried to piece things together. She wondered why John was alone.

Archie must have been out trapping.

Another thing she pondered was where the others who should have been with John were. Had he put everyone in the field, and he and Kimana and MacTavish were the only ones left at the post? *John was smarter than that. They were in Shoshone land. And Cameahwait....*

Her thoughts trailed off. *THE MEDAL.* Her interior voice screamed. *He was so proud of that medal that he wore it to the potlatch. DAMN HIM.*

She took a deep breath. And then another. Her mind spun. Her fingers tingled. She needed time with this. To consider things.

Stay focused on living.

LIVING!

But before she tucked this information into a remote place in her mind, she had one last thought: *For Cameahwait, it was an eye-for-an-eye. His brother was killed. Someone had to pay!*

Marie and the boys moved out following the route of the river that one of the men in the company had named *Malheur*, French for River of Misfortune. This river, which undoubtedly had its source in the mountains' glacial field, would hopefully lead to a trail that would take them through a pass in the mountains and then to whatever water route they could find on the downslope side of the mountains, which would lead them to the Columbia River—Wimahl. She was hoping for a shortcut. From there, they would wait for a passing fur brigade or an express canoe fleet headed to or from Montreal, then they would be off to Fort George, or perhaps they might return to Canada. Cadotte had made the Red River colony sound nice. Marie didn't want to make that decision yet.

Get the boys to safety. Bigger questions could wait.

She wished Cadotte was here. He'd know.

Maybe they'd go to Red River.

Marie had entertained the idea of canoeing to civilization for the first part of their journey. This made sense in terms of ease of travel and speed. However, Marie chose horse travel instead. You couldn't eat a canoe. Marie reasoned. She was also sure there was no continuous waterway back to the Columbia River. No, it would be horseback or, in her case, foot travel.

Walking was easy. She and the boys moved over a flat, snow-splashed plain, following the meandering river to the north and northwest. Chunks of ice floated lazily in the current. Low-slung hills sparsely covered in pines and scrub sage bordered the valley. The sun was warm; the further north they got, the less snow they encountered. They moved past a rock formation shaped like a haystack.

"Look, Mama," Jean Baptiste pointed to the formation. He sat on his horse, ramrod straight, holding the reins in one hand and wrapping his other arm around his little brother. "What is that?"

The boys' bodies gently rocked with their horse's movement.

"The elders of my mother's tribe say there was a wind cave in the *Paha Sapa,* the Black Hills, our holy place, and that the first people came from underground through that wind cave. Maybe this is another? Maybe this is how the Great Mystery put people all over the earth?" She shrugged.

She sang a song her mother had sung when Marie was very little. Her voice rose and fell in sweet, melodic waves that filled the air. Her body swayed with the horse and was in rhythm with the tune, giving the sunny day a magical feel.

"What are you singing?" Jean Baptiste asked.

"It's the bear medicine song of my mother's people. The bear is very powerful. Helps us feel better. If we are sick, it makes us well. If we are weak, the Bear makes us strong," Marie answered.

Jean Baptiste thought about that for a minute. "Are you sick?"

"My heart is heavy."

"Are you singing for Papa?" Jean Baptiste wanted to know.

"Yes, my baby. For your Papa."

Should I tell them their Papa's gone? Should the passage of time tell them?

"How will he find us?" Jean Baptiste wanted to know.

She tried to speak, but she felt her voice might crack and betray her emotions. She felt tears and knew she couldn't cry in front of the boys. After a few deep breaths, she said, "Your Papa knows how. Hold tight to Paul. Don't let him fall. You're the man now." She looked away from the boys as tears wetted her cheek.

As they walked she tried to get the boys minds' off of their father. She talked to them about her childhood travels over the frozen Canadian Shield. "When I was little your grandmother and grandfather and my sisters and I traveled by sled pulled by dogs over the snow."

Jean Baptiste spoke, "Tell us about our grandmother and grandfather."

Paul chimed in, "Tell us, tell us!"

Marie's eyes swept the horizon. She was checking for riders coming their way. Nothing. She checked the ridge tops, too. Again nothing. The Shoshone warriors, the ones that killed Pierre, John, and the rest, swept over the land like packs of wolves, devouring what they wanted and moving on. She was hopeful the Indians had gone back to their village. The fur-men had fought, so the war party would have dead and wounded to attend to. What she was searching for now was help. Maybe they would come across a friendly band of Nez Perce. Also, she watched for any sign of an oncoming snowstorm. The weather changed quickly, and she didn't want to be caught in the open.

She continued the story of her travels in Canada, "It was very cold like here. Lots of snow on the ground like here."

Jean Baptiste said, "We need a sled and dogs too!"

Paul added, "I wanna ride a sled!"

"Your grandfather was very strong and he knew the land like the natives knew the land. When the blizzards blew in, he would find a cave, always checking that there was no bear sleeping inside, or he would build a shelter from branches that would get us out of the weather."

"What about grandmother," Paul asked.

"Your grandmother sang with a voice that made the angels blush with shame! She kept us fed. She showed us how to harvest food from the wilds. She taught us to love *Wakan Tanka* and to be glad for our lives."

"What is *Wakan Tanka*," asked Jean Baptiste

"My mother's people, the Ioway believe in a universal spirit that lives all around us. Like God."

The boys went quiet. She continued to scan around them for any signs of life, food or shelter. She always wanted to be ahead of their next meal or their next place to sleep.

• • • • •

After a few days of moving over snowy, high-desert plains, with its flora of juniper and sage, the ground started to rise, gently at first, and then it took on a steeper grade. Marie noticed trees began to thicken on the hillsides. The air grew colder, and the ground, which had been covered with patchy snow, became covered entirely in white. Marie had taken to riding her horse, wanting to conserve her energy.After a few hours, they came to an opening in a basalt formation, with spires of rock that seemed to be the teeth of giants that had fallen to earth. Gazing at these spires, Marie recalled reading of the Pillars of Hercules. *Like sentries guarding the entrance to the canyon.* She watched the roiling river as it made its way between them and disappeared into the steam-obscured mouth of the canyon. Marie decided to continue to follow the land upward instead of taking the river. River banks were typically shrouded in brush or rock-strewn. Following the contour of the land promised, at the very least, a path of least resistance.

"There! The home of a dragon, Mama!" Jean pointed toward the rising steam.

Marie looked at Jean Baptiste. His eyes were wide. He stared at the billowing cloud near the canyon's opening. "No, Jean. We've been this way before. You were only four, then. This is where Satan's breath comes from below the ground." *What had Nuttall called these?* She had to think back to his talk at Fort George the night before his departure. *Volcanic vents.* Marie was satisfied with her ability to pull that information from her memory. *The cloud comes from far underground; it escapes through cracks in the ground.*

Clicking her tongue, she told the horse, "Get up!"

The horse hesitated because of the billowing cloud and moved back a bit. Marie used the excess of the rein and gave the horse a whack on the flank, letting it know who the boss was. Grudgingly, it moved forward. Jean Baptiste and Paul followed on their horse. They started to climb, still following the river as it slid through the rock canyon walls. The distance between them and the water grew until the river existed only in the roaring sound it sent upward. The horses went single file. Marie led the first horse while the boys followed behind. They topped out on a mesa. She could see for maybe a hundred miles or more. What she saw horrified her. Black clouds. The wind was picking up from the north. *Snow!*

As they moved, she kept an eye skyward. Clouds were coming. An hour or so later, the sky was leaden gray, and small snowflakes began to fall. Here and there were scattered pines and junipers. Nothing that would make a good shelter. They were moving too slowly and would be caught out in the storm. They wouldn't survive.

At the next stand of trees, she rode her horse over and tied him to a slender pine. She got the boys down and did the same with their horse. Taking the buffalo robe, she waded back into the copse and laid the robe on the ground.

"Lay down on the robe."

Paul started to cry. Jean asked, "Why, Mama?"

"Just get on the robe."

The two boys did as they were told. Paul's cry became a few choking gasps.

Marie looked at them. Paul's eyes were red. Tears ran down his face. Jean's face was like stone except for his lower lip quivering slightly. "Jean, you and your brother stay under this robe. It will protect you until I get back. You understand? Stay here until I get back." They both nodded. She covered the boys.

Grabbing her horse's mane, she swung on its back in one fluid motion. Kicking it on the flanks, the horse set out at a trot. Snow floated down as she rode. The wind and the chill stung her cheeks. Marie spotted what she had been seeking in what seemed like a short time. Through the pines, she saw a rocky outcropping. Volcanic material. Basalt. On their journey out from Fort George, Pierre had shown her a similar formation with caves. He had called them volcanic tubes. Approaching the darkened opening, the horse began to whinny and shy backward. She kicked, but the horse wouldn't go forward.

She swung down. Tied the horse to a tree. Something was in there. But she needed that space. Her boys' lives depended on it. She crept close to the darkened opening. She had thought about the pistol in her belt, but in that cave, the risk of getting hit by her own shot was too great. Hatchet in one hand and hunting knife in the other, she knelt on both knees and gave the sign of the cross.

Jesus, let me get back to my boys. She made the sign of the cross again.

She thought of the bear and its power. Raising her head, Marie peered into the opening, trying to penetrate the darkness but to no purpose.

Marie took a deep breath. Then, exhaling, she plunged into the opening. Once inside, she found she could stand in the main chamber. Her breathing was ragged, her palms sweaty, and her heart raced. Anxiety enveloped her in a cloud of numbness, making every step laborious like she was wearing concrete shoes.

Marie became aware of breathing. It was not her own. Then, a low, rumbling growl came out of the darkness.

COUGAR!

Her head turned toward the sound. Then, as padded sounds rushed toward her, she was hit and knocked to the ground. Her head smacked hard on the rocky surface of the cave floor. The growling was on top of her now. She felt hot breath. Instinctively, she swung the hatchet wildly in the dark, and luckily, the broadside hit home, stunning the beast whose jaws had just clamped around her forearm. A searing pain shot through her arm, but the blow from the hatchet had stunned the cougar, causing the animal's jaw to slacken just as its teeth sunk home. She pulled her forearm away and staggered out of the cave.

In the dim light, she saw that her dress was a deep, blood-red. She checked for wounds and found only a gash in her forearm and a head bump. She bent over, her hands on her thighs supported her weight. Gathering her breath, *I'm done fighting with cougars. Anything happens to me the boys...*

She pushed that thought away as it was nearly dark, and her only chance of getting to the boys before the dark of night was to ride out immediately.

She swung on her horse tied to the tree and kicked its flanks. The mare burst to a trot, slipping on the snow-covered ground.

Easy, easy.

She leaned in and stroked the horse's neck, saying, "Slow, baby. Slow."

She was in a hurry, but the footing in the snow and the low visibility suggested caution.

A horse with a broken leg would put me on foot.

The snowfall was picking up, obliterating her outbound track. She could hardly see beyond the horse's head. Her stomach and chest began to tighten. Breaths came in short pulls.

Scanning the snow covered clearing. *I can't find them.* She looked, her head moving wildly from side to side. Her hair flipped behind her. *I CAN'T FIND THEM!*

Her hands were sweaty. Ice pellets hit her face. She took a deep breath. She looked intently at a form in the trees.

THE PACK-HORSE! Marie, walked her gaze in from the pack-horse. Then she saw it, a rectangular shape just beneath the surface of the newly fallen snow. Walking to the spot she reached down, her hand plunged into the snow and pulled back the top layer of the buffalo robe.

"Mama, where were you? Why did you leave us!?" Jean yelled.

She grabbed both boys and wrapped her arms around them, taking care to cover the red blood on her garment with a blanket thrown over her shoulders. "Oh, my boys, I am so sorry. Mama won't leave you again!"

"Promise?" Jean had pulled away. His arms were folded across his chest.

"I'm cold," came Paul's cry.

Marie, holding Paul, looked down into his little face. He wore a pout. His eyes were searching for some comfort from his mother.

"Come here." With her free arm, she waved Jean back into her embrace. The boy came, and she hugged them both tightly. Then, pulling back, she said, "It's snowing! Look at the snow!"

She stood and, scooping snow with her cold bare hands, formed a ball and lightly tossed it at the two boys. They let out a giggle and scooped up snow, throwing snowballs at their mother in return. Soon, snowballs flew back and forth amidst the boys' giggles and laughter.

"I got you!" Paul yelled out when he got his brother with a snowball on the side of his face! Just then, a snowball from Jean got Paul, hitting the bridge of his nose and spreading across his face. Paul burst into tears. "He got my face!"

Marie went to the boy. She brushed the snow off his face. "You're okay." The boy sniffled. "If you're going to play, you gotta take what comes. Okay?" She looked Paul in the eyes. The child nodded. "Okay." She pulled him into a hug.

The snow had slackened to a few flakes drifting down, no wind disturbed them on their gentle float to the earth. She gathered the two boys to her. Kneeling down to eye-level she spoke, "I need you to go find sticks," and she held her arms wide, "This long." She nodded, "Go. Be quick it is getting dark." While the boys scavenged for limbs Marie took one of the pots she had brought from the post and started digging down in to the snow. She worked at shoveling away snow until she had a rectangular space big enough for the three of them to lie down. She used her hatchet to hack down a small Aspen tree that would serve as the center-pole of their shelter. As the boys brought limbs she would lash the limbs to the center-pole, using stripped bark to hold the limbs in place. Just as darkness curled around them she placed the last of the limbs in their makeshift home.

Standing back and admiring it she said to the boys, "We are back in the trees which will help keep the snow off of us. "Get in. Wrap the buffalo robe around you."

"Where are you going?"

"Jean it will be cold tonight. I'm going to build a fire. Okay"

The little boy nodded.

"Don't worry I will be close by."

Marie navigated her way to the pack-horse and retrieved a conk with a burning ember buried just under the surface. She blew on the ember and it sprung to life in shades of orange, a spark flew up causing Marie to jump and let out a gasp of surprise.

Wrapping a stick with cloth bandages from her kit bag, she used the ember to light her torch. She scurried around first snatching up small twigs and branches laying on top of the snow. These were a bit snowy and frosty but essentially would burn well once the fire made its way through the surface dampness. Next, she found a few downed pine trees, hacked away their branches and drug them in to a pile near the shelter where the boys lay quietly.

Working quickly, shivering against the cold, night air, steam forming with her every exhale, she touched her torch to the twigs piled up near the pine logs that formed a back stop that would reflect the heat of the fire back toward their shelter. Her fire sputtered a bit before catching as it burned into the pile, flaring up as it hit pockets of pine resin just beneath the surface of the wood.

Sitting near the fire, she dug in to her kit bag and retrieved a tin. Removing the lid, she dug in to the salve of animal fat which had hardened due to the coldness. Taking what she could scrape out she warmed the salve by rubbing her hands together until it softened enough for her to apply to her wound. She sprinkled some dill, a naturally occurring substance for healing, over the wound as well, then wrapped a bandage around the area. She tossed some additional fuel on the fire and then retreated to the shelter and the warmth of the buffalo robe.

As she lay on her back, listening to the sounds of her sleeping boys, she thought about John and Pierre. *Lord have mercy. Christ have mercy....*She didn't get far in her prayer when sleep came for her.

• • • • •

Marie's eyes snapped open at first light. She laid there for a moment listening, assessing her surroundings. The only sound came from the breathing of the two boys sleeping next to her. She slipped out of the cover, gingerly replacing it to ensure the boys stayed warm and slept on. Marie saw to the fire, and walking to the pack horse retrieved her kettle and a bundle of dough she had placed in a canvas wrap. Before long the dough was cooking in the kettle which sat on a bed of glowing coals at the edge of the fire.

She crossed her arms against the cold, glanced through tree limbs up at the sky, which showed white streaks on a field of azure. *Cold but no snow.*

The ground will be firm. Good for the horses. Marie knew their good fortune wouldn't last. *Snow will be back. Need that cave.*

"Mama?"

The sound of Paul's tiny voice brought her out of her thoughts. She strode over to him and kneeling down, smoothed his hair, "Yes, my angel?"

"Is Papa here?"

Marie fought back a tear, managed a smile, her lips turned slightly upward, trembling. "No baby. He's probably hunting a big elk." She held her hands wide over her head. "Wait here." She rose to go, then turned back, holding her index finger to her lips she gave the quiet sign. Paul nodded that he understood.

When she returned with a hunk of bread and dried elk meat she found Jean was awake also. "Good morning sleepy-head!" She handed both boys food.

In less than an hour she had the pack-horse loaded and both boys sitting on top of the other. Jean was in back, arms wrapped around Paul, his little hands held the reins. The sun was fully over the horizon to their right and as they transited a clearing she located the Morning Star. "Take us home," she whispered.

Marie pulled up short of the cave. She walked to the boys and got Paul down first. She reached for Jean.

"I can get down myself," he said as he swung his right leg over and slid down the horse's side, landing deftly on the ground.

"Big boy!" Marie smiled at him.

She unloaded the packs from the pack-horse and hobbled the other horse which moved off to graze in a copse of trees that had a patch of grass protruding from the snow. Marie positioned the boys behind a log, "Wait here." She grabbed the reins of the pack-horse and led it to a point in front of the cave. Peering into the cave entrance she saw a set of glowing eyes and heard a low, rumbling snarl.

"Whoa, baby." She gently stroked the side of the mare's face with her right hand while her left held tight to the horse's halter. Her voice was soothing as if she were speaking to a baby. Then, with a lightning-quick movement, her hand left the mare's face and dropped to the belt tied around the middle of her buffalo-hide dress and to the knife hanging there. Her blade hit the carotid, blood spurted turning the snow red. Marie stepped back as the mare's knees wobbled, then it dropped to its front knees. Then, slowly, its rear sank to the ground, and it flopped on its left side. The horse's breaths were labored, billowing clouds of steam surrounded its head.

She first opened the cavity in which the internal organs resided. She sang a buffalo kill song as she worked. She held the heart to the sky while she sang. Her voice rose and fell, undulating, the words floating on air on their way to the heavens, to *Wakan Tanka*, the Great Mystery, the life force that provided their needs. Her mother's people believed the spirit of the animal lived in the heart and that one could gain the animal's strength by eating some. She bit into the heart; blood trickled over her lips and down her chin. There was a sensation of warmth growing inside of her. She felt a surge of energy.

Marie glanced at the cave opening, then rising from a crouch she unslung her rifle and retreated to the log where the boys were waiting. She laid the barrel of the rifle on the log, cocked back the hammer and waited. She didn't have to wait long. The cougar poked its head out of the cave opening. "Couldn't say no to a meal dropped at your door could you," Marie whispered. The cougar looked around and satisfied that all was clear it trotted to the carcass bleeding in the snow. Marie whispered, "Plug your ears, boys." She took a deep breath, slowly exhaled and then the rifle exploded and bucked against her shoulder. The acrid smell of burnt gunpowder and smoke hung in the air. When the smoke had cleared she saw the cougar laying in the snow. "Wait here," she barked.

• • • • •

Marie got into a pack and took out the conk in which she had transported the previous night's embers to get a fire going quickly. Using her knife, she dug out the ember and, using twigs and sticks scattered around the cave, had a crackling fire in moments. She watched the smoke drift to the ceiling and out a small crack in the cave.

That's what I call natural ventilation.

Marie wondered why a cougar had been in the cave. *Coulda been worse. A bear probably woulda stayed til Spring.*

She'd checked for bear vents before entering the cave the first time. When no steam of a slumbering bear's breathing came from the top of the cave, she decided it was safe to go in. The last thing she expected was to find a cougar. It was then that she heard it. A chirping sound came from somewhere in the back of the cave. *Birds?*

She grabbed a small, burning stick for light. She moved to the back of the cave. "Oh my god!" From behind her came Jean's voice. "Mama, kitties!" The little boy squealed with joy. "Can we keep them?"

Marie's heart sank. *I killed a mother.* Looking at the cougar cubs. *I killed their mother.* She looked up and crossed herself. *Forgive me.*

That night, the boys went to sleep wrapped in the buffalo robe and as near to the 'kitties' as Marie was comfortable with. She'd given the boys some pemmican and bread for dinner.

Paul had cried himself to sleep. She didn't know why he was crying. She asked him but he wouldn't talk. She let him be. *Probably misses Pierre.* Marie sat in the cave's dwindling light, slightly warmed by the small fire she kept going with twigs and sticks. She could hear the wind outside and, in her mind's eye, imagined the blizzard churning everything up out there.

Her thoughts drifted away to John and Pierre. She hoped they were at peace. She said a short prayer and then began thinking of what lay ahead. As she thought about the food, the weather, and the distance they would have to cover, she felt a sense of anger rise within her. *WHY? Why these boys? Why John? Why Pierre?* These thoughts and more consumed her. Finally, she wept. Her weeping became sobbing. Sitting with legs bent, she folded her arms on her knees, laid her forehead on her arms, and gave vent to emotions she had been sitting on, tamping down. There had been too much to do, too much to think about. Her sobs continued until sleep finally overtook her.

CHAPTER SIXTEEN
THE CAVE

At first light, Marie was bustling around the cave, getting the fire going, cooking breakfast for the boys, and making a type of porridge by making the bread soggy with warm water for the kitties. She moved the cougar cubs off the buffalo robe where they had snuggled in with the boys overnight. "Here you go." At first, she was concerned that the kitties wouldn't eat, but before long, the two cougar cubs ate the mash voraciously.

While everyone ate, Marie went outside. The weather had cleared, but cold bit at her flesh. With a hatchet, she began cutting small aspen trees. She stripped the bark from the cutdown saplings, then, using her knife, she harvested long, narrow strips of bark. She gathered up the aspen trunks and bark strips. Looking at the cave opening, she laid out the small poles in a rectangular frame approximately the same size as the opening. She lashed the poles together using the bark strips, then stretched deer hides over the frame before securing the hides by looping bark strips through holes and tying them securely, creating a door for the cave. She placed the new door over the mouth of the cave. She stood hands on her hips admiring her handiwork. *That'll be fine.* As long as she kept the fire going, things would be tolerable inside the cave. Food was now the biggest issue, especially with two helpless kittens to feed. Firewood was second on her priority list.

How will the three of us last over the rest of the winter? The cubs will grow. They will eat.

She knew what needed to happen next. Tiny flakes of snow drifted down from the leaden sky. She looked toward the aspen copse, where the horse dug through the snow, trying to find whatever grass or forage it could.

She walked to the pack-horse's carcass, crouching down she reached into the cavity and pulled out the animal's innards, saving the vital organs for soup. Then, having put the organs aside, she moved to strip the animal of its hide, which she would cure and turn into something useful, like a tarp or coat, she didn't know what yet.

Marie then cut strips of its flesh and muscle. She hung these on a rack she had crafted out of tree limbs and bark. She pulled the rack up using a strap of tree bark, which she had slung over a branch. Suspending the rack in mid-air allowed the meat to dry and keep it away from wolves, coyotes, and whatever else came to investigate. Looking up at the rack of meat, she thought, "If I can find some honey and maybe berries, I can put a glaze over those strips."

Soon a fire was roaring, a pot hung over it with the bones, heart, liver, and entrails of the pack horse inside. Marie added some snow that would melt to water and would turn to a hearty broth. This would be their meals for the next several days. With the pot simmering and the boys playing, she went in the cave, retrieved the kitties and let them get their fill on the gut pile before she buried it under the snow to ward off predators.

That night, as she lay by the fire listening to the sleepy breathing of her sons, she could hear the horse whinnying and snorting. But there were other sounds of animals moving around. She didn't know what was out there, but she sprung off the hard ground bed. She gripped her pistol in one hand and poked a stick, with cloth wrapped around one end, into the fire. The cloth erupted in flame, functioning as a torch.

Gently pushing back the door to the cave, she stepped into the cold night and held the makeshift torch high. In the dim light of the torch, she saw four glowing eyes but could not determine what they belonged to. She wanted to fire off a shot but decided against waking the boys so abruptly, not to mention any Shoshone that might be in the area.

She ran to the horse that was hobbled nearby. Its head rose and fell with every whinny and snort. She spun on the four glowing eyes, sure that they were wolves. She yelled out, "Get out of here! Shooo. Shoo."

The eyes kept staring, and soon Marie, recognizing the futility of the exercise, moved the horse closer to the cave opening. She stood near the horse with her pistol in one hand and her torch in the other. Eventually the wolves trotted away. She pulled the door closed and went back inside. She added the torch to the fire and crawled back into bed.

She held the pistol, which lay on her chest, and listened for more noises, but soon her eyes flickered, her body shut down its alert status, and she slept.

The next morning, she left the cave as soon as it was light. She was greatly relieved to see their remaining horse standing, its nose nudging the snow and its hooves digging down to find food.

With the weather clear, she and the boys went out that day. The sun shone brightly. While the boys jumped and rolled in the snow, Marie searched the area for loose pieces of wood and downed limbs. Before long, she had a stack of wood in various shapes and sizes piled against the cave wall. Stacking the smaller sticks and twigs in a honeycomb design allowed air to circulate and dry things out. She had some dry tinder available that would suffice for the day and hopefully into the next day. She built a small fire circle from rocks she gathered inside the cave.

She set traps to catch more food. First, she used the only beaver trap she had, dobbing its pan with some of the grease that had arisen in the pot simmering by the fire. Then, she covered it with leaves and branches to conceal the metal. Next, she used straps, which she intertwined into a net. She hoped this would catch small animals such as squirrels, mice, and maybe a bird if they got lucky.

As the sun climbed toward midday, Marie and the boys went hiking in search of whatever vegetation she might convert into food or medicine. She harvested some dried-up fern to be added to the soup simmering back at the cave. They came across some huckleberries that had freeze-dried on the vine. These could be boiled down, mashed, and mixed into the horsemeat to make a pemmican. The sun was in the lower third of the sky as they walked out of the woods. They came to a creek that wound through a small ravine choked with aspens. As they walked, a crash of limbs and leaves erupted from the trees. Marie pulled her pistol and held it at the ready. Her eyes scanned for the origin of the sounds. Was it Indians?

Seems unlikely anyone would be up here in the winter.

She immediately recognized the irony of that statement. Still, she motioned to the boys to get down and stay quiet. She knelt on the ground, scanning the trees for whatever was making that noise.

Finally, she spotted movement.

Might be a deer making its way through the trees. We spooked it.

"Boys, ssshhhh," she noised with a finger to her lips.

"Mama, Mama." Came the plaintive cry from little Paul.

Marie took the time to pull him close. She whispered to the two boys, "There's something in there. I've got to get it so we can have food to eat. Understand?"

She saw both boys nod their understanding.

Marie said, "Good." Then, she placed an index finger to her lips to signal them to be quiet.

Marie pulled her pistol and took off at a run, going wide of the spot that the sound of crashing brush emanated from. She occasionally slipped and slid on the snow, which was icy in the shady spots, but once she got ahead of the crashing brush sound, she turned her course and slowed to a walk, hoping to intercept whatever was the cause of all the ruckus.

Slowly, she stepped, making sure not to snap a downed branch or rustle the leaves. The light breeze blew from the animal's direction toward her.

It can't smell me.

A smile grew on her face. Steamy breath rose around her. The sprint had raised her breathing rate, and she fought to get it under control. She ducked under a branch; coming out, she looked up, and about twenty yards away stood a deer. Antlers poked up on each side of the deer's head. Its breath steamed the air around its nose and mouth. It sensed something was present. Its gaze met Marie's, but it didn't see her. Marie brought the pistol up and lined up the bead at the end of the barrel. Took a deep breath and squeezed off a shot. She saw the deer's head snap in a wrenching, twisting motion before it crumpled. She gutted it in the woods, as she was away from the cave, and any predators would be drawn here instead of by their home. The boys, seeing her emerge from the trees, ran to her.

"Jean, help me drag this." She saw the boy's confused look. "Grab an antler and pull!"

As they walked back to the cave, Marie and Jean dragging the small buck by its antlers, they came across a steaming pool of water. She tested it with a finger, a toe, and then her foot. The water was hot but not too hot.

"Boys, let's take a bath!"

They stripped down and got into the water. Marie felt the warm water caress her, soothe her sore, tired muscles. As she soaked, she felt her tension ease and the ache of her body, a pain that went all the way through her, lessen as it melted into the warmth that surrounded her.

After a good soak, she and the boys stood on the snowy ground surrounding them.

"Now, let's roll!"

Marie, her body steaming, dove, landed in the snow, and sank a few inches. She felt the ice cold of the snow colliding with the warmth of her body. Rolling onto her back, the shock made her tingle from head to toe.

She yelled, "Whoooooooo hooooooo! That feels good!" She thrust her arms into the air.

"Mama, can we do it," Jean squealed. "Can we?"

"Of course!"

Jean squealed with joy. Paul hit the snow and immediately came to his feet crying, "I'm cold, I'm cold."

Marie, sitting up now, looked at him and laughed.

• • • • •

She lay beside the boys that night, recounting all she had accomplished. They had meat: venison and horse. They had shelter and firewood to stay warm. She smiled and said to the air, "Thank you, Lord, for this bounty we have received." She performed the sign of the cross.

Then her smile faded, and she talked to John. "My love. I hope wherever you are, you're happy."

CHAPTER SEVENTEEN
SPRING

Two months later

The cave had served them well over the long, arduous winter. It had been a haven against the onslaught of arctic winds and slashing snow. But now the winds had shifted, blowing from the south, and along with more sunlight during the day, warmth came to the snowy, icy landscape. The sound of dripping water could be heard as the trees lost their winter coats.

The cascading of water caused Marie's eyes to blink open. Inside the cave, there was a faint glow from the dying fire. It shined on the rock walls and the ceiling just a few feet above. The edges of the cave were darkened by shadow, places that light never touched. She lay still for a moment, listening. Outside the cave, she heard water running and the wind howling. Rising from the buffalo robe, she instinctively went to check the fire. She'd been up twice at night to add fuel—keep the cave warm. There were still red embers in the fire ring, and in a few seconds, she had a pile of sticks burning. The fire crackled in the circle of stones. Squatting before the ring, in the soft glow of firelight dancing on the walls, she glanced over her shoulder at the boys still asleep in their robes. The kitties, cuddled on top of the buffalo robe, had grown and were now cats. They also had names: Archie and Francois. She smiled at the sweetness of this scene, but despite this sweet image in front of her the cats were getting to be a problem. They ate a lot. She then turned back to the fire placing a pot with the remainder of the horse meat on some rocks near the flame.

Gazing into the flames, she remembered that the Bear had spoken to her in her dreams. Spoken wasn't quite right. The Bear had made its wishes known. It was time to leave. Now!

She had prepared for this day by drying horse meat on racks over a fire. She'd built a makeshift oven out of rocks from the cave, mudding the stones with clay-filled dirt she'd found at a nearby creek. She had baked bread in the oven, but all their flour and camas were gone. Only part of a loaf was left.

She'd been able to snare a couple of rabbits using small twigs and bark of the aspen trees to craft netting that she stretched between two trees, running across the surface of the snow. Checking her nets daily, she usually found that she had snagged a few mice. Maybe a chipmunk if she got lucky. These she fed to the cats. Thinking over the inventory, she decided there would be food for a few days, maybe a bit longer, if she managed the boys' portions and she herself didn't eat. The problem was not knowing where the next food would come from. They were more than a few days from where they might see people and be able to flag down a passing express canoe or trapping party.

Looking at the cave opening, she saw daylight spilling through the cracks in the door. Emerging into the open air, she found the wind had died down to a gentle southern breeze. Stepping outside, it caressed her face and lightly blew her long hair off the cougar-skin shawl around her shoulders. The dappled sun shone through the lodgepole and ponderosa pines. She heard the squawk of geese. Looking skyward, she saw a flock flying north, the formation was a perfect V. A smile broke across her face. Never thought I'd be happy to see them.

A loud KWUMPF from behind sent her spinning and reaching for the pistol in her belt. Her body eased when she realized it had only been a clump of snow dropping off a tree limb, thudding to the ground. Everywhere, the still, lifeless forest dripped water.

Marie ducked back into the cave. She shook the buffalo robe. "Up, up," she commanded.

The cats scattered away, looking for breakfast.

"What," came the question of the groggy Jean Baptiste.

Paul lay there, eyes blinking, trying to navigate the dimly lit cave.

"We're going. We must hurry!"

"Mama, I'm hungry," Paul whined. Curling into a ball. "I won't go!"

She bent down and smoothed his hair, running her fingers through it. "Paul. My baby. We need to go." Despite the urgency, she sounded soothing while handing him a hunk of meat to eat.

"I won't go," Paul cried and screamed. He kicked his feet as Marie dragged him out of the cave. "I won't go!" The child bit at the hunk of meat, taking his anger out.

Marie called over her shoulder, "Baptiste, roll the robe up as tight as you can!"

She picked up Paul and held him close for a minute. "Sssshhh, sssshhh," she whispered in his ear as she bounced him up and down. She hummed. After a few moments, Paul calmed down enough that Marie put him down. The child stood beside her, gnawing the strip of boiled horse meat. The cats got Marie's portion.

Deer hide straps secured the buffalo robe into a tight bundle, and Marie formed additional straps into loops, which went over her arms and shoulders, backpack-like. Her pistol and knife were in her belt, and a satchel hung at her side. John's rifle was slung over her shoulder. Marie loaded down with gear; the two boys ate on the move, as the three set off through the snowy forest.

Marie looked back at the cave entrance. She and the boys had spent the better part of two months there. It had been their home, their sanctuary from nature's violence. It had also been a place for her to heal from the trauma of the past. She thought of John every day and peeled back the layers of her love for him. While the boys slept, Marie laid awake with thoughts of what had transpired, what she could have done differently. These plagued her. Much of her time was spent thinking about John, and at first, when she reminisced, her stomach felt twisted in knots, her chest felt hollow, and tears streamed down her face. However, as the days and weeks went by, those signs of anguish faded, and she was left with memories of moments snatched here and there, instances in which they shared love, tenderness, and laughter. For the first time in a very long time, she had felt what joy was. She wondered what his last minutes had been like. It made her sad to think of him suffering or being scared or being injured. Had he thought of her? Or of Kimana? That jealous twinge made her feel guilty. Kimana was his wife. *I have no right.*

Looking back at the cave now, she said goodbye.

The going was easy.

The land was flat, but after a few hours of steady walking, the terrain sloped steeply down, making the footing on the slushy snow slippery, but not so steep that it was impassable. Marie led the way while the two boys followed single file. The cats jumped around in the snow, sometimes to the left, sometimes to the right, and sometimes out in front.

"C'mon, boys!" Marie implored them onward. They stumbled. Paul whined almost continuously. Jean Baptiste marched in stoic silence. Each step was a laborious task in which Marie, weighed down by the buffalo robe and its contents, often broke through the crusty surface, sinking to her knees. The boys' lightness kept them mainly on top of the snow, but they were also constantly slipping and falling on the slick surface.

After they had gone through snow that made the walking for Marie feel like wading through quicksand or water, she was exhausted from the physical toil. The weight of her burden and coaxing the two boys onward added to the work. Marie fell to the snowy ground--her breath coming in panting gulps. Her heart pounded in her chest. The boys, seeing their mother's exhaustion, joined her. Lying flat on the ground, the trio looked up through slender aspen poles rising like pillars supporting a canopy of blue sky.

Marie wasn't sure how far they had gone, but she knew they needed to move quicker.

Maybe three more hours of light. We need to bed down. Still good light.

She sat up, her arms draped over her bent knees.

Leaving the buffalo robe on the ground as she rose. "Jean, untie the robe and roll it flat on the ground."

Jean Baptiste blinked.

"Roll it out between those three trees," she said, pointing to the robe and the area where she wanted it positioned.

Marie strode off, leaving the two boys. She'd only gone a few feet when she found it, what she needed. She took the hatchet from her belt and whacked at a scrawny lodgepole pine tree. The tree was dead, and she broke through the trunk with three or four good chops. When it broke at the base, Marie grabbed it with her left hand to keep it from falling to the ground. She dragged the pole back to where the boys were. She repeated this step three more times.

Then she went to work on the pine logs, delimbing them until she had two poles of roughly the same length, about eight feet. Marie lashed the poles to the tree trunks where Jean and Paul had laid out the buffalo robe. She then took two horse hides, which she had cured over the winter in the cave. She tied the hides to the pine poles using aspen bark strips to make a ceiling. For the walls of their overnight shelter, she gathered pine boughs and leaned them in layers against the poles supporting the roof.

She was too tired to lash the boughs to the roof supports. *These walls will hold.*

The boys slept well that night. Marie made Archie and Francois sleep outside to begin the process of emotionally decoupling the boys from the cats. There wasn't enough food; even if there was, the cats were wild animals and needed to stay in the wild. Marie slept fitfully. The sound of snow crashing to the ground from tree limbs startled her to wakefulness more than once.

Dawn broke clear and cold, and as she barked commands at the boys, she noticed puffy steam clouds wafting in front of her face. Paul was crying about being cold and hungry. Kneeling to eye level, "Paulie, I need you to be brave. We will eat." He sniffled a bit, but the crying stopped. His eyes dried, and there was just an occasional sniffing.

Marie broke down their shelter. *How can I keep them moving. They're exhausted. Me also.* She took a deep breath to calm herself and get a moment of stillness. She closed her eyes and asked the Bear for guidance. After a few moments, an idea came to her. *Oh my God! Why hadn't this occurred to me?*

She hacked one of the longer poles in half and then cut one of the halves again. She then laid them on top and perpendicular to the longer, parallel poles.

"What's the triangle for?" Jean Baptiste asked.

Marie looked at him. "Bring me those straps," she pointed at the deer hide straps that had held the buffalo robe in a tight package.

Jean Baptiste handed the straps to her. She handed two straps back to him.

"Now tie that pole," she pointed at a pole at the other end of the structure, "Tie that pole right where I have it laid out. Make sure they stay about a foot from the ends."

Even though just six years old, Jean Baptiste had spent enough time in the wilds - helping move camp - that he was not bad at tying things off with ropes.

While Jean Baptiste tied off the bottom crossbeam, Marie worked at the middle and closer to the other end of the structure. The two length-ways poles were lashed by three crossbeams, each roughly equidistant from the other and evenly spread across the frame.

Smiling at the boys, she picked up the two longer poles. The end she grabbed was narrow so she could fit her body between both poles. The other end of the frame widened to provide a sturdy base that would not easily tip to one side or the other. "You see?"

Both boys looked. Jean Baptiste's face crinkled a bit. His head tilted to the side. Paul lay back on the robe, speechless.

"A *travois*!" Marie smiled. "Come, bring the robe."

With Paul lying on the buffalo robe, Jean said, "Get up."

"No," Paul replied defiantly.

"Mama, he won't get off the robe."

"Jean Baptiste, I need that robe!" Marie's tone was sharp, curt.

Jean bent down and, grabbing the robe, lifted the edge and pulled. The robe rolled out from underneath Paul, who was sent sprawling into the snow, white flakes from head to toe.

"Jean Baptiste!" Marie scolded. Her face twisted and blushed with anger.

Then, looking at the diminutive Paul covered in snow, her mouth creased and opened as her laughter burst into the air. She bent at the waist, clasping a knee. Paul sobbed while wiping snow from his face.

"Come here, my love." She spread her arms wide, and the little boy ran and launched himself at her. She caught him in mid-air, swung him around—pulling him up—and the two twirled to the ground in a heap of hugging laughter. Marie signaled with a hand to Jean, and he dog-piled them. All fell sprawling onto the ground. The mother hugged and tickled the two boys.

Laughter has been gone too long.

"Mmmmm. Mmmmmm. Mmmmmm," she said, hugging them.

She kissed their heads.

Rocked them.

Just like when they were babies.

· · · · ·

As they moved, the trees began to thin until a vantage point revealed a broad valley spreading out before them. Marie could see the thin, snaking line of water. There was juniper, sage, and prairie grass everywhere she looked, scattered on the snowy plain.

The geology of the Oregon country was complex. She remembered Dr. Nuttall describing how the land had been formed by millions of years of erosion. Water erosion. Wind erosion. Glacial advance and retreat. Ice dams had broken, causing massive amounts of water to rush across the land; water from the great floods had filled these basalt-lined crags, canyons, and gorges. The water flowing downhill forged an interconnected network of watercourses that all eventually flowed into the big River and, from there, to the ocean.

He also explained how clouds formed over the vast expanse of ocean to bring rain to the land, which allowed vegetation to grow, created snow that piled up in the mountains, and provided water that filled lakes. All of this water is returned to streams, rivers, and oceans, starting the process over again. He had called it the circle of life.

Looking at the vast expanse, Jean Baptiste asked, "Where's home?"

Marie knelt, looking both boys in the eyes. Then she turned back to the valley before them. "Mostly just follow that line of water. It'll go to the Columbia, the Big River." She pointed to the valley floor.

They needed to know. What if...

She didn't finish that thought.

But what if she couldn't travel, was sick or injured, or...Worse. Things happened out here. She'd seen men die in rivers and lakes and by arrow. She'd seen people get sick and die. She'd seen people break bones and die.

They both looked at her, eyes wide.

"If you lose the water, keep going north."

"How do we know which way is north?" Jean piped up.

"Pay attention to the sun. It's on our right now, meaning we've only just begun today. It also means we are traveling north."

"In the evening, the sun will be on our left, to the west." She pointed. "In the early afternoon, it will be behind us. If you remember that, you will always be traveling north. North is where the Big River is. Understand?"

Jean nodded he did. Paul with crossed arms, stomped and shouted, "NO I DON'T!"

Marie put her hands on her hips and pursed her lips at her smallest son. "What do you not understand?"

"I don't know what is right and left."

"Oh, I hadn't thought about that. Okay watch the sun. If it is coming up that is east. If it is going down, that is west and if it is warming your back that is south. Better?"

"Yes!" Paul said. "I'm hungry!'

Marie got the boys loaded on the travois again. As she walk she thought about the cats, who had the instincts to survive even when she had to abandon them. They were natural predators. The boys, on the other hand, would be helpless out here. They needed to know things, like how to get home.

"So, we are going to play a game. You boys are going to tell me if we are not going north. Understand?"

Paul chimed in, "I'll win, I'll win."

"I'm sure you will, little one." She looked out again over the land in front of them. Then she said, "C'mon, let's get down to that creek before dark.

CHAPTER EIGHTEEN
THE BEAR

The sound of running water woke her. She blinked her eyes into focus. The stars were still out. Heavy breathing next to her told her the boys were still asleep. They had made camp around the time the sun was going down. The boys had wrapped up in the cougar hide. Their youth had let them pass the night on hard, rocky ground without complaint.

Marie was not so young, and her body groaned as she rose, throwing aside what was left of the deer hide. Her back ached as she fought to stand straight. Years of packing traps, trinkets, food, and pelts were taking their toll.

Walking down to the creek, she faced east and waited for the sun. In the dim light, she could see her breath. She pulled her cougar-skin shawl tighter around her to ward off the cold. Finding the constellation of the Bear, she prayed. She stood looking at the fading light of the stars in the early morning sky and spoke, "Thank you, Father Bear, for filling my heart with fierceness to protect my sons, for ferocity in fighting the cougar, and for giving them a cave to hibernate in for the winter. We followed your path, resting, waiting for the snow and cold to return to the northland. Now, with the renewal of the Spring winds, please renew our strength. Father Bear, keep us healthy and strong so that we might get back home." She felt foolish talking out loud, so she continued to pray silently..

Wakan Tanka, you are the Great Mystery; you have provided this land. Here is an abundance from which we will find food, shelter, and warm blankets at night. Lead us to the straight path back to Wimahl, the Big River.

Then, with bowed head, she kneeled and, praying aloud, said, "Dear Jesus...let us find food...let us find our way out of the wilderness as you led the Israelites, lead us too, to the land of Milk and Honey, Amen." She crossed herself.

The sun brightened the horizon, and she prayed to the east, to the Morning Star. Looking up at the star, she said, "Thank you for bringing us through the forests to the creek that will take us back to *Wimahl* and Fort George." She stopped for a minute and, still looking at the star, said, "Or wherever our next home is."

The creek, a tributary of the North Powder River, was swollen with the spring run-off. The cloudy meltwaters raged over rocks, making a gentle, low roar while sweeping along limbs and logs. She had seen from the vantage point yesterday that the creek coursed through this broad valley in a north-northwesterly direction, and she intended to follow it.

She'd hoped to get fish from the creek, but the water was murky from the snow runoff and didn't allow her to see them as they passed. They still had a bit of dried horse meat. That would have to do.

Rising, she walked up the hill and woke the boys, and in minutes, had the travois loaded for the long walk. She picked up the poles, which served as handles, and pulled the vehicle along. Paul rode, cuddled up in a blanket. Jean Baptiste walked by his mother.

"I woke to your singing by the creek this morning. It was the Ioway language," the boy said. "Remember, you taught me?"

"Yes, I do. I was singing a Morning Star song. The Morning Star gives us wisdom and courage." She paused. Her huffing and puffing didn't allow her to speak. The travois slid well over the snow floor, but the pulling got more challenging when they hit a patch where the snow had melted away.

They hit a snowy stretch, and without the weight of the buffalo robe pack, she could glide on top of the snow; this made pulling the travois easier. Her breathing became more manageable so that she could speak without effort; she said, "Your grandmother taught me the Morning Star song long ago. It's kind of like praying to Jesus."

"My grandmother?" the boy inquired.

"Yes, my mother. She died when you were small. You never knew her. They said it was typhus."

"Typhus?"

"The burning disease is what the people call it. From the fever."

"Will I get typhus?"

"No, my son, we are away from those troubles. You needn't worry."

She stopped and set the travois down. Reaching into the pouch at her side, she pulled out two flat, rounded pieces of dried horse meat. "Take this to your brother. You eat too."

"Mama, the priest at the school, said that *Wakan Tanka* is the devil speaking to us. That it's a sin to pray to a spirit. That we will go to hell if we do."

"No one knows the world's mysteries, Jean. Keep your mind open to everything that is good!"

"How will I know what is good?"

"You will feel it." She pointed to her chest. "In here. The Holy Spirit, or *Wakan Tanka*, will come to you, and you will know."

Picking up the travois, she began walking again. Despite the warmer temperatures, the valley floor was primarily snow-covered, and the bright sunbeams reflected hard in her eyes. She looked down to cut the glare. Her eyes felt gritty, and she swept at them with her sleeve, catching the travois pole before it fell to the ground. As they topped a rise, she collapsed to the ground.

"Mama." Jean came running to her. "Are you okay?"

"Yes. I'm fine." She stroked the boy's long black hair. She was a bit winded, so it took a minute. "I'm fine. Go take care of your brother."

"Look!" Jean pointed.

Marie swung her head from the boy, following his gaze. She blinked, her eyes tearing up and making her vision blurry. "What?" She swiped a sleeve across her eyes.

"Antelope!" The boy squealed with excitement.

Marie swiped with her fingers, trying to clear her eyes. They stung. She could make out lumps in the snow field in front of them.

Snowblind!

"Okay, ssshhhh. Get down." The boy and the woman dropped to the ground. The wind was blowing from the antelope towards them, so the animals hadn't smelled them either.

Jean and Marie crawled backward away from the crest of the rise. As they approached the travois, little sounds of Paul sleeping filled the space around him. Earlier, he was hungry, so he'd cried when Marie told him there was no food left. He had finally drifted off to sleep. Other than jerked horse meat, they hadn't eaten for two days.

Marie didn't trust her vision enough to use the rifle to kill an antelope. Its sound would send the herd into a panicked flight or attract unwanted attention. With the warmer weather and the snow melting, the Shoshone would likely be more active, looking for food like she was.

Marie gently rolled the buffalo robe with her sleeping child to the ground. Paul murmured and stirred but did not wake. She began removing the crossties on the travois. She then whittled one end of the pole, creating a notch. She felt around in the bag held by a shoulder strap at her thigh and retrieved two black spearheads.

Over the long winter, when out on a walk, she had discovered an obsidian flow not far away. It looked like a jumbled mass of razor-sharp black rocks. She'd used her hatchet to knock off a couple of clumps. Over time and with much sculpting, these clumps became spearheads, each about four inches in length, very similar to the spearhead Ilchee had on her spear when she killed the cougar. Each showed the marks of her fashioning the obsidian into sharp-tipped weapons.

Marie rubbed at her itchy, watery eyes. Her vision blurred as she attempted to insert the first spearhead into the crosstie's notch. Using horsehair twine she had made during their time in the cave; she lashed one of the spearheads at the end of a six-foot pole. The other crosstie was a bit longer.

In a hushed but emphatic tone, she spoke, "Jean! Stay here with your brother. And keep quiet!"

The boy shook his head and whispered, "Where are you going?"

"To get dinner." She smiled.

She reached into the jumbled remains of the travois and grabbed a deerskin. She covered her top half and bent slightly, assuming the approximate shape of a doe. Hunched over, bent at the waist, she slowly trotted toward the top of the rise with a spear in each hand. She got down on hands and knees, crawled to the top, and peered over the hillock. The antelope was about five hundred yards distant. She estimated fifty to a hundred head. Glancing back, she could make out the shapes of Jean Baptiste, who appeared to be covering the slumbering Paul. And then, looking back at the herd, she rose, again bent at the waist, and plunged over the side of the hillock.

She trod slowly forward, looking out from under the scraggly mass of deerskin that covered her. She held a makeshift spear made from the travois crossties in each hand. Their heft felt good; their balance was about right. These spears would fly straight and true, but in her emaciated, weakened state, her vision blurred from exposure to the sun reflecting off of the snow, she had to get within twenty feet to have a chance.

Slowly, she walked. Now that cloud cover provided a respite from the blinding sun, her eyesight had cleared a bit. Looking over the herd, she saw they were busy grazing. The antelope would paw at the ground and dig under the snow to reach the grass below. She spotted a calf. It would be the easiest to knock down with a spear and the slowest to recognize danger. She corrected her course, moving slightly to her right. She raised the spear in her right hand and side-stepped closer. Within a few minutes of slow, easy walking, stopping every few feet to appear like a grazing deer, she stood within fifty feet of the calf. Marie's body was tensed, and her nerves tingled. She was like a snake coiled to strike.

Thirty feet.

The calf looked up.

She brought the spear back and prepared herself to launch. Her back arched as she hurled the spear toward the calf.

Suddenly, as if one, the entire herd leaped into action, bounding away. Marie was bewildered. She took her eyes off the flight of her spear, turning instead toward a padding, snarling sound. Almost the same instant, something pounced on her, knocking her to the ground. She rolled over inside the deerskin. She banged the back of her head on the ground and lay there for a few seconds, trying to regain her senses.

Whatever it was, it was on top of her, snarling and teeth and claws digging into the deerskin, the only barrier between Marie and itself. She felt the power of the animal's muscles, and knew it was only a matter of time until it broke through the thin deerskin that separated her from this beast. Somewhere in the air, she heard the boys' screaming. In a reflexive move, she went for the pistol in her belt, and just as she brought it toward what she believed was the creature's midsection, a paw broke through the deerskin and knocked the pistol from her hand. It wouldn't be long before the snarling, thrashing creature tore through the deerskin completely and would start tearing into her.

She was surprised at her clarity of thought. She controlled her fear, breathing deeply to calm her racing heart; instead relying on cool logic, she positioned her knee under the animal while drawing the knife from her belt. In one quick movement, Marie shoved the animal aside and flung the deerskin away as she came up, holding a spear in one hand and her knife in the other. Crouched low, she banged her knife handle on the wooden shaft of the spear. She snarled and growled at the beast, a gray wolf, that studied her from its prostrated position on the ground.

Regaining its feet, teeth showing, growling at her, he stood no more than six feet away. Its head was lowered, its back hunched up, as the wolf started moving toward her with slow, deliberate steps. Glancing briefly behind the wolf, she saw the antelope calf on the ground, her spear sticking out of its haunches. Several wolves were chasing after the antelope herd. She didn't avert her gaze long, instead locking in on the alpha male in front of her.

Marie began to sing the old wolf song of her people in their language.
In a sacred way, he makes a different pipe for me.
In a sacred way, he makes for me a wise spirit...
Her lilting voice rose and fell as she sang, sending her song to the wolf. At the same time, she backed toward the downed antelope. Moving slowly

backward, she never took her eyes off the wolf, and the wolf watched her curiously, growling and baring teeth.

Upon reaching the antelope, she knelt, her gaze moving from her work to the wolf and back to her work, she quickly butchered the animal. A quick slit across the neck cut the jugular and drained the blood. Then another cut, from the throat to the hind legs, opened the chest and stomach of the antelope's body. Reaching in, she pulled the entrails to the ground. A steam cloud rose from the warmth coming in contact with the cold air. Marie took the liver. It was warm in her hands. Then she found the gall bladder and, piercing it, showered the liver with bile. Holding the liver in her hands, she raised it to the sky. She took a bite before tossing it near the wolf, who went after it voraciously.

While the wolf ate, Marie grabbed the rear foot of the antelope and, giving the wolf a wide berth, dragged the animal toward her sons. In her other hand, she held the two spears, wore her knife and pistol tucked into her belt, and continually glanced back to keep a wary eye on the wolf.

The wolf was busy with its food.

Arriving back, the two boys bounded to her excitedly. Jean came first, took the other hind foot of the antelope, and helped his mother drag the carcass back. Paul came along slower but, as usual, had a grin from ear to ear.

"Mama, Mama," he called as he ran up. Archie and Francois, who had disappeared for a while, ran to the antelope, sniffing and pawing at its body.

"Where have you two troublemakers been?" Marie chuckled and threw them each a piece of meat.

In an hour or so, Marie had skinned the antelope calf and had the hind quarter turning on a spit over a crackling fire. She started doling out slices of steaming meat, first to Jean.

"Here." Jean took the slab, handling it gingerly due to the heat.

Next was Paul.

"Here, Paul," she said, handing him a smaller slab.

The boys bit the hot meat carefully at first, blowing on it between bites until it cooled. Then they hungrily wolfed the food down.

Marie sat on the ground near the boys. She gnawed at a piece of meat.

Looking at the boys, she said, "We will leave early tomorrow. Continue down this plain. There will be camas for fry bread, I hope."

The trio spread the buffalo robe out, and laying on their backs, feeling full bellies for the first time in days, they watched the stars.

"Mama, what are stars?" Jean Baptiste asked.

"Some people say they are people who have lived and gone to heaven."

"Do you think that is true?"

"I don't know, Jean. I heard a man who came to Fort George by ship say they got to where they wanted to go by looking at the stars."

Jean didn't say anything. He just looked up at the stars and wondered how a ship could find its way by looking at them. There must be a million lights up there. *How would they know which one to use?*

Paul was breathing heavily.

"Go to sleep now, Jean. We are starting at dawn."

Marie continued scanning the night sky. Before long, she heard the two boys' heavy breathing. When the fire had burned down to a mass of glowing coals, she got up from the bed and threw some more wood on the fire. She would get up several times at night to keep the fire going. Getting back in bed, she looked to the sky. The sailor had shown her *Ursa Major*, the bear.

Thank you for getting us this far.

Her mind wandered to the Lord's Prayer, then to Pierre. She hadn't thought about him since the first days in the cave. She wondered how he had died. She hoped death had come quickly. Tears streamed down her cheeks. Looking at the star-filled sky, she thought, *Which one is Pierre? Which is John?*

Please get my boys home. Don't let them starve out here.

She traced the outlines of the Bear in the sky. The Bear was watching over them.

In the distance a wolf howled.

· · · · ·

The next day broke clear, and a freshening southerly wind brought warm temperatures and snow melt. The sun illuminated a bright blue sky. Marie looked around the valley; tree-filled foothills encircled it. As far as she could see, there were no signs of life—no smoke from campfires, no animals grazing, not even a bird in the sky.

She'd slept well, probably because of having a full stomach. In the faint morning light, she breathed deeply. The air had a sweetness of spring that she couldn't describe. She smelled juniper, intermingled with wild prairie grass. Marie remembered she had dreamed of John last night. She couldn't recall the details, only that he was smiling at her and told her she was doing well getting her and the boys back home. He kept saying, "Follow the river."

She wasn't sure what to make of the dream.

Looking at the fire ring, she saw the fire was completely out. With the warmer nights, she was not getting up to stoke the fire. She didn't plan to build a fire, having decided that they would eat on the move today. Before waking the boys, she strolled to the top of the hill to gaze over the valley where the antelope had been grazing the day before. She saw the remnants of the gut pile from her antelope, what the wolves had left. Blood splatter and antelope carcasses dotted the whiteness of the snowy field in front of her. The carnage had been severe. From her vantage point, she counted five antelopes the wolves had brought down.

Probably the young ones. A full-grown antelope would be too fast, even for a wolf.

She'd stop at each and check for leftover meat, trim some off, and add it to their meat bag. The wolves were efficient eaters, so the pickings would be slim.

She returned to the campsite. The boys were asleep, and she let them continue. *Needed the rest.* She spent the time packing the loose items scattered around the camp. She laid out some roasted antelope meat for the boys. She didn't eat. They'd had a filling meal last night and had some reserve, but she knew they had to conserve. There was no way of knowing where the next meal would come from.

Where are those cats?

She decided they would turn up—they always did. Before long, Jean Baptiste woke and came to her. He hugged her, and they spent a moment in an embrace. She tousled his hair, saying, "Good dreams?"

The boy shrugged. "Good, I guess." He hesitated for a minute. "Why hasn't Papa come for us yet? Why hasn't anyone come?"

Marie breathed deeply and got down on one knee. She looked her son squarely in the eyes.

"I've struggled with how to tell you this. Paulie's too young."

"He's dead, isn't he?"

Marie saw strength in her son's face. His jaw was firm and set. There were no tears. "Yes, my son. I believe he is." She paused for a minute and studied the boy's face before continuing. "I believe he is in the stars. Tonight, when you are lying in bed, looking up into the night sky, talk to him. Tell him that you miss him, that you love him." She hesitated. "Know that your father loved you and was so proud of you."

The boy nodded; his eyes were watering. He turned and walked away. She let him go. He needed some time to feel sad.

Marie went to Paul. He was still sleeping. She reached down and shook him lightly. "Hey, sleepy head." She saw Paul's eyes flitter and then open. He rubbed his eyes. "Time to shake a leg!" Marie smiled at him.

"I'm hungry!"

"Yes, my little boy. You're always hungry." Marie laughed.

Marie fed the boys and put the travois together. She and the boys were moving when the sun was over the eastern mountains. The cats didn't show up that morning, but she wasn't waiting.

I hope they've gone to where the wild things live.

The land was flat and would be sloping downhill for now. Her strength was dwindling, as were their supplies. She hadn't eaten that morning. She carried John's rifle slung over her shoulder.

Marie turned and checked on the boys from time to time. They came to a rise in the land. Marie plodded and slipped on the snowy slope. Falling, her knuckles smashed into the snow-covered ground. The snow in the shade was crusted with ice. She winced at the stinging sensation in her hands.

"Are you okay, Mama?" Jean ran to her, sounding concerned.

She checked herself. Her hands and knees hurt. Her knuckles bled. Other than that, she felt fine. "Yeah, I'm good." She got to her feet. "Be careful. The snow is slippery here."

When she topped the rise, looking down at the river flowing through a notch in the landscape, the bright sun reflecting off of the snow was blinding her. She saw black spots, her eyes felt like there was sand in them. With her diminished eyesight she just could make out a couple of blobs in the distance near the riverbank. Her heart leaped a bit.

People! Could be Blackfeet. Friendly or not, I have to take the chance.

She waved her arms and yelled out. "Hello, hello!" Had they heard? She rubbed her eyes, trying to clear them. She went over the top of the hill. The speed at which she moved and the weakness in her legs caused her to tumble forward. The boys ran after her as she rolled in the snow down the hill. She heard Paul crying.

"Mama, Mama!" Came Jean's plaintive cry.

Marie lay in the snow, on her back, a forearm draped across her eyes. Her body started to convulse slightly. Then, her laugh floated into the air.

"Oh, my boys, come here."

Jean and Paul fell on top of her. She began tickling them, and soon, all three were laughing. She then rolled over and started dumping snow on them.

"Mama, stop," screamed Paul. "It's cold. It's cold."

Marie rose to her feet. She smiled broadly down at her boys. "C'mon, you two. Let's go see who those people are over there."

"People over where?"

"Jean, see them, over there across the river?"

"Mama, those aren't people. Those are bears."

Just then, Marie heard a wailing sound from one of the blurry figures. The other figure, smaller than the rest, had entered the water.

"Mama, the little bear is in the water and can't swim!" Jean was yelling and pulling at his mother's coat sleeve. "Help it, Mama!"

Marie stumbled toward the river. She could make out the small bear in the water. Its head was bobbing up and down, and then it went under. The current was pushing it further away. The mother bear followed on the opposite bank, making a high-pitched wailing sound. Marie tracked the small bear on her side of the bank while dropping her pack, rifle and jacket and kicking off her boots, she placed her pistol inside of a boot. She waded into the current, and with water at her mid-thigh, deep enough for swimming, she dove in.

She disappeared briefly but broke the water's surface in a few seconds. Blowing water out of her mouth, she went into a front crawl. With each stroke, she kicked her feet, and soon she was where she guessed the small bear would be. She dove deep, eyes open; she found the small bear and pulled it by the scruff of the neck. She and the bear broke through the water's surface. Marie guided the small bear to the opposite bank. She watched as the cub climbed the bank and reached its waiting mother.

Marie turned and swam to the other side of the river, where the boys were waiting for her. She got out on the other side and saw the mother bear standing on its hind legs, wailing in a lower-pitched tone. Her cub was at her feet.

Marie raised a hand to the mother. "You're welcome." She turned toward the boys.

One child of the bear should help another.

"Mama, you saved that bear cub," Jean said excitedly.

She shrugged.

"Mama, I'm hungry, I'm hungry!"

Marie laughed. "How did I know, Paulie?"

In a short time, Marie had her wet clothes off and had put her coat and boots on. She moved around the campsite she had chosen, on the beach by the river, gathering small twigs for a fire. She had sent the boys out for bigger sticks and other pieces. "Stay away from the river," she had told them. "I don't want to have to go in after one of my cubs!" She winked at them after the warning.

Marie scanned the valley below her and then behind her. Then she heard something coming from the distant trees. Twigs snapped. Something or someone moved through the undergrowth. Then there was nothing. *Elk probably.* She felt for her pistol.

She turned back to her work. With a fire roaring, she hung her clothes to dry and then carefully constructed a fish trap from tree branches that grew near the riverbank. She set the trap in the river current near the shore. For dinner they ate more jerked antelope meat.

In the dying light of the day, Marie went to the river. She got on her hands and knees to scoop a drink with her hand.

"Oh my...," she said.

Her hand moved to her face, which she saw in her reflection.

My face! So thin!

She looked at her sunken cheeks, her hollow eyes.

I need to eat more.

Marie rose and turned to go back to the fire. She looked over the plain. Her eyes caught movement, her hand went to her pistol. Her eyes had cleared from the snow blindness a bit and she saw a figure in the distance, maybe a quarter of a mile away. She blinked and used a thumb and forefinger to rub her eyes. Then she peered hard again into the dusky light. What she saw was the unmistakable figure of a man walking toward her.

CHAPTER NINETEEN
THE PRODIGAL SON

Marie called back to Jean Baptiste, "Bring the rifle."

"*Oui, Mama.*" The boy grabbed the weapon and, sensing her urgency, ran toward his mother.

Marie leveled the weapon at the oncoming figure. It was dusk, and her vision had not completely healed, but as she watched the figure walk, she felt a familiarity. *He's wobbly, but there's something.*

She turned to Jean. "Stay with your brother."

Jean stood for a moment. Perfectly frozen. He eyed the oncoming stranger with suspicion.

"Go on!" Marie said to Jean, her voice brusque. "Take your brother and hide!" She watched him go and then she walked slowly to meet the intruder; every footstep brought a crunch on the icy snow. She pointed the little bead at the end of the rifle at the man's chest.

The man continued to approach.

As he got closer, Marie saw that something wasn't right. He was wounded or starving. He swayed as he moved and suddenly collapsed amongst the sagebrush. Marie stepped over to him, circling wide in case he lunged at her. She came close, approaching with careful steps. Standing over him with the gun inches from the man's chest, she looked at his bearded face. She didn't know him. And then she looked into his eyes.

"Oh my God!" she screamed and threw the rifle to the ground.

Kneeling, she yelled for Jean to bring water.

"It's you!"

Jean brought the water flask as the man looked up from the ground and spoke. "Pie."

Marie laughed loudly. "YES! WE HAVE PIE!"

Leaning over, she threw her arms around Archie. Then backed away and asked, "Are you hurt?" She saw him shake his head. "Can you walk?"

He nodded that he could.

Marie got to her feet, bent over, and held out her hands to help Archie stand. "Dammit, Archie! I could have killed you!" She laughed again.

Once she got him to his feet, she checked him head to toe for blood.

Nothing. She noticed a healed-over scar on his left hand. *Maybe cut while blocking something. A knife?*

She wrapped her arm around his waist, and he put an arm over her shoulder. The two gingerly moved over the snow, picking their way through the juniper and sage to the camp. He was limping. Marie lowered him gingerly to the ground. Archie sat before the fire and soon Marie had handed him some food. He stared in to the fire, as he gnawed on some antelope meat and fry bread.

It was dark when Marie settled in front of the fire. She watched Archie eat. "Would you like more?"

"Yes...more."

She smiled, surprised at the words he was able to use. Handing him more meat. "This will strengthen your body. We have a long walk ahead of us."

Archie nodded.

"Can you tell me what happened?"

Archie stopped chewing, staring blankly at her.

"At the outpost?"

"No! Hid." Archie's head hung.

"Archie, there's no shame in that!" She waited to see his reaction. Seeing nothing in his countenance change she continued, "There were too many. All you could've accomplished is to get yourself killed, like everyone else!" She reached out and put a hand on his shoulder. He looked up and their eyes met. She could see tears. "It's okay." She rubbed his shoulder. He took a bite of the meat.

· · · · ·

Marie sat before the fire, warming herself against the cold night air. Above her, the night sky sparkled. Gazing at the stars, she became lost in thoughts.

He can't travel yet. Too weak. His speech is better. How?

She decided to spend the next few days resting and feeding Archie. She hunted, fished, and looked for camas root, she found the previous spring's berries still on the bushes. Archie's appetite was voracious. Every day, he grew stronger until, on the fifth day, he was up and playing hide and seek with the boys.

He's ready.

Once she decided to move on, Marie scurried about the camp packing bundles while the boys and Archie slept.

Archie can share in hauling our supplies. The boys can walk on their own.

She stopped for a moment and considered how things had changed over time since they left the cave. She remembered having hauled the boys and their supplies on a travois. But now the boys were bigger and had grown stronger. Paul's whining had lessened, and Jean Baptiste had grown half a hand.

He eats constantly.

Then there was Archie. He was a puzzle to Marie.

Satisfied that she had the packs ready and that they could move first thing, she sat down by the fire and listened. Like all the previous evenings since Archie had shown up, she had sought clues in his night-time ramblings. Mostly, when he spoke, it sounded like gibberish. She could sometimes hear a name amongst the strings of sounds. Once, she heard Ida's name. Tonight, as she listened, a cacophony of sounds gently caressed her senses: the running river gurgled, crickets chirped, and somewhere in the distance, a wolf howled. Archie rambled.

She moved around the fire to a pile of limbs, grabbing a handful and arranging them strategically on the fire. All the while, she kept an ear to the wind to take in the sounds of the night. As she laid the last stick on the fire, she heard it.

What did he say?

She froze, hoping he would say it again.

Then he practically yelled, "CAMEAHWAIT."

Oh, Lord! How would Archie know that name?

She retook her place in front of the fire. She glanced over at Archie; he was thrashing. Again, there were more loud words, mostly gibberish, with words intermingled.

"NO."

She thought for a while, wracking her brain to recall if Archie could know that name.

He hadn't been to the potlatch with Pawashtimane back by the rapids.

She finally decided that Archie could only know that name if he had encountered Cameahwait at the burned-out trading post. She reached into her pocket and pulled the chain attached to the Lewis and Clark peace medal. The medal twirled and dangled in front of her eyes.

Son-of-a-bitch.

The following morning, Marie was up early, getting food together. This morning's meal was roasted salmon with a berry sauce drizzled over the top. Fry bread. She'd been giving Archie tea made of valerian root, which she was using to calm his mind and his fears. As the boys and Archie ate, she strolled toward the river and basked in the early morning daylight that was beginning to bathe the valley floor. There was a warm, southerly breeze that kissed her skin.

As she watched the flow of the river, she took stock of all she'd accomplished since Archie had shown up. Besides getting as much food in him as possible, she had repaired his clothing, which had rips and wear and tear of months in the wilderness. Smiling, she remembered the sheepish look on his face when she told him to take off his pants. He'd gone out in the sagebrush, got down on the ground, completely out of her sight, and the next thing she knew, his pants were flying over the brush to her. It took her an hour or so to make the necessary repairs, but when she had gotten done, she simply lobbed his pants back over the sagebrush. In a minute or two, he emerged, fully dressed.

They had gone to ta hot springs near the river she'd found on one of her hunting forays. She bathed the boys and herself. The water soothed aching muscles and bruised bones.

Archie was told to bathe once she and the boys were done.

"Take all your clothes off! Then get in the water. Soak! Understand?"

Archie nodded his understanding.

"Good because, friend, you don't smell good."

He looked confused.

She pointed at his chest and held her nose with thumb and forefinger, "Peeyew!" She handed Archie a small flask of soap made from mountain lilac, ground into a powder. and mixed with some elk fat. Then she and the boys went back to camp. He showed up a while later. His wet hair was a sign he had done as requested.

Marie and the boys went back to the campsite. She soon had a pot cooking over a fire. The boys ran and played and laughed. Her mind began to wander. *Where had Archie been and how did he find us. Would've been like finding a needle in a haystack.* She reviewed their travels since the cave and knew she hadn't covered their route of travel. Each day moving north she'd become less concerned about the Shoshone, as she and the boys were moving constantly away from Shoshone homeland. *Archie had been in the wilderness for a long time. He knew how to track and he was able to survive alone.* She concluded that he had come over the mountains at the break of winter and picked up their trail somewhere on the downhill slope. Maybe he found their tracks in a snowfield close to the cave.

Just then Archie's arrival caused her attention to snap to the present.

She walked up to him and sniffed him. "Very good. You don't stink!"

Archie smiled.

"Come sit by the fire." Marie sat next to him. She pulled her knife from its sheath and worked to sharpen it on a whetstone. A pot of water heated near the fire. She ran a finger on the edge of the blade. "Turn toward me." She splashed some of the warm water on his face, and kneeling before him, she moved in toward his face, brandishing her knife.

"No, NO!" He tilted away and raised his arms, grabbing her hand that held the knife.

Marie was shocked that Archie had said something other than 'pie.' She moved back, wrenching her hand free, then sat on the ground. She looked up at him, saying, "Archie, look at me. Do you trust me?"

Archie's eyes met hers. He nodded that he did.

"I'm just going to shave you." She looked into his eyes as she spoke. "Alright?"

Again, he nodded.

"We've got to get you handsome for Ida, right?"

Archie's eyes lit up, "Ida."

Marie saw his eyes watering. She took his hand.

"Archie."

She could sense his excitement at the mention of his fiancée. "We're going to get you home to Ida." She thought about the letter she'd mailed.

I hope she got it.

Then, in her mind, she saw Cadotte. His big, reddened face was hidden under his mostly gray beard. His gleaming teeth. Smiling.

She noted Archie's improved energy level yesterday. The boys and Archie had spent the day playing hide-and-seek and chasing each other in the warm spring sun. The snow was almost completely gone.

Weather's good.

She heard a familiar sound, "honk, honk." She glanced skyward, spotting the flock of geese flying in a V formation. She smiled. *Well, even the geese are heading north. Hate 'em!* She smiled at that. *But I'd be happy to eat one now!*

"Let's go boys!"

Over three days of walking Marie noticed slight changes in the landscape. The snow was gone, mostly, just patches in the shade. The juniper and sage lessened, eventually giving way to grass-filled prairies. The wind rustled the grass, pushing on their backs. The sun warmed them, and they were now consistently walking downhill. Off in the distance, Marie thought she saw the winding Snake River. Back in 1810, with the expedition from St Louis, she recalled following the Snake to its confluence with *Wimahl*, the Columbia. They'd gotten lost in the canyon country. They were forced to walk the canyon rims, following the river but never able to get down to it. It was hot, the land like a desert. They ran out of water. It was a near catastrophe. Eventually, Pierre had found an Indian trading route.

He earned his pay that day.

Marie looked at the position of the sun in the sky. She roughly calculated that they had been walking for several hours. They started when the sun was in the east; it had swung to the south, and she guessed that it was now in the southwest - starting on its trajectory to sunset in the west. Using this logic, she estimated where north-northwest would be. She knew they could avoid the dangerous and deep canyons of the Snake if they veered a bit and headed toward the more friendly banks of the Columbia. Going off in the new direction would mean leaving the river they had been following. It had been a source of food and water. She loaded the flasks with water, and then, finding a shallow ford, she led the boys and Archie on their new course.

The boys were running ahead, and she and Archie walked side by side. "Archie," she said, looking at him. He turned to look at her. "Do you know the name Cameahwait?" She saw his eyes widen, and he stopped walking. She grabbed his hand. "It's okay." She took his other hand in hers and stood facing him. "Did Cameahwait kill John?" she asked. "Archie?" She felt his body tighten; his tension flowed through their fingertips. She studied his face. His forehead wrinkled, forming horizontal lines that met at a vein that popped in the middle. A tear ran down his cheek.

"It's okay, Archie. You just told me." she said soothingly. She brought him to her, wrapped her arms around him, and held him close. She whispered soothingly into his ear and stroked his hair. "It's okay, sweetheart." After a few moments, Marie released him and saw more tears running down his cheek. Holding his face in her hands. "Please know this. If you hadn't hidden you'd be dead too and Ida would be alone forever. Remember that!" She looked at him, "It's okay." She turned away. Gave him a moment to collect himself and then, without turning back to him, said, "Let's go."

The boys had skittered out a bit. "Boys! Boys!" she yelled, and when they both turned to look at her, she waved them back in. "Not so far." She watched them return to what they were doing, ignoring her request.

"Hey!" Her voice was louder and had an edge to it.

"Come in!"

"But Mama, we're playing a game. Just a minute," Jean called.

Marie acquiesced. She had moved closer anyway, so she let it go. The boys were still digging at something when she caught up to them.

"What do you have there?"

"It was sticking out of the ground," Jean said.

Marie chuckled, "Congratulations. You've just harvested your first camas root! I'll make bread if you can find more," she said, looking at their eager, dust-streaked faces. Putting the root in her shoulder bag, she began walking. The boys ran ahead, looking everywhere for more camas.

That'll keep 'em busy.

She looked over her shoulder to make sure Archie was following. "Hurry up, slowpoke!" She chuckled. "The boys are outrunning you!" She saw Archie's head pop up, and his pace increased.

He must have seen it all! God how terrible. Just him. Hiding. Watching. Indians everywhere yelling and war cries piercing the air. How frightening.

Just before sunset, they came to the edge of a steep downhill stretch. Looking out over the vista, Marie's heart quickened, feeling something like excitement.

"Mama, the grass is burned," observed Jean Baptiste.

"Yes, Jean." Marie walked back from the edge of the defile and started to set up camp.

"Mama! The grass!"

"Sit down, and I will explain something to you. Okay?"

Jean and Paul sat. "There are no trees nearby, so we will have a cold dinner tonight." Archie plopped down on the ground next to the boys as she spoke. He leaned against his pack. She gave Paul a hunk of dried venison. Jean preferred fish, so he got a smoked trout. He bit off the head. Marie looked at him with a cocked eyebrow. "Eating the head, Jean?"

"Papa and Cadotte taught me to eat it this way."

"Yes, I know. Be careful of the bones."

She looked at Archie. She handed him venison and fish.

Then, looking at her boys, she said, "The blackened prairie is a sign we are close to people. You see, the Indians here and even our people back east burn the prairies after they harvest the camas."

"Why do they do that?"

"Well, Jean, it makes the prairie more fertile."

Jean scrunched up his face.

"If the ground is more fertile, then more camas grows. Did you notice some blue flowers in the field amongst the black?" The boys shook their heads. "Well, that's the camas flower. Understand?"

"Yes," replied Jean. Paul nodded.

"I asked you to harvest some earlier today. Remember?"

The boys said, "Yes, mama," in near unison.

"You've got to pull the root, just like you did. Don't just pick the flower. Understand?" She looked for understanding in their eyes. Their heads moved up and down. "Go get some then." She patted little Paul's bottom as he scurried after his big brother.

• • • • •

The next morning, they headed across the burned-out plain and eventually came to a small ravine with a creek meandering through it. Marie decided to walk in the small wash. Being below ground level would help them avoid any hostiles in the area. Again, the boys formed the vanguard, and she and Archie walked together. Marie began to hum one of the rowing songs she recalled, saying the words in her head.

En roulant ma boule roulant.

En roulant ma boule.

Her humming turned to singing out loud. Then, to her surprise, Archie joined in at the end. "*Derrier ches nous y a-tun-un tang. En roulant ma boule!*"

"You know that song!" She walked and looked sideways at him. "Archie, you are full of surprises, my friend."

She hummed, and he sang the words, over and over, until they stopped at midday to eat.

"Why a bunch of grown men want to sing about a ball and a bunch of ducks is beyond me!" She looked at Archie and laughed. "Do you know what the words mean?" Archie's eyes blinked, but he said nothing. "Well, amongst the rolling of a ball, there is a king's son who shoots a duck, and no one is happy about it, especially the duck." She laughed at her own joke. Archie blinked.

It's nice to have someone to talk to, even if he doesn't talk back.

She considered that maybe she was getting through on some level.

Kind of like a metaphor for my marriage. She let out a belly laugh, then tears formed in her eyes, surprising her with a deep emotion she didn't know existed within her.

There were tree trunks and branches scattered about, probably carried down from the snow runoff in the mountains. She set the boys to gather twigs and sticks for the fire. Before long, she had frybread baking and meat sizzling in a pan. She made Archie some tea of valerian root. He sipped it slowly.

They continued walking down the wash. About an hour later, clouds appeared out of nowhere. Darkness filled the sky. Lightning slashed. Thunder boomed. Rain poured down in buckets. The wind roared down the wash. The boys' light-hearted scampering slowed to trudging in mud.

Paul cried, "I'm coooooooolllld!"

Marie saw his teeth chattering.

Got to find shelter. Where?

Marie heard it first—the roaring sound of rushing water. She grabbed the two boys by the backs of their shirts and began running.

"RUN, RUN, ARCHIE," she called over her shoulder.

Her eyes scanned the sides of the wash for an escape route. The sides were perfectly straight up. No way out. She was tired. Her breathing was rapid. She looked back for Archie. He was keeping up, but behind him was an onrushing wall of water. Time's up. Marie pushed Paul up the wall to the upper edge.

"PULL YOURSELF UP," she yelled. She was happy to see his little legs clamber over the top.

"You're next, Jean."

"What about you?"

"Take care of your brother. I'll be along." She boosted Jean, and. once he was over her head, she shoved his feet and watched him scramble out of the wash.

"Archie, you're next."

Again, she used her hands to form a step. She could hear the loudness of the onrushing water increasing. Archie stepped with his right foot into her hand. She struggled to lift, but finally, he stepped on her shoulder and extricated himself. He turned back. Looking at her, he reached his hand down to help her up. It was no use. She couldn't reach his hand. She held out her rifle. Archie grabbed its steel barrel and pulled.

Marie began to rise, but the muddy walls were too slippery. Her legs thrashed, and her feet sought purchase, but she slipped back down. The wind whipped her wet hair. Rain pelted her face. Marie eyed the wall of water that was getting closer. She sighed. Removed her backpack and flung it over the edge of the wash. She saw Archie grab the pack.

Above the sound of the approaching torrent of water, she yelled, "GET THE BOYS TO SAFETY, ARCHIE!"

She saw him acknowledge by nodding his head. She looked at the approaching water. She said a Hail Mary, crossed herself, and braced for the force that would sweep her to her death.

Lord, get my boys home!

CHAPTER TWENTY
SALVATION

Just as the water was about to sweep her away, a pole struck Marie on her right shoulder. Her body jerked with surprise. She took hold of the pole and held tight. Her feet scrambled against the walls of the wash to assist Archie's attempt to save her. She was two-thirds of the way up when the water made contact. Its mighty power knocked her left hand from the pole and pushed her lower body along with the current. She gripped tightly with her right hand and grabbed the pole again with her left. She could see Archie straining, and the rising flood waters were lifting her to the edge of the wash. Soon, she kicked to scramble up the remainder of the wash wall. Upon extricating herself, she sat on the edge of the wall with her legs dangling and her breath coming in gulps. She heard a voice.

"Guess I came along at the right time."

Marie spun around. "ILCHEE!"

She ran to the Clatsop princess and threw her arms around her. Stepping back a bit, she added, "Oh My God! How!? Where did you come from?"

"I heard rumors," she said flatly.

"You came running out here based on rumors?"

"The Indian trade network. I heard...people were dead." Ilchee's eyes avoided Marie's look. "I came to see for myself."

"Thank God. I've thought about all the ways I could die out here. I was drowning in a wash because I forgot not to be in one during a rainstorm...well, I hadn't considered that one." Marie smiled back. "Thank you."

"And don't forget him," Ilchee pointed at Archie. "He got the boys up and out of that wash!"

Marie looked toward Archie and hugged him tightly. "Thank you, my friend."

He looked at his feet, blushed, and said, "Pie."

"So, tell me. How'd you come to be out in a storm like this one?" Marie asked Ilchee.

Ilchee put her free hand out, palm facing the sky, and said, "Let's get out of this rain, and I'll tell you."

· · · · ·

Ilchee had horses she'd traded for with the Nez Perce. Marie and Paul rode one of Ilchee's appaloosa horses. Marie wrapped the child in a deer skin to ward off as much of the slashing rain as possible. Archie and Jean rode another. Ilchee, on her mount, led everyone through the rain. She stopped the party when they came to a copse of aspens that stood out like a beacon on the flat prairie lands. The sun was on the horizon, nearly set.

Swinging down from her horse, "I camped here on the way out. The shelter is still up."

She looked up at Marie, "Quickly, let's get the children in to shelter."

Darkness had fallen that evening, so Ilchee and Marie sat by a fire. The sound of raindrops dripping off the trees filled the air. The wind had died down, and Marie could glimpse stars splashing in the night sky through the leafy branches.

"You asked how I had found you?"

"Yes. How?"

"The Nez Perce told me where to find you. They've been watching you for a while. They keep tabs on strangers in their country.

That told Marie they had come the right way. Nez Perce country was north of Shoshone territory, bordered by the Snake and Columbia Rivers. "Okay, but a bigger question. How did you know to leave home to come in the first place?"

Ilchee chuckled, saying, "You whites do not understand us." She looked at the fire as she spoke. "You come here. Hand out trinkets. Smile, and you think we are your friends."

"Your father has embraced us," Marie stated.

"Concomly, my father, he is a survivor. He knows we cannot fight you. He has seen the ships with the big fire sticks that go boom!" Ilchee's arms spread upward to emphasize the explosion of cannon fire. "So, he makes accommodations."

"I see." Marie looked at Ilchee.

Ilchee met her expression. "You have enemies here, true. You also have friends. You don't always know which is which." Ilchee paused. "For thousands of years, the people here have traded, fought, inter-married to make alliances. We are interconnected. What happens by the ocean, where I come from, is known here in the high desert. Word travels. Do you understand?"

"Yes. You heard what exactly?"

"I heard that some Shoshone had killed your men. When your party split, some of you went north, and your group, which you and the boys were with, went further into Shoshone lands. When I heard, I came to find you. Something told me you would survive."

Marie took out the peace medal. "I found this at the burned-out trading post," she said, holding the chain, letting the medal dangle. "I saw a Shoshone warrior wearing this or one like it when we attended a *potlatch* at Pawashtimane's village. Did you hear which Shoshone did it?

"Yes." Ilchee looked down at the ground. "His blood burns for a brother the white's killed.

Marie looked into the fire. "Damn," she said in a barely audible whisper. She shoved the peace medal into her pocket. "Cameahwait!"

* * * * *

The following day was clear, the sky blue, pockets of steam rose with the sun blazing on the water-logged land. With Ilchee leading the way, the little party rode for that day and part of the next. They topped out on a slight rise and gazed downhill to the river, Wimahl. A grove of cottonwoods hugged the bank. At the edge of the trees were tipis, smoke curling out most of the tops. They were arranged in rings. There were three rings with each of eight tipis. Marie calculated a population of a hundred or more Indians. She breathed deeply, and her chest muscles loosened. The tension she didn't know was there left her shoulders feeling like a hefty burden had been lifted from them.

We made it. Thank you God! Thank you Wakan Tanka! Thank you Bear!

As they rode downhill toward the village, Ilchee spoke, "These are the Walla Walla people. Hunters and fishers. You'll be safe here."

· · · · ·

Chief Kellepit came out of the village. He had a blanket draped over his shoulders. Marie noted it was a four-point blanket that the fur traders at Fort George routinely handed out. Kellepit and his family greeted the newcomers at the edge of the village.

"*Bonjour*!" He made the sign of peace.

"*Bonjour*," Marie replied. "We have come from over the mountains." Marie pointed at the white-capped mountains behind her. "We were with a group of hunters."

"Ilchee told us that she would be going that way to look for you. There has been talk amongst the people also." Kellepit paused. "We will prepare a lodge and food for you, but come, sit under the trees, and we will talk."

Marie, Ilchee, and Kellepit, along with the tribe's leading men, sat on the ground in the shade of maple and oak trees. Sunlight filtered through the leaves above. Marie sent the boys to play.

"Thank you for your hospitality."

"It is a joyous time when we get visitors. Not long ago, some men came from the east. They gave us a piece of cloth with colors and this medal I wear on my neck." Kellepit held up the medal for all to see. "Since then, more whites have come. They bring things to the People that help us live." He lifted the blanket, holding the fabric out for all to see. "The whites are our friends." Kellepit looked at Marie and saw the fabric of her tattered dress, the rifle laid by her side, the pistol in her belt. "But you are not white. And you are not of the People."

Marie spoke, "This is true. The whites are your friends. My mother was Ioway Indian. My father was a French trapper and trader. This is back in the land of the Grandmother, Canada. My boys's father was part Lakota. So, you see, I and the boys straddle two worlds. I walk through the world with two ideals, both of which I have made to work together, just as whites and the People can work together." Marie let her words be heard. Then she added, "There will be white men coming from the land of the Grandmother. They will take us home to Fort George by the ocean."

"You and your children will be our guests until that joyous day arrives. Come. Your lodge and some food will be ready soon." Kellepit barked some commands at the women standing nearby. Marie did not understand the language, but she guessed he ordered them to take their guests to their lodge and for roasted elk meat prepared for a meal.

After examining their accommodations, Marie and the boys settled in. Before long, a meal of elk meat was brought to them. There were also steamed roots. The roots reminded Marie of the yams she had eaten at Fort George, and fry bread made of camas was smothered with berries.

Marie spent the next several days eating, resting, and growing stronger. She and the boys spent much time by the river, basking on the sun-strewn sandy beach. Today, she watched the boys splashing in the water; the sounds of their laughter filled the air and her heart with joy. Looking at the sky, she let out a deep breath.

This is good.

She heard footsteps behind her, and turning to look over her shoulder, she saw Ilchee approaching.

"The boys are having fun!"

"Yes. They love the water."

The two sat together in silence. The only sound was those the boys were making in the river. "You're losing your touch." She smiled at Ilchee, who looked confused by the comment. "I heard you coming!" Marie laughed.

"Ah," Ilchee nodded and smiled. "You seem...."

"What?"

"I dunno, lost in your thoughts." She said it more like a question than a statement.

Marie looked down at the sandy beach for a moment. Then she looked at Ilchee and said, "Been trying to think of what comes next."

"That makes sense. Any ideas?"

"Only one that makes sense, but I'd need a big favor from you."

"From me?"

"I want you to take the boys and Archie back to Fort George. You're going back home, right?"

"Why aren't you taking the boys to Fort George?"

"Because I am going after him."

"What!?" Ilchee understood the need for retribution; it was a basic human emotion. "You can't be serious? Cameahwait is a proven warrior. Tested in battle. How do you propose...?"

Marie cut her off. "Honestly, I don't know."

"Then why do it? Take your boys. Go home. Start over."

Marie looked down at the ground. Her hands were folded in her lap. "He killed the man I loved. I can't let that go unaddressed." She paused. "Also." She hesitated and looked at Ilchee.

"There's more?"

"Yes. He killed the boys' father, too."

"Ah, I thought that is what you meant by the man you loved."

"Yes, I suppose I loved their father. But he was a cruel man. Mean. I fell in love with another man. A good and decent man."

Marie told Ilchee about her marriage to Pierre and the mistreatment she had suffered at his hands. She told her of John and his gentle spirit and many kindnesses.

"He sounds like a wonderful man."

"He was that. I loved him very much. Unfortunately, by the time I figured out what I wanted, it was too late." Marie bowed her head. She could feel tears running down her face. She brushed at them. "There's something else, too."

"What's that?"

"Since I was a girl, I have followed the path of the Bear Spirit. This is a strong deity among my mother's people, the Ioways." Marie looked up at Ilchee. "During our darkest days in that cave in the mountains, when we were almost out of food and shivering from the cold, I prayed to the Bear, and I told him if he saved us, I would do whatever He asked."

Ilchee nodded. Her face showed lines of worry and focus, or how someone looks when they seek to understand.

"Last night in my dream, the Bear came to me. He didn't say anything. He stood there looking at me but held a spear in his right hand."

"And the spear signifies war?"

"Yes. I can't read it any other way."

Ilchee looked out towards the river. She didn't speak for a time. At last, she said, "No. I cannot take your boys back to Fort George."

Marie stammered, "Wha`? Why not? You're going that way anyway."

"No. I'll go with you. Who knows what kind of trouble you'll get into without me!" Ilchee chuckled. "Besides, I'm a good tracker; you'll need that to find Cameahwait. Archie can take the boys."

Marie smiled. She extended her right hand to Ilchee.

Ilchee firmly took Marie's hand and looked into her eyes. "Yes, we are like sisters. You and me."

CHAPTER TWENTY-ONE
FOUND!

Marie stepped from the tipi into the bright light of the morning sun. The air smelled of the river and the sweet fragrance of hyacinth. She walked to the shoreline, where the boys were busily building a sand fort.

"Look, Mama, it's Fort George." Jean's smiling face beamed at her.

"It's a grand-looking fort, my boyos!" Marie stretched, arching her back and viewing the slow-moving river before her. "There's meat in the pot when you're hungry."

Behind her, she heard the padding of footfalls.

"It's a wonderful view, this river."

Marie spun to see Chief Kellepit approaching. "It is that. Where I come from, the land is dry, the rivers, small."

"Yes, I have seen the lands over the mountains. We hunt buffalo there."

"Hmmm." Marie nodded.

"For us, though, the river is life. Water is life. The salmon that swim provides sustenance. No river. No life." The old man paused. "I have heard you will go after some Shoshone."

Marie looked Kellepit in the eyes. His long hair was streaked gray, and scars on his bare chest attested to a life spent battling for his people. "A very specific Shoshone. Cameahwait. Do you know him?"

"The Shoshone and my people are enemies. Eyes are everywhere. Words fly through the air." He reached into the air as if catching a fly in mid-flight.

"What do these eyes and words tell you?"

"The man you seek is in the valley of the river of trees. The Frenchmen call it the *rivière du bois*. After the long winter, their food supplies will be low and the Shoshone will be hunting."

Marie nodded. "Very similar to my mother's people, the Ioway." She stopped and thought about how to seek this old warrior's aid. "You have seen many things in this life. You have fought your enemies. You have seen loved ones die." The old man nodded. "I am going after this man because he killed my people. People that I loved. My husband."

The chief was quiet. She assumed that he was thinking about what she had said.

She went on. "I will need horses. I have nothing to trade."

"I have spent time in the sweat lodge, fasting, seeking guidance from the Great Spirit," said Kellepit. "About you." He pointed a bony finger at her.

Before the man could finish, Marie heard Jean yelling, "*Arrêter, arrêter*!!!" She turned back toward the boys and broke into a trot. As she was preparing to call out to her son, she heard men singing—Frenchmen. She turned to look upriver. Her face broke into a wide smile. She jumped up and down, arms extended, waving, "WE'RE HERE, WE'RE HERE!" she screamed.

Three canoes glided down the river with the current flowing toward the ocean. Sails were deployed to assist the oarsmen who rowed in unison. Each man wore the traditional red felt hat with the ball on the peak flopped to one side. Their shirts were blue or red and made of linen. The shirts fit loosely to accommodate the rowers' almost constant motion.

As the oarsmen hauled the canoes up to the riverbank, the excited boys yelled in unison, "Uncle Cadotte, Uncle Cadotte!"

Marie ran to the giant steersman. His face wore a wide grin. He lifted Paul over his head and gleefully said, "Your Uncle is back, little one!"

Paul let out a giggle. Setting Paul down, he lifted Jean Baptiste and hugged the boy. "It is so good to find you here! You had me worried."

"We were fine. Mama took care of us," said Jean.

Marie came to Cadotte and leaned in to him, her head rested on his chest. "Oh, Francois! I've thought of you often." She stood back a little and looking up at Cadotte, their eyes met.

"*Oui*, me as well." His face reddened. He broke off his look from Marie, looking instead at the ground.

Marie released Cadotte, who, in turn, set the boy down. "As soon as I heard what happened, Madam Dorion, I jumped on to the next canoe fleet headed for Fort George. I was coming to find you, but look, you have found me instead!" Cadotte let out a belly laugh.

"Yes, Francois, and you are a sight for sore eyes." Her hand reached out to touch his shoulder. Tears ran down her cheeks.

Francois Cadotte bowed slightly. "I am at your service! You and the boys."

"They've been through a lot." She paused. "I need to ask a favor."

"But of course. Anything!"

"We'll talk tonight. While you're smoking your pipe down by the river."

· · · · ·

Later that evening, Marie found Cadotte down by the river, watching the water flow by, a small fire to ward off the night chill, and a bowl of burning tobacco in his pipe. She sat on the ground across the fire from him. "How was Red River?"

"Red River? I would not know Madam Dorion. I only got as far as Fort Colville. We stopped there for the winter. When Spring came, and we were getting ready to sail, I heard you and the boys were lost." He puffed at his pipe, blowing smoke into the air. He hung his head and looked at his feet. "My heart was broken. Thinking of you and the boys. I barely slept." He paused to puff on his pipe. Slowly he exhaled a cloud of smoke, which trailed away, carried by a slight breeze coming off of the water. "But I said if anyone can get out of the wilderness, it is Marie Dorion. So, I came to see for myself. And here you are!" Francois Cadotte's face beamed with a huge smile that was just visible in the fading light.

"Francois, it was terrible. Many times, I thought...." She brought her hands to her face to hide the tears. Her body shook slightly. Neither of them spoke. Removing her hands from her face she sniffled. Rubbing her nose with her hand, she looked at Cadotte, saying, "I thought we'd never make it out. Or something would happen to me, I'd get sick, and then what would become of the boys? I thought about those kinds of things every day. A thousand different ways we were all going to die."

"Madam Dorion," he said, then paused. "Marie, I have worked in some of the most god-forsaken places imaginable. Up in the northern country of Canada." He swung his pipe in the air to indicate the general direction north. "It starts snowing there in September. We would ice fish in the lakes to supplement the food. If winter ran too long, which it did quite often, men were reduced to eating their boots, moccasins, and whatever they could get their hands on because the food had run out, the horses and dogs had been slaughtered, and it was all that was left before we started in on each other. Thankfully, it never came to that." Cadotte puffed his pipe. "My point is we always found a way. And you found a way. Be proud of that."

"I'm happy the boys are safe." Her head tilted slightly as she confessed, "But I couldn't save John. I couldn't save Pierre." She looked up and into Cadotte's eyes as she wiped her face with her sleeve. "I couldn't save any of them."

"You saved the boys, yourself, and Archie. That's enough."

She nodded in agreement. "There's something else that needs doing. I'm going back out there."

Cadotte clambered off of the log he had been sitting on and rose to his feet, yelled, "YOU'RE WHAT!?"

Marie was shocked at the speed with which Cadotte moved; she raised her arms, her palms pointed at Cadotte. "Hold on. Hear me out. There's a Shoshone warrior, name of Cameahwait."

"Never heard of him."

"We encountered him first at the *Dalles*. Pawashtimane's village. You remember where we picked up Kimana?"

"Yes. She...I don't know the words. She made me feel funny."

Marie considered her thoughts on Kimana and then said, "Anyway, he's responsible, and I will make sure he pays."

"Pays? Ah, that's a tricky one there!" Cadotte held the bowl of his pipe. "Ya see...."

Marie couldn't catch her anger. She cut him off, yelling, "ARE YOU GOING TO QUOTE SCRIPTURE TO ME?"

Her words came out angrier than she had intended. She took a deep breath, "I'm sorry Francois." She waited for a calmer moment to overtake her. "Vengeance is mine and all that crap!? Look, Francois, I didn't go looking for this; it came to me, and I know John and Pierre...well, I think they'd want to see their killer repaid in full!"

He puffed at his pipe. "I see there's no talkin' you out of this."

"I need a favor, Francois."

Cadotte leaned in.

CHAPTER TWENTY-TWO
DOWN RIVER BY CANOE

Marie stood at the river's edge as the canoe with Cadotte, Jean Baptiste, little Paul, and Archie pushed off and drifted backward in a vast, arcing path toward the current that would carry them to Fort George.

She huddled against the chill of the morning. Arms folded across her chest.

Am I doing the right thing?

"You're doing the right thing," Ilchee said.

Marie looked at her. "Reading my mind now?"

They both chuckled. Ilchee walked away toward camp. She called back at Marie, "I'll get the horses fed and ready."

Marie nodded without turning or taking her eyes off the canoe gliding toward the ocean.

Standing and watching the canoe get smaller and smaller, Cadotte's remarks about Kimana haunted her. She saw him in her mind's eye, holding his pipe in one hand, exhaling smoke as his words spilled out, "Never trusted her. She's in this somehow."

Stop watching. They're gone.

It was then that it occurred to Marie that except for the few days out on the prairie when she had stayed behind to give birth, she and the boys had never been away from each other for an extended period. She pushed those thoughts out of her mind, knelt by the river, and, speaking out loud, asked the Lord for protection. And added, "...as you say, I am seeking an eye for an eye. I don't know if this is a sin, but I seek it. Forgive me. Amen."

She rose to her feet, took one last look toward the canoe that no longer sat there, felt a pang in her heart, and walked to the village.

She found Ilchee checking the supply pack on a petite but sturdy-looking horse with strong, solid shoulders. This horse's stature was typical of the Nokota breed, a Lakota variety used to pull travois. Its gray coat glistened in the onrushing sunlight, and its bushy forelocks hung almost to its eyes.

Kellepit and his two wives came to see them off. "The Great Spirit favors you," he said to Marie. "He spoke to me in a dream again last night. He is pleased with the horses we have provided. They are strong. The Appaloosa: fast and sure-footed. The Nokota: strong and steady."

"Chief Kellepit." She nodded at his wives. "I thank you for giving us food and shelter and letting us rest before our journey."

"You should take some of our warriors."

"That would attract a lot of attention. Walla Walla warriors in Shoshone country." She looked at Ilchee, who was now seated on an Appaloosa. She was riding with an Indian saddle, which had a wooden frame covered with tanned hide stuffed with fur. The stirrups were made from leather straps that held the wooden footbed where the rider stepped to mount, dismount, and rest their feet while riding.

"I suppose that is right," replied Kellepit.

Marie swung up to sit her horse. Her rifle was held in place by leather thongs at each end. "We'll be back soon." She reined on her horse to avoid the chief and gave it a kick. The horse sprung forward. Ilchee rode up next to her. Ilchee led the pack horse.

"Cadotte, last night, said something I can't get out of my mind."

"What's that?"

"He thinks Kimana is somehow involved in the attack."

"Did he say why he thinks this?"

"He just said he felt it in his gut." She paused. "He went on to say his gut is rarely wrong."

"What does gut mean? His gut?"

Marie recalled that while Ilchee's English was serviceable, it wasn't her first language. "It's a saying that whites have. It means that he has a feeling that she is involved. It means that he has bothersome thoughts about her. Make sense?"

"Yes. I see." Ilchee considered this for several moments. "What does your gut tell you?"

"I don't know. Once she and John were married, I distanced myself. I couldn't..."

Marie's thoughts went to John. She missed him—his laugh, his strength, the way his body felt next to hers. She looked skyward.

I hope you can see me. I know I can't bring you back. I know you would not want me to put myself in danger.

Her gaze returned to earth, to the trail they were following. Ilchee had moved out in front, riding single file.

Had she sensed my need to be immersed in my thoughts? Marie looked skyward again. *Protect me now like you always did when you were here. I know it's my pride leading me on, leading me to ignore your clear instruction. Vengeance is yours. And not mine.*

Shortly after leaving the village, they started climbing a long, broad ridge with juniper, sage, and wild grasses flowing down its sides. They followed a narrow trail topped out on a butte covered in pine forest. After a few days of traveling east, they struck the top of the river canyon that the Snake River ran through. Occasional stands of aspen were interspersed among the pines. The visibility in the forest was excellent, as there was little in the way of underbrush. They stopped to eat some huckleberries that were lining the trail.

"I love these berries," Marie said. "So sweet."

"I've been seeing lots of signs of passing. Lots of unshod ponies. Could be Shoshone."

Marie nodded.

"We are on a trade route, so not surprising." Ilchee waited for a reply, but Marie was distracted picking and eating berries. "There's a lake a ways ahead. We can stop there tonight. Water the horses. Good grass, too."

• • • • •

They followed the Snake River canyon for several days, then veered off at its confluence with the *Riviere du Bois*. Marie and Ilchee followed this river, which was lined with cottonwood trees and generally headed south and east. The weather was good, with warm sunny days. The water was plentiful as the snow melt had filled the river with crisp, cold water. Grass grew along the banks and flowed onto the lush meadows of the floodplain. Whenever she spotted the little blue flowers of the camas plant, Marie would dig some and other roots for food and medicinal purposes.

On their seventh day out, Ilchee speared a doe. It was small but Ilchee made the most of the available meat.

They camped after dark but lit no fires. The moon came up late. It lit the land almost like daytime. They traveled until dawn was starting to creep over the distant mountains. They camped. In a copse of trees.

Marie and Ilchee sat in the near-dark. Their horses tied to stakes pounded into the ground.

Marie whispered, "There is a meadow a day or so ahead. I visited it a few years ago. We'd come through this area on our way out from St Louis."

Ilchee replied in a whisper, "What about the meadow?"

"The field will be full of camas at this time of year. We should find women there harvesting." She paused. "We can start there."

Moving across the land like ghosts, making no noise, leaving no trace. They moved into Shoshone land undetected. Ilchee and Marie followed the river for two more days until they came to a well-worn trail from the River of Trees to the meadow they sought. They topped a rise, and Marie's eyes grew wide when she saw the smoldering, blackened meadow. "Damn! They've harvested and gone already."

"We should be able to pick up their trail," Ilchee answered, hoping her words would comfort Marie a little. She reined her horse to skirt the edge of the burned-out meadow.

After a short distance, Marie got her attention, "Psst."

Ilchee looked back, and Marie signaled that she saw people at the bottom of the meadow. Ilchee looked where Marie was pointing. Through the smoke, she could make out the shapes of several people, probably women.

Ilchee signaled back with a raised palm toward Marie, which meant she wanted Marie to wait.

Marie rode back to the river and dismounted. She let her horse and the pack horse wander back toward the river to eat some grass and drink a bit. She found a driftwood log and sat in the warm sun; the water gurgled over small rocks. Her thoughts went back to a sunny day near Fort George.

God, that seems so long ago.

Fort George.

Is it real or a dream she had once?

She was basking in the sun when she heard male voices speaking, but couldn't understand their words. Rolling off of the log she lay flat hoping she was not visible.

She peered over the log and saw two warriors riding the trail she and Ilchee had been on minutes before. She watched as they slowly descended the trail. She couldn't understand what they said, but she could tell by how they moved their hands and arms when they spoke that they were excited about what they were discussing.

If they ride down into that meadow, they may find Ilchee. If they see me, it's two of them against me.

She moved crawled on all fours and then rose moving toward her horse and the rifle in the scabbard. She had decided to ride behind them, and if Ilchee was discovered, she could take them from behind.

Just as they began to take the hill that would lead down to the burnt field, one of her horses whinnied. The two warriors paused their conversation and turned at the sound. One pointed at the pack horse, probably thinking of the loot they might garner.

Marie, quickened her pace toward her two horses. She reached them just as the two warriors began to gallop toward Marie. Then, seeing her, the warriors whooped and spurred their horses toward Marie, who had just gotten to her horse and pulled her rifle from its scabbard. She swung the gun around, the butt pressed on her shoulder, and she drew a bead on the lead rider, who was now within a few yards. She remembered being taught to take a deep breath and then squeeze the trigger. KABOOM. A cloud of smoke belched out from the barrel and slowly drifted into the air. Her nose stung from the acrid scent of burnt gunpowder. As the air cleared, she saw a riderless horse sprinting over the hill toward the burnt field. The other warrior had left his horse and ran at her on foot. He yelled a war cry, holding a lance in a throwing position as he approached her.

Marie pulled her pistol out of her belt, aiming at the oncoming warrior. "STOP. STOP," she called.

The warrior, seeing the pistol, stopped, lowering his weapon. Just then, the first warrior rose from some brush. He held his right shoulder, which was splattered in blood. She couldn't tell if his shoulder was broken or dislocated.

The second warrior wore a grin. "Two of us," he said in French. "One shot for you."

"You're next. Your friend over there doesn't look like he's in any condition to cause trouble."

Just then, she heard Ilchee's voice.

"And then there's me," Ilchee said as she swung her left leg over her horse and slid to the ground. Her lance with an obsidian tip was poised. Both warriors looked toward Ilchee, assessed the situation, and then looked back at Marie.

"Where the hell did you come from?" Marie asked the air. Then, looking at the warriors, she commanded the warrior who was standing, "Sit." Marie waved the pistol up and down.

The second warrior moved to his friend and sat.

"Ilchee, come here."

The women walked away a bit, and Marie said in a tone just above a whisper, "What do we do with these two?"

"No idea."

"Do you speak their language? The second one speaks tolerable French, but I'm unsure how far we'll get."

"They're Snakes, so I can manage. Their tongue is similar to the tribes on the lower river."

Marie wandered off to collect her horse and the packhorse while Ilchee worked on the Snake warriors. Luckily, the gunshot had not spooked either of the horses into a run, and she found them grazing on the grass near a copse of cottonwoods.

Marie held the reins at the bit and looked her horse in the eyes. "Good boy," came out in an almost whisper. She patted the side of the horse's head. She moved around to his right side, her hand caressing his neck. Then she noticed the scars on the upper-left front of the horse's shoulder.

War horse. No wonder he didn't spook.

Marie sat by the river, watching the water flow. She could feel the stress of the fight wearing away, and her thoughts turned to the boys.

They'd be back at Fort George by now or close. Maybe they're having some of Jack's apple pie. God let me get back to them despite this folly I am insisting on.

That thought made her smile. Her vision of Paul's pie-smeared face disappeared at the sound of a rider coming from behind her. Her head turned, and as she spotted Ilchee, she could feel her face relax. "Where are the two gentlemen I left you with?"

"They're gone."

"WHAT!?" Marie was shocked.

"I let them go."

"Yes, I understood that, but why?"

"Here. Look at this." Ilchee swung down from her horse. She pulled a rifle from her scabbard. She took the gun and held it out to Marie.

Marie looked and stumbled backward. One of her heels caught the edge of a rock, and she landed on the ground with a thud.

Ilchee ran to her. "Are you alright?"

"Yes, yes." She raised her hands toward Ilchee. "Give me the rifle." Taking it in her hands, she turned it around and upside down, finding the initials PD on the underside of the rifle barrel. "Pierre always scratched his initials on his rifles. See?" She held the rifle up for Ilchee's inspection. "Which one of them had this?"

Ilchee saw Marie's face redden, could sense Marie's anger, and felt heat rising from her. "He didn't do it. Just hear me out."

Marie took a deep breath. Then nodded, saying, "Okay. Talk."

As they rode, Ilchee filled Marie in on the information she'd gotten from the women harvesting roots and burning the meadow and then what she'd learned from the two Shoshone warriors.

"How do you know anything those two Snakes had to say is trustworthy?"

"Because the stories match pretty well. The women, the warriors. Same story."

Marie considered that for a minute. She felt the movement of the animal beneath her. She swayed with the horse's steps. "So, Cameahwait is disgraced? Kicked out of his band?"

"Yes. He lied about the events with Pawashtimane's people, hoping his lies would enrage his people against the whites and they would follow him to destroy the white traders' posts.

"And Kimana?"

"She and Cameahwait have known each other since they were kids. They were supposed to marry, but then the marriage arrangement between her tribe and Pawashtimane's, well, you can figure the rest of that out."

"Okay, why are we riding back the way we came?"

"Cameahwait is not with the tribe. The women and the men both agree on that. He's an outcast. He has ten warriors and Kimana. Probably most of the warriors have their families, so figure forty or fifty in his village."

"Okay, but where are we going?"

"One of the warriors mentioned that he might still be around your trading post. He told me it is a sacred area for the Shoshone people."

"How'd they happen to have Pierre's rifle?"

"The wounded Shoshone?"

Marie nodded.

"He met a follower of Cameahwait and traded for it. Three horses. And good ones, he said! I could tell he was mad about losing the horses and now the rifle."

"Huh." Her mind sifting through all the information she'd just been given.

· · · · ·

They stopped riding short of dusk. Ilchee had lanced a boar, and they risked a fire to roast a hindquarter. They strung the rest in a tree to let the meat cure for a few days. As they ate, Marie noticed the moon edging over the mountainous horizon. It was not full yet, but it would be in a few days. "We'll ride through the night. Sleep a bit." The hot meat felt good in her stomach. She couldn't remember the last time she had this much food in one sitting. They doused their fire and swung up on their horses. "Moon's gonna be big and beautiful tonight!"

"Yes, a wonderful light to guide us through the night," Ilchee said.

The next morning, as the sun crept over the mountains, flanking them in the east, they came upon a copse of trees near a river. "Let's let 'em graze and drink a bit, then hobble 'em while we sleep," Marie said.

Before they drifted off to sleep, Ilchee said, "I picked up a fresh trail of ponies. When we wake up, I think we should follow it. See where it leads."

Marie nodded. Wrapped in a blanket, she laid her head on her saddle. She got halfway through her *Our Father* before she fell asleep.

They slept for a few hours and were back in the saddle before the sun was in the southern part of its daily arc to the horizon. Ilchee led as they followed the pony trail, which ran in a meandering but generally southwesterly route. Marie started recognizing the terrain; remarkably, she noted the volcanic vent she and the boys had passed on their way to the Columbia River. Next, they came to the river they had followed last winter to the mountains. Her stomach felt queasy, then alternately tied in knots as memories came and went.

Ilchee halted on a rise. From this vantage point, they could see every crease and fold of the high desert landscape before them. Marie rode up beside her. She scanned the land in front of them. "See something?"

"I know where they're going. This river is fed from a lake that sits up on that bench of land over there." Ilchee pointed towards the flat-topped land feature that was still several miles away.

Marie looked. "The country is wide open. They'll see us coming."

"We'll swing wide. Go along that. You see?" Ilchee pointed to a ravine, a remnant of some ancient flood that snaked through the land, passing close to the eastern slope of the bench.

Marie followed where Ilchee pointed and saw a small, rutted defile that led to a deeper ravine. The ravine ran due south, almost directly past the bench of land that was their target.

"See those trees? There on the eastern slope?" Ilchee continued without waiting for an answer. "We'll come out of that gulch and use those for cover. Leave the horses. Scout on foot."

"See what we see," added Marie.

"If I had to guess, we'll see the village of Cameahwait and his followers."

Ilchee led off toward the ravine. Marie followed with the packhorse in tow.

• • • • •

They'd followed the ravine to a small pool of water, remnants of the spring runoff, and had left the horses there to drink and eat whatever grass or other vegetation could be found. Then, with the horses secured, they climbed out of the ravine on foot and up the eastern slope of the bench until they reached a spot that provided cover from view. There they sat in the dark eating frybread and wild boar haunch left over from the other night, no fire, a cold dinner. A word had not passed between them for several minutes. Marie broke the silence. "Ilchee?"

"I know what's coming, and it's a bad idea."

Marie explained, "I'm going to do something that...." She paused, searching for a way to explain Christianity to a woman whose cosmology was based on animism and a belief that all living things harbored spirits – good or bad. "In my life, I have been taught that to take life is a bad thing.

My God says it is a mortal sin to kill. And also, my God says that vengeance is for Him to take care of. Do you understand?"

"It is interesting that your people believe in one person to rule the world. We believe that spirits are everywhere, in everything."

"My mother was an Ioway Indian who lived far over the mountains. Her people believed in something that was the Great Mystery, the essence that runs the universe but cannot be understood by the people."

Ilchee nodded.

"I cannot ask you to do something that I know is morally wrong according to my God and the God of my father and his people."

Ilchee was silent. Several minutes passed without a word. "I am here. I decided, not you."

Marie wrapped up in a blanket and lay on the bare earth, looking at the stars through the tree limbs. Sleep came quickly.

CHAPTER TWENTY-THREE
ALONE

Marie crept through the pine forest, stepping carefully so as not to snap twigs and the dry tinder on the ground. Her way was clear, there being little in the way of underbrush. She had John's rifle slung over her shoulder, a pistol in her belt, and her right hand held one of Ilchee's spears with an expertly carved obsidian arrowhead. Ilchee had insisted she take it. "Just in case the others fail you. This never will."

Marie was trying to control her breath, which was coming in gulps due to the exertion of the uphill climb and the thinner air at that altitude. She stopped briefly and leaned on a tree, waiting for her breathing to normalize. Her mind drifted to her conversation with Ilchee an hour ago. When she returned, Marie had asked her to check in on the boys, and Ilchee had promised to do so. Then Ilchee said something that surprised her, "You are my sister. Where you go, I am there." Marie threw her arms around her and thanked her for everything she had done.

Then Ilchee climbed up in her saddle. Her last words to Marie were, "Remember, the spear will fly straight and true. Don't aim; look where you want it to go."

Marie resumed her climb. Slowly. Steadily. She trudged on, one foot in front of the other, for what seemed like hours. Eventually, she topped out on the bench of land. Once on top, she was surprised at the terrain. She had expected a flat butte. Instead, she stood on the rim of a bowl, and at the bottom of that bowl was the lake that Ilchee had talked about. She saw the river that left the lake, flowing through a gap in the rock wall of the bowl. She scanned a treed area near the lake, looking for signs of life. Her eyes tried to peer through the foliage of the aspen trees that grew near the bank.

Nothing. Ilchee was wrong.

She was turning to go when she heard it. A dog barking. Then a horse whinnied. She stopped and stood completely still.

Had the dog sensed her? Was she discovered?

She made the decision to move slowly to the ground. She lay in a prone position on her stomach. John's rifle was ready as she aimed it at the aspen copse. Marie observed from her perch. Before long, a slender trail of smoke rose from amongst the leaves and branches. Then another. She knew the signs of a village awakening. Her heart pounded. She felt an electric surge of excitement pulsing through her.

I've got him.

She rolled onto her back and gazed up at the clear blue sky. Finding the Morning Star in the east she prayed.

Wakan Tanka. Great Mystery. Please give me the courage to do what is needed. Give me the heart of my Bear guardian.

Marie slowly crawled backward from the bowl's rim, retreating into the pine forest from which she had emerged moments ago.

Rest now. Watch later. Take my time.

She lay between two recently fallen trees in the stand of pines. She gathered some pine boughs using her hatchet to cut lower limbs. Before long, she had a shelter for sleeping that screened her from view. If someone happened by, it looked like a couple of downed pines. She peered through her shelter's roof to the sky as she lay on the forest floor.

John, my love. I go now to avenge you. I know you would advise against this. You were always so protective of me. But there's no one to protect me now. Soon, Cameahwait will join you in Heaven. I don't believe in a place called Hell, so even his sort will be with you and Pierre bathing in the Light of the Loving God of All. I miss you every day. I hope you and Pierre are behaving.

She felt a smile creep across her face.

. . . . .

Marie awoke with a start, and a gasp slipped out despite her efforts at quietude. She lay, listening to the world around her. She recalled her dreams. John had been in them. He was smiling but didn't say anything. There was a growling bear in her dream, too. Then there was something like a specter, a ghost. She recalled it being dark like a shadow but wasn't sure what it meant. She knew that in her mother's culture, dreams meant something. She wondered if John's smiling face was a sign of his approval. The growling bear meant her spirit guardian was with her and would strengthen her when she needed it most. She couldn't come up with any notion of what the shadowy figure symbolized for her. Even in the Holy Roman Church culture, it was thought that the dead visited in dreams to deliver messages. The problem was: what had John meant to get across?

She resumed her position at the edge of the rim. Gazing down, she heard and saw a beehive of activity. Women worked in the grassy area near the river. Children splashed and laughed. Dogs barked. Thoughts of her boys started to creep in, but she pushed them out.

Not now.

Her mind eased that she hadn't been discovered. She noticed a woman off from the group. She stood by the river briefly and then began walking back to the aspen grove.

KIMANA! Screamed in her mind.

Although a long way off, Marie had seen Kimana enough over the months to recognize how she moved. How her arms swung in unison with her hips. Her mind raced with a thousand thoughts colliding together at once. She stayed still, trying to sort through the information in her over-excited mind. Then Cadotte's words, "She wasn't quite right. Something was off."

She decided to move closer, never taking her eyes off Kimana, watching as she moved up a trail on the backside of the aspen grove. With a closer look, she was sure it was Kimana. Marie scrambled to get to that trail. She needed to be careful.

Retreating to the trees and following the forest edge, she kept the bowl's rim in sight as she moved toward the trail. It took over a minutes of slow, careful movement to get to where she estimated the trail ran. Her eyes peered through the tree trunks. She sat waiting and watching. After a few some time, she heard a woman singing in what she assumed was the Shoshone language. Before long, the voice switched to French. She recognized the hymn immediately: "*Je vous salue, Maria...*"

Damn, she's Catholic!

Marie followed the voice. She reached a point where the words were clear and loud enough to be easily understood. Pistol in hand, she stepped out of the trees into the small clearing and saw Kimana sitting at the edge of a thermal pool. Her skin glistened, and the pool's water caught the dappled sunbeams filtering through the trees and highlighted her face, which was framed by hair that flowed down over her shoulders and onto her torso.

Kimana's face lit up with surprise.

In French, Marie said, "Don't scream or you're dead. Understand?"

Kimana nodded that she did.

It was then that Marie noticed something else. "My God, you're pregnant." Kimana's hands went to her swollen abdomen. She looked down. "Is it John's baby?"

"Oui," Kimana replied. "But Cameahwait says it must be disposed of. It is a white child, and he will have no part of that."

"Oh, God," Marie crossed herself.

"He's become terrible. I am afraid of him." Kimana's shoulder shook as she began to weep.

A twinge of empathy ran through Marie. Most of all, she knew about being wrong about the man she had fallen in love with.

"Alright. Get dressed." Marie ran through her options. None seemed good. She could do what she had vowed, to kill Kimana as a traitor to John. But then John's baby would be gone. She felt like Kimana was in danger. She could take Kimana with her.

What if she's lying?

Marie's thoughts were racing in a loop. She couldn't come up with a solution that seemed right. Just then, she heard a man calling for Kimana. Marie put a finger to her lips to signal Kimana not to say a word, and then Marie melted back into the woods. Her spear rested against the trunk of a tree. She held John's rifle close and knelt out of sight.

Marie watched. She had to restrain herself from letting out a loud shriek and charging at the sight of Cameahwait. She felt a surge of anger; her face became hot. She listened as he spoke to Kimana. She didn't speak Shoshone but could tell by the volume of his words and the sharpness of his tone that he was angry.

Kimana said something back; Marie imagined it was something like, "I'll come back when I'm ready." Cameahwait, feeling his authority challenged, yelled, and grabbed the woman by her hair, pulled her to her feet, and dragged her back down the trail. When Kimana screamed and yelled, he turned and hit her in the face with his fist, forcing her to the ground. Marie's body trembled, not with fear, but with anger. She remembered the beatings Pierre had given her over the years. She remembered the humiliation, the loss of dignity, being made to feel worthless, and those feelings fed the fire of her rage. John had remedied that and made her feel valued and significant. And this evil man before her, Cameahwait, had ended that for her when he took John's life. He had taken away everything. And she knew she couldn't hold back any longer. She would be there for Kimana in a way she couldn't be there for herself.

As Cameahwait started for her with eyes full of hatred and anger, Marie burst out of the trees. "Stop right there!"

Cameahwait didn't understand, but the sight of Marie and the sound of the hammer of her rifle clicking into place got his attention.

"Kimana, come stand over here by me," she commanded.

Starting to walk toward Marie, she halted when Cameahwait spoke sharply.

"What did he say?" Marie asked.

"He said he will kill you, and then he'll give me mine later," Kimana said, fear and indecision showed in darting eyes that could not focus on Marie.

Cameahwait pushed Kimana to the ground and pulled a knife from his belt. The steel sang as it cleared the sheath. Its large, long, stainless blade gleamed in the sun that filtered through the tree leaves. He began striding purposely, let out a war whoop, and then broke into a run toward Marie.

He was closing ground quickly. Marie held her rifle on him but did not get off a shot before he crashed into her, knocking the rifle to the ground. She hit the ground hard, landing on her back; her head snapped backward and smacked the ground. She fought to maintain consciousness, but her eyes couldn't get it right, her world was swimming; she wondered if she were in a dream. One thought kept coming to the top of her mind: *Pistol.* She started to get up, pulling the pistol from her belt, but Cameahwait knocked her down again, and the pistol went flying. It clanked as it hit a rock. She crawled, her hands sweeping the ground around her for her rifle. She couldn't find it. She felt herself being rolled over; looking at the sky, she saw Cameahwait standing over her, a sneer on his face. Just then, Kimana rammed into him with all her might; the warrior went sprawling, knocked over more by the surprise of the collision more than the collision itself.

"Marie," she yelled.

Marie looked up to find her rifle flying toward her. She reached with both hands to grab it, then leveled the gun at Cameahwait, her right elbow resting on her knee to steady her aim. Cameahwait struggled to get to his feet. He had lost his knife. Marie trained the rifle on him as he arose and stood before her. Marie said to Kimana, "Translate, so this evil stain on humanity knows why he's about to die."

"A man named John. A good man. A man that I loved. You killed him. He didn't deserve to die, but you killed him."

Kimana repeated Cameahwait's reply. "He and your husband wept like dogs as we hunted them down. They begged for their lives."

"Yes, you're a brave man. Killing men who are alone, unsuspecting. Three or four of your men to one of them." Marie didn't know if the sarcasm would translate, but she hoped it would. She listened to Kimana finish the words in Shoshone. Then Kimana spat on him.

He wiped the spit from his face. He stood in front of Marie unphased. No emotion on his face. Unrepentant. Arms folded across his chest.

"Kimana, give him his knife."

"What?"

"You heard me. Do it."

Kimana found the knife and handed it to Cameahwait. He grabbed it angrily. Turning to Marie, he smiled his crooked smile and began running and whooping. Marie aimed, took a deep breath—for some reason, she would remember later, the smell of oil and metal—and squeezed the trigger. The gun exploded fire out of the barrel. She looked up from the rifle and saw Cameahwait crumple to the ground. She had caught him square in his chest, knocking him to the ground, flat on his back. Blood oozed across his shirt.

Marie heard the snapping of twigs and the rustling of brush behind her. She turned just in time to see Ilchee step out of the trees, her spear at her side. Marie's face eased in relief. She dropped her rifle and bent over at the waist, hands on knees, taking deep, ragged breaths. Finally calmed again, she straightened to a standing position and managed, "I'm so glad it's you! What brings you here?"

"Just in case!" Ilchee laughed.

The three women stood over Cameahwait. The wound made it hard for him to breathe. He gulped for air as he bled out. His eyes flickered and then closed. His body heaved one final time. Marie pulled the Lewis and Clark Medal of Peace out of her pocket. The same medal she had found hanging at the burned-out trading post those many months ago. She tossed the medal on Cameahwait's chest. *There's your peace.* She looked at the sky, said a quick Our Father, and then crossed herself.

Kimana spat on his body. She started to deliver a kick to his rib cage but pulled up, "UUUUUUUUHHHHHHHHHH!" She bent at the waist as the contraction rolled over her abdomen, and pain shot throughout her body. Kimana's knees buckled, and she started to fall. Marie grabbed her and steadied her. "Oh god, I can't do this."

"Yes, you can," said Marie, adding, "That baby of yours is ready to come! But it can't come here! Come on." She put an arm around Kimana and led her away from the carnage.

"I brought the horses around. They're down in a draw at the bottom of this hill," Ilchee said.

"Kimana, can you ride?" Marie asked.

"Yes, I think so."

Marie and Kimana, arms draped over each other's shoulders, trudged downhill. They didn't move fast, but before long, the three women were sitting on their mounts and riding steadily away from what; it did not matter. What mattered was gaining distance before Cameahwait's body was found.

Kimana said, "I know a place. Up ahead by the river. There are trees and soft grass near where the river slows and pools. It's a good place. Good spirits are there. OOOoooooooooo." Another contraction and surge of pain swept over her. When she recovered, she added, "It's a place that John and I walked to sometimes just to be away from the post and all the busyness."

Marie recognized jealousy at that statement, but quickly swept it aside. She had told John to take care of his wife and he had. A smile broke across her face. "Let's go," Marie said.

The sun was getting low in the sky when they reached the river glade where Kimana had directed them. Marie helped Kimana down from her horse. A jarring landing caused her to wince through clenched teeth. Marie spread a blanket on the ground for Kimana to lay on. Then they waited.

Marie spoke quietly to Ilchee in the near dark, "Why'd you come back?"

Ilchee thought for a moment and said, "Your god would be mad if you had done it. My gods expected it to be done." Ilchee looked at Marie and continued, "I could not let my sister take the brunt of the punishment from an angry god." She hesitated again. "You're not a killer."

Marie analyzed this comment, "Yes, but I killed him. And I expected to feel joy at his death."

"Do you?"

"No. Not joy. Something else I can't describe. Like you said, something needed to happen, and it happened."

Just then, Kimana let out a groan. This one was deep and guttural.

"It's coming," said Marie.

• • • • •

That evening, when Cameahwait and Kimana did not return to camp, a young warrior named Pocohote was sent to find the people's leader and his wife. As Pocohote approached the thermal pool, he found Cameahwait dead on the ground with a spear in his chest and a curious medal with a leather strap. There was no sign of Kimana.

CHAPTER TWENTY-FOUR
THE LONG ROAD HOME

Marie woke to a baby crying, a sound she had not heard in a long time. She went to Kimana, but the baby had latched on, and the new mother had everything firmly in hand. Marie sat down next to her while she nursed.

"This place was special for John and me. We talked about many things here. He told me of Scotland and his home there. His brother Jamie. His mother. His son." Kimana broke down in tears. "I am so sorry that I played a part in his...." Her words trailed away. "I was a fool!"

"Kimana, a son?"

"Yes, John had a son with an Indian woman who died shortly after giving birth. You did not know?"

Marie felt as though she had been punched in the stomach. "No." She looked at the ground. "He never told me."

"His son was sent to his brother in Scotland."

The women sat in silence. The baby ate.

"It sounds like you and John were coming together. He must have loved you very much."

"No," Kimana said. "He took care of me. Never mistreated me. But he loved you. I could see it in his eyes whenever you were around. It made me envious."

Warmth spread over Marie's body, and a smile creased her face. "Get some rest. We have to move in the morning."

At sunrise, Ilchee gathered, saddled, and readied the horses to move out. Then she led the way. When they came within sight of a cinder cone, Marie called to Ilchee, "Hey, wait!"

"What?" Ilchee asked.

"There's something that needs to be done. Follow me."

They deviated to the west from due north for about an hour. Marie shuddered at the sight of the burned-out trading post. She watched Kimana for her reaction to being back and saw Kimana raise her hand to cover her mouth. Despite this a gasp escaped. More of the timbers had fallen and only one wall stood supported by the chimney. Marie took the baby from Kimana, who slid from her saddle to the ground. Marie handed the baby to Kimana.

"What are we doing?" Kimana asked. "This place is evil."

"We're going to introduce John to his son."

The two arrived at the grave site. Marie got on her knees and straightened and re-stacked some of the rocks that had fallen away. The cross she had erected was askew, so she straightened that up. Looking down at the grave, she stood and began talking, "John. I don't know if you can hear or see us, but I have come, and Kimana has come to introduce you to your son. John Junior."

Kimana stepped forward with the baby cradled in her arms. "John, this is our son. I gave him your name. I promise you I will do everything in my power to protect him and care for him and when he is older, I will tell him stories of his strong, brave Papa."

The women and the baby lingered for a moment. They looked down at the grave, not at each other. Each swiped at tears on their cheeks.

Marie turned to Kimana and said, "I came here to kill you and Cameahwait. My blood burned hot. But I think John would forgive you. So, I am going to forgive you. I will give you the second chance that we all should get." She paused momentarily, then said, "Can you give me a moment alone with John?"

"Of course." Kimana turned to go and then stopped. Looked at Marie, "He loved you very much." Then she was gone.

Marie couldn't keep the cry from escaping despite trying to cover it with her fingers. Her cry turned to a blubbering. "John," she said once she could trust her voice. "He's a fine boy. I'll keep my eye on them."

That night, Marie and Kimana were alone. Ilchee had turned in for the evening. They had made enough distance from the Shoshone to feel safe having a small fire and a hot meal. Neither spoke. They stared into the flames. Marie occasionally tossed on a small stick to keep the fire going as the season was advancing and the nights got cold. Off in the distance, a wolf howled.

"Tell me everything," Marie said.

"I don't want to go through it all. I'm ashamed."

"Kimana. You must do this. I need to know, and your son someday is going to want to know how his father died. What will you say?" Marie hesitated. "You better prepare for that day."

"He'll hate me."

"Maybe. But just be honest." Marie went silent. Waiting. She blushed as she recognized her own hypocrisy.

"Cameahwait and I were raised together. We were inseparable. All the people assumed we would be married. But then the day came when Komkomis struck a deal with Pawashtimane that I would be the bride of Pawashtimane's son. Cameahwait and I were devastated. When Pawashtimane's son was killed, Cameahwait saw an opportunity. He hated the whites for what they had done to his brother. Hanging is not an honorable way for a warrior to die. You know this."

Marie nodded. "That was a terrible thing. John and I agreed that the man that hanged those warriors should've been punished severely."

"I need you to understand that I loved Cameahwait deeply. How can you love someone so much and then they become a monster, and you wonder where the love has gone."

"My husband was much like your Cameahwait. Not a murderer, but he had his demons."

"Cameahwait instructed me on what I was to do. At the *potlatch* hosted by Pawashtimane, I was to ask to be the wife of the white leader; this would be seen as a peace offering to the whites and put them off their guard. Cameahwait watched your party move up the big river, Wimahl. He saw you split in two. Then, the outpost was built, and John sent the men out to trap. That was my opportunity to signal Cameahwait so he and his followers could attack. I arranged to be gone when it happened."

Marie, her legs bent and arms folded on her knees, rested her forehead on her arms. She stayed like that for several minutes. "Kimana, I'm going to sleep now."

"Okay."

"We will never speak of this again." Marie arose, walked toward a grassy spot, rolled out her blanket, and, lying down, looked at the stars as she spoke to John.

What should I do? How will Kimana ever be reconciled with your son? My heart hurts.

· · · · ·

In a few days of steady riding, the women rode into the Walla Walla village on the banks of *Wimahl.* They were greeted by the chief Kellepit and a few of his headmen. The people of the village came out but stayed back a bit.

"This is a great day. Our friends have returned, and their enemy, our enemy, has been vanquished!" Women's voices trilled in unison. Drumbeats pulsed through the community, and the men cried out in war whoops.

"Chief Kellepit, thank you so much. These fine horses served us well, and we will return them to you now," Marie said.

"Who is this Shoshone woman?" Kellepit asked.

Marie looked at Kimana and said, "She is a friend and was very helpful to us."

"Come, we have set up a tipi for you to rest."

As they walked to the tipi, Marie asked, "Have the canoes come by?"

"No canoes."

"Do you have any contact with tribes downstream that might take us to Fort George?" Marie looked at the chief. His brown eyes fixed on her. He was slightly taller than Marie. His long hair hung over his back. The skin around his eyes was wrinkled but the rest of his face was flawless, save for a small scar on his right cheekbone.

"I've sent a runner to Pawashtimane. Asked him to send canoes and a few men. Rest." He held open the tipi flap for Marie, Ilchee, Kimana, and the baby to enter.

• • • • •

A few days later, two canoes and four men showed up on the shore by the village of Kellepit. When they saw Ilchee, they bowed in reverence. "I guess you're a big shot." Marie smiled and winked at Ilchee.

"Huh?"

"Important person."

"Ah, my father is important."

"I think you underestimate your sway with people."

In an hour, after Marie had said goodbye to Kellepit and the People, the two canoes glided along the river's flow. Ilchee rode in one canoe, and Marie, Kimana, and the baby rode in the second canoe. The sun and the wind were at their backs, and they made excellent time. Marie took in the basalt cliffs and the soaring eagles. She watched the oarsmen at work and noted that they didn't sing like the *voyageurs*, but she smiled at their happy-sounding banter going back and forth occasionally. But mainly, they were focused on the work at hand, and their powerful arms and backs were bent to the task. The canoes bucking over the whitecapped water made for a bumpy ride. That night, they slept under the overturned canoes wrapped in blankets.

Marie laid on her back looking up at the stars. "Dear Lord watch over us as a make our way to our new home. Keep us safe. Amen." *The dalles du mort awaits. We should wait above the falls. Let the men rest a night before going through them. They'll need their strength.* She fell asleep to the sound of river water lapping at the sandy bank.

Ilchee and Marie took one canoe on the second day, while Kimana took another. Just before they pushed off the riverbank, Kimana kissed her baby on the forehead, whispered in the boy's ear, and handed him to Marie. "I had a dream last night. John was in it and he wanted the baby to ride with you today."

Marie held out her arms as John Junior entered them, cozy and warm in his blanket.

The river was smooth; the wind had died down, and the native rowers knew the river's currents that soon sent them gliding toward Fort George.

About midday, with the sun high in the sky, Marie heard the faint roar of the Dalles—the rapids. As they proceeded, the roar grew louder. Marie was surprised that the native rowers were not putting into portage as her *voyageurs* would.

"Ilchee!" Marie yelled.

Ilchee turned to Marie.

"Why are they not putting in?"

"These rowers know the river. They know ways through even these rapids," Ilchee called back over the deafening sound of the powerful water.

Marie grabbed tightly to the side of the canoe with one hand her other hand clutched the baby's blanket tightly and her arm pressed the baby close to her chest.

The first canoe with Kimana led the way, diving into a narrow chute.

Soon, only the upraised stern of the craft was seen before it plunged over the side.

God save us!

Marie sensed her craft tilting steeply forward as the river pushed it into the chute. The rest was like gliding down a snow-covered hill, fast and smooth. Marie watched the first canoe; she saw Kimana sitting midway on the craft. The two oarsmen were using their oars now to push away from the basalt rock sides. Again, the craft in front went over a drop; Marie's canoe followed. It landed in a pool of churning, spinning water. Marie looked for the first canoe, but it was nowhere to be found. The sound of crashing water was all around her. She turned from side to side but to no avail. The men at the oars of her craft were barking back and forth, trying to communicate over the roar. They paddled hard, taking long, powerful strokes, and soon, they emerged out of the pool and back into a calm stretch of river.

Marie yelled, "KIMANA? KIMANA?" Her eyes scanned the water, looking for any sign of the first canoe and its passenger and crew. Nothing. She called out again. "KIMANA?"

Ilchee touched her shoulder. "They're gone."

"No! Her son...." Marie brushed a tear from her cheek, cuddling John Junior tighter toward her breast.

That night, they pulled into a place known by the *voyageurs* of the North West Company as Tea Prairie, as it was a popular place to stop for morning breakfast with a cup of tea. Marie, Ilchee, and the baby sat on the beach. "One minute she was there, the next she was gone!"

"I lost two men also, remember that," Ilchee replied. She hesitated for a minute, "One of those men was a friend I had known since I was a child. He was like a brother."

"Ilchee, I am very sorry." Marie reached out to Ilchee, putting a hand on her forearm. "I have prayed for their immortal souls as well as Kimana's. In our way of thinking, they are all with God now, in a place so wonderful that it is beyond imagination."

"Save your prayers. We don't believe that our dead leave us."

Marie smiled and blushed, understanding it was naïve of her to think that all people believed in an afterlife. "Where do people go when they die in your world?"

"These men, their ghosts, will come to our village at night. When I get back, I will need to make sure that we take their most important possessions and set them adrift in their favorite canoe."

"Do they need this in the afterlife? Is that why you set their possessions adrift?"

"The ghosts of these men come back to make sure no one is using their possessions." Ilchee paused for a moment. "Your people believe in a place of beauty where your spirits go. We believe we have already lived in such a place. Like this!" Ilchee raised her arms as if to display the beauty of their surroundings.

She kept quiet for a moment, appreciating the beauty of the land and the grandeur of nature with its life-giving power. "Yes, I like this very much."

The two women smiled at each other as the baby slept in Marie's arms.

Ilchee, looking down at the baby and then at Marie, said, "I guess you're little John's mother now."

Marie said, "No. I'm not his mother." She paused for a few heartbeats. "This child's parents are together now." She looked at the sky. "Be happy."

Later that night, sitting at the edge of the river, Marie cradled the sleeping baby. "Kimana. I promise you I will take your son and raise him as my own. But I will not be his mother and I will tell him the stories that I know of you. I will tell him that you were a good person. A heart filled with love. As angry as it made me that you were with John. As angry as it makes me that you were responsible for his death, I will keep your memory alive for your son. Go with God!"

Two days later, the canoe rounded Tongue Point, giving Marie her first view of Fort George in over a year. Her heart raced excitedly as she thought of the boys and the big hugs that she would give them. As they approached the dock, she saw Cadotte with the two boys and Archie watching their approach. The boys were jumping up and down, yelling, "Mama, mama!"

Many others were there, among them Concomly, with his wives. After hugging the boys and covering them with kisses, Marie was introduced to the new Chief Factor of Fort George, James Keith, a Scotsman who had served the company for years in Canada. He'd been recently posted to Fort George a few months earlier.

Marie offered her hand, which Mr. Keith took, bowed, and kissed it lightly. "Madam Dorion, your reputation proceeds you and is much deserved. Will you join us for dinner in the main hall tonight?" He saw a look in her eyes that he could only interpret as hesitation. "Come, please regale us of your adventures in the backcountry of Oregon."

Marie replied with her two boys clinging to her at the hip, "It was hardly glorious but I would be happy to, Mr. Keith." She smiled at him, "However, I must get these rascals fed and to bed first." She spun on the boys. Wrestling and tickling them to the ground.

Standing over the heap of bodies, "Of course, Madam. At your convenience." Mr. Keith turned and walked toward the gate of the fort.

Cadotte approached her and picking the boys up from the ground he said, "Let us get you to a room, Madam Dorion."

"Just one moment Cadotte." Marie walked over to where Ilchee was conversing with her father and mother.

Concomly said in broken English, "Thank you. Daughter returned to me."

Marie laughed, covering her mouth with one hand while holding the baby with another. "Without her, Chief Concomly, I would not be here."

Marie turned to Ilchee and said, "I have no words to express my love for you, my sister. I cannot tell you how thankful I am for all you have done."

"You sound as if we will never see each other again. I will see you soon."

Marie turned and walked to the fort. Her boys peppered her with questions about the baby. "Is he our brother?" Marie hesitated. *What do I tell them.* "Soon, my loves. We will talk soon."

That evening, after the sun had set, Marie and the boys lay on the bed in their room. The baby slept in a small crib-like structure that Cadotte had put together in a matter of hours using a shipping container that had come by sea from London, according to the markings stenciled on the side.

"You see, my loves, the baby's parents have gone to be with God...Adieu!"

"Like our Papa?" Jean looked at her with big, tear-filled eyes.

Marie hesitated to answer. "Yes, my sons, your Papa has also gone to God."

Jean buried his face in his mother's arm and sobbed. "I hate God," he blurted into the air.

"No, no, my love. God works in ways we cannot understand, but He loves us, and we love Him! Your Papa is happy now. And he is waiting for the day when we will all be together again in Heaven."

"What is Heaven?" little Paul asked.

"We will talk of these things later. Jean, are you okay?"

The boy sniffled and replied, "Yes, Mama."

"Okay, sleep now, and we will talk in the morning. I will be back soon. Cadotte is right outside; you know the place where he smokes his pipe?"

The two boys nodded that they did.

"If you get scared, Uncle Cadotte will be there. And Mama will be back to sleep with you tonight. Okay?"

"Yes, Mama," came the boys' reply.

On her way across the courtyard, she saw Cadotte walking toward her.

"I was just coming to your room. I forgot to give you this earlier." He held out an envelope.

Marie took it from him, looked at the return address, and then quickly opened the envelope, pulling out a single piece of paper. She read. Her face broke into a smile, and a tear ran down her cheek. Her open mouth was covered by her free hand.

Dear Madam Dorion,

Thank you so much for your letter concerning my beloved Archie. After receiving no answer from him for several years, I assumed the worst. Please tell him that Ida is here in Spartanburg waiting for him to come home. Also, please let him know I'll have one of his favorite pies ready when he gets here. He loves apple pie. Maybe he told you?

Sincerely and with Respect,

Ida Freeholder

Marie folded the letter and put it in the pocket of her dress. She began walking to the main dining hall.

Oh yes, my dear Miss Freeholder, I know he loves pie.

Marie burst out in laughter.

Marie entered the kitchen area. Jack and Tom were busy working. "Hey, fellas, did you miss me?"

The two men turned. Their mouths agape, eyes wide open, they soon broke into smiles and spoke to each other rapidly in their native language.

"Madam Dorion, we are so pleased!"

"Me too," Marie replied. "I thought of you often."

"Did you hear anything about Tom's cousins?"

"No. I'm sorry I didn't." She looked down at her feet. Then up at the expectant faces of the two Owyhees. "There was evil that took your cousins. Do you understand?"

Jack translated for Tom. "That's okay. We are happy to have you here!"

She smiled at the two. Grasped each by hand. "I have to go upstairs for dinner. I'm the guest of honor. How fancy!"

She walked up the servants' stairs, and the noise of the gentlemen's chatter subsided when she entered the hall. "You could hear a pin drop in here," Marie exclaimed.

"Please, Madam Dorion." Mr. Keith showed her a chair next to his at the front of the table.

Marie spent the next hour or so telling the tale of the John Reed expedition to a rapt audience. When she was done, Mr. Keith stood.

"A toast, gentlemen, to Madam Dorion. A brave and determined woman."

Someone yelled, "I'll drink to that."

All cups were lifted. Mr. Keith leaned over to Marie. "I admire everything you've gone through to safely get your boys, you, and Archie home. You are a most resolute woman!"

Marie felt her face. It was hot from a blush breaking out. "Thank you, Mr. Keith. That is very kind. I feel like I did what any mother would do for her children."

"Perhaps that is right, but how many mothers have the skills to survive a wilderness ordeal such as yours? You passed a great test."

"Yes, but I lost the great love of my life."

"Ah yes, Pierre, right. Wasn't that your husband's name?"

"Yes, that was my husband's name." Marie waited a minute before she said, "But it was John Reed that I loved."

Mr. Keith spit out a bit of his drink in surprise. "I see. Well, I'm not sure what to say to that."

"No words are needed. Love is enough." She paused to let what she said settle amongst those who heard.

Mr. Keith stood and tapped his silver spoon on the side of his crystal glass. The room quieted. "I'd like to invite our guest of honor to share some words with us. How about it, Madam Dorion? Any words of wisdom gained from your experiences in the wild?"

Marie stood. "Thank you, Mr. Keith." She scanned the crowd and continued, saying, "Funny, I'm used to serving food in this room, not being served." Light chuckles erupted. "As many of you know, my husband, Pierre Dorion, my two sons, and I left this place last October. We left here under the leadership of John Reed to establish a trading post or two amongst the native peoples to the east." She picked up the crystal glass in front of her, sipped her drink, and set the glass down. "We left here with 51 men; 30 would continue to Montreal, and 21 of us would continue on Mr. Reed's great adventure. And as it turned out, it was more than we bargained for. Besides myself, my children, and Archie Devlin, seventeen men, my husband, and John Reed included, all died at the hands of a rogue warrior named Cameahwait." She looked at the men seated to her left and then to her right.

"Once I got my children to safety, I went looking for this Cameahwait. I hated him, and I wanted him dead. I forgot the words, 'Vengeance is mine; I will repay, sayeth the Lord.' Actually, I didn't forget I shoved them out of my mind. Lord, forgive me." She crossed herself. "Who of us is wise enough to mete out justice? Vengeance? I discovered that in killing the men in our party, Cameahwait was meting out some vengeance of his own. I don't know how many of you recall, but a few years back, one of ours hung four native boys for stealing glass beads and other worthless trinkets. One of these boys was Cameahwait's brother." Marie paused. Murmurs were heard throughout the room. "The point I am trying to make is that we are allowed to defend ourselves. But the thing I keep thinking is that one man's rash actions set off a chain reaction that resulted in the deaths of many innocent people." She paused to let her words sink in. "We are here as guests in a strange land inhabited by people who do not understand our ways, and we do not understand theirs. We, as guests, bear a great responsibility. I would ask each of you, when you're out there, before reacting impulsively or without due consideration, just take some time to understand the people you're dealing with and understand that there might be another way to resolve things. Another perspective that you have never considered before. Thank you."

Marie took her seat to applause and shouts of, "Here, here!"

Marie smiled and mouthed the words thank you to her audience. Then, leaning over, she asked, "May I ask a favor, Mr. Keith? I hate to ask anything more from you since you've been so kind to us."

"Nonsense. We're family here. We look out for each other. Lord knows that we are all we have out here in the wilderness."

"Are there any ships bound for New York or London coming soon?"

· · · · ·

The next day, the solitary figure sat on the dock. Wind, coming off the fast-flowing river, swirled over and around her. Blowing from the east, the wind kept the usual fall storms from sweeping in from the ocean. The prior weeks had seen gloriously bright sun-filled days and the bluest blue skies, typical for this late summer. Marie Dorion's long, black hair whipped behind her like silken ribbons rising and falling with the waxing and waning of the breeze. Despite the sun, the lateness of the day brought a coolness that raised goose bumps on her flesh. She rubbed her arms. Her gaze drifted toward *Wimahl* – The Big River. The surface churned and roiled, topped by white caps. Evergreens, sweeping uphill from the river, swayed on the distant bank and blanketed the faraway ridges and mountains. Green alder leaves among the firs and pines spoke to the uniqueness of the biome of this land.

She pushed herself up to stand, arms folded over her chest, and thought, *God!* She felt warmth spreading over her, and a smile crossed her face. "Dear God, I love this place."

Repeating a ritual she had performed often, she loosened some strands and dropped her buckskin dress to her feet. On her chest, a silver cross dangled from a simple leather thong tied behind her neck. This she never took off, ever! She stepped out of the garment and dove into the choppy water. Her muscles tightened at the shock of the instant cold. Her skin tingled. Reflexively, she kicked off the sandy river bottom, gliding to the surface and breaking through. Her breath came in shallow gulps. Her chest was tight. Stroking with her arms, she made her way through the chop of the whitecaps. She felt like she was flying over the water, fast as a flat rock skipping. Eventually, she tired and returned to the dock. Overhead, a flock of geese flew south.

What I wouldn't have given for one of those back in the cave.

She chuckled.

She stood and dressed, walking back to the fort; she stopped momentarily at the path to where she and John had made love for the last time. A nagging notion told her that all would be good if she just went down that path. John would be there waiting for her. A tear rolled down her cheek, and she walked to the fort. "HELLO," she yelled and waved an arm. "It's an Indian, but a friendly one!"

"Very funny, Miss." Then the guard yelled, "Open the gate!"

CHAPTER TWENTY-FIVE

Six Months Later
Scotland

The coach rolled along the gravel and mud highway, which was the main road between Inverness and the hamlet of Dingwall; the Reed estates were outside the latter. Through a window, the woman inside watched the Scottish landscape roll by. Undulating hills covered in windswept grass with pockets of snow hung on in the shady spots. It was a sunny January day, but the sight of snow and the cold wind blowing off the North Sea reminded her that it was winter. Inside, Marie Dorion was surrounded by sleeping boys, the littlest of them all, John Jr., whom she held in her arms.

I'm going to miss you little one.

Marie's mind went to the events of the past several months. In her mind's eye, she recalled the tear-filled goodbyes she had said to Ilchee and Francois Cadotte. There were promises to see each other again, but she knew in her heart that she had probably gazed upon those two people for the last time. She had exacted a promise from Cadotte to get Archie back to Ida Freeholder in Spartanburg, Connecticut. She smiled as she recalled his reply. With a deep bow, with his hat in one hand nearly sweeping the ground, he said, "If it is with my last, dying breath, your wish is my command!"

"Why Francois," she had replied, "For a man of your girth, you are quite nimble!"

"Ah, madame, I held back and only had two pieces of pie with supper tonight! What good is a skinny *voyageur* anyway!"

Then there was Ilchee, with whom she had shared so much danger and who had saved her on more occasions than she wanted to count. Marie recalled saying something like, "I don't know what to say. Thank you seems inadequate."

"What is meant by *inad...inadeke*t?"

"It means not enough. Too little compared to what I have received."

"You, Marie, have given me much. Much that you will never know. It is I who feel like the inadequate one."

Marie watched from the ship's railing as it pulled away from Fort George until the tiny figure of Ilchee disappeared from view.

To Archie, she could only pat his cheek and hug him tightly. "Ida's waiting, Archie." She took out the letter and handed it to him. She remembered being astonished that he looked at the paper for a long while, and tears ran down his cheek. He had seemed to be reading the letter.

Then he said something that shook her to her core, "Pie."

Marie laughed a bit while choking up. "Yes, my dear Archie. Pie!" She hugged him and whispered, "Francois will get you home; he will get you back to Ida." She stepped back, her arms extended as she held both his arms. "Goodbye, Archie. I hope you and Ida are happy and blessed with many children." She felt tight in her chest as her heart was filled with love and joy for this man.

They'd sailed over the Columbia River bar in August, stopping in Hawaii to take on food and fresh water supplies. She and the boys had roamed the sandy beaches, splashed in the surf, and felt the gentle caress of the Trade Winds. She had marveled at the expansive greenness of the island and now understood a bit more how Jack and Tom could grow things even in the rainy, cold, and windswept slopes of Fort George. The native women wove mats and baskets made from the local vegetation, harvested food from trees and bushes, chased after children who ran over the sand, swimming and diving. She saw a catamaran and canoes that the Hawaiian people used to fish and hunt for food.

"No wonder the Owyhees were in such high demand by the North West Company," she thought upon seeing them at work in their ocean.

There had been stops at other ports of call, but none as fascinating as the Owyhee Islands or, as the captain had called them, the Sandwich Islands.

A few months later, they came to the docks of London on the Thames. The waterfront bustled with activity. The ship's Captain, Thomas Rogers, insisted on escorting her and the boys through London and seeing to their accommodations until they could acquire transportation to Dingwall. The streets of London, near the docks, were filled with a mass of humanity that seethed forward, seeming to fill every empty space. She kept the boys close and John Jr. in her arms. They passed the famed coffee shop, Lloyds of London, as the captain informed her that coffee shops were the fashion now. "More international shipping business is done in these venues than in any trading house on the wharf."

He took her to the headquarters of the North West Company. Her first introduction was to Andrew Colville, which the trading post Fort Colville was named for. The express canoes from Fort George had carried messages destined for London through Montreal. In one of the dispatches was a request made by Mr. Keith for Marie Dorion to be accorded all the hospitality and privileges the company could muster. The dispatch also outlined the hardships she'd endured along with the services rendered to the company.

"Pleased to make your acquaintance," Mr. Colville said as he kissed her hand. "Looking up into her eyes, he said, "Your reputation proceeds you, Madame Dorion!"

"Marie's got quite the story to tell," said Captain Rogers. "You should hear it."

"Yes, I've received a written report from Mr. Keith." Still looking at Marie, "Awe-inspiring stuff!" Then he added, "There's a board dinner tomorrow. Perhaps you'd be good enough to attend?"

"I'd love to, sir, but right now, I'm trying to get this lad to his uncle, and I'm afraid I have not yet secured accommodations or transportation."

Colville assured her that he would see to everything, and he was as good as his word. Marie and the boys had remained in London, lodging in the home of Andrew Colville and his lovely wife, Charlotte.

The board had been quite taken with Marie and her story of survival. Vanquishing the fierce warrior Cameahwait seemed to garner enthusiastic approval based on the applause and the gift of 50 pounds sterling as a reward for heroism and the loss of her husband.

The board hired a coach with two coachmen.

"The first one'll drive ya, the second will ward off any bandits," Andrew Colville had said. Then he added, "Although after what I heard last night, maybe we should send someone to protect the bandits from you!"

He and Marie chuckled.

A hard bounce as the coach hit a pothole knocked Marie off balance. She quickly recovered, and the toddler John in her arms slept unperturbed.

As the distance to the Reed Estates shortened, her stomach tightened. Mr. Colville had sent a dispatch rider with a message to expect them in four days.

We won't be a complete surprise. But what if he doesn't want the child, and we're sent headlong back to London? Should I have the coachmen wait? After all, I'm a Metis, half-blood, brown-skinned. Maybe he regards me as his brother's whore, nothing more? Had John even mentioned me?

Those thoughts weighed on her as the coach jostled its passengers down the road.

An hour later, the coach turned off the highway onto a long, straight roadway. She looked out the window. Manicured grounds of grass and hedges and trees and plants rolled by. There was even a white stone fountain in the middle of it all. A waterspout shot up from the middle. Then she saw the home, headquarters of the Reed estate. It was three stories tall; the façade was the color of the White Cliffs of Dover, which she had seen before their ship entered the Thames and docked in London. But mostly, the front of the home was windows framed in darker wood, like the color of the basalt cliffs of the Columbia River. A glass dome sat in the middle part of the roof.

As they approached the home and rounded the circular drive, Marie whispered, "Well, it's too late to turn back now." She reached across the coach and jostled the two boys awake. Jean brushed his eyes with his hands. Paul looked around and then laid his head back down.

"Paul, PAUL, time to wake up," Marie said sternly. Reaching over, she shook him a little. "C'mon, sleepy head. Up and at 'em."

Just then, the coach door opened, and the footman, as Marie learned he was called, said, "Here we are, miss."

"Thank you," she said, stepping from the coach. The footman held her hand to help her down. The boys jumped down on their own. Paul began rolling on the ground and giggling. Marie quickly barked, "Stand up; you're getting your suit dirty." She sounded gruff but chuckled a bit once he was on his feet. I *can't blame them. We've been cooped up for days.*

Before she could advance to the doorway, the door swung open and out stepped a very proper-looking man dressed in a coat and bowtie. His face sported a scowl, and his tone was gruff.

"The lady Marie Dorion, is it?"

"Yes, I am Marie Dorion."

"Follow me if you would."

There was no hint of the Scottish brogue. His English sounded as if he was from London. Marie and the boys followed her and stepped into the home. The entryway was cavernous but well-lit. Marie looked up. Instead of seeing a ceiling, she saw the glass dome visible from the roadway. A set of glossy, marble stairs led up to the second floor. She guessed the third floor was for the staff and was probably served by hidden staircases in the back of the home.

"Wait here." Then, looking at the boys, he pointed and said, "And don't touch anything."

Marie smirked a bit.

Telling an eight-year-old and a five-year-old not to touch anything is like telling bees not to make honey.

"We'll do our best," Marie said with a smile. She held John, who had somehow slept through all the commotion. His head rested on her shoulder.

The man scowled and disappeared through an overly wide and tall doorway. She glanced around at the niches filled with statues of famous Roman and Greek gods. She spotted her personal favorite, the goddess

Artemis, she knelt on the ground, her bow bent and arrow notched. She thought of Ilchee. From upstairs, a man's voice was now heard.

"For god sake, man, we've got guests arriving. Get these rooms made up. They'll be tired."

Then he appeared at the top of the stairway. Marie's breath left her. Her knees buckled. "John?" Her knees landed on the floor before losing her balance and landing on her back. The toddler John rested on her chest. Then everything went black.

• • • • •

Marie awoke to the feeling of a cold cloth on her forehead and someone holding her hand. Her eyes blinked open. She looked at the face above her. It was smiling, it was John. "But how?"

"I see my brother neglected to mention we were identical twins."

"Yeah, he didn't say anything about you."

"I came out first, so all of this is mine!" He held his arms spread wide. "He came out second, so he was sent by our father to make his way in the world."

Suddenly, panic coursed through her and she cried, "The baby!"

"Not to worry. The governess has taken the boys to meet John's other son. Ya know, to get them acquainted."

"John's other son?" Then she recalled that Kimana had mentioned him. "Oh yes. His son."

"Let's get you on your feet, love. Then we'll talk."

Marie got to her feet. She was wobbly, so the man held her with an arm behind her back and his free hand holding one of hers.

"George, we'll be in the study. Bring some tea, eh?"

They reached the study, and the man helped her to a divan. He took a seat in a cushioned chair opposite her.

"As you might've guessed, I am John's older brother Jamie."

"Oh well, I wasn't prepared for how much you look like him." Marie felt her cheeks warm. "Sorry."

"No need to apologize. John wasn't great with the details sometimes."

"Tell me about his son."

"Aye."

"How old?"

"He just turned fifteen. Leaving for university next year. Edinburgh. I don't have children, so he'll inherit this. But I felt some education and a little seasoning out in the world would help a gentleman in managing these lands and all that goes with that."

"His name?"

"John."

She smiled. "Oh. His little brother is John also. So, was John, your brother, married before?"

"I guess he didn't fill you in on much of his life beforehand."

"Well, I know he went to the seminary."

"Yes, our father's idea. John hated it and hated him for sending him there. After a bit, he ran off. Caught a ship up in Stornoway, headed for Canada."

Marie watched as Jamie arose and went to a desk. He opened a drawer, withdrew a piece of paper, and returned to the cushioned chair. He leaned forward and handed the paper to her. Marie accepted it and, looking at Jamie, asked, "What is this?"

"A letter from my brother. It came about three months ago. Soon after his death notice from the company arrived."

Marie read through the letter, and tears ran down her cheeks. Then she handed the paper back.

"You keep it. He loved you very much and would want you to have it."

Marie, her head bowed, replied, "Thank you."

"The baby, then? You and John?"

Marie's eyes widened, and a sound escaped her mouth that was somewhere between a laugh and an expression of shock or surprise.

"Oh, I guess I'm the one who hasn't communicated the details well." She looked down into her lap, thinking about how to tell this story. "No. It's complicated, but you're half right. He's John's son."

"Complicated, eh?"

"Back to John's first wife," Marie questioned.

"Ah, yes. John hadn't been in Canada for over a year, maybe two. He took a country wife; I think is the term?"

"Yes, white fur trappers and traders marry native women. It's quite common. Usually, they stay together. Sometimes, when the contract ends, the man returns to civilization and washes his hands of the family he created. My father and mother were similar, but my father chose to stay with his family. So therefore, the result of their marriage, me and my sisters are called daughters of the country."

"I see." Jamie saw something in her face, a slight wrinkling around her mouth and eyes. "You seem conflicted about that arrangement."

"They fought a lot. Sometimes, my sisters and I would run to the woods to escape it. Come back in a couple of days."

"Hmm. Sounds like you and your sisters took care of each other. John and I were the same. If there was a scuffle, the other one jumped in. That kind of thing."

"I took care of his last scuffle," Marie said matter-of-factly. Her jaw was clenched.

"The company sent word." He looked down at his hands as he spoke. Then, looking her in the eyes, he added, "Thank you for that. And thank you for bringing his son to me."

Marie used a handkerchief to dry her eyes. She sought to change the subject. "John was married before?"

"Yes, John was married. He wrote to me right after John Jr. was born. The first John Jr. Didn't say a lot about the mother. He did write a couple years later to say she'd died of a fever and asked me to take the boy. Get him educated, which I agreed to with great joy. Anyway...." Jamie clapped his hands. "You've got to be tired. Let's get you settled and get you some rest before dinner."

"That sounds like a fine idea, but I'd like to meet John first, if I might, and check on my boys. And little John."

"Certainly." Jamie rose from his seat and walked to the staircase. "OPHELIA! Please bring the boys here."

• • • • •

Sitting at a vanity that night, Marie watched in the mirror as she brushed her hair out.

He has John's lower jaw and piercing blue eyes. He must favor his mother mostly. He's beautiful.

Tears began to flow down her cheek as she thought about John and his two sons and the missed opportunity to spend time doing what fathers and sons do.

Pierre. Even him. He did with his sons. Showing them how to stalk a deer. Let them watch him clean his rifle.

But while she was crying in bed for John that night, she realized she was also crying for her sons and Pierre.

CHAPTER TWENTY-SIX
THE LAIRD AND HIS CASTLE

In the morning, Marie checked on the boys and found them still asleep, so she walked down the staircase, taking care to raise her simple cotton dress so as not to trip on the ankle-length garment. She stopped in the manor's entryway, taking time in front of a mirror to admire the dress, a gift from Charlotte Colville. Marie twisted from side to side, pleased with how the green, pleated dress moved, how it followed the contours of her shoulders and then gathered at her waist. She was delighted with how she had changed from the gaunt, waif-like figure she had been when she emerged from the wilderness.

She wasn't sure where to go but decided to wander on the main floor until she encountered one of the staff or perhaps Jamie Reed. She glanced toward the study and saw a lamp light. Seeing Jamie at his desk, she walked to the doorway and said, "Good Morning!"

Jamie looked up from his work; his glasses were down on his nose. He reached to remove them. Papers were strewn about, and he held a pen in his right hand. Waving his glasses, "Damn things. Damn old age." Then he laughed a deep laugh that reminded her of John. "Come, have a seat." He gestured toward the leather chair in front of his desk.

Marie took a seat in a leather-padded chair. She felt her body sink slightly into the cushion, which felt good.

"George, George," Jamie yelled out.

Within a few blinks, George appeared at the doorway. "Yes, sir?"

"George, bring us some tea and ask Gretta if there are more of those biscuits from dinner last night."

"Yes, my lord." George bowed slightly and turned to go.

"Oh, George?" Jamie called out.

George turned back to the doorway. "Yes, sir?"

"And do bring some honey with the biscuits. Good man."

George said nothing. He bowed and turned, walking away to the kitchen.

Jamie looked at Marie. "He's a bit stodgy, but he runs this house like a regiment of His Majesty's army." He smiled.

Marie giggled. "Yes, a bit stodgy seems about right."

"I have asked Ophelia to include your boys in the lessons she administers to John; I hope that is alright?"

"That's very kind of you. Are you sure it's no trouble?"

"Not at all. She is well versed in the classics."

"She'll have those boys reciting Livy in Latin in no time, I'm sure." Marie smiled at him.

"You know Livy?"

"Yes. And Catullus. And Virgil and Ovid."

"Impressive. Tell me, Marie, how a woman from the wilds of Canada has such an impressive, erudite background."

"Do you mean to ask how an Indian came to be educated?"

Jamie squirmed in his seat. Then, sitting back, said, "Actually, I believe I asked how a woman, with seeming limited opportunity, came to be educated. That's something we Scots do but is not universal."

Marie glanced down at her lap. Then she gazed at Jamie and said, "Forgive my impudence."

There was a period of silence while Marie searched for what to say next. The awkward tension was broken when George came into the room. The slight rattle of the teacups in saucers announced his arrival.

"Tea, sir." He nodded at Marie, "Miss, do you take sugar and milk?"

"Thank you, yes," Marie replied.

When George left the room, Marie started. "I am the product of a French-Canadian trapper and a Ioway mother. I can speak French and English fluently. My husband was Lakota, I can get by in Lakota and Ioway. And the priests at the various villages where I grew up taught me Latin by having me translate the works of the gentlemen I just mentioned."

"I see. But Ovid? Priests? He's a bit naughty, don't you think?" Jamie smiled.

"I think secretly they enjoyed Ovid the most!" Marie laughed. Jamie joined in.

They sipped their tea.

"Hmmm." Marie savored the tea.

"Yes," Jamie said.

"I was just thinking, in the cave, when we were hunkering down during the winter in the mountains, I would have given anything for a cup of tea with milk and sugar." Marie looked down at the cup she held with both hands.

"I can't even imagine." Jamie set his cup down and putting his elbows on the desk, he leaned in.

"What is the work you are doing?" Marie asked.

"Oh all of this," his hands gestured at the piles of paper strewn about the desk. "There are a million details to running this place. The lands. The tenants. It all requires constant attention."

"The tenants?"

"Yes. I have ten families working and living on my lands – Crofters, they are called. They raise crops on their share. They give me some, and they keep the rest for their use. Sell the extra."

Marie remained silent. Sipped her tea.

"If you feel up to it, I will give you a tour of the operations while the boys receive their lesson for today."

"That would be lovely. I'd like that."

· · · · ·

After breakfast, Marie and Jamie went to the stables. There were two horses saddled, the reins held by the groomsman for the estate.

"What's this," Marie pointed at her horse.

"It's one of my finest mares," came Jamie's reply.

"I don't mean the horse. I'm half Indian and we don't ride side-saddle." She let a chuckle slip. "Note my change of clothes?" Her eyes twinkled at him, as she faux-bowed her one hand swept over her riding pants.

Jamie blushed, a smile crossed his face, "I see what my brother liked about you."

They rode horseback through the fields of his holdings. "You see, many lords are turning the Crofters out. The estates have decided to focus on raising sheep which currently pays more than wheat. If they don't raise wheat, the crofters aren't needed, so they are being evicted all around this part of the country."

"Where do they go?"

"They go to the cities. Living in gutters and alleyways and counting on the church to feed them."

"That sounds terrible."

"Aye." Jamie paused for a minute. Pointing toward a grouping of small huts. "They live here. Better than life in the city for sure."

"You don't want to raise sheep?"

"Their parents, their grandparents, and on and on back in time, they have worked this land for my parents and grandparents and so on. That's not nothing."

"No, it isn't."

"Adam Smith. You heard of him?"

"No, who is he?"

"He was a brilliant Scotsman. Bet you thought John and I were the only ones!" He chuckled.

Marie blushed a bit. She looked down at the reins in her hands, mostly because she didn't know where else to look.

"Well, Adam Smith said, and I'm loosely paraphrasing here, 'We come together and organize for the financial benefit of the group.' So, my Crofters and I will stay together for everyone's financial benefit. We're all good Scots!" He laughed that belly laugh that reminded her of John.

"Too bad your neighbors don't share Adam Smith's views."

"There's a man. His name is Thomas Douglas. He and I were at The University of Edinburgh together. He's organizing the displaced Crofters and sending them over to agricultural colonies in Canada. Prince Edward Island was the first. He's founded a bigger colony in the middle of the Canadian prairie, where you're from. Red River. Have you heard of it?"

"Yes, I know Red River. Retired *voyageurs* go there to live when their service to the company is done." She gazed at the small huts across the way. "Can we meet them?" Marie nodded toward the huts scattered along the crest of a windswept ridge.

"The Crofters? Aye."

Jamie explained as they rode toward the huts, "As I told you, us Scots are very committed to education. We're an erudite people."

"I recall you mentioned that the girls get educated too."

"Yes. Everyone learns at least reading and writing and working with numbers."

Arriving at what could be called a small village, the huts were arranged in two rows on either side of a minor road. Marie was reminded of the cart trails she had traveled in her fur trade travels. She noticed a woman with ruddy cheeks and shoulder-length red hair outside washing clothes with a washboard and tin basin. She was hanging a pair of trousers on a line.

"Ay, Martha," Jamie called.

Martha looked up, and a smile came to her face, "Aye me lord such and such! To what do we owe this grand privilege?" She laughed.

"Now, Martha, make me look like a Grand Scottish Laird in front of our honored guest!" He smiled and laughed back at her.

"Yes, my Laird. You are all-powerful and all-knowing!"

Jamie swung down from his horse, and he and Martha exchanged a hug. They talked in a low tone, and with the wind, Marie could not make out what was being said.

As she approached, the two turned to face her. Martha took her hand. "A friend of the Laird's is welcome here, Ma'am." She curtsied.

"Martha, it is my pleasure. I am Marie Dorion."

"A French woman, eh? The Scots and the French share much in common. We're intelligent people, and we both think the English are scoundrels!"

Marie laughed. "I've met some scoundrels and some not so bad! I am from Canada and sailed here from a land far away on the shores of the Pacific Ocean."

"A world traveler then, are ya?"

"I guess so."

"Would you like some tea?"

"I think we need to be going. I just wanted to meet you. Maybe I can come back again?"

Jamie chimed in, "Why don't you have tea with Martha now? I've some business with her husband, and I can attend to that while you get acquainted."

Marie looked at Martha and said, "Sounds like we're having tea."

"Come on," she motioned to Marie. "I'll put the kettle on."

The two women sat at a table of rough-hewn wood. Marie's chair wobbled a little, but she didn't mention it.

"That chair's a bit off," Martha said, looking at the legs.

"It's fine." Marie sipped her tea. "I grew up in Canada. My father was a fur trapper and trader. I lived in cabins much like this one. It reminds me of home."

"You dear? Live in a hovel like this?"

"It's lovely. It's warm and comfortable."

"Yes, we like it here. The Laird is a good man."

"He is."

"How did you and he come to know one another?"

"That's a long story. I was a friend of his brother John."

"John? You know our other prince of the manor?"

"I did. I loved him very much."

"Why do you talk of him in the past tense?"

Marie swallowed some tea. She looked down at her cup. "He died. I brought his son to Jamie, uh the Laird, so that he could raise him."

Martha's face twisted, and she put a hand to her mouth. She swatted a tear from her cheek.

Marie reached out and took Martha's hand. "I'm sorry. I should have been more delicate. I didn't realize you knew John."

"Oh yes, Ma'am. I have lived here since I was a wee lass. These two boys, Jamie and John, and I, my brothers and cousins, used to play in these fields together. Their father encouraged the classes to mix, so to say." She got up from the table. Taking a minute, she stared away. Then turning, with a sniff, a hand sweeping her cheek, she smiled at Marie. "John gave me my first kiss. We were quite smitten."

"He was a bit of a scoundrel." Marie smiled. "But a good scoundrel."

"Aye, miss he liked the lasses for sure." They both laughed, taking a quiet minute to remember John.

The two women had a second cup of tea. Marie had many questions about their lives on the lands of Jamie Reed. Marie had just finished the second cup when she heard a horse ride up outside. Jamie knocked at the door, and on entering, he smiled. "Okay, you two, Marie and I need to get back. George will be apoplectic if we are late for dinner."

Marie said to Martha, "I had a lovely time. Can we do it again sometime?"

"Of course, dear. You come by anytime. I will fill you with tales of this yahoo and his brother when they were young!"

Jamie said, "Easy. Remember, I have gotten respectable and all!"

The three shared a laugh.

· · · · ·

On the ride back, Marie's thoughts were spinning around in her mind. She had found Martha to be charming, intelligent, and witty. She thought of a question and decided to ask Jamie but did not want to assume anything. She wanted to ask him if she could spend some time teaching the classics to the children of the Crofters, the older ones, to prepare them for life and maybe university. She tried to ask several times, but each time she was about to ask, she had nagging doubts and shrank back.

Am I overstepping my role as a guest? Would I be violating local mores? She decided to wait.

• • • • •

Marie and Jamie sat at the dinner table. The children had eaten and were being herded toward bed by Ophelia. Marie considered different ways to broach the subject that had come to mind while visiting with Martha. Jamie spoke before Marie had a chance.

"Are you enjoying your time here?"

"Yes, you've been very kind in opening your home to me and my boys."

"Marie, I'm a man who speaks plainly. So, I will just come out with it." He raised a crystal glass to his lips and sipped some wine. Setting his glass down, he looked her in the eyes. "My brother loved you. He loved your boys. To me, that makes you family."

Marie reached a hand to her mouth to stifle a cry. Tears ran down her cheeks. "I loved your brother with all my heart. I just recognized it too late." She sniffled. "I will never forgive myself for that."

"My brother loved you. That was enough." He took another sip. "My home is your home, Marie. You and your boys are welcome here, and I hope you will accept this invitation."

Marie blinked at Jamie for a moment. "That is a very kind offer." Marie's question eased its way forward as she said, "I would like to ask a further favor."

"Anything."

"I would like to instruct the children of the Crofters."

Jamie cleared his throat. "They already have a teacher."

"Yes. They are being taught to read and write and work on numbers. What I am talking about is providing them with a Classical education. Latin. Roman and Greek literature."

Jamie swirled his wine in his glass, watching the liquid rise to the rim of the glass and then recede as the revolutions slowed. "To what purpose?"

"You, yourself, have said that the Crofter way of life is ending."

"True." He nodded as he spoke.

"I think the Classics makes the world seem bigger. Reading what ancient people thought, I feel that…."

"It inspires?" Jamie arched an eyebrow while studying Marie's face.

"YES!" Her response was more enthusiastic than she intended. "When people see their thoughts are similar to what people thousands of years ago thought…." She searched for the right words, then added, "It's freeing or validating. At a minimum this knowledge provides another point of view."

"I see." He paused, thinking how to make it work. "We'll have to ask the Crofters."

Marie smiled. "Of course."

CHAPTER TWENTY-SEVEN

Thirty Years Later
Fort Vancouver, Oregon Territory

Marie's steps down the wet gangway were halting and gingerly taken. She scanned the shoreline, seeking familiar faces. She saw none. No one she knew. Reaching the bottom of the ramp, she set foot in the Oregon Territory for the first time in many years. Her gaze went to a tall, white-haired gentleman approaching her. Reaching her, he bowed, took her hand, and kissed it, saying, "Madam Dorion, it is an honor to meet you." He spoke fluent French, "I am Dr McLoughlin, the Chief Factor of Fort Vancouver and His Majesty's representative in this area."

She replied in French, "It is a pleasure, Dr. McLoughlin. I have recently come from your ancestor's homeland – Scotland."

"Ah yes, my father. My mother was French."

"By the way, my name is Mrs. Reed. But please call me Marie."

"But of course. Please come with me. I have instructed the men to bring your bags."

The doctor and Marie strolled casually along a two-rutted cart road. She gazed at the apple trees in the orchard. She could hear the children's laughter coming from the village of cabins off to the west. Dogs barked. It took her thoughts back to the Crofters on the estate.

"You know, on our way out, with that last trapping expedition?" Marie asked, needing to share the memory that had splashed through her mind.

"When you were stranded?" Dr. McLoughlin asked, interested in hearing all she wanted to share.

"Yes," she said, looking at him and realizing that he knew more about her than she did of him. "We overnighted here. This was just a rolling plain along the river. Lakes were there. Trees over there. Now, you have wheat fields, cattle grazing, and orchards. It's changed."

"We've built a self-sustaining enterprise. And what you see here is just a fraction. We have a dairy, sawmills, a ship-building yard."

"Very impressive."

"Thank you. By the way, your sons are driving cattle up from California. They sent word they are delayed. In the meantime, I hope you will accept the hospitality of the Hudson's Bay Company. We have quarters set up, and we have a dinner planned in your honor for this evening."

"That's very kind," she said. They walked through the south gate of the fort. The cacophony of industry and movement of men first caught her attention. The sounds of clanging metal rang from what she supposed was the blacksmith's shop. Carpenters were pounding nails. Men were pushing carts loaded with bales of furs toward the fort's storage warehouse. "This is a lively place," Marie exclaimed.

· · · · ·

Marie was seated next to Dr. McLoughlin in the middle of the twenty-foot-long dinner table. She sat to his right, his wife Marguerite and his daughter Eloisa sat to his left. The gentlemen of the fort sat on the opposite side of the table and at each end. Candles burnt in holders hanging on the wall; each holder was backed with a polished metal that reflected and amplified the light of each candle. A candelabra hung over the table and held more candles. The room was heated by a cast iron stove that burned wood. Marie enjoyed the crackle and popping of the wood as it burned. It was the sound of warmth. She watched as the officers of the fort filed in and took their assigned places.

Dr. McLoughlin stood and tapped his crystal wine glass with a spoon; the room quieted. "Today, we have an honored guest amongst us," he said. "A woman who needs no introduction and whose story is familiar to us all." Those gathered at the table clapped politely. "Marie, would you honor us with a few words?"

Marie rose to her feet, looked at the doctor and his wife, and began. "Thank you, Dr. McLoughlin and Marguerite, for your kind hospitality." Her gaze went to the men sitting in front of her. "I am very happy to be back in Oregon. My, so much has changed." She took a sip of water. "You all know my story. I was the second woman to come to Oregon overland. Sacajawea being the first. It was a wild and untamed place back then." She scanned the men at the table. She could tell by their faces that they were listening. "Not many of you may know that I spent the last several years in Scotland. My husband, the late Lord Jamie Reed, and I spent the last 30 years raising children and caring for the land and the tenants on that land. But our proudest accomplishment is that my husband and I founded a private school, one dedicated to educating the poor and unfortunate of the Scottish Highlands."

As Marie hesitated for the applause to die down, she scanned the crowd to see all the people who were there to listen to her words. "Many of you here at this table are from Scotland, or your ancestors were from there. As such, you know the Scots' commitment to education." There was more applause. "I have come back to Oregon to reunite with my two sons but also to continue that work and to build a proud tradition of education here." Marie looked at Dr. McLoughlin. "As this territory fills with more and more people, it is critical for the populace to be educated, especially as they build communities and the political structure that goes with it. Thank you."

Marie took her seat. Dr. McLoughlin stood and said to Marie and those in attendance, "Marie, please know that the full power and prestige of our company and our settlement will be at your service as you pursue your dream of educating the residents of the Oregon Territory."

"Thank you, sir," Marie said as she looked up at Dr. McLoughlin.

There was a rustling sound near the entry to the dining area. She looked toward a man with gray hair, a little bent over and thick in the middle, standing in the doorway between the entryway of Dr. McLoughlin's home and the dining area.

"Forgive me for being tardy, Dr. McLoughlin," the man said.

"Nonsense. I believe you know the guest of honor. I think you knew her as Madam Dorion."

"I'm sure Madam Dorion doesn't recognize me as I have changed much since our last time together." Marie recognized the voice but couldn't place it. The man's appearance was no help. He hesitated as he looked over his shoulder at a woman behind him. She joined him, but neither one of them looked familiar to Marie. She squinted her eyes, cocked her head, and tried to think back on all the people she knew over the years. Shaking her head, she couldn't place him.

"Madam Dorion, I'd like some pie," the man said.

Marie's heart jumped at these words. Her chair toppled backward to the floor with a loud bang as she leaped to her feet. She disregarded the chair and quickly rushed to the man on the other side of the room. She flung her arms around him, and he wrapped her in his.

"My God, Archie! What are you doing here?"

The man embraced her, stepped back a half step, and looked her in the eyes. Then he turned to the audience at the dinner table. All eyes were locked on him and Marie. "If not for this woman, I would not be here today. I owe her my life."

Marie looked at him, astonished. "I don't think I've ever heard you say a complete sentence before!"

Dr. McLoughlin said, "Archie has been one of my finest managers for over 15 years. His wife Ida runs the primary school."

Just then, the woman stepped up from behind Archie. "Madam Dorion, I am Ida Devlin. It's a great pleasure to meet you!"

Marie wrapped her arms around Archie and Ida. Marie wept as she thanked the Lord for this reunion. After dinner, walking alone in the fort courtyard, she looked into the sky. She traced out the Bear in the sky with her index finger, Ursa Major. "Thank you for getting me home." She walked to her quarters. She stopped to gaze at the night sky. Using her index finger, she again traced the constellation of the Bear. "Thank you," she whispered.

That night, she dreamt of Ilchee. She had died a few years before, a victim of the malarial fever that had swept away a vast majority of the native population that used to teem along the banks of the great river – Wimahl. In her dream, Ilchee and John stood in a sunny, flower-filled meadow. Both looked happy. They smiled at her.

ACKNOWLEDGEMENTS

I could not have completed this book without the help of many people. First, I want to thank my wonderful editor, Amy Weber for guiding me as I wrote. She helped me keep the narrative flowing straight and true! Next, my friends and family that were willing to read my book in its nascent stages and offer advice as well as criticisms. These people are all very special to me in some way. Lacey Acklin, Sharon Sorenson, Adele Weber, Ann Bryant and Louise Hill. Thank you all so much!

ABOUT THE AUTHOR

R.R Hill is an almost native of the Pacific Northwest, having spent some early years in California before moving to Washington. He's wandered the highways, byways, and lonely mountain trails of the region, and what he lays before the reader is a beautiful tapestry of what the region looks, smells, and feels like.

R.R. Hill is the father of three, a grandfather of three, and a person of interest to a very rambunctious Vizsla. He holds a Master's in history, is an avid reader, and enjoys sports and being outdoors.

NOTE FROM R.R. HILL

Word-of-mouth is crucial for any author to succeed. If you enjoyed *The Morning Star Shines Brightest*, please leave a review online—anywhere you are able. Even if it's just a sentence or two. It would make all the difference and would be very much appreciated.

Thanks!
R.R. Hill

We hope you enjoyed reading this title from:

www.blackrosewriting.com

Subscribe to our mailing list – *The Rosevine* – and receive **FREE** books, daily deals, and stay current with news about upcoming releases and our hottest authors.
Scan the QR code below to sign up.

Already a subscriber? Please accept a sincere thank you for being a fan of Black Rose Writing authors.

View other Black Rose Writing titles at
www.blackrosewriting.com/books and use promo code
PRINT to receive a **20% discount** when purchasing.